Dropping
the mayor went [illegible] convulsions. . . .

Tom Womble finally caught up to the rest of the group as they reached the Canyon city limits. A large crowd was already assembled in the town square. While they waited for the parade to begin, they browsed the fairgrounds and the vendor booths.

Two Texas Rangers, mounted on identical palomino stallions and carrying the Stars and Stripes and the Texas State flag, led the parade. Just as they reached the center of the square, the aircraft arrived in formation. The spray planes were ten abreast as they roared over the crowded square, leaving a cloud of atomized, highly toxic VX gas in their wake.

As the deadly spray wafted down on the unsuspecting crowd, the odorless fog seemed little more than a light mist.

"What the hell are those morons up to?" Mayor Robert Dunst asked. "They're not scheduled to do the flyover for another ten minutes."

"They aren't part of the Air Force," Police Chief Green said.

"My God, that burns," the mayor shouted, choking and rubbing his eyes.

But before he could say anything further, he was coughing uncontrollably. Dropping to his knees, the mayor went into convulsions.

BY KEN SHUFELDT
FROM TOM DOHERTY BOOKS

Genesis
Tribulations
Rebellion
Rage
Blood of Tyrants

BLOOD OF TYRANTS

KEN SHUFELDT

A TOM DOHERTY ASSOCIATES BOOK
NEW YORK

This is a work of fiction. All of the characters, organizations, and events portrayed in this novel are either products of the author's imagination or are used fictitiously.

BLOOD OF TYRANTS

A Forge Book
Published by Tom Doherty Associates
175 Fifth Avenue
New York, NY 10010

www.tor-forge.com

Forge® is a registered trademark of Macmillan Publishing Group, LLC.

ISBN 978-0-7653-8169-9

Our books may be purchased in bulk for promotional, educational, or business use. Please contact your local bookseller or the Macmillan Corporate and Premium Sales Department at 1-800-221-7945, extension 5442, or by e-mail at MacmillanSpecialMarkets@macmillan.com.

First Edition: June 2017

Printed in the United States of America

0 9 8 7 6 5 4 3 2 1

To all the brave men and women
who have given of themselves to ensure
our great nation continues to provide
liberty and justice for all.

BLOOD OF TYRANTS

CHAPTER 1

William Trussle, the president of the Country Club of Virginia, had been expecting a big turnout for Richard Wilkes's sixtieth birthday celebration. As the line of Mercedes-Benzes, Range Rovers, Jaguars, and Cadillacs filled the circular drive, he said, "Marty, get everybody that's not working the party out here to help out."

Richard Wilkes's great-great-grandfather had founded the club back in the 1800s, and Richard was one of its most esteemed members, so William didn't want any of his guests having a bad experience if he could help it.

Richard was a world-renowned businessman, and many of the guests had come in from all over the world to attend. Normally the club only allowed the members to book the main ballroom for parties, but due to the large number of attendees, they were using the adjoining rooms to accommodate the crowd.

There was a distinct chill in the air, and there was a light mist falling from the dull overcast skies. They had roaring fires going in the twin fireplaces, and the web of LED lights draped from the twin crystal chandeliers cast a spiderweb of light across the ballroom's highly polished wood floors.

Richard had been a member of Yale's national championship–winning rowing team, and he was on the twelve-member executive committee of the Yale Alumni Fund Board of Directors. Rachel, Richard's wife, had every room decked out with all types of Yale memorabilia, and they'd set up a small stage near the center of the ballroom where several of Richard's college teammates took turns sharing their favorite stories about him during dinner.

After dinner there had been a constant stream of guests coming by Richard's table to wish him well, but by ten o'clock the party had started to wind down. He was left sitting on the far side of the ballroom, contemplating how his life had turned out.

He'd intended to enter politics when he finished his MBA at the Yale School of Management, but his father's untimely death in a boating accident had forced him to assume the reins of the family empire. In the thirty-odd years since he'd taken over, he'd more than doubled the already vast family fortune, but he still lusted for the recognition and power that a political career might have afforded him.

Richard had been on the country club's board and membership committee for many years, and after the last of the guests had left, William Trussle dropped by to introduce their newest member.

"Richard, I'd like to introduce you to Charles Trowbridge," William said.

"It's very nice to meet you, Mr. Trowbridge," Richard said. "I noticed on your membership application that you're a political campaign manager."

"I hope you're not going to hold that against me," Charles said.

"Not at all. I once considered a career in politics myself."

"It's never too late to start," Charles said.

"I'm afraid I wouldn't have the energy for it anymore."

"I hope that's not true, because that's actually why I asked Mr. Trussle to introduce us. I know that your family has made significant financial contributions to the GOP over the years, but the party is in serious trouble for the upcoming presidential election."

"How much do they want this time?"

"This isn't about money. I've spent the last six weeks consulting with the Republican National Committee to help them vet the potential presidential candidates, and we don't have a viable candidate."

"I could name at least four off the top of my head, surely one of them will step up."

"I've spoken with all of them, and none of them are willing to run against President Tidwell."

"He's a popular bastard, but I don't understand how he can still command that much loyalty considering the sorry shape the country is in."

"I know this is going to sound crazy, but given your reputation for getting things done, we think you would have a realistic chance of winning the party's nomination."

"Given the current political climate, I doubt that any Republican could unseat President Tidwell, let alone a complete unknown."

"Would you at least consider it?"

"I'd be seen as some sort of Don Quixote."

"I promise we wouldn't let that happen."

"It seems like a fool's errand to me, but give me some time to think it over," Richard said, even as his heart raced at the thought of it.

"Of course, but don't take too long. The longer you wait the harder it's going to be."

Three days later, Richard Wilkes sat down at Charles's table while he was eating lunch at the club.

"I'll do it," Richard Wilkes said.

"Great."

"Will you be my campaign manager?"

"That's up to you. I've managed a lot of senatorial campaigns, but I've never run a presidential campaign."

"I've done my homework on you. You can do it. Give me a call when you're ready to get started."

"We can get started this afternoon."

CHAPTER 2

Four months later, Richard had been named the GOP's candidate, and he was on the road, hustling between a grueling series of campaign stops. Charles had hoped Richard's campaign might catch fire after the convention; however, the latest polls showed that his numbers were continuing to decline.

Richard had just finished a major outdoor event at Klyde Warren Park in Downtown Dallas and was on his way back to the airport. When the black Lincoln limo stopped at the side entrance to the Signature Flight center, Special Agent Taylor, the head of Richard's Secret Service detail said, "It's going to be another half hour before we can take off. Does anyone need to use the facilities?"

"I sure as hell do," Richard Wilkes said.

The driver got out to open the door, but Richard was already out the door and heading inside with his four-man Secret Service detail following closely behind.

When the ground crew finished loading their luggage, chief pilot Pete Dawkins asked, "Is everyone ready?"

"We're all here," Special Agent Taylor said.

Pete motioned to the girl behind the desk, and she hit

the button to unlock the door to let them board their aircraft.

They had to be escorted by one of the flight crew, but the FBO patrons didn't have to go through the formal TSA security check.

Pete Dawkins was giving them an overview of Richard's new aircraft as they made their way to the plane.

"This is just the second Global 8000 that Bombardier has delivered, and we just got back from picking it up from the plant in Montreal," Pete Dawkins said as he led them up the aircraft's stairs. "It has a range of seventy-nine thousand nautical miles and is designed to cruise at an altitude of fifty-one thousand feet at five hundred and seventeen knots. It can hold up to nineteen passengers, but this one is configured to seat ten, not counting the flight crew and the cabin attendant. The chairs are flat, fully electric and are managed by an aï-zen remote-control panel. We have the newest version of Gogo's high-speed satellite Wi-Fi, and all of the wing tables have an iPad mounted to them for Internet access and to control the in-flight entertainment systems. This is the forward cabin, and it has seating for four, along with the bar, the forward bathroom, and the galley," Pete said as they continued aft. "This is the middle cabin, which also seats four, and on this bulkhead there's a small conference table that can be folded out when needed."

"You were a Yale man?" Special Agent Taylor asked Richard.

"And a member of the national championship Bulldogs rowing team."

Richard's lean, muscular, six-foot-one frame looked like he could still row a few miles. His sandy blond hair was starting to thin, but he was holding up pretty well for sixty years old.

The captain glanced at his watch and said, "We'll be taking off in a few minutes, and so if the rest of you will follow me, I'll show you to your seats."

After Richard and Charles had stowed their carry-on bags, Richard noticed that Janice Peoples, the cabin attendant, had left the latest issue of *The New York Times* on his seat. He was about to pitch it in the trash when he noticed that his picture was on the front page.

Shortly after takeoff Charles reclined his chair to try to catch a quick nap.

As Richard started reading the *Times* article he was half expecting a hatchet job, but to his surprise, the article was lucid, well researched, and surprisingly balanced. The in-depth article was four pages long, and it detailed Richard's family history, his academic career, his tenure leading his family's corporate empire, and finally the brutal rounds of negotiations and deal making at the GOP convention that had led to him winning the nomination.

The final two paragraphs detailed the challenges Richard faced trying to defeat the well-heeled incumbent and the disaster of a platform that had come out of the convention.

Charles was asleep when Richard nudged him.

"What's up, boss?"

"I just finished an article in the *Times*, and they're saying I don't have a chance in hell."

"Good, something finally got through to you. You've got to go after Tidwell with all guns blazing, and we've got to partner up with some of the super PACs so we can get your agenda in front of the American people."

"I don't want to owe those bloodsucking bastards if I win."

"Then you're going to lose."

Richard closed his eyes and leaned back against the

headrest. After several seconds, he opened his eyes and said, "Fine, who would you suggest?"

"Larry Ragsdale's group, Conservatives for America, is still calling."

"See if you can set something up."

Charles tapped the screen of the iPad mounted to the table and started typing.

Twenty minutes later it chimed as the response to his e-mail came in.

"Larry Ragsdale wants us to meet him for dinner tonight," Charles said.

"Let's see what he wants."

CHAPTER 3

When they landed in Phoenix, there was another limo waiting on the tarmac.

As the ground crew loaded their luggage, Sumitro Choudoury, their limo driver, got out to open the door for them. He was wearing dark blue slacks, a white shirt with a SKY LIMO logo on the pocket, and a bright yellow tie. He had black hair and dark brown eyes, and with a distinctly Indian accent he asked, "Where to, sir?"

"We've got an eight o'clock dinner meeting at Café Monarch in Scottsdale," Charles Trowbridge said.

"No problem. I'll have you there in plenty of time."

When the limo stopped in front of the restaurant, Sumitro opened the sliding glass window and said, "Here's my card. Just give me a call when you're ready to leave."

The light brown adobe building had a red tiled roof and a porch that covered the reservation desk by the front entrance.

"Do you have a reservation?" the maître d' asked.

"Yes, we're meeting Mr. Larry Ragsdale," Richard Wilkes said.

"Mr. Ragsdale hasn't arrived yet, but Paul will show you to your table."

The waiter led them through the restaurant to the outdoor seating area. The patio was paved with multicolored stone tiles, and there were steel cables crisscrossed overhead with water misters and lanterns hanging from them. The wrought-iron tables were covered with white tablecloths, and each of them had a large candle as a centerpiece. The waiter guided them to their table next to an ivy-covered redbrick wall and said, "Enjoy your dinner. Rene will be your waiter for tonight."

"I hope Ragsdale shows," Richard Wilkes said.

They'd been sitting there for about ten minutes when Richard spotted Paul guiding Larry Ragsdale to their table. As they made their introductions, Richard was trying to size Larry up. He certainly wasn't what he'd expected from reading his bio. Larry was a Harvard Law and Wharton School of Business graduate, and at forty-two he was one of the youngest leaders of a super PAC in the country. However, he was only five eight, and a bit pudgy. His light brown hair was already showing traces of gray, but Richard had seen the fire in his hazel-colored eyes when they'd shook hands.

After the waiter took their orders, Richard Wilkes said, "I'm sorry, but I've never heard of your organization."

"We're relatively new, but I can assure you we're the real deal, and that we've got the ability and the money to obliterate Tidwell with a multimedia blitzkrieg."

"I'm listening."

Larry put his MacBook Pro up on the table and jumped into his pitch.

Richard was expecting a PowerPoint presentation, but Larry had a full-blown interactive presentation, and after thirty minutes of his over-the-top presentation style, Richard was blown away.

"Well, what do you think?" Larry Ragsdale asked.

"If you can pull off even half of that, I'm in, but what you just described is going to cost a hell of a lot of money," Richard Wilkes said.

"The members of my organization will spend almost any amount of money to move their agenda forward."

"Good to hear, but what do they want in return?"

Larry opened the file containing their requests and said, "I'll e-mail you the file with the details, but I'll cover the big-ticket items. To start, they want to cap the top tax bracket at twenty-eight percent. They want to reduce the long-term capital gains tax and the qualified dividends tax to five percent for all tax brackets, and shorten the minimum time you have to hold the investments to six months. They also want to modify the oil depletion allowance calculations to allow a two hundred percent recovery of the original investment. And lastly, they want Congress to repeal the employer fines for not offering affordable health insurance."

"That's a hell of a wish list."

"Please don't misunderstand. If we do this we'll expect you to institute every one of these once you're elected."

"Understood," Richard said.

People in hell want ice water, but I'll play along for now, Richard Wilkes thought as they got up to leave.

CHAPTER 4

The next week the super PAC launched an all-out media blitz to discredit President Tidwell. After spending almost a billion dollars they managed to turn the tide of the election. The popular vote had been a virtual tie, but Wilkes was able to eke out a narrow win in the electoral college.

Five weeks after his inauguration, President Wilkes and Vice President Regal were in the newly redecorated Oval Office, waiting on Larry Ragsdale to arrive for a 6 A.M. meeting. During his first week in office, President Wilkes had sent Larry Ragsdale's list over to Jack Woods, the head of the congressional budget office, to run the numbers, and this was their first meeting to review them.

The vice president was nothing like the president. He was a career politician with over thirty years as a senator, and would turn seventy-one in two weeks. He was six two, a hundred and sixty pounds, and his gaunt frame made him look almost anorexic. However, as the LED lights in the recently redecorated Oval Office reflected off of his neatly combed silver hair, his blue eyes were twinkling with the excitement of his new job.

The president was sitting at the Resolute desk as they waited on Larry Ragsdale to arrive. The ornate wooden desk had been a gift from Queen Victoria to President

Rutherford B. Hayes in 1880, and had been crafted from the timbers of the British Arctic exploration ship, HMS *Resolute*, and the president had jumped at the chance to return it to the Oval Office.

The president's assistant, Mary Counts, brought him his morning coffee and opened the gold drapes covering the three bulletproof windows behind his desk. Mary had never married, and she was forty-one years old with light blond hair, green eyes, and a voluptuous figure. She'd been his executive assistant for twenty years, and he depended on her to take care of all of his day-to-day needs.

"The office turned out nice, but it seems like I've seen this carpet before," Mary said.

"You have. The damn decorators wanted me to pick out everything, and so I went with an exact replica of the blue and gold carpet that President Clinton used."

"This desk is amazing," Mary said, putting his coffee down, "but where did they find these butt-ugly chairs?"

"If you don't like them, get with housekeeping and pick out something else," President Wilkes said.

The president took a sip of coffee from his Yale Bulldog mug and asked, "Have you looked over Jack Woods's numbers yet?"

"I've discussed them with him and his team, and I don't like any of it," Vice President Regal said as he sat down. "Their initial estimates peg the potential revenue loss at eight hundred and fifty billion dollars. The loss attributable to the changes to oil depletion calculation is three hundred billion dollars, the reductions to the capital gains tax will cost two hundred and fifty billion dollars, and capping the top tax bracket at twenty-eight percent accounts for the rest. However, I think they're being overly optimistic, so I had them put together some recommendations on what to cut, and I just e-mailed it to you and Larry Ragsdale."

"This will explode the deficits to the stratosphere," President Wilkes said.

"Reagan, George W., and Obama taught us that deficits don't really matter," Larry Ragsdale said as he came in.

"Perhaps," the president said, "but the team has identified the amounts and the areas where the cuts will have to be made." He handed Larry the summary page from the VP's report.

"Where you make the cuts doesn't much matter to us, but we need you to move this forward as quickly as possible," Larry Ragsdale said as he scanned the list.

"We'll see what we can do. Do you have any feedback on my cabinet?" President Wilkes asked.

"You'll need to replace Aryeh Behrmann, the secretary of defense, with Robert Taylor, and name Jim Rutherford as the assistant to the president for national security affairs."

"I'm not shocked that they dislike Behrmann, however, I'm not going to replace him. He did a stellar job for the previous administration, and he'll do the same for me. I don't know Mr. Rutherford, but I'm willing to take a look at him."

"My organization is going to be pissed if you leave Behrmann in place."

"Let's move on."

"We'll revisit the Behrmann issue another time, but we're okay with the remainder of your team," Ragsdale said.

"Good, and as soon as we have the budget details finalized I'll set up another meeting," President Wilkes replied.

Six days later Larry Ragsdale called President Wilkes to check on their progress.

"How much longer is this going to take?" Larry Ragsdale asked.

"We're ready to submit the legislation, but we're short twelve votes in the House, and seven in the Senate."

"I told you to call me if you ran into any problems," Larry Ragsdale said as he hung up.

The next morning Larry Ragsdale called back. "You can submit your bills," he said.

"But we're still short votes," President Wilkes said.

"Just put them through."

To their amazement several members of the opposition switched their votes, and the new legislation sailed through both houses.

Six days later Mary Counts came into the Oval Office and said, "Aryeh Behrmann, the secretary of defense, would like to speak with you."

Secretary Behrmann and his older brother Lieb had been born in the U.S., but their parents were naturalized citizens who had emigrated from Israel. Aryeh had graduated from West Point with a master's degree in mathematics, and had been an officer in the United States Army Security Agency (ASA) for twelve years before he'd left the service to take a position with the NSA. After five years of service with the NSA, he'd been named the director of the NSA/CSS Threat Operations Center, and was responsible for all the cryptologic efforts to identify and counteract the adversary's cyber-attacks.

When President Tidwell was first elected, his friend Terry Pebbles, the director of the NSA, had convinced him to consider Aryeh for his secretary of defense. When President Tidwell had first appointed him, a lot of people had questioned his choice. However, Aryeh had risen to the occasion, and exceeded all of their expectations. Before leaving office, President Tidwell had made a point to reach out to President Wilkes to convince him to leave the secretary in place.

"What can I do for you this afternoon?" President Wilkes asked.

"Mr. President, I've just made my first pass through your numbers, and we might have to cut our head counts by twenty-five percent to hit the new budget number. I want to go on record that this is a terrible mistake."

"Noted, but everyone has to do their part. Did you get the invitation for the cabinet meeting?"

"I'll be there."

The next morning President Wilkes had just sat down in the Oval Office when Mary Counts handed him a folder.

"What's this?" President Wilkes asked.

"The background investigation you requested on Jim Rutherford."

"How's he look?"

"Impressive," Mary Counts said. "He graduated with honors from Michigan State with a degree in political science, and he was a Fulbright scholar. He's a former Brookings Institution fellow, and has been the United States ambassador to the United Nations. He's also served on the staff of the National Security Council, and as the assistant secretary of state for the Bureau of African Affairs."

"I'm sold. Let's get him in here so I can ask him to join the team."

Late that afternoon, Mary Counts came into the Oval Office and said, "Mr. Rutherford is here."

"Thank you for coming in on such short notice," President Wilkes said.

"When the president calls, you come," Jim Rutherford said.

Jim Rutherford was a fifty-year-old black man who had earned everything he'd ever gotten in life through hard work and perseverance. He was six feet tall, a hundred and eighty pounds, and in his younger days, the top-ranked Golden Gloves middleweight in the country, until a detached retina ended his career. His dark black hair had streaks of gray around the temples, but he still kept himself fighting trim.

"Jim, it's late so I'm going to get right to it. I'd like you to be my national security advisor."

"It would be my honor," Rutherford said.

"That was easy enough, and I look forward to working with you," President Wilkes said as they shook hands.

The following Monday Secretary Behrmann scheduled their budget meeting at the Pentagon in a small second-floor conference room. Carpeted with a tightly woven dark brown Berber carpet, in the center of the room was a large hardwood conference table with twelve wheeled, dark brown leather chairs. At the far end of the table there was a wall-mounted ninety-six-inch monitor that could be used for videoconferences or presentations.

Secretary of Defense Behrmann was seated at the head of the table, and as the commanders of the army, navy, and air force took their places, he was mentally rehearsing his approach. General Lehman, the chief of staff of the army and the current chairman of the Joint Chiefs, was seated to his left. General Lehman was fifty-eight years old, six five, and weighed two hundred and sixty pounds. His dark black hair had turned to a brilliant shade of silver, which further emphasized his gunmetal blue eyes. Admiral Donnelly, the chief of naval operations, was seated next to him. He had brown hair, light gray eyes, and had been a navy SEAL in his younger days. General Gibbs, the chief of staff of the air force, was seated next to him, and he'd been an F-15C Eagle jockey. He still ran at least six marathons every year, and his wavy blond hair and movie-star good looks belied the fact that he'd turn sixty on his next birthday. Secretary Behrmann was ex-military himself, but he was quite a contrast to the others. He was smaller than the rest of them, but he'd just earned a seventh-degree black belt in aikido. "Good morning. I hope you came prepared to work," he said. "During the next two days we've got to cut at least twenty-eight percent out of your budgets." He let them vent for a few seconds before he said, "That's enough. This isn't up for discussion. Congress has mandated these reductions, and it's up to us to get it done."

He put a chart up on the screen and said, "This shows the breakdown of our combined spending for the next year. The original budget was six hundred and twenty billion dollars, but we're going to figure out how to cut approximately a hundred and seventy-four billion dollars out of it without destroying our ability to defend this country."

When they finished for the day, Secretary Behrmann said, "We've made a lot of progress today. We'll reconvene at oh-nine-hundred, but I'll need you to send me your numbers by oh-seven-hundred so I can go over them before we resume. I don't expect you to have all the details worked out, but I need to see your approach in every area."

When they resumed the next morning, Secretary Behrmann said, "Good morning. It's evident that all of you had a productive evening. I've summarized the notes you sent me, and I'll start with the air force. From an equipment perspective, they'll cancel the remainder of the F-35 orders and mothball the F-22s and the F-35s that are currently in service.

"On the manpower side of the ledger, they'll execute a reduction in force of eighteen percent, or a little more than fifty thousand personnel. Since the army doesn't have a lot of equipment in this year's budget, they'll release approximately two hundred and fifty thousand soldiers, which is approximately forty-six percent of their total headcount. I haven't run all of the different scenarios, but we may make deeper cuts in the officer corps, since their salaries are more substantial. The navy will cancel all their contracts for new vessels and their portion of the F-35 production schedule, and reduce their spare parts budget by fifty percent. Combined, the navy and the marines will lose approximately a hundred and fifty thousand personnel.

"That's all we're going to cover for today, and I'd like to commend all of you for the work you've done so far," Secretary Behrmann said. "However, from this point forward, I'll be working with each of you individually to get your plans implemented."

Six months later, Harvey Gabriel, the White House press secretary, was in the Oval Office for a 6 A.M. meeting to brief the president on the firestorm they'd set off. Harvey was forty-six years old and had graduated from Brown University with a degree in political science. When the president had recruited him to be his press secretary, he was the CNN global affairs correspondent, covering U.S. foreign policy and international affairs for the network.

"How bad?" President Wilkes asked.

"That depends on your point of view. Your supporters are touting the benefits of the tax cuts and the ten percent rise in the Dow. However, every major newspaper in the country is accusing you of targeting old people with the cuts you've made to Social Security and the Medicare/Medicaid programs, and they claim you're impoverishing children."

"That seems a little unfair."

"It gets worse. Fox News is blaming the rise in civil unrest and terrorism around the globe on our military cutbacks."

"They can't pin that on me."

"They're sure as hell trying."

CHAPTER 5

As he was beginning the second year of his presidency, President Wilkes was struggling to deal with the surge in domestic terrorism even as the intelligence community and the military attempted to manage the chaos breaking out around the globe.

Colonel Tompkins, the deputy commanding officer for the Army Special Operations Command (USASOC) in Fort Bragg, North Carolina, was sitting in his office in the command center when the director of the CIA called.

"I need a team for a top-priority mission," CIA Director Joshua Bright said.

"What have you got?" Colonel Tompkins asked.

"I've just sent you an overview of the situation."

"This doesn't tell me crap," Colonel Tompkins said.

"That's all I can share, but Jeff Trimble, the Bagdad station chief is going along, and he'll brief them on the way. I'll have a C-5 at your location by oh-four-thirty tomorrow morning and it will be wheels up at oh-five-hundred."

"They'll be ready."

"Lieutenant, I need Major Franks," Colonel Tompkins told his aide.

"Come in, Major," Colonel Tompkins said. "A group of Syrian ISIS fighters have kidnapped four members of Doctors Without Borders, and they're threatening to behead them in five days."

"Those bastards again. Have you got a briefing folder?"

"No, that's all the CIA would tell me."

"Spooks. How the hell is that supposed to work?"

"I know it's total bullshit, but the CIA is sending a C-5M Super Galaxy to transport your team to Incirlik, and the Bagdad CIA station chief will brief you en route."

Major Deke Franks was six one and a hundred and ninety pounds, with closely cropped light brown hair and gunmetal blue eyes. As he walked briskly across the parade grounds toward his office, he was the consummate image of the modern fighting man, but he'd had a rough start to life.

Deke had never known his parents. The nuns had found him one dark, snowy, New York night, wrapped in a thin blanket outside the front entrance to St. Patrick's Cathedral. The nuns had raised him, so he'd gotten his education in the Catholic schools. The archbishop had taken a personal interest in him, and when high school graduation came, he'd gotten his friend Senator Dominique to arrange an appointment to West Point for Deke. After graduation, Deke entered the army as a second lieutenant in the 160th Special Operations Aviation Regiment (Airborne), also known as the Night Stalkers.

When Major Franks reached his office, he called his XO. "Lieutenant Burke, we've caught another mission."

"Damn, we just got back," Lieutenant Burke said. "What is it this time?"

"All I know so far is that we're headed to Turkey,

and then Syria to rescue some hostages. The Bagdad CIA station chief will be on board, and he's supposed to brief us on the way over."

"What do you need me to do?"

"We're shorthanded so I need you to see if you can commandeer a couple of Major Sullivan's men. Then pass the word that everyone needs to be geared up and in the main hangar by oh-four-thirty."

Frustrated that he was being asked to put his men in harm's way without a plan, Major Franks opened his laptop and started laying out some basic mission parameters, but as he did, he flashed back to the mission that had earned him the Defense Meritorious Service Medal and put his career on steroids.

It had taken place over six years ago, but the vivid memories came rushing back. The mission was supposed to have been a simple snatch-and-grab "rendition" operation. They'd located the number two man in the Taliban leadership living in a three-story walled residence in Mianwali, the capital city of Mianwali District, Pakistan, about 388 km from the Afghanistan border, and they were going in after him.

They'd been in the air for almost an hour, and as they approached their target the mission leader, Major Binge said, "We'll be landing in five, all teams report."

"Team two good to go," Captain Rime said.

"Team three ready," Lieutenant Franks said.

"Team one will approach the compound from the east, team two will approach from the north, and team three will follow team two in."

"Stay on team two's tail," Lieutenant Franks told his pilot, Captain Wayne.

Hoping to catch them by surprise, they'd timed their attack to occur just before dawn, but as they sped through the moonless night sky, a shoulder-fired SAM slammed into Captain Rime's chopper, temporarily blinding them.

"Shit," Captain Wayne said as he banked hard and managed to narrowly avoid the second missile streaking up at them, but it exploded near the rear of the helicopter, severely damaging their tail rotor.

"Brace yourselves, we're going down," Captain Wayne yelled before he managed to guide the wounded chopper down to a hard landing.

They'd barely skidded to a stop when a Russian Kord heavy machine gun riddled the cockpit with bursts of 12.7 mm metal-jacketed slugs, killing Captain Wayne and his copilot.

"Sergeant Todd, take two men and silence that machine gun," Lieutenant Franks said.

As Lieutenant Franks and the rest of the team took cover behind the wreckage, multiple 72 mm RPG rounds hit Major Binge's chopper as it was coming in for a landing.

The chopper slammed into the ground near their position, and the furiously burning wreckage illuminated the shredded, smoldering body parts scattered around the crash site. The prevailing wind carried the smoke toward them, and as the stench of the burning flesh swept over them, Lieutenant Franks couldn't stop the vomit from spewing from his mouth.

Lieutenant Franks was embarrassed, but he realized they were all going to die if they stayed there. So he straightened up, wiped the bile from his cheek, and when he saw Sergeant Todd's team take out the machine gun, he shouted to his men, "Follow me."

When they reached the twelve-foot-tall gate to the compound's courtyard, he said, "Blow that door."

All the blast did was knock the massive door askew, but Lieutenant Franks and his team managed to slip through the narrow opening.

As they entered the courtyard Lieutenant Franks took two AK-47 rounds to the chest. His ranger body armor stopped both of the slugs, but the impact knocked him off balance. He steadied himself against the wall and put a five-round burst from his 30 mm HK MP7A1 submachine gun into his assailant's chest.

Their target was in his third-story apartment, but as they started up the stairs, his six-man security team opened up on them from the second-story landing.

"Thomas, take those assholes out," Lieutenant Franks said.

Corporal Thomas was carrying a Heckler & Koch M320 Grenade Launcher Module, and it only took him a few seconds to lob two low-velocity 40 mm rounds onto the second floor.

When they reached the third-floor residence, the door was locked, but Sergeant Todd used a M1030 breaching round from his 12-gauge shotgun to blast the door open, and threw an M84 stun grenade inside.

Lieutenant Franks was the first one through door, and when the still-disoriented bodyguard tried to raise his AK-47, he put three rounds in his chest and said, "That dirtbag in the corner is the one we're after. Tie his hands and get him downstairs.

"Command, all of our aircraft are inoperative, and we have many causalities to transport," Lieutenant Franks said as they started down the stairs.

"Roger that, we have replacements on the way and should be at your location in thirty."

"Sergeant Todd, take some of the men and start gathering up our casualties; the choppers should be here in thirty minutes."

"Sir, let me take a look at that," the medic said when he saw the blood on his shirt.

"Fine, but be quick about it," Lieutenant Franks said.

When the replacement choppers arrived, Lieutenant Franks said, "Sergeant Todd, take the prisoner and the walking wounded, and get the hell out of here."

Once they were on their way, Lieutenant Franks and his men helped the aircrew load the rest of their dead and wounded onto the other choppers.

"Is that the last of them?" Lieutenant Franks asked as they loaded two more body bags onto the chopper.

WHEN HIS DESK phone rang it jerked Major Franks back to reality.

"Major Sullivan's team caught another op, so I couldn't get anyone," Lieutenant Burke said.

"Damn, we'll just have to make do," Major Franks said.

CHAPTER 6

At 0445 the next morning Major Franks's team was walking up the cargo ramp sticking out of the front of the Super Galaxy, but the station chief was nowhere to be seen.

That asshole had better be on board, Major Franks thought.

Major Franks and his team were sitting in the upper flight deck of the massive aircraft, and shortly after it leveled off, Jeff Trimble walked out of flight operations and sat down beside Major Franks.

He opened up his laptop and said, "Major Franks, I'm Jeff Trimble."

Trimble was five ten and two hundred pounds with dark brown eyes and hair. He spoke with a heavy Middle Eastern accent, and together with his stocky build had Major Franks wondering if he was a native Iraqi.

"Mr. Trimble, I need you to fill me in."

"We'll land at Incirlik Air Base in approximately twelve hours. The hostages are being held at an abandoned government compound on the north side of Kobani, Syria. General Burr will have a squadron of MH-60 Black Hawk helicopters standing by to take us the rest of the way."

"I've only got forty men. How many terrorists are there?" Major Franks asked.

"That's more than enough."

"Answer my question," Major Franks said.

"There shouldn't be more than a hundred."

"Weapons?"

"A few vehicle-mounted heavy machine guns, RPGs, and AKs."

"Do you have a layout of the facility?"

"I've got satellite footage of the twenty-five-acre compound, and the building layout where they're holding the hostages," Station Chief Trimble said as he turned his laptop toward the major.

"Could I borrow this?"

"Take your time. I haven't slept in two days," Trimble said as he rolled up his coat to use for a pillow and reclined his seat.

Major Franks spent almost an hour with Lieutenant Burke mapping out their tactics before they briefed the rest of their team.

"That should do it, men," Major Franks said when they finished. "It's going to be several hours before we land, so try to get a little rest."

Ten hours later they landed in Turkey, and when the nose of the gigantic aircraft opened up, Major Franks saw the MH-60 Black Hawk helicopters lined up on the tarmac.

Major General Burr, the base commander, met them as they walked down the ramp.

"This has got our latest intel, and Iraqi Colonel Bashara needs to speak with you before you take off," General Burr said as he handed Station Chief Trimble an encrypted jump drive.

Colonel Bashara and Station Chief Trimble moved to one side and started a heated discussion.

"Trimble is sure fluent in whatever the hell it is they're speaking," Major Franks said.

"It's Kurdish, but Trimble is also fluent in Arabic, Dari, Pashto, and at least four other languages spoken in this hellish part of the world," General Burr said.

"Have you got everything I requested?" Station Chief Trimble asked when he finished with Colonel Bashara.

"We've got eight MH-60Ms for your team, and two CH-47 Chinooks for your passengers," General Burr said.

"Good deal, but there's been a new development, and I'm going to need air support."

"Colonel Bashara gave me a heads-up, so I've been working on it. Give me just a second and I'll see how we're doing," General Burr said.

"There are ten MH-60L Direct Action Penetrator gunships en route to the target," General Burr said when he returned.

"That's a lot of firepower," Major Franks said. "And what are the Chinooks for? I thought you said there were only four hostages."

"I'll explain once we're in the air," Station Chief Trimble said. "General, may I have a word in private?"

They'd been airborne for about ten minutes when Major Franks asked, "What the hell are you getting us into?"

"I apologize for the subterfuge, but this had to stay need-to-know until the last minute," Station Chief Trimble said. "Most of the high-ranking ISIS and Taliban leadership in this part of the world are holding a summit meeting in Kobani, and we're going to capture or kill as many of them as we can."

"Is the number of fighters and the layout you gave me still good?" Major Franks asked.

"The layouts for the compound and the building are

accurate. However, Colonel Bashara just informed me that the ISIS leaders brought in two ten-man teams for additional security," Station Chief Trimble said.

"We're going to be outnumbered three to one."

"That's what I was discussing with General Burr. The gunships are going in ahead of us to soften them up."

The MH-60L DAPs were an hour ahead of Major Franks's group, and they were outfitted with M230 chain guns, 30 mm automatic cannons, rocket pods, and door-mounted M134D miniguns. When they reached the compound they began laying down a horrific barrage of fire on the terrorists, and by the time they finished their fifth pass, there was a thick cloud of black smoke over the compound.

Major Watkins, the gunship commander, made one last pass to check their handiwork, and said, "This is Night Stalker One, and the compound is as clear as we can make it."

"Roger that, but keep an eye out for reinforcements," Major Franks said.

All of Major Franks's team was wearing headsets, and as they neared their objective, Major Franks said, "Check your gear, we land in five."

Their chopper had just slid to a stop when Station Chief Trimble screamed, "Follow me," as he bolted out the door.

"Let us take the lead," Major Franks said, but Trimble never slowed.

After the last chopper had landed, Major Franks ordered, "First and second squads on me. Lieutenant Burke, get some men up on that wall, and set up a perimeter around the entrance."

When they entered the compound, Major Franks saw that six enemy guards had Jeff Trimble pinned down.

The guards were using a rock wall for cover, so Major

Franks said, "Corporal Todd, clear those assholes out of there."

Corporal Todd took a knee and vaporized the wall and the guards with an FGM-148 Javelin shoulder-fired missile.

"The leaders are in the main auditorium, and it's this way," Trimble said as he rushed ahead.

As Major Franks and his men followed Trimble toward the center of the sprawling complex of buildings, they ran into one of the elite ten-man ISIS squads, who immediately opened fire with AK-12s and RPGs.

"Take cover," Major Franks said as he returned fire with his MK-17 7.62 mm Fabrique Nationale FN Scar.

The firefight only lasted a few minutes, and as the last fighter fell, Major Franks radioed, "We've got three men down, and we need a medic in here."

"Are you hit, Mr. Trimble?" Major Franks asked when he saw the blood on Trimble's left shoulder.

"Flesh wound, I can keep going."

The airstrikes had killed half of the guards, but the survivors were gathered at the front of the building.

The teams finally caught up with Trimble as he was approaching the main hall, but the guards opened fire, and they had to dive behind a half wall surrounding a small reflecting pool in front of the building.

They returned fire, but when the guards took out a portion of the wall with an RPG, killing three of his men, Major Franks said, "Lieutenant Burke, I need another squad in here ASAP."

Major Franks lost two more men before the reinforcements arrived, but once they had the enemy in a crossfire they made quick work of the remaining guards.

"They should be in here," Station Chief Trimble said as he tried to open the front door to the building.

As Major Franks watched him struggling to open the

massive door with one arm, he said, "Why don't you hang back, and let my men do their job."

There was another savage firefight as they entered the auditorium, but once they'd neutralized the guards, they started tying their hands behind their backs with plastic zip ties.

"Heavy one, we've got twenty-two prisoners ready to transport," Major Franks said.

"Heavy one and two are inbound," the Chinook commander said.

"Get the prisoners moving, the transports are on their way," Major Franks said. "Lieutenant Burke, get all of our casualties loaded up and on their way back to base."

After Lieutenant Burke had left, Station Chief Trimble said, "I'm going to ride back with the prisoners."

"Fine, we'll hang here until everyone is safely away," Major Franks said.

Major Franks kept one of the MH-60L gunships and one of the MH-60Ms with him, and once the rest of the choppers were well out of sight, Major Franks said, "Mount up, we're getting the hell out of here."

The two choppers were flying nap-of-the-earth using their AN/APQ-174B terrain-following radar to avoid detection, but as they neared the Turkish border a heavily armed ISIS patrol spotted them.

"Take them down," the ISIS commander said.

Several of the fighters stood up in the back of the moving pickups and fired their Russian-made SA-24 rocket launchers.

Less than three seconds after the Black Hawk's missile warning system squealed its warning, one of the missiles blew a gaping hole in the front of Major Franks's chopper, killing both the pilots.

"Where the hell did those come from?" asked Captain

Terry Tubbs, the gunship pilot. "There the bastards are," he said as he banked and unleashed a salvo of M261 FFAR 2.75-inch rockets at the convoy.

The rockets blew the small convoy of vehicles into shattered pieces of flaming junk, but Captain Tubbs circled back to strafe them with his M230 30 mm cannon and miniguns. When he was satisfied the threat had been eradicated, Captain Tubbs put his chopper into a violent turn and circled back to the crash site.

"Command, Arrow One is down," Captain Terry Tubbs said. "We've neutralized the threat, and we're landing to check for survivors."

Major Franks had been thrown clear of the furiously burning wreckage. He was unconscious and badly injured.

"Command, we've got one survivor, and Night Stalker One is inbound," Captain Tubbs said.

"Night Stalker, be advised that we're currently experiencing a severe sandstorm, with near zero visibility, and we strongly suggest that you divert to the Niğde airport until it passes."

"How's he doing?" Captain Tubbs asked the crewmen in the back.

"I'm no doctor, but he's hurt bad," Corporal Jett said.

"Command, I need direct clearance to the hospital helipad."

"Granted, but the visibility is extremely poor and getting worse."

"Understood, but we've got to get this soldier to the hospital."

"Your call. We'll dispatch a team to retrieve the other causalities once the weather clears."

They were still fifteen miles from the base when Captain Tubbs caught sight of the eight-hundred-foot-high wall of sand sweeping across the countryside.

"How the hell are we going to land in that?" the copilot asked.

"Carefully," Captain Tubbs said as he began throttling back.

Their airspeed was down to thirty knots, and the visibility was less than a hundred feet as they approached the helipad, but Captain Tubbs managed to land safely. The trauma team was crouched behind the wall of the elevator shaft to escape the wind-driven sand, but they came rushing out to meet the chopper as soon as it touched down.

"Let me take a quick look before we move him," Dr. Denning said as one of the aircrew opened the door.

"Is he going to make it?" Captain Tubbs asked.

"Hard to say," Dr. Denning said as he started an IV in the major's arm. Once he had the IV set, they slid him through the door and onto the gurney.

The surgical team met them as they wheeled the major out of the elevator across the hall from the surgical suite. They already had the surgical instruments laid out, and the head surgeon, Dr. Pennington, and the anesthesiologist, Dr. Thrush, were standing by. Dr. Pennington was an army reserve officer, and was doing a one-year stint of active duty. He'd graduated from Northwestern University Medical School, and was one of the leading brain surgeons in the world. In his civilian life, he was the lead surgeon at the Barrow Neurological Institute, which was located at Saint Joseph's Hospital and Medical Center, in Phoenix, Arizona.

"The patient is unresponsive, blood pressure is ninety over fifty-eight, and his pulse is seventy. He has multiple head injuries and a third-degree burn on his left arm," Dr. Denning said as they transferred the major onto the operating table.

After they'd finished cutting his uniform off, Dr. Pennington took a quick look at the worst of the charred areas on the major's body and said, "Dr. Denning, I need you to treat those burns while I'm working on his head wounds."

"That should do it," Dr. Pennington said as he finished closing up the head wounds.

"Doctor, his cranial pressure is spiking," one of the nurses said.

"I was afraid of that. I'll have to put in a shunt."

When he finished inserting the shunt to relieve the pressure, Dr. Pennington said, "Dr. Thrush, I'll need you to keep him in a barbiturate coma until the bleeding stops."

After they'd dressed his wound, Station Chief Trimble had waited around until Major Franks was out of surgery. "How's he doing?" Trimble asked when he saw Dr. Pennington come out.

"He'll live, but I had to put in a shunt to relieve the pressure to his brain."

"Brain damage?"

"We won't know for a while yet, but we're going to keep him sedated until the cranial swelling subsides," Dr. Pennington said.

"When can I speak with him?"

"No way to know."

"Too bad, he was a fine soldier."

"He's not going to die," Dr. Pennington said as he paused to make a notation on the chart, but when he looked up, Trimble was already gone.

Twenty-one days later, they woke Major Franks up.

"What the hell is going on?" Major Franks asked when he saw the doctor and two nurses standing around his hospital bed.

"You've been injured, and you're at Incirlik Air Base in Turkey."

"Turkey?"

"Do you remember anything?"

Major Franks thought for a moment, "The last thing I remember is being summoned to Colonel Tompkins's office for a mission briefing."

"Memory loss, particularly short term memory, isn't unusual with a traumatic brain injury."

"When can I get out of here?"

"We'll give your wounds a few more days to finish healing before you start your physical therapy. That will give my colleague, Dr. Benjamin Waltershide, our clinical psychologist, time to complete his assessment of your condition."

"How long?"

"That depends on what he finds, but you've been laid up for a while, so your physical therapy will take some time."

"Well, did I pass, Doc?" Major Franks asked when he'd completed the first battery of tests.

"It's not about passing or failing," Dr. Waltershide said. "You graded in the top ten percent on the IQ tests, and the personality tests didn't show any major abnormalities."

"Abnormalities?"

"Everybody's unique, but the personality tests try to evaluate five areas: openness to experience, conscientiousness, extraversion, agreeableness, and neuroticism."

"What the hell does that have to do with me?"

"Probably nothing, but I'd like to do a few more tests."

Three weeks later, Dr. Pennington decided he was ready to begin his physical therapy.

At 0600 the next morning, Tom Ridge, the physical therapist, had the major out of bed and walking around the nurses' station in the center of the ward. Tom was six feet tall and two hundred and twenty pounds of rock-hard muscle from working with the patients every day.

"You can do it," Tom said as he steadied Major Franks from behind.

"I can't believe how weak I am," Major Franks said.

"You've been out of commission for quite a while, but we'll get you whipped into shape."

Five grueling weeks later, Tom Ridge said, "Great job. Thirty reps benching two-fifty is amazing."

"Let's get the running out of the way so I can get the hell out of here," Major Franks said.

"I'm finished with my physical rehab," Major Franks said when he sat down with Dr. Waltershide the next morning. "How about you?"

"At this point we've got to assume that your short-term memories may never return, but other than that, you don't seem to have any cognitive dysfunction."

"That's good, isn't it?"

"Absolutely, but I am a little concerned—no, puzzled—by some of the shifts I've seen in your personality tests."

"Care to explain?"

"You no longer have the same levels of compassion, empathy, or emotional responses that most people do."

"Is that a problem?"

"There's no way of knowing, but I'd like you to continue seeing a psychologist."

"Anything else?"

"No, and I'm going to release you for full-duty status."

CHAPTER 7

"Where are you off to now?" Dr. Waltershide asked as Major Franks was checking out of the hospital the next day.

"Haven't heard yet, but I've got a call with my CO, Colonel Tompkins, at fifteen hundred hours."

An hour later, Dr. Waltershide answered a page. "This is Dr. Waltershide."

"Doctor, this is Colonel Tompkins, Major Franks's CO. I wanted to get your professional opinion on his condition."

"He's been cleared for full duty."

"Let me be clear. I'm about to send him into a combat situation, and I need to know if he's up to it."

"Physically he's at a hundred percent."

"Why the qualification?"

"He still has short-term memory loss."

"He has brain damage?"

"I didn't say that. His cognitive abilities are excellent, but you just never know with an injury like his."

"Is he fit for combat?"

"I wish I could say no, but I can't."

Colonel Tompkins wanted to be able to see Major Franks's reactions, so he held the call on a high-definition video feed.

"You've been laid up for quite a while," Colonel Tompkins said. "Are you sure that you're ready to come back?"

"I feel great, and besides, to me it never happened."

"Good, then here's what I've got. There's a special ops team out of Ramstein, Germany due to arrive at your location in three hours. Major Tuttle is in command, but he's developed a blood clot, and I need you to take over for him."

"What's the mission?"

"I don't have any of the details, but Major Tuttle's XO, Lieutenant Percy, will fill you in."

When the special operations team landed, the medics took Major Tuttle off in an ambulance, and Major Franks walked out to meet the team.

"I'm Major Franks, I'll be filling in for Major Tuttle, and I'm going to need some gear."

"I'm Lieutenant Percy, and you can use Major Tuttle's."

"I've never seen a vest like this," Major Franks said as he was gearing up.

"It's a prototype that the major was supposed to be field-testing," Lieutenant Percy said.

"Whatever," Major Franks said. "Tell me everything you know about the mission."

"There's not a hell of a lot to tell," Lieutenant Percy said. "All we were told was that an unidentified group of assailants has abducted the governor of the Diyala Province, and they think he's being held in a small village about ten miles west of Karbala."

"How many hostiles, and do we have the layout, or at least a description of the building where he's being held?"

"Afraid not, all they gave us was a satellite map of the village."

"This blows. I'll be right back."

"What's up, Major?" Colonel Tompkins asked.

"What nitwit put this op together?" Major Franks asked.

"It was a direct request from our ambassador to Iraq."

"It's completely FUBAR. We don't know which building he's in, and we don't know how many hostiles we're facing. Hell, he may not even be there."

"Are you scrubbing the mission?"

"I am, unless you order me to move forward."

"Not my decision to make. Hang on."

A few minutes later the colonel reappeared.

"The president has made this a top priority. The governor is the brother of Mr. Rafi, the Iraqi president, and President Wilkes has promised that we'll make every possible effort to rescue him. I did find out a little more background. They've received a ransom demand for a million dollars, and they're now certain it's a group of local criminals, not a terrorist group."

"Well?" Lieutenant Percy asked.

"I tried, but I couldn't get it scrubbed," Major Franks said. "So we might as well get loaded up, and get to it."

General Burr had provided ten specially modified versions of the Sikorsky MH-60M helicopters for the mission. They'd added extra blades on the tail rotors, and several other noise reduction measures. The choppers had also been reskinned with hi-tech low observable materials similar to those used in the stealth fighters.

It was a moonless night, and as the choppers neared their destination, they went to quiet mode and prepared to land.

"We're not picking up any heat signatures on the scopes," Captain Rudd said.

"Put us down in that clearing, and we'll hump it the rest of the way," Major Franks said. "We'll try to get in and out without raising a ruckus, but we'll give you a shout if we run into problems.

"Lieutenant Percy, take alpha squad and work the north side of the village, and I'll take bravo, and work the south, and we'll meet back here in one hour," Major Franks said.

They'd been at it for about thirty minutes when Major Franks said, "This is taking too long. Break up into two-man teams, and let's get the rest of these buildings checked out."

As they dispersed to continue their search, Major Franks and Corporal Dodge turned down a trash-strewn dirt path to one of the larger houses in the village.

"Corporal, keep an eye out while I check this out," Major Franks said as he unsheathed his Busse Boss Jack knife, and pried the door open.

He had his night vision on as he entered, and he immediately spotted a bolt action rifle leaning against the far wall and thought, *That can't be good.*

When he heard a noise from down the hall, he considered calling the corporal in to help, but he decided he could handle it on his own. He paused to attach the silencer to his Heckler & Koch Mk 23 Mod 0 pistol and started down the hall toward the first bedroom.

A few minutes later, Lieutenant Percy reported, "Major Franks, we have the governor, and the kidnappers have been eliminated."

"Get him to the chopper, and we'll be right behind you," Major Franks said.

Major Franks had intended to debrief the team after the mission, but it was complete chaos when they landed back at Incirlik Air Base.

"We'll take President Rafi's brother off your hands," Iraqi Colonel Masri said.

"Great job, Major," General Burr said. "Lieutenant

Percy, they need your team back at Ramstein ASAP, and we've got your aircraft refueled and standing by."

"Before you run off, let me give you Major Tuttle's gear back," Major Franks said.

When Lieutenant Percy's team got back to Germany, Master Sergeant Sanderson met them as they walked into their barracks. "Pile your gear up over here, and we'll get it checked out. You're wheels up again at oh-six-thirty," he said.

"I'll take that one, it's not going back out," he said as he picked up the prototype vest.

Unknown to any of them, Major Tuttle's vest was outfitted with a video camera, which had recorded every moment of the mission.

While his men hustled to get the team's gear ready for their next mission, Master Sergeant Sanderson pulled the solid-state hard drive out of the vest, and began reviewing the recording.

"Sir, I need you to come over here and take a look at a video I just processed," Sergeant Sanderson said.

"Just put it on the server, and I'll have a look when I get time," General Broward said.

"Sir, you really need to see this."

"I'll be over in a few minutes."

"Have you told anyone about this?" General Broward asked after he'd viewed the footage.

"No, sir."

"Make sure it stays that way. I'm going to take the hard drive with me."

When the general got back to his office he told his aide, "I need Major Randall."

Major Randall was in charge of their communications and technology section, and when he got there, General Broward said, "Major I need you to encrypt the file on this drive and put it in my secure folder on the server. When you're done, bring it back here, and I'll lock it up in my safe."

When the file was on the server, General Broward called the judge advocate's office.

"General Broward, what can I do for you?" asked General Pibbs, the judge advocate general of the army.

"I've just sent you a secure link to a video recording of a special ops mission in Iraq, and I need you to take a look at it."

"They took a photographer on a special ops mission?"

"No, it's from the solid-state hard drive in a prototype RBA."

"What am I looking for?"

"You'll know."

As the video played out, General Pibbs was horrified as he watched Major Franks slipping from room to room to slaughter the sleeping men, women, and children.

"Was that one of our men?" General Pibbs asked.

"It's a recording from Major Deke Franks's vest camera."

"Send me the drive by courier, and we'll handle it from here."

"I need you to pull the service jacket for a Major Deke Franks," General Pibbs told his aide, Major Lowery.

As the general studied the major's service jacket, he wished that he could just sweep the whole thing under the rug and move on, but the horrific atrocity demanded justice.

"Major Lowery, I want you to dispatch Colonel Jefferies's team to interview everyone involved in this mess. Then I want you to contact Major Franks's commanding officer, Colonel Tomkins, and have him come in so I can brief him."

General Pibbs had been the judge advocate general for seven years, and had just celebrated his thirtieth year in the army. For the most part he was in great shape for his age, but there was a weather front sweeping over D.C., and an old football injury to his right knee was really acting up.

"I appreciate you getting over here so quickly," General Pibbs said as Colonel Tompkins sat down in the wheeled leather chair in front of the general's massive oak desk. The general's office was on the fifth floor of the Pentagon, overlooking the plaza at the center of the massive complex, and it was filled with the memorabilia he'd accumulated during his army career.

When the colonel saw the case displaying an army football jersey bearing the number fifty-five, he said, "You played football at West Point."

"I was a linebacker, but days like this remind me that there's a price to be paid for everything," General Pibbs said as he painfully extended his right leg, trying to find a more comfortable position.

"But enough small talk," General Pibbs said. "How well do you know Major Franks?"

"He's worked for me for the last three years. He's a good man and a fine officer."

"Tell me a little bit about him. I've read his service jacket, and I didn't see any disciplinary actions."

"Of course not. He's led one of the most effective special operations teams we've ever had. Besides that, he's a highly decorated war hero, and his character is above reproach. But why all the questions?"

"I'm going to show you something that will answer your question, but you can't discuss it with anyone."

When the video ended Colonel Tompkins felt like puking.

"You all right?" General Pibbs asked.

"Not really, but that just can't be Major Franks."

"I'm afraid it is."

"Is there anything I can do to help him through this?"

"I'm not sure yet, but when we finish our investigation I'll bring you back in before we move forward."

Ten days later, General Pibbs called Colonel Tompkins back to his office to share the results of their investigation.

"Colonel Tompkins, this is Lieutenant Colonel Myles. He's going to be representing Major Franks, and I've asked him to sit in with us."

"That doesn't sound good," Colonel Tompkins said.

"It's not," General Pibbs said. "We've completed our investigation, and we're going to court-martial Major Franks and charge him with eleven counts of murder."

"I can't say that I'm surprised after what you shared with me last time, but why didn't he disable the camera?" Colonel Tompkins asked.

"He didn't know it was there."

"Colonel, are you ready for trial?" General Pibbs asked.

"Yes, but I don't have a hell of a lot to work with," Colonel Myles said.

The next morning General Burr met Major Franks at the entrance to the Incirlik operations center and said, "Good news, Major, your orders came in last night, and I've got you a seat on a C130 that's headed back to the States."

"It sure will feel good to get back to the States."

"Your flight leaves in an hour, so you'd better grab your gear and hustle back," General Burr said.

When Major Franks's plane landed at Andrews Air Force Base, four burly MPs were waiting for him.

"What's up, boys?" Major Franks asked.

"Sir, you need to come with us," Lieutenant Stevens said.

"Why?"

"You're under arrest."

"I think you've got the wrong man."

"Sir, I've got my orders. Please don't make any trouble."

"No reason to, I haven't done anything."

When they arrived at the stockade, the MPs fingerprinted him, and one of them handed him an orange jumpsuit and said, "You need to put this on."

"I want to speak with a lawyer," Major Franks said.

"The JAG has already appointed one for you, and he's waiting for you in the interrogation room."

"I'm Lieutenant Colonel Myles, and I'll be representing you at your court-martial."

"For what?"

"You're being charged with eleven counts of murder."

"I haven't murdered anyone."

"They've got a video of you slaughtering all the members of an Iraqi family."

"Video?"

"There was a camera in the vest you were wearing during your last mission, and it recorded every move you made."

Shit, that's not good, Major Franks thought.

"As your lawyer, I can't repeat anything you tell me, so just between us, why did you murder those people?"

"They could have queered the mission, and besides, who cares what happens to a bunch of illiterate ragheads?"

Good lord, he means it, Colonel Myles thought. *And I don't sense that he has a shred of compassion for those poor souls.*

"I'll do the best I can for you, but I'm going to have to get creative to keep you off death row."

"Well, what do you think?" Colonel Tompkins asked when Colonel Myles came back out.

"He's a coldhearted bastard," Lieutenant Colonel Myles said.

"I know him pretty well, and while he's always been

a ferocious warrior, he'd never hurt anyone that he didn't have to."

"You wouldn't say that if you'd seen the look in his eyes when he told me that slaughtering those civilians didn't mean a damn thing to him."

"This is all my fault. I should have never rushed him back into combat," Colonel Tompkins said.

"Back into combat? Did something happen to him?"

After Colonel Tompkins had related the story, Colonel Myles said, "I don't understand why I'm just now finding out about this, but it might explain his actions. I'll subpoena his medical records, and have our investigators interview everyone that treated him in Turkey. While I'm waiting on that, I'll have an outside team of doctors do a full physical and psychological workup on him."

Three weeks later, General Pibbs held a follow-up meeting at JAG headquarters with Colonel Tompkins and Lieutenant Colonel Myles.

"I've read the reports from the staff in Turkey, and your medical experts' conclusions," General Pibbs said.

"Then you saw that the report clearly stated that the major's actions, and lack of remorse, could reasonably be attributed to the head injury he suffered," Lieutenant Colonel Myles said.

"Does that mean you'll give him a lighter sentence?" Colonel Tompkins asked.

"The report was also quite clear that the changes to his personality were quite likely permanent," General Pibbs said.

"So what, he wasn't himself when he murdered those people?" Colonel Tompkins asked.

"I don't disagree, but they've not only certified him as medically incompetent to stand trial, they've concluded he should be considered a permanent danger to society," General Pibbs said.

"Major Franks has dedicated his life to this country,

surely you can cut us some sort of deal," Colonel Myles said.

"The best I can do is a lifetime commitment to the mental ward at Fort Leavenworth in Kansas," General Pibbs said.

"We'll take it," Colonel Myles said.

"Major Franks would never agree to that," Colonel Tompkins said.

"He's incompetent, so I won't be asking him," Colonel Myles said.

"The major was a fine soldier, and he sure as hell doesn't deserve to be locked away in a cage for the rest of his life," Colonel Tompkins said.

"That did come out during the background investigations, but he can't be allowed back into society," General Pibbs said. "And if the law allowed, it would be far kinder to have him put down."

"Harsh, but he'd probably agree," Colonel Tompkins said.

"They're going transport him as soon as we're finished. So if you'd like to say good-bye, you'd better do it now," General Pibbs said.

"I'd rather remember him as he was," Colonel Tompkins said.

At 4 A.M. that morning, Colonel Tompkins received an urgent call.

"This is General Pibbs. Major Franks has escaped."

"Escaped, what the hell happened?" Colonel Tompkins asked, still half asleep.

"The Missouri Highway Patrol found the transport van on fire at a roadside park near the Missouri state line. The guards' bodies and the van were badly burned in the fire, so it was several hours before they figured out who to call. Since they had no way of knowing the circumstances, they didn't put out an all-points bulletin until after they'd contacted us."

News of Major Franks's escape was all over the media for weeks as they frantically tried to apprehend him. He even made the FBI's most wanted list, but after several months without any leads, the publicity faded, and they stopped actively looking for him.

CHAPTER 8

A year later, Walter Jefferson, a multibillionaire from North Dakota, was touring one of the drilling rigs he had working in the Beaufort Sea, just south of the Arctic Ocean.

There was a powerful storm sweeping into the area, and as Walter peered down at the frigid arctic waters, he could see the whitecaps on the wind-driven swells. "How's the weather looking?" he asked.

"Not good," answered Harold Close, the pilot of Walter's impeccably appointed Sikorsky H-92 Superhawk helicopter. "The front has unexpectedly turned south, and we're going to be stuck out here until it moves through."

When the massive semisubmersible drilling platform came into view, Harold Close said, "That's the biggest damn rig I've ever seen."

Like a proud parent, Walter Jefferson started reciting the rig's pedigree. "It's a Diamond Offshore Drilling CS60, ultradeep-water, semisubmersible drilling platform. It has accommodations for a two hundred and ten man crew, and it can operate in ocean depths of up to twelve thousand feet, and drill to a depth of forty thousand feet."

"That's quite impressive," Harold Close said. "But

you'd better cinch up tight, because we've got crosswinds of over fifty knots."

"I think you're going to be pleased with this setup, boss," Todd Scruggs, the deep-water drilling supervisor said as he guided Walter across the windswept helipad. "How long are you going to be with us?"

"I'd only intended to spend the day, but my pilot said we'll have to wait out the storm."

"We've got plenty of room, although it might not be as fancy as what you're used to."

That night Walter had dinner with Todd Scruggs in the rig's galley, which was austere but functional. The long aluminum tables and the benches were bolted to the metal floor, and everyone had to walk through the serving lines to get fed. The galley was getting crowded when one of the rig hands came walking by. Walter could tell he was ex-military by the way he carried himself, so he said, "We've got room, why don't you sit with us?"

His name was Terry Robertson, and they struck up a spirited conversation over dinner, so they decided to continue it over drinks in the ship's pub. The pub had a long wooden bar, three dartboards, six pool tables, and a small wooden dance floor. In the center of the room there were fifteen metal tables and benches bolted to the floor, along with several booths bolted to the walls. The pub was crowded with off-duty rig hands, but after a few minutes' wait one of the booths came open, and they sat down to continue their discussion.

Before he'd gone on to law school, Walter had completed a double major in pre-law and clinical psychology, and he was a master at reading people. Sensing that there was more to Terry than met the eye, Walter kept probing, and after another hour, he said, "Terry, if that's really your name, how'd you like to come to work for me?"

"I believe you own this operation, so technically, I already work for you," Terry Robertson said.

"I meant more directly."

"Doing what?"

"Whatever I need, but I've got to stay over for another day, so we can talk some more tomorrow."

When Terry left, Walter picked up Terry's glass, and took a high-resolution picture of his fingerprints with an app on his phone.

"I need you to run these prints," Walter Jefferson said. "And no matter what comes back, this stays between us."

"I understand," said Special Agent Jenkins, the lead investigator with the FBI's Bismarck, North Dakota office.

When the results came back, Special Agent Jenkins immediately e-mailed them to Walter. He hadn't intended to look at the results, but his curiosity got the best of him.

"Oh shit," he said before he deleted the file and the history off his computer.

Walter was eating breakfast as he read the file, and he was so excited that he almost choked on his eggs. *I've got some work to do, but this is just the man I've been looking for,* Walter Jefferson thought.

That night after dinner Walter Jefferson and Terry Robertson returned to the pub to continue their discussion.

"I'd like to formally offer you the job we were discussing last night," Walter Jefferson said.

"Doing whatever?" Terry Robertson asked.

"That's the one."

"I'm in. It's too damn cold out here to suit me. Besides, there's damn poor pickings for broads."

"Good, and I can solve the bimbo problem as well. We take off at oh-five-hundred, so be ready to go.

"I'm stealing one of your hands," Walter said after Terry excused himself to go pack.

"I thought that's what you were up to," Todd Scruggs said. "He keeps to himself, but he does whatever the job calls for and never bitches about it."

When they took off the next morning, the chopper was getting tossed around pretty good, but it didn't seem to faze Terry.

"There's not much that upsets you, is there, Major Franks?" Walter asked.

"How'd you find out?"

"I had one of my FBI contacts run your prints."

"So I'm headed to jail?" Deke Franks asked as he glanced around the luxurious cabin, weighing his options.

"Hardly."

"Then where do we go from here?"

"You're a deserter, and on the FBI's most wanted list, so the first thing we're going to do is fix you up with a new identity."

"How's that work?"

"I have a doctor in Santiago, Chile that I use from time to time, so I'm going to fly you down there and let him work you over. When he's done, they'd have to run a DNA test to ID you."

"What's the catch?"

"None, other than you shouldn't question any task I give you."

"Won't be an issue."

"Then we have a deal. This could take a couple of months, but when you return, I'll put you to work. Oh, by the way, you'll need another alias. Do you have any preferences?"

"Nope."

"Umm, how about John Jay?"

"Wasn't he one of the original founding fathers?"

"You know your history. Will that work for you?"

"Doesn't make a difference to me. When does this all start?"

"I've already arranged for one of my other aircraft to pick you up in Anchorage."

Later that evening, Walter's spare G650ER Gulfstream touched down at the Comodoro Arturo Merino Benítez International Airport in Santiago, Chile. There was a car waiting for John, and it took him directly to Dr. Torres's clinic in downtown Santiago.

In order to guarantee anonymity, the clinic was completely self-contained. It took up half a city block, and housed Dr. Torres's offices, an in-house pharmacy, two surgical suites, a chef's kitchen, and eight elegantly appointed private rooms for his patients. Walter Jefferson had been adamant that there be complete secrecy for John's visit, so they'd cleared out the facility for the duration of his stay and limited the staff to the bare minimum.

"Mr. Jay, it's a pleasure to meet you," Dr. Torres said. "I'm going to skip the explanations since you're here at the request of Mr. Jefferson, but if you do have any questions, I'd be happy to answer them for you."

"How long is this going to take?"

"The entire process will require six different procedures. Everybody responds differently, but if you don't have any complications, you should be back to normal in eight to ten weeks. Now, if you don't have any more questions, you can follow Nurse Sanchez, the head nurse, and she'll get you prepped."

Nine weeks later, John Jay (aka Deke Franks) was sitting in courtyard garden in the center of the clinic, enjoying the warm sunlight. As the soothing sound of the waterfall spilling into the koi pond filled the air, he was contemplating his options to resolve the issue he'd discovered a couple of nights before.

He'd been unable to sleep, so he'd been wandering around the facility, looking for something to occupy his time. When he'd come to Dr. Torres's office he decided to see what the doctor had tucked away. It only took him a few seconds to defeat the locks on the filing cabinets, and as he'd riffled through the files, he'd discovered the doctor was keeping a before and after file on every patient he'd ever worked on. "The bastard shouldn't be keeping this kind of shit," John muttered.

"It's a beautiful day," Dr. Torres said as he sat down.

Jolted back to reality, John said, "It is. Tell me, Doc, how much longer do I have to hang around here?"

"You can leave anytime you'd like."

"Great, I'd like to leave as soon as possible."

"I'll be right back," Dr. Torres said.

John was pacing the courtyard when Dr. Torres returned and sat down at the table. The doctor was talking as he composed a text message on his phone.

"Mr. Jefferson's jet will be here in the morning. Don't worry about transportation, Nurse Sanchez will take you to the airport."

John didn't say a word as he slid in behind the doctor and snapped his neck. He eased the doctor's head down on the tabletop and went inside.

Nurse Sanchez was in the kitchen when John came in, and she asked, "Is the doctor still in the courtyard?"

"Yes, he is," John said as he crushed her windpipe with a savage blow to the throat.

John picked the nurse up off the floor and stuffed her body into the kitchen pantry. After he'd retrieved the doctor's body and put it in with the nurse's, he spent the rest of the day destroying all of the doctor's records.

The kitchen was just down the hall from the front entrance. So when the taxi arrived the next morning, John blew out the pilot light to the Wolf gas stove in the kitchen and turned on all of the burners. He stopped to get a bottle of water out of the Sub-Zero refrigerator before he lit a candle and placed it on a table in the hall. He locked the front door behind him and jumped into the waiting cab.

As Walter's Gulfstream rose over the city, John could see the thick black smoke rising from the raging inferno consuming Dr. Torres's clinic.

Eight hours later, John's plane landed at Walter's private airfield on his North Dakota ranch, and Larry Duke, Walter's longtime ranch foreman, was waiting to take him up to the main house.

"If Dr. Torres hadn't sent me a picture I would never have recognized you," Walter Jefferson said when John walked in. "How are you feeling?"

"No complaints," John Jay said.

"Is there anything you'd like to tell me?"

"Concerning the doctor?"

"Correct."

"He'd been keeping before and after photos of all his patients, so I took care of it."

"Initiative, I like it. But from now on, clear that sort of thing with me first."

"I didn't think you'd have a problem with it."

"I don't, it's a control thing."

"It won't happen again. What now?"

"I'm going to take a few days to bring you up to speed on some of my long-term plans," Walter Jefferson said.

"From what I've seen so far you've already got everything money can buy," John Jay said.

"I do, but money isn't what drives me. This country is well down the road to ruin, and I intend to do something about it."

"Fine words, but you're just one man."

"True, but the militias have plenty of manpower."

"Militias! They're nothing but a bunch of rednecks with guns."

"A fair assessment at the moment, but I'll rectify that once I gain control of them."

"How's that going?"

"Not that well, but I hope to get a meeting with Roger Newsome, the leader of the North Dakota militia in the near future."

"How can I help?"

"I need you to put together a plan to expand his group."

"What did you have in mind?"

"I want you to list the types of skills you'd want if you were putting together a special ops team, the training regimen you'd use, and the equipment and supplies you'd need."

"No problem, but what do you intend to do with all of this if you're successful?"

"I want to be able to help defend our way of life if the need arises."

Two months later Walter Jefferson finally got his meeting with Roger Newsome.

He'd spent the previous two years and several million dollars trying to get hooked into the militia subculture, but this was the first militia leader that had agreed to meet with him.

"Why in God's name are you meeting with this nutcase?" asked Larry Duke.

"He's the head of the North Dakota militia," Walter said.

"Everybody knows that, but you don't need to be seen with the likes of him."

"I'm trying to gain some credibility with the militia leaders in the United States, and I thought he might be able to help."

"Again, why?"

"It's really none of your damn business, but I'm working on a plan that may require the help of men like them."

Duke recognized the tone in Walter's voice, so he decided to shut up.

"It's about damn time," Roger Newsome muttered when he caught sight of the tree-lined road that led to Walter's house. He'd lived next to Walter's spread his entire life, but this was the first time he'd ever been to his house.

Walter was standing by the massive fireplace in the great room when Larry Duke brought Roger Newsome in. Despite Larry's criticism, Roger wasn't one of the rednecks-with-guns types; he'd been a captain in the Delta Force until he'd lost his left foot to an IED. He was six feet tall, with brown hair and brown eyes, and even though his injury made it more difficult, he still kept himself in top-notch shape.

Roger had felt out of place in the sprawling ranch house, but when he saw that Walter was in boots and jeans, he relaxed a little.

As they shook hands, Roger was a little surprised to see that Walter was only five foot five and weighed maybe a hundred and thirty pounds. His fair complexion was quite a contrast with his black hair and brown eyes, which were so dark that they looked black.

"I wouldn't have agreed to the meeting if I'd known it was going to take me an hour to get here," Roger Newsome said. "What the hell do you want with me anyway?"

"You're the leader of the North Dakota militia, aren't you?"

"Yes, but why would a rich bastard like you care?"

"If we can come to a mutual understanding today,

you'll be leaving with a duffel bag containing ten million dollars in cash, and a yearly salary of five hundred thousand dollars."

"Who do I have to kill?" Roger asked.

"No one, at least for now," Walter Jefferson said.

Shit, he's serious, Roger thought when he saw the expression on Walter's face. "What then?"

"I want you to use the money to expand your organization."

"What do you get out of it?"

"I'll want to take an active role with your organization, and I want you to arrange a meeting for me with all the other militia leaders."

"That might be doable, but I'd like to hear some of the specifics before I agree."

Walter spent almost an hour covering the plans that he and John Jay had been working on.

"Well, do you think can we work together on this?" Walter Jefferson asked.

"I'm in, but the other militia leaders aren't a trusting lot, so it may take me some time to convince them to meet with you," Roger said.

"Trust me, I understand that. Here's your money, and I look forward to a long and mutually beneficial relationship," Walter said as he handed Roger the bag of money.

Roger unzipped it and said, "Damn, I sure never thought I'd see this much cash."

Sixty days later, Roger received a phone call from Walter.

"How's the recruiting going?" Walter Jefferson asked.

"We've already signed up nine thousand new recruits."

"How?"

"After those shit-for-brains congressmen cut their

budgets, the military gave most of them an early discharge."

"I know you weren't expecting that many. What do you need?"

"I don't have enough room for us to drill, or to hold maneuvers."

"I've just purchased the old Steel spread just north of you. I'll build you some barracks and put up some barns for storage."

"We could use some more uniforms."

"Anything you need."

"Why are you doing all of this?"

"There will come a time when these people will be needed."

"We'll be ready. I'm still waiting to hear back from a couple of them, but I should be able to get the other militias to meet with you by the first of the year."

CHAPTER 9

As President Wilkes was beginning his fourth year in office he was growing concerned about his chances of being reelected.

"Thanks for coming in," President Wilkes said when Larry Ragsdale sat down in the Oval Office. "Quite a lot has changed since the first time we met in here," he said.

"True, but what's up? Your assistant said it was urgent," Larry Ragsdale replied.

"As I feared when your organization strong-armed me into instituting them, the tax cuts haven't performed as advertised. The unemployment rate is over nine percent, inflation is over ten percent, and we haven't had positive growth in the GDP since I took office."

"Okay, but how is that urgent?"

"I'm up for reelection, and I don't have much of a track record to run on."

"Sure you do. The stock market is at an all-time high, and corporate profits are through the roof."

"True, but the average citizen is much worse off."

"And your point is . . . ?"

And they accuse me of being a coldhearted bastard, the president thought. "The point is that I still need their votes."

"Not to worry, we'll be able to herd the sheep again."

Even though he'd offhandedly dismissed the president's concerns, his words had struck a chord with Larry. He'd always been quick to defend the group he worked for, but in truth, he'd never actually met, or even spoken with the people he worked for. Each week a courier service would bring him his instructions for the coming week and a cashier's check to cover his expenses and salary.

The weekly courier was scheduled for the next morning, so that night he typed up his concerns and included them in the pouch. He'd never sent them an unsolicited communication before, so he didn't know if they'd reply, but to his surprise two days later he got an early morning phone call at his home in Bethesda, Maryland.

"Hello, Mr. Ragsdale, I'd like to discuss your note."

"Okay, but who the hell are you?" Larry Ragsdale asked.

"My name is John Jay, and our employer has asked me to set up a face-to-face meeting to discuss your concerns and clarify their expectations."

"When do you want to meet?"

"Right now, if that's all right?"

"Where?"

"If you'll let me in your front door, we can get started."

When Larry opened the door, John Jay was standing on his front porch.

"John, this is more than a little disconcerting."

"My apologies, but they felt this needed to be handled ASAP."

After John answered Larry's questions, he spent the next three hours detailing their expectations for the upcoming campaign.

"So, Larry, is there anything you didn't understand, or need clarification on?"

"Why are they so adamant about replacing Secretary Behrmann?"

"They have several reasons, but the biggest rub is his role in the selection process for the Unified Combat Commands. Anything else?"

"Jim Rutherford was their man, why do they want to replace him?"

"His level of commitment hasn't been what they expected."

I guess they don't like that he can actually think for himself, Larry thought.

THE NEXT DAY Daoud Mansouri, the worldwide leader of the Islamic State, was on his way to his office of the day in his armored BMW X5 M.

His father had been the head of the Iraqi Republican Guard until he had a falling out with Saddam Hussein and had been forced to seek asylum in England. Daoud had been raised in England and had graduated from Cambridge. He'd been studying for the bar until the Israelis assassinated his father. After he'd buried his father, he'd returned to Iraq and joined the Islamic State to seek his revenge.

Three weeks before, Daoud had been delayed by an accident on the way to his office, and he'd just missed being killed when an American B1-B Lancer had imploded his downtown office building with a JDAM.

However, that wasn't the first time the Americans had almost killed him. He still walked with a limp from an injury he'd suffered during an MQ-9 Reaper Hellfire missile attack that had killed the previous leader of the caliphate, Abu Mohammad Al-Qaradawi.

As a result of the latest attack, Dizhwar Akram, his right-hand man, had assembled a mobile office that they moved to a different location every day. Dizhwar was a massive man at six eight and two hundred and eighty pounds, and had once been a rising star in the Syrian army until he'd become disillusioned with Bashar al-Assad's brutal repression of his people. He'd joined the Islamic State.

When Daoud's small convoy of vehicles stopped in front of the trashed library building on the east side of Mosul, his security team quickly escorted him inside.

Daoud Mansouri was five six and a hundred and twenty-five pounds, with a light brown complexion, dark brown eyes, black beard, and closely cropped black hair, but his haggard appearance made him look far older than forty-five.

The rioters had overturned the library shelves, and Daoud could see the scorch marks from where the rioters had torched the books. As they made their way through the debris the stench was almost overpowering.

"Sorry about the smell, but it's the best we could do for today," Dizhwar Akram said.

"How'd we fare yesterday?" Daoud Mansouri asked as he sat down in the makeshift office.

"Not well, those damned American drones killed the two men we sent to Yemen."

"Already? How the hell did they even know they were there?"

"NSA, CIA, who knows? I'd cautioned both of them to stay off their phones and the Internet, but they were both young, so I doubt they listened."

"Send two more. We need to get those new groups organized before they lose heart and go back to the local al-Qaeda chapter."

"We've got plenty of willing volunteers, but speaking of volunteers, we need to come up with a plan for all the inquiries we're receiving off of the new website."

"It's working?"

"Too well. We've received over two hundred new

requests since it went live this week, and over half of them are from North America."

"So what's the problem?" Daoud Mansouri asked.

"If we don't keep them engaged, we'll lose them."

"Suggestions?"

"We need a physical presence in the country."

"Right now that would be problematic, but how about Canada?"

"Possibly, but why not Mexico?"

"The Americans have a lot more surveillance on their southern borders."

"You're right, Canada would be a lot easier," Dizhwar Akram said.

"Then let's work that angle for now. I've had a couple of calls with Prime Minister Rodney Douglas, and I think I'm close to working out a mutual accommodation with him."

"What does that even mean?" Dizhwar Akram asked.

"It means I've guaranteed that we won't cause him any more trouble if he'll look the other way on our activities."

"He'll never go for that. The Americans would rip his balls off if they ever found out."

"Then I'll just have to get his attention. I think it's time that we reengage your favorite mercenary," Daoud Mansouri said.

"I can't believe you'd use that asshole again. The man is an apostate, and we should be making an example of him, not giving him millions of dollars to do our dirty work."

"I know he's a pig, but he gets things done."

"What's the job?"

"I want him to assassinate three of their parliament members."

"Which ones, and how do you want it done?"

"I don't care who he offs, but I don't want it to resemble one of our attacks."

"It may take a few days to make the arrangements."

"Okay, but it needs to happen before the end of the month. On the website thing, I want you to personally handle the interactions with new recruits, but if you find one that's got potential I want you to involve me."

To his surprise, Dizhwar made contact with Hani Aboud on his first try, and he reluctantly agreed to take the contracts.

"He'll do it, but he wants a million dollars apiece," Dizhwar Akram said.

"Pretty steep for a simple hit, but go ahead," Daoud Mansouri said.

After the last attack Daoud and Dizhwar never slept in the same location twice, and they were staying in a small villa near the center of town. Hani Aboud called three nights later.

"It's done," he said.

"Good," Dizhwar Akram replied as he opened an app on his phone. "The money should be in your account."

"I see it. Good doing business with you."

"Hani Aboud just completed his contract," Dizhwar told Daoud.

"It's about time. Now I can call the prime minister."

"You're nothing but a low-life murderer," Canadian Prime Minister Rodney Douglas said.

"You forced my hand," Daoud Mansouri replied. "Are you ready to reconsider my offer?"

"Hell no, and I'm going to track down and kill every one of you murderous bastards."

"You really should reconsider."

"Go to hell."

"Did you get your accommodation?" Dizhwar Akram asked when Daoud hung up.

"No, but I will. Call your favorite mercenary back, and have him kidnap the prime minister's oldest brother and his family."

"How much ransom do you want to ask for?"

"Ten million, but he can keep the money if he gets it."

"He'll still want money up front."

"Pay whatever he asks, but tell him not to make a move until I give the word."

Two days later, Prime Minister Douglas was sitting down to dinner when his cell phone rang. "What the hell do you want now?" he asked.

"I'm giving you one last chance to do as I ask," Daoud Mansouri said.

"Go to hell."

At 3 A.M. the next morning the phone beside the prime minister's bed rang. "Yes?" he said, still half asleep.

"There's been an incident at your brother's home on Prince Edward Island," said Terrance Wells, the head of the Canadian Security Intelligence Service.

"Incident?"

"A large number of intruders killed the security team guarding his estate and abducted him and his family."

"How could you let that happen?" Prime Minister Douglas asked.

"I've got no excuses, but what do you want us to do if we receive a ransom demand?"

"Forward it to me."

"You're going to negotiate with them?"

"Hell no. I want every available resource on this, and to be perfectly clear, I don't care what sort of methods you have to use."

The prime minister had just gotten to his office the next morning when his cell phone rang.

"You bastard, you'd better not hurt them," Prime Minister Douglas said.

"Are you ready to deal?" Daoud Mansouri asked.

"Hell no."

"Then their blood is on your hands."

"If you harm them I'll—"

"You'll what? If you don't play ball, this will just be the beginning. If you change your mind you can reach me at this number."

"I just received a demand from the kidnappers," Prime Minister Douglas said.

"What did you tell them?" Terrance Wells asked.

"I told them to go to hell, but you need to get off your ass and find them."

The next day was a Saturday, and Prime Minister Douglas was sitting in the study of the twenty-two-room Rideau Cottage drinking his morning coffee and reading the overnight dispatches.

"Sir, were you expecting a delivery?" asked Larry Williams, the prime minister's butler.

"No."

"Well, there's a courier outside with an express shipment."

"Just take care of it," Prime Minister Douglas said.

When his butler returned with a large Styrofoam container, the prime minister asked, "What the hell have you got there?"

"It's marked for your eyes only, so I didn't open it."

"Put on the table. I'll take a look when I get a moment."

When the prime minister finished reading the CSIS updates, he poured another cup of coffee and muttered, "I wonder what the hell that is," but as he did, a cold chill came over him.

"Oh dear God, no," he exclaimed loudly. "Williams, get in here and open this damned thing up for me."

The Styrofoam lid was jammed in tight, and when Williams pried it out, it made a horrible screeching sound.

"What's in there?" Prime Minister Douglas asked.

When Williams didn't answer, the prime minister rushed over to see for himself. The dry ice was holding the decapitated heads in place, and when he saw the cold dead eyes of his brother and his family staring up at him, he fainted.

As Charles Dudley, the prime minister's head of security, waved the smelling salts under his nose, he asked, "Are you all right?"

"What happened?" Prime Minister Douglas asked as he tried to sit up.

"Easy, you've got a nasty gash in your head."

"Oh, God. Tell me it's just a horrible nightmare," he said as his head started to clear.

"How I wish I could. We've removed the package, and we'll have the forensic team examine their remains."

"Doesn't much matter now. Help me up, I need to make a phone call.

"I swear by all that's holy, I'll hang your sorry ass someday, but for now I'm forced to go along. Just don't hurt anyone else."

"You have my word, as long as you hold up your end of our agreement. The Americans will eventually find out what happened, so I'm going to give you the location of a couple of the al-Qaeda cells you can take down to make it look like you've taken care of the situation."

"Why would you do that?"

"Neither of us need them poking around up there."

CHAPTER 10

Two weeks later, Walter Jefferson was standing on the front porch of his rustic, eighteen-thousand-square-foot ranch house in North Dakota, enjoying the crisp January air. As he waited for his guests to arrive, he was contemplating how he'd reached this point in his life.

A descendent of Thomas Jefferson, he'd spent most of his adult life pursuing his vision of the world. Small in stature but with a prodigious IQ, he'd suffered from what his father had loved to throw in his face all his life, his "little man syndrome."

His father had been a tyrant, a scoundrel of a man, but he'd managed to carve out a vast empire in the oilfields of North Dakota and Canada while becoming a billionaire many times over. His mother had died while giving birth to him, and Walter had often thought that was why his father had been so rough on him as he was growing up. In spite of the abuse, Walter had managed to graduate at the top of his undergraduate class at Harvard. From there he'd gone on to graduate summa cum laude from Harvard Law School, and had been recognized as one of the finest orators to have ever graduated from the university.

As Walter thought back over his life, a memory of one of those pivotal events came rushing back.

"I wish you could have attended the ceremony," Walter said.

"It was just a graduation. Hell, you're a grown man, I don't need to hold your hand for everything," said his father, Jerry Jefferson.

"I worked my ass off to be top of my class, and I was hoping that you'd at least come to graduation."

"Quit busting my chops, that's all in the past. So where are you going to practice?"

"I wanted to discuss that with you. I'm considering going into politics instead of practicing law."

"Over my dead body. Politicians are nothing but a pack of money-grubbing, self-serving losers, and that's the end of this conversation. I'll call my friend Tubby in Bismarck first thing in the morning, and I'm sure he'd be more than happy to let you join their firm."

"Dad—"

"Don't 'Dad' me, you sniveling little pussy. Just shut the hell up and do as I say."

Disgusted, Walter shook his head and plopped down in one of the overstuffed chairs in front of the roaring fire in the great room.

"Don't get too comfortable, we're going quail hunting on that new spread that I just bought."

"You know I don't like to hunt."

"I don't give a shit. Get off your dead ass and go get changed."

When Walter came downstairs, his father had gotten their shotguns out of the massive glass gun cabinet in the great room.

"Here's your gun, and I've already filled your vest with shells."

"Great."

"Quit sulking and try to make the best of it," Jerry Jefferson said.

As they walked down the stairs to the circular drive in front of the house, Larry Duke pulled up in a brand-new, jacked-up four-wheel-drive crew cab pickup.

"She's all gassed up and ready to go. There's a couple of coolers in the backseat with some brisket sandwiches and a case of beer."

"Thanks, Larry. We should be back by dark," Jerry Jefferson said.

Neither one of them said a word as they made their way across the rugged, unspoiled countryside that separated the two ranches.

They'd been hunting for several hours, and were about a mile away from their truck when Jerry Jefferson said, "We'd better head back, it'll be dark in another hour."

"Sure, Dad, whatever you say," Walter Jefferson said. "Then maybe we can discuss my future."

"Shut your pie hole. I've already told you what you're going to do, and that's the end of it."

"Sorry, bastard," Walter muttered under his breath.

"Spit it out if you've got something to say," Jerry Jefferson said.

Neither said a word as they made their way back to the truck, but Walter's mind was filled with years of repressed rage. Screw this, *he thought.*

Walter stopped, and as his father continued walking, he dropped to his knees, jammed the gun's butt into the ground, and pulled both triggers on his silver-plated, over-and-under Benelli shotgun.

His father was only a couple of feet away when the birdshot ripped through his back. He fell face-first, screaming in agony.

"You clumsy little bastard, you've shot me," Jerry Jefferson screamed.

Jerry was already going into shock, so he didn't notice when Walter bent down and took the cell phone out of his vest pocket.

"Son of a bitch; that hurts like hell." Jerry moaned as he fumbled for his phone. When he couldn't find it, he said, "Call Luke and tell him to get his ass out here and pick me up."

When Walter didn't respond, Jerry managed to roll over onto his side to demand, "You stupid little shit, call Luke."

Walter didn't say a word, but he took out his phone and started tapping the touch screen.

After another minute, Jerry asked, "When's Luke going to get here?"

"Not coming."

"Quit being a smart-ass. How long?"

"Haven't called him yet," Walter said as he continued playing his game.

"You little imbecile, get me some help."

Jerry was fading fast, but just before he passed out he managed to gasp, "Help me, I'm dying . . ."

"Good," Walter muttered as he got up and started walking slowly back to the truck.

Walter flinched as the sound of the Gulfstream's engines jerked him back to reality.

"Is that our guests?" Walter Jefferson asked.

"It is, and they're just about to land," Larry Duke said.

Larry had worked for his father, so Walter knew he had to be getting up in years, but his rugged features and the old cowboy hat that never left his head made it hard to tell how old he really was.

"Is everything ready?"

"Of course, but what are you up to this time?"

"I'm meeting with the leaders of every meaningful militia in the United States."

"More militias? Your dad is probably rolling over in his grave."

I hope the miserable bastard is burning in hell, Walter thought.

"Roger Newsome and some of the boys are going to bring them up to the house," Larry Duke said.

"Gentlemen, please come in, and thank you for coming," Walter said as Roger Newsome led them into the conference room. The conference room was located just down the hall from the great room where he'd first met with Roger, and it was quite a setup.

The walls of the windowless thirty-six-hundred-square-foot room were covered with massive 8K monitors, and there were speakers everywhere, so there wasn't a bad seat.

After they'd made their introductions, Walter took his place at the head of the massive mahogany table and said, "Find a seat and we'll get started."

"Damn fine setup you've got here," said Clarence Booth, the commandant of the North Carolina militia.

Clarence was sixty years old, five foot nine, with white hair, a ruddy complexion, and was at least fifty pounds overweight, but his family controlled a goodly portion of the tobacco production in North Carolina and was immensely wealthy.

"Thanks. This is the main house. It sits on sixty-five sections of land, and it's the first property my father purchased when the oil boom hit."

"Damn, man, what the hell do you need with us?" asked Terry Gould, the leader of the Idaho militia. "You're already living the American dream."

Terry had been a fifth-generation farmer until the drought had wiped him out. He was a gaunt six foot five, a hundred and seventy pounds, and he'd seen the militia as a way to regain his dignity. His whole life revolved around it.

"I do have everything money can buy, but I didn't invite you up here to discuss money. This is about what's happening to this great nation of ours, and what we might be able to do to get it back on the right path. My ancestor, Thomas Jefferson, was one of the founding fathers, and I'll not stand by while this country gets ripped apart by Islamic terrorists, illegal immigrants, and the liberal wack jobs who are trying to take away our religious freedoms."

"Amen, Brother Jefferson," said Lee Davis, the head of the West Virginia militia. "But what the hell can we do about it? They've got all the power, and we've haven't got a pot to piss in or a window to throw it out of."

Lee Davis was one of the rednecks with guns that John Jay had been alluding to. After the FBI had taken down the local KKK chapter, Lee had moved on to bigger and better things, and his group was now the biggest meth manufacturer and distributor in the South.

"A little redneck Southern humor, I like that," Walter Jefferson said. "There'll come a time when men like us will have to step forward, as our forefathers did, and put it all on the line. Borrowing a little of Lee's Southern wit, it's more akin to the fable about a ham and egg breakfast: 'The chicken is involved, but the pig is committed.'"

They all laughed, but Clarence Booth said, "It's not going to be all that humorous if we fail. I'm more than willing to sacrifice my life for the cause, but I can't stand the thought of this country falling into the hands of those damned ragheads."

"Well said. We're going to spend the next three days discussing some of my initiatives, and how we might be able to work together to achieve them. However, before we get started, I've prepared a nondisclosure agreement that I need each of you to read and sign before we continue."

"What if I'm not comfortable signing this?" Clarence Booth asked when he finished reading it.

"Then I'll have my plane take you home, and there'll be nothing more said about it. However, if you do choose to sign, and break your promise, there will be ramifications."

"That sounds like a threat."

"It is. This is far too important to allow anyone to jeopardize it."

Waiter's eyes were such a dark shade of brown that they often looked black, and as Clarence Booth tried to stare him down, it felt like Walter's eyes were peering into his very soul.

"Okay, I'll sign," Clarence said, looking away.

Once they'd all signed, Walter said, "Let's get started."

They worked twelve hours a day for the first two days, and on the afternoon of the third day Walter closed his laptop and said, "Gentlemen, I think we're done for now. Do any of you have any further questions or comments about the roles you're being asked to fill?"

"I do," said Lee Davis. "How do you expect me to talk the owners of the Greenbrier hotel into letting me do all of those renovations to their property?"

"That won't be an issue. I bought it last month, and the new manager is one of my men."

"Shit, that place must have cost a fortune."

"Enough, but as I said when we started, money's not going to be a problem. Gentlemen, I can't thank you enough for spending this time with me, and from time to time I'll be contacting you to give you further assignments.

"I almost forgot to mention it, but I'm going to be making a run at the presidency as an independent, and I hope I can count on your support."

They were all quick to assure him of their support, and after a few minutes Walter said, "I'm sorry to have kept you so late. My men have already loaded your luggage, so have a safe journey home, and we'll be talking again in the very near future."

The militia leaders were discussing the meeting at the airport when Clarence Booth asked, "What just happened?"

"What do you mean?" Lee Davis asked.

"We were the independent leaders of our organizations when we arrived, but now it feels like we're Walter Jefferson's lackeys."

"I sure wouldn't put it like that," said Jeb Butts, the leader of the Texas militia. "To me it feels like we're all part of something much bigger." Jeb's family owned three of the largest cattle feedlots in Texas. Jeb had graduated from the Air Force Academy, but his once promising career had been cut short by a training accident that had destroyed his left knee.

"He's a charismatic bastard for sure. Several times I found myself getting goose bumps when he'd get all wound up," said Jerome Rappaport, the leader of the California militia.

"Same here, and I was pleasantly surprised to see that he didn't come across as a bigot," Jerry Garcia said. Jerry's grandfather had snuck his family across the border to escape the cartel's violence, but Jerry's father had been born in the U.S., and Jerry had been a twice-decorated career marine until a sniper's bullet had severed the nerves in his right arm.

"I agree," Willy Wood said. "As a black man leading a militia, it has been an issue at times, even in New York."

Willy was five eleven and almost three hundred pounds, but even at that weight he was surprisingly agile in a tussle. He'd had a brief career as a professional wrestler, but the militia had given him a renewed sense of worth.

"It's going to be a diverse group for sure," Jerome Rappaport said. "I'll bet none of you ever expected to have a Jew as part of your group."

Jerome's ancestors had left Germany just ahead of the Holocaust, and his father had been a wildly successful Wall Street banker. Jerome was six foot three and two hundred pounds, with blond hair and blue eyes. He'd graduated from MIT at the age of nineteen with a doctorate in physics, and was currently working on a nuclear fusion project with General Electric.

"I don't care what your religion is as long as you hate Muslims," Melbourne Turner said. His family had owned several large plantations and had been a fixture in Georgia society since the Civil War. His militia was filled with white supremacists. He was small for a man at five foot five. He weighed a hundred and thirty pounds and had angular features and a shaved head.

"Whoa, let's be clear here, this isn't about hating all Muslims, this is about stamping out the Islamic State," said Clyde Thomas, the leader of the Nevada militia. "I've got several good friends who are Muslims." Clyde had been a major in the marines until his father had been killed during a holdup at one of their liquor stores in Las Vegas. He was an only child, so he'd resigned his commission and returned home to help his mother run the family business.

"I'm definitely in agreement with that," Jerome Rappaport said. "My people have been on the wrong end of that kind of hate before, and it isn't anything I'd want to be a part of."

"I agree, but let's change the subject for a minute. I

can't understand how Walter could have known some of the stuff he shared with us," Jeb Butts said.

"I asked him about that last night after dinner," Clarence Booth said. "All he would say is that he has people embedded throughout the government, military, and intelligence communities, but he wouldn't give me any specifics."

"Don't blame him," Lee Davis said. "You've got to protect those kind of assets, and as the old saying goes, 'If more than one person knows, it's not a secret.' "

"Some of the scenarios he laid out were quite frankly terrifying," Clarence Booth said.

"The truth often is." Jerry Garcia nodded. "But he didn't say anything that I found surprising or even hard to believe they could happen."

"The Liberty Tree scenario was by far the most disconcerting," Willy Wood said.

"It was disturbing, but I can imagine a time when the military might have to take charge, at least for a little while, to reestablish the government," Lee Davis said.

"Let's pray that never happens," Terry Gould said.

"The one thing that I know for sure is that Walter Jefferson expects us to have his back, and I didn't sense that he's a man to be trifled with."

That night, as was often the case, Walter Jefferson's dreams were filled with images from his troubled youth. On this night, it was about the last time he'd seen his best friend, Jamie Robinson.

Jamie's dad was a wealthy rancher, and Walter's dad hadn't hit it big in the oilfields yet, so Jamie got to do a lot of things that Walter's family couldn't afford. They were both freshmen in high school, and Jamie was raising show rabbits to enter in the Future Farmers of America's livestock show. One morning when he went out to check on them he found Walter standing beside his prized rabbits' overturned hutch.

"Walter, what the hell are you doing out here?" Jamie asked.

"Nothing you need to worry about, but you'd better go back inside."

"What have you done?" Jamie asked when he saw the blood on Walter's hands. He ran over to the hutch, and when he saw the bloody carcasses, he screamed. "You've killed them. You sorry little bastard, I'm going to kick your ass."

Walter turned to walk away, but Jamie grabbed his shirt and spun him around. Walter hadn't intended to hurt him, but out of sheer reflex he lashed out with the razor-sharp knife in his hand.

With his throat slit from ear to ear, Jamie dropped to his knees on the manure-laced straw. He looked up at Walter and struggled to speak, but all he could manage was a horrible gurgling sound. Jamie struggled to breathe for a few seconds with blood gushing down the front of his shirt before he passed out and fell facedown on the barn floor.

"You should've left," Walter said.

What the hell have I done? *Walter thought. Desperate to cover his tracks, Walter frantically looked around the barn, until he remembered Jamie's dad's warning to them the previous day: "I've got a sow penned up in the barn, and she's meaner than hell when she has babies, so stay out of there."*

The old sow was half asleep and lying up against the fence feeding her babies, so Walter was able to grab one. When he snapped its spine so it couldn't run away, it started squealing in agony. Walter rolled Jamie over onto his back, laid the screaming piglet on his chest, and folded Jamie's arms over it to hold it in place. By then the enraged sow was throwing a fit to reach her baby, and when Walter pulled the gate open, she went straight for it.

Once Walter saw the sow savaging Jamie's body, he hurried out the back of the barn.

When Jamie's dad heard the commotion, he grabbed his rifle and came running out to see what was going on. When he saw the sow ripping chunks of flesh out of Jamie's body, he screamed, "Oh dear God, no. Get off of him, you bitch."

He kicked her in the side to get her off of Jamie, but she let out a squeal and came after him. "Oh hell no," he said as he shot her dead.

When he heard the shot, Walter muttered, "Son of a bitch, that was close." He kept walking, but he stopped when he heard Jamie's dad wailing in agony.

"Oh well, shit happens," Walter remarked as he turned and walked away.

When Walter woke the next morning and remembered the dream, a wry smile creased his lips.

CHAPTER 11

A couple of weeks later Daoud Mansouri's office of the day was set up in the corner of a massive clothing warehouse in downtown Mosul. The workers hadn't shown up yet, so they had the immense building to themselves.

Dizhwar Akram had been refining their mobile office, and he'd mounted the office furniture, communications, and office equipment on large pallets that they could have unloaded and up and running in less than thirty minutes.

"This new setup works a lot better," Daoud Mansouri said when he walked in with his bodyguards. "Was the new video what you had in mind?"

"It was very powerful, but I'm not sure it was a good idea to threaten the Americans like that," Dizhwar Akram said.

"They're a plague to all that's holy to us, and until we can strike them down in their own country they're never going to take us seriously. How's the new website going?"

"It's getting a lot of hits, and I think one or two of them are actually going to step up and do something," Dizhwar Akram said.

"Has Ehsan Hashmi arrived yet?"

"He's waiting outside."

Ehsan Hashmi was twenty-eight years old and six foot two, with long black hair and dark brown eyes. He'd been a rising star in the Pakistani Special Services Group until the president of Pakistan had his father executed during a purge. Fearing the same fate, Ehsan had fled the country, and he'd eventually ended up in Pretoria, South Africa, where he'd been recruited into the Islamic State. After two years working with them, he'd garnered a reputation as a strong leader, a meticulous planner, and a master tactician.

"You've had remarkable success in South Africa, but I need your help to begin launching strikes against the American homeland," Daoud Mansouri said as he motioned for Ehsan to take a seat beside him. "Although, at least initially, you'll be based out of Canada."

"I didn't think the Canadian operation had ever amounted to much."

"It hasn't, but you and I are going to rectify that."

"I'll do whatever you ask."

It took Daoud Mansouri over two hours to convey his expectations, and when he finished he asked, "Any questions or concerns?"

"No, and I will not fail you," Ehsan Hashmi promised.

Six days later, President Wilkes was working out in the White House gym when Mary Counts came rushing in. "Sir, there's been an incident in Los Angeles."

"What now?" the president asked. "It had better be important, because I'm tired of wasting my time on petty bullshit."

"I'll let you be the judge of that, but Nancy Baker, the secretary of homeland defense, made me promise that I'd get this to you right away."

"Let's see what you've got," he said as he stepped off the treadmill.

"Is this for real?" he asked.

"Yes, sir, and there are already dozens of videos of the attack posted to YouTube."

"I'm going to take a quick shower. See if you can find a good video for me," he said as he walked away.

"Let's see what you've got," President Wilkes said when he reached the Oval Office.

"This is from a permanent webcam on EarthCam .com, and it will give you a good perspective of what happened," Mary said.

After a few seconds President Wilkes said, "I don't see anything other than a bunch of tourists gawking at the stars on the Walk of Fame."

"Focus your attention on the palm tree across from the Sephora sign," Mary Counts said. "There. Do you see that?"

"What the hell is that?"

"One of the blogs said it's an off-the-shelf drone."

"I think it's going to hit the crowd . . . oh my God, it exploded," President Wilkes said. "Any causality estimates yet?"

"LAPD is reporting ten people killed and another twelve wounded."

"I need Nancy Baker. Get her on the phone for me," he told Mary.

"Thanks for the heads-up," President Wilkes said when he had Nancy on the phone. "Do you have any details yet?"

"No, but my team just arrived at the scene."

"Any idea who did it?"

"No, but if it had been the Islamic State, they would have already taken credit."

"Thank God for that, I've already got enough to deal with from them. Do you think it's another one of those self-radicalized assholes?"

"Possibly. The attack wasn't very sophisticated.

We're estimating the size of the explosive charge at less than a pound, and the drone used in the attack is a commercially available model and small enough to be carried in a suitcase or duffel bag."

"I need to make some more calls. Do you have anything else for me?" President Wilkes asked.

"That's all I know, but I'll let you know if we discover anything new."

The president had just hung up when his cell phone buzzed with an automated reminder.

The timing really sucks, but I might as well get this over with, he thought.

"Mary, I need Jim Rutherford, and don't run off, this won't take very long."

"What's up, Mr. President?" Jim Rutherford asked.

"Jim, I've decided to replace you," President Wilkes said.

"May I ask why?"

"I'd rather not get into it. It's just something that I have to do, but I'll be happy to give you any sort of reference you want."

"That won't be necessary, and I hope it all works out for you."

"He sounded pissed," Mary Counts said.

"I don't blame him, he's done a damn fine job."

"Then why replace him?"

"Sometimes you're forced to make deals that carry baggage, and this was one of those. Now I need to talk with Director Clawson," he told her.

"Rod, I need your expert advice," President Wilkes said.

"Sounds like a setup, but shoot," said the director of the NSA/CSS.

"I'm sure you're already aware of the California attack."

"Yes, and it's just another reason we should be going

after those Islamic State thugs with everything we've got."

"That's your opinion, but if I were to listen to all of you war mongers, we'd be blowing up half the world," the president said.

"Even if they didn't directly carry out the attack, it was undoubtedly a result of their recruiting efforts."

"You could be right, but that still doesn't give me a strategy to stop them."

"The only way to stop them is to put boots on the ground," Rod Clawson replied.

"There's got to be another way."

"There is, but I know you won't be willing to do it."

"Let me be the judge of that," said the president.

"We could use nuclear weapons to eradicate them."

"I may be desperate, but I'm not willing to kill millions of people."

"Not that kind of nukes. Tactical nukes. There would still be a fair amount of collateral damage, but it should be within acceptable limits," said Director Clawson.

"By whose standards? I'll not go down in history as a mass murderer."

"Then we're pretty much screwed."

"I refuse to accept that," said the president before he hung up.

It was almost midnight when Walter Jefferson received a call from Andrew Milliken, the secretary of state.

"Sorry for the hour, but that gutless piece of shit we've got for president isn't going to do a damn thing to protect our country," Milliken said.

"I warned you," Walter Jefferson replied.

"I know, which brings me to the reason for my call. You can count me in."

"I hope you realize there's no going back if you make that sort of commitment to me."

"I do."

"Good. I can use men like you. Please keep feeding me anything you think might help."

"I will, and let me know if there's something specific you need me to do."

"Would you try to convince the president to reassign General Drummond and Admiral Crawford?"

General Lawrence Drummond was six foot two, two hundred and fifteen pounds, with short gray hair and green eyes. He was the unified combatant commander of the European Command, and had just been named the supreme allied commander of the Allied Command Operations. He'd been in the army for thirty years, and his previous command had been the U.S. Army Intelligence and Security Command.

Admiral Crawford was six feet tall and a hundred and eighty pounds, with light brown hair and hazel eyes, and was the current UCC of the Pacific Command. He was a career submarine officer, and a twenty-eight-year naval veteran. He'd graduated with distinction from Annapolis with a degree in engineering, and held a master's degree from Yale. He was a world-renowned expert on logistics and battle tactics, and was rumored to be next in line to replace Admiral Burton as the commander of the United States submarine force when he retired.

"I'm willing to try, but they're exemplary officers and have the secretary of defense's full confidence, so I doubt he will."

CHAPTER 12

A few months later, Daoud Mansouri's small convoy of vehicles stopped in front of a boarded-up building in downtown Mosul. His portable office was set up in the center of the dance floor of the abandoned nightclub, and as he sat down at his desk, Dizhwar Akram said, "The daily reports are in your folder, and I've finally finished the report on Hashmi's operation you asked for."

Daoud was drinking his morning cup of thick black coffee and snacking on a plate of dates as he worked through the pile of papers on his desk. However, when he finished Dizhwar's analysis of the Canadian operation, he threw the report aside and said, "This is total bullshit. We've poured a ton of money into his operation, and we should have seen some results by now."

"I told you he was a perfectionist," Dizhwar Akram said. "And I think you should replace him."

"I'm frustrated, but we've already dumped a ton of time and money into this, so we might as well see how it plays out. However, before I forget again, I've been working with that group of converts in Texas that you passed on to me, and they're going to mount an attack on the Fourth of July that will definitely get the Americans' attention."

"That's only few days from now, and if it's going to be that big of a deal I should have been working on our messaging for weeks."

"No, I don't want you to do anything that would validate our involvement."

On the morning of July 4, Tom Womble stopped by the Walmart Supercenter on the south side of Amarillo, Texas, to pick up his friend Jack Portman when he got off work. Tom was nineteen and had just finished his first year of college at West Texas A&M in Canyon, Texas. He was six four, two hundred pounds, with blond hair and blue eyes, and had been the star quarterback in high school. His daddy was a wealthy farmer, and he'd had the best of everything growing up until he and Jack had gotten hooked on crack cocaine and their lives had fallen apart.

"I'm not sure I can go through with this," Jack said when he got in the pickup. Jack had been the equipment manager for the football team, and he and Tom had been best friends their whole lives. He was five foot five, weighed a hundred and sixty pounds, and had brown hair and brown eyes. Tom had always protected him when the other jocks had tried to pick on him.

"We've been planning this for weeks. You can't weasel out on me now," Tom said.

"This isn't one of our video games, real people are going to die if we do this," Jack replied.

"So, most of them think we're drug-crazed animals anyway."

"I suppose. Shit, look what time it is. We'd better get moving."

Their flying club only had a Cessna 150, so they'd been stealing spray planes for months to use in the operation, hiding them at an abandoned private airfield between Amarillo and Canyon, Texas.

When they arrived at the airfield, their friends had

the planes lined up on the grass beside the runway. Their coconspirators were standing beside a large tank truck, smoking and talking with the two drivers that had brought the deadly load up from Mexico.

"We were beginning to think you'd lost your nerve," Carl Earlock said when they walked up.

"Are you assholes high?" Tom Womble asked as they tried to hide their joints.

"We were bored, but don't sweat it, we're all good to go. It's a good thing you got here when you did, because these wetbacks are getting antsy and were about to bug out."

"You shouldn't say shit like that, they might hear you," Jack Portman said.

"I don't give a shit if they do, but neither one of them speaks any English."

"Well, we're here now," Tom said. "Let's get to work, but be damned careful because this is some really nasty shit."

It took them almost two hours to fill the tanks on the spray planes, and by then Jack Portman looked like he wanted to puke.

"What's the matter with you?" Carl Earlock asked. "You aren't backing out on us, are you?"

"Don't sweat it, asshole, I'll hold up my end of the deal."

"Get off his back," Tom said.

They huddled together for a group prayer before they went to their aircraft.

"It's time. We'll meet back here when we're finished," Tom said.

Once he was in the open cockpit, Tom leaned over the side and told George Brinks, "Get the van gassed up. We'll hit the road as soon as we get back."

They circled the airfield until all ten aircraft were airborne, and when Tom joined the group he said, "You all know the grids you've been assigned, but we'll stay together until we make our run over the courthouse square."

Tom Womble was at the rear of the formation, and once the rest of them were on their way, he threw his aircraft into a sharp turn. As he made a low level pass over the airfield, he flipped the switch to start the deadly spray.

"Look out, the silly bastard's dumping that shit on us," George Brinks said.

The ground crew made a run for their fifteen-passenger Ford van, and when the truckers saw what was happening they jumped into their truck and hauled ass.

The truckers were headed south on I-27 toward Canyon and had just passed Kimbrough Memorial Stadium when the driver became deathly ill, veered off the road, and overturned.

George Brinks and the rest of ground crew took I-27 back toward Amarillo, but as they reached the overpass to the city limits, George passed out. The van veered off the road and went tumbling down the concrete embankment, and when it hit the access road it burst into flames.

Tom Womble had to go to full throttle, but he managed catch up to the rest of the group as they reached the Canyon city limits.

A large crowd was already gathered in the town square to enjoy the vendor booths selling crafts and fair-type food while they waited for the parade to begin. As the aircraft lined up for their pass over the square, the parade was just getting started. As tradition dictated, it was being led by two Texas Rangers mounted on identical palomino stallions, and they were carrying the Stars and Stripes and the Texas State flag.

The spray planes were ten abreast as they roared over the crowded square, leaving a cloud of atomized

VX gas in their wake. As the deadly spray wafted down on the unsuspecting crowd, the odorless fog seemed little more than a light mist.

"What the hell are those nitwits up to?" Mayor Robert Dunst asked. "They're not scheduled to do the flyover for another ten minutes."

"They aren't part of the Commemorative Air Force," Police Chief Green said.

"Then get somebody to run their asses out of here before we have a disaster on our hands," Mayor Dunst said.

"I'm on it," the police chief replied.

"Holy crap, that stings," the mayor exclaimed as he started coughing and rubbing his eyes.

The chief stopped to see what the yelling was about, but before he could say anything, he started coughing uncontrollably. His coughing quickly grew worse as he fell to his knees and went into convulsions.

"That should take care of the parade," Tom Womble said. "You know your assignments, so spread out and get to it."

On the north side of town, in a small park adjacent to the Palo Duro Creek Golf Course, the Ortiz family was having a cookout. They'd just lit their grill when one of the spray planes swept overhead.

"Look at the plane, Daddy," Melissa Ortiz said.

"Honey, is that smoke coming out of the plane?" Carlota Ortiz asked.

"It looks like a crop duster to me, but I don't know what the hell they'd be spraying."

"Daddy, my eyes hurt," Melissa screamed a few minutes later.

"José, check on Melissa while I see what's wrong with the baby," Carlota said.

She started toward the picnic table where the baby's carrier was sitting, but she'd only taken a few steps before she bent over and threw up.

"Honey, are you all right?" José asked as he bent over to comfort Melissa.

"Oh, God," he said as he felt his chest tighten up. "I can't breathe," he said before he gasped a couple of times and fell to the ground.

"That's it for me, I'm empty," Jack Portman radioed twenty-five minutes later.

"Me too," Carl Earlock said.

"Head on back and I'll meet you at the hangar," Tom Womble said. Tom made one last pass over the West Texas A&M campus to kill a little time before he turned north toward the airfield.

"Boy, are they going to remember this day," Carl Earlock said as they gathered together on the grass where the truck had been parked earlier.

"For sure, the Fourth of July is going to have a whole new meaning from now on," Jack Portman said.

"Damned straight," Sally Mitchell said.

"I wonder where the hell George and them went off to?" Carl Earlock asked. "Tom is going to be super pissed if they've run off and left us."

As Jack Portman started walking over to his plane to give Tom a call, his eyes started watering from the VX toxin covering the ground.

Jack turned to go back to the group, but by then his chest was beginning to tighten up. As he fell to the ground gasping for breath, he thought, *Damn, some of that shit must have leaked out of the truck.*

The rest of them were starting to experience symptoms when Carl asked, "What the hell is Tom up to?" as Tom's plane came roaring overhead, spewing its deadly mixture behind it.

"Let's get out of here, the dumb-ass forgot to turn off his sprayer," Carl screamed.

They all made a run for their aircraft, but none of them made it off the ground.

Even though he knew it meant his death, Tom landed his aircraft and hurried over to where his lifelong friend lay dying in agony.

"Why?" Jack managed to ask before more vomit spewed from his mouth.

"I'm sorry, but this was the plan all along, I just never told you. We weren't supposed to be taken alive," Jack said as he collapsed beside his friend.

PRESIDENT WILKES WAS sitting at a small table in the Rose Garden drinking a glass of iced tea when Special Agent Taylor came rushing out and said, "They need you in the Situation Room."

"There's been a terrorist attack in Texas," said air force Colonel Ridgeway, the officer in charge of the White House Situation Room, when President Wilkes walked in. Colonel Ridgeway had only been in place for a short time, and this was his first real emergency. He was six four, with wavy light blond hair and blue eyes, and he looked like he'd just stepped out of a recruiting poster. Unlike most of the officers that had preceded him, he'd never seen combat. He'd spent his entire career in logistics, but he had friends in high places and had been handpicked for the assignment.

"Where? It's a big place," the president asked.

"Sorry. Canyon, Texas, it's about—"

"I know where that is, it's just south of Amarillo. Now what's going on?"

"They've had over a thousand confirmed deaths and they're expecting that number to climb."

"Good lord, did they get nuked?"

"They think it was some sort of gas attack."

"Get the team on the video channel," he commanded.

"General Lehman, do you have an update?" President Wilkes asked when the team appeared on the screen.

"I do, and it isn't good," the chairman of the Joint Chiefs said. "The local authorities are completely overwhelmed, and people are still dying."

"Do we know what happened?" President Wilkes asked.

"They thought it was sarin gas, but that would have dissipated by now," said General Willowby, the commandant of the marines.

"You know your gases," General Lehman said. "It was VX nerve gas, delivered by crop dusters."

"This could be catastrophic," President Wilkes said. "What are they doing with the casualties?"

"They were sending them to the regional medical center in Amarillo, but the casualties overwhelmed both of their hospitals, and they've started sending them on to the trauma center in Lubbock."

"How can we help?"

"They're in desperate need of supplies," Admiral Donnelly said.

"They've burned through their limited supplies of antidotes, but it's too late to help most of them anyway," General Lehman said.

"Maybe so, but I think we should send them all the auto-injector nerve-agent antidote kits we've got," Admiral Donnelly said.

"Do it," President Wilkes said. "Do any of you think there could be more attacks?"

"This may answer that for you," Colonel Ridgeway said, handing him a note.

When the president finished reading it, he said, "The Randall County Sheriff's Department has identified the perpetrators."

"Islamic terrorists?" Nancy Baker asked.

"I suppose they could be, but they were all locals, and none of them were older than twenty."

"'Were'?" General Lehman asked.

"They're all dead. Whether by design or by accident, they all died from VX gas exposure."

"Good riddance," Nancy Baker said.

"Agreed, but I wish we could have interrogated them," President Wilkes said.

"Even if there aren't any more attacks, I'm afraid the pain has just started," General Willowby said. "VX is roughly a hundred times more lethal than sarin gas, and it's much more persistent."

"Persistent?" President Wilkes asked.

"Its rate of evaporation is roughly equivalent to oil, and since it's heavier than air, it tends to accumulate in low-lying areas. We'll need a way to safely dispose of the bodies and their clothing, as well as a plan to decontaminate the affected areas."

"Explain," President Wilkes said.

"Buildings, vehicles, hell, even the grass will have to be decontaminated."

"How do you decontaminate an entire town?" asked Admiral Kennedy, the vice chairman of the JCS.

"I don't have an answer yet, but Nagasaki and Hiroshima will look like a cakewalk compared to this," General Lehman said.

"It can't be that bad," President Wilkes said.

"Much worse. With a nuclear attack, emergency response and cleanup personnel can tolerate a certain amount of exposure. With a nerve agent like this, any exposure can mean almost certain death without immediate treatment."

"What the hell do we do?" President Wilkes asked, clearly frustrated.

"Evacuate the entire area."

"Abandon the city?"

"Worse than that. We'll need to cordon off a security zone of at least . . . hell, I really don't know how far, but at least several miles in all directions."

"Colonel, put a map of the area up for us," President Wilkes said.

After they'd studied it for a minute or so, President Wilkes said, "We could be talking about at least a portion of Amarillo."

"Since it's airborne the prevailing winds could carry it over a large portion of Amarillo, so we should evacuate the city to at least the I-40 corridor."

"That's over half the city," General Willowby said.

"It's not unusual for them to have sustained winds in excess of twenty miles per hour at this time of year," Colonel Ridgeway said. "So you might want to evacuate all of Amarillo."

"Good point," General Lehman said. "Just to be safe, let's evacuate all of Randall and Potter Counties."

"Shit, the press is going to have a field day with this," President Wilkes muttered under his breath.

"Sorry, I missed that," General Lehman said.

"It was nothing, just thinking out loud," President Wilkes said. "Issue the mandatory evacuation orders," he said. "General Lehman, we need to brief FEMA, homeland, and Jim Perkins, the governor of Texas, on the plan. I'm going to declare the entire Texas Panhandle a disaster area, and I want you to work with the local authorities to institute a dusk-to-dawn curfew for the entire area."

"That's a huge chunk of land, and I doubt the locals are up to it," Vice President Regal said.

"Then I want General Stenson to establish the quarantine, and we're going to hold daily meetings until this is over. Now get to work."

CHAPTER 13

Five days later, Josh Tindle, a veteran New York state trooper, was setting up a speed trap with his rookie partner, Trooper Chase Selvedge. They were parked behind a grove of trees at a roadside park fifteen miles from Plattsburgh, New York, and the traffic on Route 9 was light for a weekday morning. So when sixty-five identical white vans flew by, it got their attention.

Trooper Tindle checked their speed and said, "One-oh-five. I'll make my whole month's quota off of these morons." He started the cruiser, flipped on the emergency lights, and tore off in pursuit.

"Shit, it's a cop," said Major Mohsen Mouradipour, the leader of the group.

Major Mouradipour had black hair and dark brown eyes, and was one of ninety battle-hardened Iranian special operations officers that were embedded with Daoud Mansouri's forces around the world.

"What should I do?" the driver asked.

"Just keep going," Major Mouradipour said. "Corporal Qazwini, prepare to fire."

"They're not stopping," Trooper Chase Selvedge said.

"Even better, I'll throw in resisting arrest," Trooper Tindle said as he floored the cruiser.

"You want me to call for backup?" Trooper Selvedge asked.

"Nah, we can handle these morons."

"What the hell is he doing?" Trooper Selvedge asked when he saw a man's head pop up out of the top of the van.

As the corporal swiveled the tripod-mounted heavy machine gun toward them, Trooper Tindle realized what it was and slammed on the brakes.

"Take them out," Major Mouradipour said.

As smoke billowed off the cruiser's tires, the corporal opened fire. The stream of 12.7 mm metal-jacketed slugs from the Russian Kord heavy machine gun riddled the engine and then the passenger compartment of the cruiser. The corporal continued firing until the hood flew up and the police car skidded off the road and went tumbling end over end into the pasture.

They were monitoring the emergency frequencies, so Major Mouradipour asked, "Did they call for backup?"

"No. I can't get this damn thing to retract," Corporal Qazwini said as he struggled to lower the machine gun.

"Leave it, you're going to need it again," Major Mouradipour said.

When they reached the Plattsburgh city limits, Major Mouradipour said, "All units execute, and we'll meet back here in ninety minutes."

As the convoy dispersed, the vehicles assigned to the ATMs and the banks used their preprogrammed navigation systems to locate their objectives. The remainder of the vans were carrying assault troops armed with AK-12s, RPG-32s, and 9K34 Strela-3 shoulder-fired missiles. They began setting up ambush points along the known routes of the emergency responders.

When Major Mouradipour's van reached its target

his driver wasn't paying attention and had to slam on the brakes to keep from running over the curb in front of the bank. As the van came to a tire-smoking halt in front of the one-story bank branch, Major Mouradipour said, "You idiot."

"Oh shit," said Tom Peoples, the security guard, when he spotted the machine gun sticking out of the top of the van. As he ran to try to lock the door he said, "Dial nine-one-one, we're about to be robbed."

"In the doorway, take him down," Major Mouradipour said.

The Kord's metal-jacketed slugs shattered the bank's tempered glass entryway and ripped Tom Peoples almost in half.

"Dear God," exclaimed Eric Post, the bank manager. "Dial nine-one-one, and trigger the alarm."

The heavily armed robbers were wearing black jumpsuits and their faces were covered with ski masks when they came charging through the shattered doorway.

"Just give them what they want," Eric Post said.

When Major Mouradipour entered the lobby he motioned to the customers and said, "All of you get down on the floor and keep quiet."

"I've got alarms going off all over town," the 911-dispatcher for the Clinton County Emergency Services said.

"Me too," the second dispatcher said. "And I've already transmitted the locations to the first responders."

"What now?"

"I'll handle the calls, if you'll call Supervisor Wilson."

"Disembark, but hold here," Sergeant Boustani said as the troops began spilling out of the vans.

"Have the dispatchers alerted all of the other agencies?" Sergeant Boustani asked.

"Affirmative."

"Black One, execute phase two," Sergeant Boustani said.

A few seconds later, six missiles from the Soviet Mi-28NE Night Hunter attack helicopter orbiting overhead struck the building, and it erupted in a series of towering explosions. The powerful blasts leveled the flagpoles in the front of the building and knocked several of the assault troops off their feet.

"Bravo squad, sweep the area for survivors," Sergeant Boustani said.

A few minutes later they returned and said, "There was one survivor, but we cut her head off and left it in the driveway."

"American bimbos bring top dollar so don't kill them, we'll take them with us. Now, load up, we've still got a lot of work to do."

"Dispatch, this is Officer Scruggs. I'm at Second and Main, and there are two fire trucks on fire, and I think there's a sheriff's cruiser that's been shot to hell. I'm going—"

Officer Scruggs never finished his sentence as an RPG blew his cruiser in half, and twenty minutes after the first alarm, every first responder in town had been slaughtered. Major Mouradipour's men all had predetermined tasks, so as one group went to clean out the vault, another one started emptying the tellers' cash drawers. When Sally Trimble, one of the tellers, didn't move fast enough, one of the goons slammed her in the face with the butt of his machine gun.

"You didn't have to do that," Eric Post said.

Major Mouradipour moved to the middle of the lobby and said, "Shut the hell up. The rest of you need to get out here, and lay facedown on the floor."

The man who'd clubbed Sally grabbed her by her

ponytail and dragged her limp, bloody body into the lobby.

"All of you close your eyes and keep your mouths shut," Major Mouradipour said.

When the major nodded, his men pulled out their razor-sharp combat knives and started beheading the hostages. When they finished decapitating each victim, they placed the severed head in the middle of the room and moved on to the next one. As the blood gushed out of the bodies and flowed across the polished marble floor, it made for a truly gruesome scene.

"Time's up, let's move," Major Mouradipour said as he shot the last two patrons in the head and started toward the door. When all of his units were accounted for, he said, "All units move out and stay together."

They'd snuck into the U.S. one vehicle at a time via the I-84 crossing, but the convoy was leaving en masse via the lightly trafficked Churubusco/Franklin border crossing.

"Sergeant, let us know when it's safe to proceed," Major Mouradipour said.

"Roger that," Sergeant Boustani said as his van raced ahead.

"Pull over, we'll get out here," Sergeant Boustani said when they were a hundred meters from the checkpoint.

The sleepy little crossing only had four guards, and they died quickly and quietly at the hands of his team.

"The port is clear," Sergeant Boustani reported.

Not long after they'd cleared the border, news of the attack finally reached the authorities.

"Director, you need to see this," said Jennifer Wallace, the on-duty operations officer at the New York Department of Homeland Security and Emergency Services.

"Sure, Jen," said Betsy Turner, the commissioner of

the DHSES. She read the alert and asked, "When did this go down?"

"Almost two hours ago."

"Why are we just now hearing about this?"

"The power is out all over the city and the Clinton County Emergency Services Center was destroyed during the attack, along with the sheriff's office."

"Can we trust any of this?"

"Yes, one of the undersheriffs has a home generator, and he used his ham radio to make the report."

"If his assessment is correct, it's catastrophic, but it's almost inconceivable it could be that bad."

"Excuse me, Commissioner, but we just got an update from Terrance Mayberry, the director of operations at the Plattsburgh International Airport," the shift supervisor said.

"Let's hear it."

"When they heard the first explosions he immediately instituted a complete lockdown, and suspended all flight activity."

"Did they contact the nine-one-one center?"

"They tried, but they were never able to reach them. Once the attack was over, Director Mayberry dispatched a team to check it out, and they're reporting a hundred and seventy-five emergency services personnel killed, and close to twice that in civilian causalities."

"I want every available resource headed their way twenty minutes ago."

"COMMISSIONER TURNER NEEDS to speak with you," Nancy Baker's assistant said.

"What's up, Betsy?" asked Nancy Baker, the secretary of homeland security.

"There's been a major incident in Clinton County," Commissioner Turner said.

"Incident?"

"There have been a series of bank robberies in Plattsburgh, and—"

"Why are you bothering me with bank robberies?" Director Baker asked.

"If you'll let me finish, I'll explain."

"Fine, but be quick about it."

"The perpetrators beheaded more than a dozen people, and killed pretty much every emergency responder in the county. Hell, they even blew up the emergency management center."

"Are the attacks still occurring?"

"We don't think so, but the state police have dispatched helicopters and ground units, so we should have something more definitive within the hour."

"SECRETARY BAKER, WHAT can I do for homeland today?" President Wilkes asked when he answered his direct line in the Oval Office.

"I believe there's been a terrorist attack in Clinton County, New York."

"I just watched a Fox News report on that, but they're saying it was a series of bank robberies gone horribly wrong."

"There have been a number of robberies, but given the high number of casualties and the level of destruction, it has to be more than robberies."

"Even if you're right, I have every confidence that your team can handle it."

"I was hoping you'd declare martial law, or at least a state of emergency, and send in troops."

"That shouldn't be necessary. I've already talked with Governor Grady, and he's called up the New York National Guard. He'll be coordinating their efforts with your office."

"Fine, but I'd still like to see us do more."

"The press is going to go crazy with this, and I sure as

hell don't need that," President Wilkes told Harvey Gabriel, the White House press secretary. "Work up a press release praising Governor Grady's actions, and announce that I've asked the FBI, NSA, and the CIA to put every available resource into finding the perpetrators."

"That's all you're going to do?" Harvey Gabriel asked.

"You too?"

By the time Harvey Gabriel issued the president's press release, details of the incident had already leaked to the press and the Internet was abuzz with all sorts of wild theories.

"Mr. President, I really think you should consider a more forceful response to the New York incidents," Harvey Gabriel said when he sat down at the president's desk.

"Harvey, it's late. Let's continue this in the morning."

A couple of hours later, General Albert Stenson, the Northern Command, Unified Combat commander called Director Baker. General Stenson had spent most of his long and storied career as a combat officer. He'd never married, and had dedicated his life to defending the country he loved. Before being named a UCC he'd been the commanding officer of the Fort Bragg, Special Operations Group. He was sixty-two years old, but his bright red hair, light complexion, and freckles made him look much younger.

"How can we help?" General Stenson asked.

"I appreciate the offer, but I'm afraid it's out of my hands. The president is convinced the locals can handle it, but I really think he doesn't want to do anything that might jeopardize his reelection campaign."

"If he says stand down, we stand down, but I damn sure don't have to like it."

Just after midnight, the satellite phone on General Albert Stenson's nightstand rang.

"I've been expecting your call," General Stenson said.

"Am I that predictable?" General Lehman asked.

"I knew that mess in New York would get your dander up, particularly when I found out the president wasn't going to do shit."

"I'd intended to call you earlier, but I was trying to track down enough intel to make some sense of it."

"What did you find?" General Stenson asked.

"Nothing definitive, but I think it was an element of the Islamic State."

"Then why haven't they taken credit?"

"I can't answer that," General Lehman said.

"Even if it was them, we can't do shit without the president's backing, unless you've changed your mind about reaching out to Walter Jefferson."

"I hate to, but see if you can get us another meeting."

"He's going to be in town next week for a fund-raiser at the convention center. I'll see if he'll give us some time."

The president was back at work in the oval office by 5 A.M. the next morning.

"It was a fairly quiet night, but I included a couple of news articles that you might take a look at," Mary Counts said as she handed him the morning briefing folder.

"Thanks, and would you have the kitchen bring my breakfast in here?"

There hadn't been any more serious incidents so that part went quickly, but when he finished reading the news articles, he hit the intercom button. "Track down Harvey Gabriel, and get his ass in here," he said.

"Have you seen this piece of shit?" the president asked as he handed Harvey the offending *Wall Street Journal* article. "Who the hell does Burgess think he is? He had the gall to call me a do-nothing political hack and a coward."

"I tried to warn you," Harvey Gabriel said.

"Whatever, but what can we do about it?"

"If you change course now, it would validate everything he said about you. However, if General Lehman is right, and this is just the start of something bigger, you're going to have to respond."

"I'll deal with that if it happens."

That night after dinner, President Wilkes called the Canadian prime minister, Rodney Douglas.

"President Wilkes, what can I do for you tonight?" Prime Minister Douglas asked.

"You can track down and kill the terrorists that just hit us in New York," President Wilkes said.

"I've got my best people working on it."

"I'm getting a lot of pressure to go in after them."

"That wouldn't be wise. We'll handle it."

"You'd better, or I may have to turn them loose," President Wilkes said.

"It would be unfortunate if that incident a few years ago at my brother's estate on Prince Edward Island were to come out."

"Are you trying to blackmail me? You know that was an accident."

"True, but a young woman is dead, and you never reported it."

"Bastard. I'll hold my people off, but it's not going to be easy."

President Wilkes finally got to bed a little after midnight, but after tossing and turning for almost two hours, he sat up, and muttered, "This is bullshit. They got me into this mess, and they can help get me out of it." He picked up the phone.

"President Wilkes, it's awfully late, what's up?" Larry Ragsdale asked.

"I need your help with these so-called news people."

"Did you have something specific in mind?"

"I was hoping that you could come up with something."

"I'll see what I can do, but if we go after them it could backfire on us."

"I'm counting on you to not let that happen, and while you're at it, see if you can do something with NAPO. I don't need law enforcement on my ass too."

"I'll try, but since we're talking, we'd like you to reconsider reassigning General Lehman, General Stenson, and Admiral Crawford."

"Don't you people ever give up? Secretary Behrmann is fully committed to General Stenson and Admiral Crawford, so they're not going anywhere. General Lehman and I don't always see eye to eye, but I'm not going to change him out at a time like this."

When they finished, Larry Ragsdale called John Jay.

"Working late, or up early?" John Jay asked.

"I just got off the phone with President Wilkes, and he's all worked up. He wants some help with the press, and he's pissed off about the National Association of Police Organizations' article in *The New York Times*."

"I'll send you some more money. See if you can pay off the really vocal ones."

"That could blow up in our faces."

"Most of them are slime, they'll take the money."

The next morning, Aryeh Behrmann was just sitting down to breakfast at his three-story home in Arlington, Virginia, when his cell phone rang. When he saw who it was, he went out on the patio and closed the door behind him, "Hello, brother."

"I just wanted to see how you're holding up," Lieb Behrmann said.

"In comparison to what? I'm doing all right, but these terrorist attacks have everyone unnerved."

"Welcome to my world, but that's not why I called.

Have your intelligence agencies picked up anything on a Pakistani by the name of Annas Elmaleh?"

"Doesn't ring a bell. Anything specific you're looking for?"

"We got a tip that he was working on some big deal, but before we could validate it, we lost track of him."

"What's the four-one-one on him?"

"He used to be one of the most sought-after contract killers in the business, but we've heard that he's started brokering high-end arms deals."

"Arms brokers are a dime a dozen."

"How true, but it's rumored that he's focusing on WMDs."

"Damn, we sure don't need that right now. I'll see what we can find."

CHAPTER 14

The next week General Stenson and General Lehman met Walter Jefferson in one of the break-out rooms in the Walter E. Washington Convention Center. The room was set up to seat a hundred, so they pulled three chairs together at the end of one of the conference tables.

"We appreciate you taking the time to meet with us," General Stenson said.

"I apologize it can't be longer, but they've got me on a very tight schedule," Walter Jefferson said.

"Then I'll cut to the chase," General Lehman said. "Since we last talked, our nation has suffered a series of horrific attacks, and we're extremely concerned with President Wilkes's leadership, or should I say lack of leadership."

"His lack of leadership was what drove me to make this somewhat quixotic run for president. I knew there wasn't a chance in hell I could get elected, but I'd hoped to pull enough votes away from Wilkes to allow Peterson to take the election."

"How's that going?" General Stenson asked.

"Not well, but let's talk about why you're here. I'm convinced our nation is about to experience an upheaval unlike anything we've previously undergone, and I've spent the last year and a half trying to prepare for that eventuality."

"We're in agreement on the challenges, but what can any of us hope to achieve?" General Lehman asked.

"If a worst-case scenario were to occur, and our government were to fall, I want to have the resources to help regain control. We've been stockpiling supplies and weapons, but you two represent the finest this country has to offer, and I would like you on our team."

The arrogant little bastard is sure full of himself, General Stenson thought. "That's all well, and good, but that won't be much good without manpower," he said.

"I'm working on that aspect as well. In fact we've been able to recruit a little over twenty thousand new militia members since I've been traipsing around the country."

"Impressive, but without the backing of the military, your little private army still wouldn't stand a chance," General Lehman said.

"Of course you're right, and I didn't mean any disrespect."

"None taken, but none of this helps us with our immediate problem," General Stenson said.

"True enough, but before we go any further with this conversation, I need to know how committed you are to helping me save this country from ruin," Walter Jefferson said.

"Could you be more specific?" General Lehman asked.

"How far are you willing to go?"

The generals looked at each other, and said as one, "If the need arises, we'll do whatever it takes."

"Perfect. I often like to quote one of my ancestors, Thomas Jefferson, who so famously stated, 'The tree of liberty must be refreshed from time to time with the blood of patriots and tyrants.' "

"Words to live by, but we need something to solve our current dilemma," General Lehman said.

"I share your frustration, but the country isn't desperate enough to accept the types of changes that will have to be made. However, we've been working on a solution to one of the worst-case scenarios we've been modeling, and I'd like your input on it."

"We'd be happy to take a look."

"Excellent. And before you go, John Jay will give you a couple of laptops and encrypted satellite phones so we can communicate without fear of being intercepted."

"I think you're being a little naive to think you can circumvent the NSA's scrutiny," General Lehman said.

"Actually I got the technology from one of my contacts in the NSA, and he's in charge of all of their encryption/decryption efforts."

Neither general said anything, but they were quite impressed.

Walter glanced at his watch and said, "I'm sorry to cut this off, but I've got a press conference in ten minutes. Please don't forget to let me know what you think of the plan."

"Is this guy for real?" General Stenson asked as they drove away.

"He's definitely full of himself, but he's the real deal, because this is some sophisticated shit he just gave us," General Lehman said.

As Walter was about to walk out on stage, he told John Jay, "I'd like to hold a short meeting tonight with as many of the militia leaders as possible."

"I'll take care of it. I'm supposed to catch a flight to Philly at eighteen hundred hours, but I can reschedule."

"Not necessary. I'll fill you in later."

It was midnight by the time Walter got back to his hotel suite, and the militia leaders were there waiting.

"I thought you had a plane to catch," Walter Jefferson said when he saw John Jay sitting at the table.

"I decided this was more important."

"My apologies for the hour, but I wanted to share a pivotal event that occurred earlier this afternoon," Walter Jefferson said.

"Your numbers went up in the polls?" asked Clarence Booth, the commandant of the North Carolina militia.

"I wish. No, I just had a meeting with General Lehman, the chairman of the Joint Chiefs, and General Stenson, the Northern Command's Unified Combat Commander."

"What's the big deal?" Melbourne Turner asked. "You've met with them before."

"They requested the meeting."

"For what purpose?"

"They feel that President Wilkes is leading the country down a path to ruin, and they were adamant that they'd do whatever it took to keep this country safe."

"I wouldn't have expected less from men like that, but how does that help us?" Clarence Booth asked.

"Once I was sure they were serious, I took the opportunity to ask for their input on the Liberty Tree scenario."

"Are you out of your rabbit-ass mind?" Clarence Booth asked. "They'll have all of us down at Gitmo if that gets out."

"Watch your mouth," Walter Jefferson said with a cold glint in his eye. "I had to know if I could trust them, and if they rat us out, I'll simply explain it away as a war game scenario."

"This could be a huge win if they really do embrace our plans," added Terry Gould, the commandant of the Idaho militia.

"Without a doubt. Even our best-case scenarios require a significant portion of the military to come over to our side to have a chance in hell of pulling it off," Walter Jefferson said. "I've got another piece of good news. We've acquired a pair of Soviet Mi-28NE Night Hunter attack helicopters, like the ones the Islamic State has been acquiring, and we've captured two of their operatives."

"I've got plenty of room if you need someplace to store them," Terry Gould said.

"Thanks, but we've stashed them on a small farm in Virginia. Lee, how are you coming with your assignment?"

"We'll be ready when the time comes. However, I didn't want to draw any attention, so we'll wait to install the new equipment until it's needed," replied the commandant of the West Virginia militia.

"Good thinking. It's late, let's call it a night."

Three weeks later, Harvey Gabriel came storming into the Oval Office and asked, "What have you done?"

"What the hell are you babbling about?" President Wilkes asked.

"*The Washington Post* just published an exposé claiming that we've been paying off journalists to keep them quiet."

"That's bullshit."

"Well, someone is doing it."

"It wasn't me," President Wilkes said.

When Harvey left, President Wilkes called Larry Ragsdale.

"You incompetent bastard, your people really screwed the pooch this time," President Wilkes said.

"I just saw the article, but all you need to do is issue a strongly worded denial. We've covered our tracks and there's no way they can prove you were involved."

"You're certain they can't pin any of this on me?"

"Absolutely."

At 5 A.M. the next morning, President Wilkes was eating breakfast in the Oval Office before he went to his daily meeting with the Joint Chiefs. He'd been up until almost midnight reviewing the latest reports on the mess in Texas, but he'd been unable to see a way out of the situation. When he finished, he took the elevator down to the Situation Room on the basement level underneath the West Wing.

"This whole Canyon/Amarillo mess has gone on for far too long, and I want a plan to get it behind us," President Wilkes said as they started the meeting.

"We've got one, but it's not a pretty," General Lehman said.

"Any progress is better than nothing."

"If you'll give the go-ahead, we'll use twenty DC-10 and 747 firefighting aircraft to spray down the entire area with a concentrated solution of aqueous sodium hydroxide. Then we'll repeat the process with hydrogen peroxide."

"Both of those solutions are extremely caustic," President Wilkes said.

"It's going to trash pretty much everything, but over time the rain will dilute it enough for it to be safe to reenter."

"Implement your plan," President Wilkes said. "Did we ever determine why those young people did it?"

"Homeland claims they were homegrown terrorists, similar to the Oklahoma City bombing," General Lehman said. "However, the NSA and the CIA say they were indoctrinated via the ISIS websites and were communicating directly with Daoud Mansouri."

"Why haven't we blocked or shut down their sites?" Admiral Kennedy asked.

"God knows we've tried, but they have them back up in a matter of minutes," General Lehman said.

"I don't give a shit what they have to do, I want those sites taken down," President Wilkes said.

"I'll tell them, but I don't hold out much hope they'll be able to pull it off," General Lehman replied.

CHAPTER 15

Eleven days later, Daoud Mansouri's BMW stopped in front of a three-story mansion on the outskirts of Mosul to spend the night. As his bodyguards led him inside the luxurious residence, Daoud said, "This is more like it."

As he sat down to eat dinner, Dizhwar Akram joined him.

"I hate to admit it, but you were right about Hashmi. First thing in the morning, I'm going to terminate the Canadian operation," Daoud Mansouri said.

"You may want to rethink that," Dizhwar Akram said as he handed him the message from Ehsan Hashmi.

"*Allah Eazim* (God is great)," Daoud Mansouri said when he read the note.

A FEW HOURS later, Janice Adams, the 911 operator for Flathead, Montana asked, "Nine-one-one, what's your emergency?"

"There's been an explosion at the Kalispell City Hall."

"Is anyone injured?"

"Hell, lady, half the block is gone. I'm going to—"

Janice was almost deafened by the sound of the explosion before the line went dead. She selected the address for the Kalispell City Hall, entered what little information she had, and clicked the icon to dispatch the appropriate fire, police, and medical units.

Fire station eight was only a few blocks away, and when the alarm sounded Captain Little ripped the information off the printer and yelled, "Gear up, there's been an explosion at the courthouse."

When the first engine arrived, the driver radioed in. "Dispatch, we're going to need more units. The entire block is an inferno." As the driver stopped at the nearest hydrant, a 105 mm RPG blew the front end off the truck, and another one hit the Starbucks across the street.

"What the hell?" said Sergeant Williams, the police field supervisor, when he saw the explosions. He slammed on his brakes. "Dispatch, reroute all units to the two hundred block of First Avenue East. Ladder eight was just destroyed by some sort of a rocket and—"

He never finished, as his car was shredded in the crossfire from two Kord 12 mm heavy machine guns, mounted on the top of the black Ford one-ton, dually, crew cab pickups.

"Sergeant Williams, you got cut off. Please repeat," the 911 dispatcher said.

The dispatcher tried several more times before she radioed, "All units respond to a fire and explosion at two-oh-one First Avenue East. Proceed with extreme caution, because we've had reports of gunfire and explosions."

"Here comes another one," Sergeant Totah said when he saw the fire truck racing toward them. "Take it out, but don't hit the damn buildings this time."

Seconds later multiple RPG rounds struck the fire engine as it was racing toward the courthouse.

All the patrons in the barbershop were gathered by the front window watching the fires when the barber said, "Oh my God, look out," as the flaming wreckage rammed through the front of the shop, killing everyone inside.

As the teams assigned to take out the emergency management center approached the building, two of the dispatchers were outside on a smoke break.

"What the hell is going on over there?" Marge Stoddard said when she saw the black-clad men running toward them.

"Let's get back inside," Chad Mertz said as he turned to open the door.

"Take care of those assholes," Major Dweck said, and three of the terrorists opened fire on the terrified dispatchers.

The security cameras were monitored in the dispatch center, and when Margret Turnbow, the head dispatcher, saw her coworkers gunned down she said, "Oh my God." Margret's heart was racing, but she managed to trigger the alarm and lock down the building.

When she broadcast the alert over the PA system everyone could hear the terror in her voice. "Attention all personnel, panic alert in zone one. This is not a drill. All panic team members need to respond to zone one immediately. Everyone else needs to lock your doors and await further instructions. I repeat: this is not a drill. Panic alert in zone one."

By the time their response team reached the lobby the highly trained intruders had blown open the doors and were entering the building. The five-man panic team was wearing body armor and carrying MP5s, and when they ran into the terrorists, a vicious firefight ensued. Two minutes later the panic team was dead, along with three of the terrorists.

"Corporal Jabra, get those bodies loaded onto the trucks, and the rest of you have twenty minutes to finish up," Major Dweck said as the two-man teams scattered to sweep the building.

"All available units, the EMC is under attack and requires immediate assistance," Margret Turnbow broadcast on all the emergency channels. When she saw the intruders sweeping through the building, killing everyone they encountered, she took a deep breath, unlocked her desk drawer, and retrieved her Glock.

"All units, be advised that the Flathead emergency center is under attack, and I'm going off the air to try to help out."

As she swiveled her chair to get up, one of the terrorists emptied his 7.62×39 mm AK-12 assault rifle at her through the glass separating the dispatch area from the hallway. The gunman paused to change magazines before he and his partner continued down the hall, slaughtering everyone they encountered.

"Let's get in the air. I need to see what the hell is going on," Lieutenant Sharp told the pilot of the sheriff's office's helicopter.

As they approached the courthouse, Lieutenant Sharp saw one of the pickups stopped in the middle of an intersection machine-gunning a fleeing crowd of civilians.

"Make a pass over that bastard," Lieutenant Sharp said.

As the helicopter banked and swooped low over the pickup, the lieutenant opened the side window and opened fire with his M16.

He managed to kill the gunner before the terrorist commander said, "Somebody take care of that son of a bitch."

Seconds later the helicopter exploded like a Roman candle when two shoulder-fired missiles blasted it out of the sky.

"Phase one is complete," Colonel Fakhoury said. "Begin phase two."

The Wells Fargo bank in Kalispell was about to close

for the day when two pickups skidded to a stop in front of the bank.

"What the hell?" said bank manager Mildred Thames when she saw six heavily armed men wearing black masks running toward the bank.

The bank's security guard rushed to lock the doors, but a hail of bullets ripped him to shreds. There were only two customers in the lobby, and as the first man inside kicked the shattered glass panels out of the way, he yelled, "Everybody get down on the floor, and keep your mouths shut."

There was an old woman with a walker standing at the counter, and she turned and froze in terror.

"I said to get down."

Her hands were shaking as she grabbed the edge of the counter and tried to ease herself down to the floor.

"I don't have all day you, crippled up old hag," the man said as he shot her in the head.

"You didn't have to do that," screamed the young man who'd been standing behind her in line.

He was lying on the floor, but the black-hooded thug ran over and began clubbing him in the head with the butt of his machine gun. The boy was already dead when the thief pulled him up by his hair and began slashing at his neck with a large knife. After three savage cuts he was left holding the boy's head as his body fell, spraying blood across the highly polished floor. The bank employees screamed in horror as the terrorist slammed the bloody head down on the counter and said, "That's what happens if you don't obey."

Three of the robbers entered the vault carrying large duffel bags. As Major Dweck started raking the stacks of cash into the bags, the others started prying open the safety-deposit boxes.

"Just load up everything, we'll sort it out later," Major Dweck said.

While they were cleaning out the vault, the rest of the team was executing the rest of the employees. When the major finished he glanced at his watch and said, "Time's up, let's move."

Two hours later they'd sacked every bank and ATM in town, and were formed back up on the edge of town.

"That's everybody, let's move out," Colonel Fakhoury said.

When they reached their base in Canada, Ehsan Hashmi was waiting for them.

"Well done, Colonel. We'll take the money off your hands. I need your team at these coordinates."

"We're moving?" Colonel Fakhoury asked.

"Yes, we've leased several farms south of Winnipeg, and we'll be launching our next mission from there."

President Wilkes was working late in the oval office when Colonel Ridgeway called.

"You're needed in the Situation Room," Colonel Ridgeway said.

"What's up this time?" President Wilkes asked.

"We've received reports of a possible terrorist attack in Montana."

"Shit, I'll be right there. Get the rest of the team on video."

"Everyone's on," Colonel Ridgeway said when the president sat down.

"Let's see what you've got," President Wilkes said.

"We don't have many details, but an undetermined number of heavily armed bandits have robbed every bank in Flathead County, Montana," Colonel Ridgeway said.

"Bank robberies, what a waste of our time," Vice President Regal said.

"Bear with me for a moment," said the director of national intelligence, Frank Gillespie. "Colonel, put up the video of the Wells Fargo robbery."

When the video ended Vice President Regal looked like he might throw up as he said, "My God. That was the most barbaric thing I've ever seen."

"That's a typical Islamic State terror tactic, and we should exterminate every one of the vermin," General Lehman said.

"I agree with the general," Secretary Behrmann said. "And I can have a team of General Volkey's men in the air within the hour."

"To what end? We've got no idea who or where to attack," President Wilkes said.

"Take your pick, we know where they are in Iraq, Syria, or Afghanistan," Secretary Behrmann said.

"It's taken us years to extract ourselves from all those no-win ground wars. I'm not falling into that trap again."

"I think you're setting a horrible precedent by not hitting back," General Lehman said.

"Not going to happen."

"Gutless bastard," someone muttered.

"I don't know who said that, but if you don't want to be on the team, I'll be happy to replace you," President Wilkes said. "Unless one of you can come up with something that's actionable, I think we're done for now."

He waited a few seconds for a response before he motioned the colonel to kill the video feed. "Colonel, I want you to go through the record of this call, and see if you can identify who made that last comment," President Wilkes said.

At 3 A.M. the following morning the encrypted satellite phone beside Walter Jefferson's bed rang. "What's up?" he asked.

"I wanted to discuss what happened yesterday in Montana," General Lehman said.

"Horrible stuff."

"Agreed, but once again the military was ordered to stand down, and we've got to do something about it."

"This isn't the time to act rashly, but while I've got you, what did you and General Stenson think of our plan?"

"Some would consider it treason."

"Probably true, but there have been several instances throughout history where the military had to step in to stabilize a government."

"Not in this country."

"Hypothetically, how much time would you need to get ready?"

"Forty-five to sixty days."

"Then you'd better get started, because I fear we're about out of time."

"Then we're on it, and after yesterday it can't come any too soon."

The next night, General Lehman and General Stenson met for dinner at il Canale, a small Italian restaurant in Georgetown. As their waiter led them to their table they passed by the brick wood-fired oven where cooks were preparing their renowned thin-crust pizzas.

"This was a great choice," General Stenson said. "I can't remember the last time I had a decent pizza."

"This place is great, I just wish it wasn't raining. I love sitting out on the rooftop terrace," General Lehman said.

Once they'd ordered, General Stenson asked, "So what's with all the secrecy?"

"We need to make our preparations for Liberty Tree," General Lehman said.

"Then it's time that I involve General Lacy," General Stenson said.

"Do whatever you need to, but we need to be ready when the time comes."

"I'm going to be at Fort Bragg on Thursday, and I'll brief him while I'm there."

CHAPTER 16

The next morning President Wilkes was working in the Oval Office when Mary Counts buzzed him and said, "I've got Scott Brambly, the governor of Montana, on line one."

"Governor, what's on your mind?" President Wilkes asked.

"I've got demonstrations blowing up all over the state, and I need you to send in some troops until this blows over," Governor Brambly said.

"Why aren't you using the National Guard?"

"We are, but there's not enough of them to go around."

"I'd love to help, but I don't believe the situation requires the military's involvement."

"I don't know why I bothered to call. You have a nice day."

"I think I pissed him off," President Wilkes said.

"I can see his side of it," Mary Counts said. "I was just watching a Fox News report, and several of the demonstrations turned violent."

"I'm sure it will blow over in a day or two."

As Governor Brambly was struggling to restore order, Ehsan Hashmi was trying to decide whether he should delay their next operation. He was staying at the Holiday Inn and Suites in downtown Winnipeg, Canada, and he was eating breakfast on the balcony of his suite as he studied the daily status reports from his field commanders.

"I don't understand why the Americans didn't respond," Ehsan Hashmi said.

"I don't think they were expecting another attack, and we've heard from several sources that the president doesn't believe we're behind the attacks," said his aide, Lieutenant Taruh Basara.

"I'm afraid they're just laying back to lure us in, so they can wipe us out in one fell swoop. Is your brother Amir still leading the cell in Mexico?"

"Yes."

"Could you get me in touch with him?"

"Sure, they're using the same communication gear as we are."

"Thank you for taking my call," Ehsan Hashmi said.

"Taruh has told me all about you, but I'm sure you didn't call to chat," Colonel Amir Basara said.

"I need your help."

"My group isn't very large, but I'm willing to try. What do you need?"

"I need you to kill as many American cops as you can," Ehsan said.

"I don't have the resources to do much, but I've hooked up with a group of Mexican army soldiers, and they'll do anything if the money's right."

"Let me know how much cash you need, and I'll wire it to your account. When do you think they could get started?"

"As soon as I get the cash," Amir replied.

Eleven days later Mary Counts put a CIA briefing folder on the president's desk and said, "The director of national intelligence sent this over, and he needs to speak with you."

"What's up, Director?" President Wilkes asked.

"There have been twenty-eight more police officers killed since we last talked," Director Gillespie said.

"Damn, how many does that make?" President Wilkes asked.

"Ninety-five in the last five days, and the attacks seem to be escalating."

"Tragic, but what am I supposed to do about it?" President Wilkes asked.

Good lord, man, you're the president of the United States, Director Gillespie thought. "The governors of Texas, New Mexico, California, and Arizona are requesting additional funds to beef up their border patrols."

"Not going to happen."

"They're going to be pissed, but I'll let them know."

"Why are they reaching out to you? They should have run a request like that by homeland," the president asked.

"They knew we were in the same fraternity in college, and they'd hoped that I could convince you to pony up some more cash."

"You need to watch this," said Harvey Gabriel, the White House press secretary, as he turned on the television.

"I'm on a call, can't it wait?" President Wilkes asked.

"I don't think so."

"Director, I'm sorry, but I've had something come up."

"No problem, but do think about it."

"Okay, now what the hell is so urgent?" the president asked.

"All the networks have been airing footage from the rioting that took place overnight," Harvey Gabriel said.

"How is that an emergency?"

"Walter Jefferson addressed the national convention of the NAPO last night, and shortly afterward the police forces in New York City, Chicago, Baltimore, and

Washington, D.C. began staging a sickout to protest your lack of support for law enforcement."

"Jefferson's no threat, but I can't have him turning law enforcement against me. Get me Tim Phillips, and I'll see if I can talk some sense into them."

"Mr. President, I thought you might call," said Tim Phillips, the head of NAPO.

"What the hell are you trying to pull?" President Wilkes asked. "I've always been a supporter of NAPO."

"Lip service, we need some real action out of the federal government. Someone is targeting law enforcement, and we need money and manpower to put a stop to it."

"It's probably just some of the drug cartels with a hard-on over our interdiction efforts."

"Bullshit, the attacks were cold-blooded executions, and while drug cartels will kill when they have to, they've never wanted to stir up that much animosity with the police."

"Whatever, but I don't understand why you're so spun up. None of the attacks have been anywhere near New York."

"We're all brothers in arms, and it's just a matter of time before they make it up here."

"I'll have Nancy Baker and Charles Berkley look into it," President Wilkes said.

"Fat lot of good that will do. Homeland and the FBI haven't done squat so far."

"Best I can do."

"I hope you know what you're doing, because sooner or later law enforcement will take matters into our own hands."

"Is that a threat?"

"Simply an observation."

"Boy was he pissed," Harvey Gabriel said.

"He was, but I'm still not doing anything until after the election."

CHAPTER 17

After their last attack Ehsan Hashmi had moved their base of operations to an isolated farm they'd leased south of Winnipeg, Canada. The farm gave them a place to work without fear of discovery, but their next operation was behind schedule.

"Where to?" the driver of the Unicity cab asked when he picked him up at his hotel.

"Parkside Ford at two thousand Main Street."

"Have you got the rest of the pickups I ordered?" Ehsan Hashmi asked when the sales manager met him at the door.

"Yes, and I'm terribly sorry about the delay," John Mallory said. "We just finished prepping them, and they're parked in the back lot with the rest of your order. If you're ready for them, I'd be happy to have them delivered wherever you'd like, at no charge."

"No need, I'll have my men pick them up. How much more do I owe you?"

"Let's see, you've already paid me four-point-seven million dollars, so the balance is eight hundred thousand."

"You still all right with American?"

"Absolutely."

Ehsan Hashmi opened his briefcase and counted out the rest of the money in hundred-dollar bills.

"It's been a pleasure doing business with you, but if you don't mind me asking, what the hell are you going to do with a hundred and five pickups?" John Mallory asked.

"We're starting a delivery service."

They'd worked night and day to get the vehicles ready, but it had taken longer than they'd expected and Ehsan wasn't pleased.

"Are you finally finished?" Ehsan Hashmi asked when he arrived at the farm.

"We finished up late last night."

"How about you, Colonel?"

"We've modified the trailers as you asked," said Colonel Fakhoury, the group's commander. "But it seems like a waste of time since the Soviet S400 missile batteries are self-propelled."

Colonel Fakhoury was six feet tall, weighed two hundred pounds, and was another one of the Iranian special operations officers. His closely cropped brown hair exposed the scars on his head that he'd gotten in a helicopter crash a few years before. He was one of the best officers Hashmi had.

"I know that, but they're not fast enough to keep up."

"Have you seen anything we've missed?" Colonel Fakhoury asked.

"Make sure you get the battle flags mounted," Ehsan Hashmi said.

"Will do, and are we still scheduled for midnight?"

"No, I had to adjust the timing of your attack. I need you to jump off at twenty-two hundred, and the second attack will follow ninety minutes later," Ehsan Hashmi said. "I also need you to extend your operation."

"It's a little late for changes."

"It's not a huge shift. I still need you to draw all of the Americans' attention to your column, but instead of stopping at mile marker one hundred, I want you to continue down I-29 toward Grand Forks. Once the authorities find out about your attack they're going to set up a roadblock at mile marker one-eighty to stop you. They'll have no idea how strong your force is, so once you've taken care of that, I want you to stay there and draw their fire until I contact you."

"How could you know that?"

"Need-to-know, but are you clear on my expectations?"

"Of course, but I'd like to add a few more fuel tankers and a couple more sets of missiles for the SA-21s."

"That's entirely up to you."

"I need to brief the team on the changes, so I'd better get moving," Colonel Fakhoury said.

At 2155 Colonel Fakhoury said, "Major Fawzi, take six units forward to take out the guards."

"On our way," said Major Fawzi, the Night Hunters squadron commander. Egyptian by birth, he'd gotten his flight training from the Russians, and had spent the first six years of his career flying close air support for the Russians during the rebellion in the Crimea.

The American side of the Pembina, North Dakota crossing was open twenty-four hours a day, and it had four lanes for autos and three for commercial vehicles, but at that hour there were only a couple of trucks passing through.

The Mi-28NE Night Hunters were flying low and dark, and when they had the checkpoint bracketed in their night vision displays they unleashed a salvo of missiles at the unsuspecting border agents. The massive explosions illuminated the countryside as they obliterated the buildings and collapsed the overhead walkway that spanned the multi-lane highway. While Major Fawzi's group was taking care of the checkpoint, the rest of the squadron was strafing the vehicles in the parking lot and the adjacent buildings with their 30 mm Shipunov 2A42 auto cannons.

"Oh, shit. Attention all units. Follow me, we're going to have to cut through the field," Colonel Fakhoury said when he saw the collapsed walkway blocking the highway.

Everything at the port had been shot to hell, but one of the agents had been outside on a smoke break, and he'd managed to find a working radio in one of the trashed patrol cars. "We have a code black at the Pembina customs port. The main facility has been destroyed, and we've suffered heavy casualties. I repeat: we have a code black in progress. A large number of heavily armed pickups, semitrailers, and an unknown number of helicopters have crossed the border and are headed southbound on I-29 at a high rate of speed. I repeat—" The transmission ended abruptly when a missile hit the squad car he was broadcasting from.

As the convoy was getting back up to speed, Colonel Fakhoury said, "Major Fawzi, take ten units and clear the road ahead of us."

"On our way," Major Fawzi said as they pulled out of formation and accelerated away.

"Lieutenant, here's a transcript of a code black alert we just received from the Pembina port," said Jill Tooney, one of the highway patrol dispatchers.

"Get me somebody up there to talk to," ordered Lieutenant Nuell, the highway patrol shift supervisor.

"We've already tried to contact them on the radio and by phone, but nobody picks up."

Lieutenant Nuell studied a map of the area for a few seconds and said, "Have the nearest unit find out what's going on. Then I want you to get every available unit to mile marker one-eighty on I-29, and have them set up roadblocks in the north-and southbound lanes. While you're taking care of that, I'll get the word out to the emergency services center."

"Yes, I've got it, and thanks for looping us in," said Roger Halstead, the night supervisor at the North Dakota Department of Emergency Services. As soon as he'd hung up, he escalated the incident to homeland security.

"That's all the information we have at this time," he told Benjamin Turnbow, the regional director for homeland security.

"Forward everything you've got to our command center, and I'll take care of alerting the other agencies," Turnbow replied. *Thank God we just finished the contingency plans for something like this,* he thought.

"I was expecting your call," said Harry Thorn, the homeland supervisor. "We just received the alert from the NDDES."

"Good, and I'm instituting Alpha Dog protocol," Director Turnbow said. "They may already be aware of the situation, but make sure that U.S. Northern Command is in the loop."

"It didn't sound like that big of a deal."

"Just do as I ask."

"This had better be important," Chuck Ludwig, the governor of North Dakota, said when he answered his cell phone on the nightstand.

"Sir, this is Roger Halstead with the NDDES, and we've had a terrorist attack at the Pembina border crossing on I-29."

"When?"

"About thirty minutes ago, and they've reported heavy casualties. The highway patrol is establishing roadblocks at mile marker one-eighty on I-29."

"You said a terrorist attack, but how big of a force

are we talking about, and why are they putting up roadblocks?"

"I'm not sure who made that decision, and we've haven't been able to verify the data, but the initial report said that there was a large group of armed vehicles headed southbound on I-29."

"Doesn't matter who, but we need to make damn sure they get them stopped," Governor Ludwig said. "I want you to send every available resource to shore up those roadblocks, and then I want you to contact the Grand Forks Air Force Base and see if the commander will put a drone up over that area."

"Okay, but if we pull that many units in it's going to leave the rest of the state unprotected."

"Have there been any other incidents reported?" Governor Ludwig asked.

"No, but—"

"No 'buts,' send everything, and make sure you keep me updated."

"Understood."

"It's been over an hour since I've heard from anyone, what the hell is going on?" Governor Ludwig asked Roger Halstead.

"I'm terribly sorry, I thought we'd given you a status update," Halstead answered. "I've got the highway patrol superintendent on the line if you'd like to speak with him directly."

"Put him on."

"Sorry for the confusion, Governor, it's been a crazy evening," said Colonel Michaels, the superintendent of North Dakota Highway Patrol.

"I understand, but I need to know how we're doing."

"The Grand Forks chief of police, Jeremy Thomas, is onsite at the roadblock, and he's running the show. They've blocked both sides of the interstate, and he assures me they're going to show these bastards not to mess with us," Colonel Michaels said.

"What else should we be doing?"

"I think we're good. They should have more than enough manpower to get the job done. Every sheriff, highway patrolman, game warden, and city cop that could get there is on the line."

"Be sure and let me know when it's over."

The scene at the roadblock was sheer pandemonium as they scrambled to finish their preparations. They had vehicles stacked three deep on both sides of the interstate, with just enough room between them for their men.

They'd ended up with 240 members of law enforcement manning the makeshift barricades, but other than the SWAT teams' MP5s and sniper rifles, all they had were shotguns, pistols, and a hunting rifle or two.

When Chief Thomas finished surveying their positions, he said, "I think we're ready."

"I still think we should have held my men in reserve," said Lieutenant Jefferson, the SWAT commander. "If they get past us, there's nothing to stop them from trashing the city."

"I hear you, but it's my call," Chief Thomas said.

When Colonel Fakhoury's command reached mile marker 170, he said, "Captain Shaaban, halt the column.

"Major Fawzi, execute Whirling Dervish," Colonel Fakhoury said.

On his command, four of the helicopters carrying S-8DF high explosive missiles separated from the column and began climbing as the rest of the Night Hunters slowed to a crawl. When the helicopters reached a thousand feet, the pilots centered the targets in their heads-up displays and signaled their weapons officers to fire. When the sixteen missiles struck the front line of the amassed police vehicles, the blasts turned them into tumbling balls of fire.

As the survivors milled around in shock, Chief Thomas said, "Hold your positions. You are free to fire when you have a target."

The RQ-4 Global Hawk from the Grand Forks Air Force Base had arrived a few seconds before the first missiles hit, and it had recorded everything.

"Forward this video to command," said the drone pilot, Airman Scott, after watching the carnage unfold.

The officers manning the blockades still hadn't spotted the enemy aircraft, but the drone's sensors located them in seconds.

"There they are," he reported. "I've got two groups about two thousand yards out."

"How many?" Lieutenant Sparks asked.

"There are four in the first wave, and fifty or more in the second wave."

"Drone at twelve o'clock," the lead helicopter called.

"Take it down," Major Fawzi said.

"There's only one, I'll handle it," the lead pilot said as he fired an R-74M2 air-to-air missile at the drone.

"Incoming," Airman Scott said.

He tried to dodge the missile, but the highly maneuverable Soviet missile took down the drone with ease.

For the next ten minutes the helicopters pummeled the roadblock with missiles and cannon fire, until there was nothing left but dead bodies and shattered burning vehicles.

"Cease fire. All aircraft are ordered to land immediately," Major Fawzi said.

As soon as the choppers had landed on the interstate, the trucks came rushing up to refuel and rearm them with R-74M2 air-to-air missiles.

"Ready the SA-21 missile launchers, and make sure they're all dead," Colonel Fakhoury said when the rest of the convoy arrived at what was left of the roadblock.

President Wilkes had just gotten to sleep when the phone beside his bed rang.

"Yes," he said groggily.

"There's been an incident in North Dakota, and you're needed in the Situation Room," Colonel Ridgeway said.

"What's going on this time?" President Wilkes asked.

"According to the NDDES, a large group of terrorists have crossed the Canadian border at the Pembina port, and are headed south on I-29."

"Sounds like hyperbole from some overly excited local," President Wilkes said. "Why isn't law enforcement handling it?"

"They've tried, but they've been getting their butts kicked."

"Incompetents. They should be able to handle a few terrorists."

"You might rethink that once you've seen the video taken by an air force drone on the scene."

"Who authorized that? Never mind, I'll be right down."

The president threw on some clothes, and took the elevator to the basement level. After he had watched the video, he said, "How long before the rest of the team is available?"

"Secretary Behrmann and General Lehman have just joined on the videoconference line," Colonel Ridgeway said.

"Secretary Behrmann, what's the current situation?" President Wilkes asked.

"General Stenson has raised the FPCON to level delta and has authorized air strikes to contain the situation," said the secretary of defense, Aryeh Behrmann.

"That seems extreme," President Wilkes said.

"Extreme? Didn't you watch the video?" General Lehman asked.

"Calm down," President Wilkes said. "I've seen it, but an air strike on American soil hasn't been done before."

"General Stenson is responsible for North American security, and we need to go with his assessment of the situation," Secretary Behrmann said.

"What's done is done, but I don't want any further escalation without consulting me first," President Wilkes said. "Do we have anybody up there we can trust?"

"No. I think we should have General Lacy dispatch a rapid response team right away," Secretary Behrmann said.

"Let's hold off on that until we can get some facts," President Wilkes said.

"I agree with Secretary Behrmann," General Lehman said.

"And I think it's an overreaction. We'll wait," President Wilkes said.

When General Lehman's phone rang, he muted the video call to take it.

"I've got a team standing by on the tarmac," General Lacy said.

"Have them stand down," General Lehman said.

"We need to get moving."

"I agree, but the president shot us down. If anything changes I'll let you know."

"Are we a go?" Colonel Tompkins asked.

"We've been ordered to stand down, but keep your team at the ready," General Lacy said.

Walter Jefferson was eating a late-night snack when Larry Duke burst into the kitchen. "Boss, there's some heavy shit going down up by the Pembina border crossing."

"Slow down and take a deep breath. Now, what's happening?"

"I just heard the news on my ham radio. There's a big-time invasion going on up there."

"I doubt it's an invasion, but as soon as I'm finished, I'll check it out."

A few minutes later, he picked up his phone. "Roger, have you heard anything about an attack up by Pembina?"

"Sure have. I was about to holler at you to see if you wanted us to try to help out," Roger Newsome said.

"See if you can get me some actual facts first, and I'll make a few phone calls as well."

When General Lehman returned to the call, Secretary Behrmann, said, "Bathroom break, but I'll be right back," before he muted his line and stepped out of the camera's view. When he was out of sight he called General Lawrence Drummond, the head of European Combat Command. "General, this is off the record, but I think you should consider raising your alert levels again," Secretary Behrmann said.

"Why hasn't the president already done it?"

"Equivocating as usual."

"Damned politician. I knew he was weak, but that's almost treasonous."

After the secretary finished briefing the general he asked, "Would you mind briefing Admiral Crawford for me? I've got to get back."

"No problem, Sam and I go way back," General Drummond replied.

"Admiral Crawford, General Drummond needs to speak with you. He says it's urgent."

"What's up?" Crawford asked.

"The secretary of defense just briefed me on a terrorist attack that's taking place in North Dakota."

"How bad?"

"NORTHCOM has declared a FPCON delta condition, and has authorized air strikes to gain control of the situation."

"Damn, why haven't they raised the DEFCON level?"

"The president won't do it."

"Shithead."

"Exactly. Secretary Behrmann left it up to my discretion, so I've already placed my commands on FPCON charlie."

"Then I'll do the same."

"Excellent, but you're not going to win any points with the president when he finds out what we've done."

"Like I care."

"Good man. I'll keep you updated as we learn more."

"What about the other commands?"

"I'm going to contact all of the other UCC commanders, and make the same recommendations."

CHAPTER 18

While Colonel Fakhoury's Pembina attack was drawing all of America's attention, the main thrust of Ehsan Hashmi's plan was about to kick off at the little-used Westhope/Coulter crossing in North Dakota.

"Damn, I'm hungry as hell. I hope the old lady has something ready to eat," Jerry Tubbs said as he turned off the lights and locked the door to the Westhope customs office.

"At least you've got an old lady," said his coworker, Tim Sears, as he walked toward his old pickup.

"Now," Sergeant Boustani ordered.

The snipers squeezed off 9 mm rounds from their silenced Vintorez "thread cutter" sniper rifles, and Jerry and Tim dropped in their tracks.

"The port is clear," Sergeant Boustani said.

"Air One, execute lights out," Colonel al-Jabiri said.

Colonel al-Jabiri had been a commander in the Egyptian army's counter terrorism unit 777 until he'd killed a fellow officer in a drunken rage and been forced to flee the country. He'd worked as a gun for hire for a time before he'd ended up in Syria, where he'd joined up with the Islamic State. He was the most aggressive commander Hashmi had ever encountered. He had a dark complexion, brown hair and eyes, and was only five foot eight and a hundred and sixty pounds. He was vicious killer with absolutely no compassion for anyone.

On his command, sixteen helicopters in the rear of the formation broke away and accelerated toward Minot to take out the infrastructure targets.

"All units move out," Colonel al-Jabiri said when the helicopters were on their way. As the column was getting up to speed he said, "Set your GPS units for the route marked Minot, and make sure that you don't lose sight of the vehicle in front of you."

When the GPS unit had them turn off of Highway 83, the colonel's driver asked, "Why don't we just follow the road we're on?"

"Minot Air Force Base is up ahead, and I don't want to chance alerting them."

The Minot 911 dispatch center had been running on emergency generators for several minutes when Margaret Turner, the dispatch supervisor said, "I guess one of those crazy oilfield truckers knocked down a power pole again."

"Don't think so," said Pete Tower, the other dispatcher, as he took his fourth call. "I've had two reports of explosions, and one of them was at the main power substation."

"What the hell is going on?"

"Hard to say, but I've got Officer Thompson headed that way, so we should know something shortly."

"Dispatch, this is Officer Thompson. The substation is blown all to hell."

"Could you be a little more specific?" Pete Tower asked. Before Officer Thompson could respond, one of the Night Hunters spotted his car and shredded it with its 30 mm cannon.

"Dispatch, this is Officer Duffy, and I think I just

spotted that group of terrorists we received the alert on," said the on-duty highway patrolman.

"Not a chance, they were last reported headed south on I-29," Pete Tower said.

"I've lost count, but at least a hundred heavily armed vehicles just passed my location, and they've got what look like helicopter gunships with them," Trooper Duffy said.

"Calm down, I'll send backup."

"Air One, there was a police car parked in that rest stop we just passed," Colonel al-Jabiri said. "Have your men take it out."

Two of the helicopters opened fire with their chin-mounted 30 mm Shipunov 2A42 auto cannons, and within seconds they'd shredded the highway patrol cruiser and the three RVs camped for the night, along with every tree and picnic table in the park.

"Execute Clear Trail," Colonel al-Jabiri said.

The squadron immediately broke into groups of four as they began the next phase of the operation.

"Officer Duffy, what is your situation?" Pete Tower called several more times. "Officer down. I repeat: officer down. All units respond to the roadside park on northbound Highway 83. Possible shots fired, proceed with extreme caution," he said.

"Nine-one-one, what's your emergency?" Pete Tower asked.

"I'm at the roadside park off of Highway 83, and it's been shot all to hell. You need to get an ambulance out here because there's several people hurt, and I think the highway patrolman is dead."

"Sir, please stay on the line and I'll get right back to you.

"All units, confirmed officer down at the roadside park on Highway 83. I repeat: officer down at the rest area on northbound Highway 83. Assume this is an active shooter situation.

"Sir, could I get your name?" Pete Tower asked.

"Charlie Billings. You need to tell them to hurry."

"Help's on the way. Are you hurt or in any current danger?"

"I've got a couple of cuts from the flying glass, but nothing serious."

"Is the shooter still in the area? Could you tell what type of weapon he was using?"

"It wasn't a singular shooter. They looked like some sort of army helicopters, and they were using one hell of a gun because it blew huge holes through the RVs and the cop car."

"Dispatch, I'm under attack, and—"

"Come back. Who was that?" Pete Tower asked.

"That was Sheriff Grady, and he's probably dead, because his car just went up like a Roman candle when the missile hit it."

"Who is this?"

"This is unit ten, Sergeant Tibbs. Oh shit, they're coming after me."

"Unit ten, unit ten, come back, unit ten. Please repeat your last."

Realizing the situation was completely out of hand, Margaret Turner hit the speed dial for the North Dakota Department of Emergency Services, but before they could answer, she heard the distinctive thump of a chopper's rotor blades, followed by the sound of cannon fire.

"Margaret, get under the counter," Pete Tower screamed as the missiles started hitting the building.

They made it under the counter, but it was in vain as a wave of fire, followed by tons of debris rained down on them.

"I just had a dropped call from the Minot nine-one-one center, and now all the lines are down," the NDDES operator told his supervisor, Bill Kennedy.

"Keep trying, and I'll see if the phone company can tell us anything." Bill Kennedy said.

After all of the helicopter squadrons had reported in, Colonel al-Jabiri, said, "All units execute Operation Windfall."

Their vehicles had been waiting on the outskirts of town. They split into their assigned groups and headed off toward their targets. Ninety minutes later they'd cleaned out every bank and ATM in town, and returned to their rally point on the outskirts of town.

"Move out. We're running behind, so we need to pick up the pace," Colonel al-Jabiri said as the convoy sped toward Bismarck. "Captain Shaaban, we can't afford any more delays. Leave me eight aircraft and take the rest, and clear the way," he said.

"On our way," Captain Shaaban said.

"Glasgow, what's up?" asked Lt. General Glasgow, the commanding officer of the Minot Air Force Base when he answered the phone on his nightstand.

"NORTHCOM has just instituted FPCON delta," said Captain Biddle, the duty officer.

"Damn. I'm canceling all leaves effective immediately, and issuing an immediate recall for all off-base personnel. Make sure the gate guards know that civilians aren't allowed back on base until this is over."

There wasn't much traffic at that time of night, but the Night Hunters used their 30 mm cannons to destroy every vehicle they encountered.

"All units, execute Lights Out," Captain Shaaban ordered as they approached the Bismarck city limits.

"We must be having communication glitches," the on-duty dispatcher in the NDDES center said.

"What's going on?" Roger Halstead asked.

"Several units have tried to contact the nine-one-one dispatcher, but they keep getting cut off. My brother-in-law, Larry, is on duty tonight, but I couldn't raise him either."

Before Roger could respond, a ball of fire swept through the room as ten air-to-ground missiles pounded the building into a heap of flaming rubble.

By the time the main column reached the edge of town, the reflections from the burning vehicles and buildings were flickering across the low-hanging clouds over the city.

"Captain, I need a status report," Colonel al-Jabiri said.

"We've eliminated the nine-one-one and emergency management centers."

"How about the patrols?"

"There might be a few stragglers, but we've taken care of everything we could find."

"All units, execute operation Gold Digger," Colonel al-Jabiri said.

As the vehicles in the column set off to carry out their assignments, Colonel al-Jabiri said, "Pull over, we'll wait here."

By two thirty in the morning, they'd completed their assignments.

"All units present or accounted for."

"All units move out," Colonel al-Jabiri said. "Air One maintain air cover until we reach the border."

As the column sped away, the night sky was glowing bright red from the flames sweeping across the city, but no one was coming to fight them because the police and firemen lay dead in the ruins of the city.

"We should reach the border in about an hour," Colonel al-Jabiri said.

"Right on schedule," Ehsan Hashmi said.

As Colonel al-Jabiri's men were leaving Minot,

Colonel Fakhoury's ground crews were hurrying to get their helicopters refueled and rearmed.

When the screens on the S400's consoles lit up, Lieutenant El-Shennawi said, "Radar's up."

"Stay alert, they should be along shortly," Colonel Fakhoury said.

The S-400's 91N6E acquisition and battle management radar was designed to track up to three hundred targets at a distance of 600 km, so they had plenty of warning when the F-16s first appeared on radar.

"I've got eighteen incoming aircraft at five hundred and fifty kilometers out, at an altitude of fifteen kilometers," Lieutenant El-Shennawi said.

"Air speed?" Colonel Fakhoury asked.

"Two thousand, two hundred and fifty kilometers."

"Fighters, ready the long-range missiles," Colonel Fakhoury said. "When they're four hundred and fifty kilometers out, start giving me a countdown every fifty kilometers."

When the aircraft had closed to 300 km, Lieutenant El-Shennawi said, "Target two missiles per aircraft, and fire on lock."

As the missiles streaked away, the flames from the missiles' exhausts momentarily blinded them.

"I've got a missile warning," said Lieutenant Birch, one of the F-16 pilots.

"Break right, and take evasive action," Captain Gold said.

"All targets destroyed," announced Lieutenant El-Shennawi.

"Reload and stay sharp. There'll be more," Colonel Fakhoury ordered.

"We heard Captain Gold's missile warning, but nothing since then," said the air traffic controller.

"There's no way in hell terrorists could have taken

down a squadron of F-16s," said Air Force General St. James.

"I hear you, but they hit them while they were still over a hundred miles out."

"Damn, that's some serious shit. There's got to be more to this than we've been led to believe. How many squadrons did we scramble?"

"Four, and the other three should be on target in about twenty-five minutes."

"Have them kick it in the ass, and tell whoever's in command that they are free to engage at will," General St. James said. "And when you're done with that, let's go ahead and put Holloman and Langley on alert."

"Red Dog Two and Three, continue on your present course and speed."

"Red Dog One, slow to four hundred knots until the others can join up. All flights, Red Dog One is in command, and you're to go to burners as soon as possible."

"Roger that, but we'll be bingo on fuel," said the Red Dog 1 squadron leader, Reserve Air Force Colonel Tobias.

"Understood. We'll vector you to an alternate location when you've completed the mission. You're cleared to engage, and be advised that the hostiles have long-range surface-to-air missiles."

"Roger that, Red Dog One out," Colonel Tobias said.

As soon as the other F-16s fell into line behind Red Dog 1, they immediately went to full afterburners.

As they were nearing the target, Colonel Tobias said, "We'll begin the attack at a hundred and twenty-five miles out. We'll be going in a squadron at a time. Red Dog One will take the lead, followed by Red Dog Two and Red Dog Three. I want at least ten miles separation, so drop back when we begin our descent. Command has advised that they have SAMs, so stay alert and maintain your spacing."

"I'm shocked they haven't hit us again," Lieutenant El-Shennawi said.

"Trust me, there are more coming," Colonel Fakhoury said. "How long until the aircraft are ready to go?"

"They're just finishing up. Do you want to put them in the air?"

"Have them start their engines and stand by for orders."

When they'd closed to a hundred and fifty miles, Colonel Tobias said, "Red Dog One, follow me."

As they began their descent from fifty thousand feet, Lieutenant El-Shennawi said, "We've got multiple bogies approaching from the east at twenty-two hundred kilometers."

"All batteries prepare to fire on my command. Lieutenant, let me know when they're within a hundred kilometers," Colonel Fakhoury said.

"Enemy aircraft are at a hundred kilometers," the lieutenant said.

"Fire two missiles per aircraft," Colonel Fakhoury ordered.

When the missiles' fiery trails had disappeared, the colonel said, "All aircraft, ascend to six hundred meters and await my orders."

When his missile warning went off, Colonel Tobias said, "Incoming missiles, take evasive actions and press the attack."

Red Dog 1 and Red Dog 2 threw their aircraft into violent twists and turns, but they were unable to outmaneuver the deadly swarm of highly sophisticated Soviet 9M96E2 missiles. As the pitch-black night sky turned bright red from the explosions and the burning aircraft spiraling downward Major Williams, the commander of Red Dog 3 said, "All aircraft disperse. Let's take care of these bastards."

"We're still reloading, and there are still several aircraft approaching from the south," Lieutenant El-Shennawi said.

"Major Fawzi, have your men take care of them," Colonel Fakhoury said.

"Alpha One, fire as soon as you have target acquisition," Major Fawzi said.

Seconds later the hovering helicopters had acquired radar lock on the incoming F-16s and fired their R-74M2 air-to-air missiles at the fighters.

The surviving F-16s had managed to unleash their ordnance, but they couldn't evade the barrage of missiles, and as Colonel Fakhoury watched the fiery pinwheels dropping toward the ground, he said, "Arrogant fools! Reload the missile launchers. We're not done yet."

"What did you find out?" Walter Jefferson asked when Roger Newsome called him back.

"There's been a hell of a firefight on I-29 around mile marker one-eighty. From the sounds of it the police have been wiped out."

"Is it still going down?" Walter Jefferson asked.

"No way to say, they've lost touch with the whole bunch. But that's not the worst of it. Evidently a second group slipped across the border while that was going down, and they've sacked Minot and Bismarck."

"Damn it to hell, those dumb-asses can't do anything right. Where are they right now?"

"They were last seen hightailing it toward the Canadian border on Highway 83."

"That means they're going to come right by you. Round up everybody you can and see if you can take a chunk out of their ass."

"We're on it," Newsome answered.

"All right, boys, grab some of those Stingers and some of the Carl Gustaf recoilless rifles and let's go kill some dirtbags," Roger Newsome said.

Roger only had a hundred men that stayed at the ranch full time, but they were in their pickups and on their way in less than twenty minutes. As they neared Highway 83, Roger's cell phone rang.

"Good deal, we're just coming up on the highway," Roger said.

"Who was that, boss?" Richard Low asked as he stopped by the barbed wire fence that ran alongside the highway

"That was Herb. He said that they just came by his place, running like bats out of hell," Roger said.

"That should give us at least ten minutes," Richard Low replied.

"Spread out and take cover, but don't open up on these assholes until I give the word," Roger Newsome said.

"I've got heat signatures up ahead, and it looks like troops," Captain Shaaban said.

"I doubt there would be any soldiers out here, but don't take any chances. Take them out," ordered Colonel al-Jabiri.

The helicopters were flying four abreast, and the commander reported, "All units, we have hostiles at two thousand meters."

It only took the pilots a few seconds to lock onto the heat signatures from Roger's men and signal their weapons officers to open fire.

The helicopters were flying dark, so Roger's men didn't have any warning before the 30 mm rounds from the Shipunov 2A42 auto cannons begin ripping them to shreds.

"Holy shit," Roger screamed as he saw his men being slaughtered.

"Where's that coming from?" Richard Low asked.

"There the bastards are," Roger screamed when he spotted the muzzle flashes from the cannons. "Fire everything you've got."

By then, there were only seventeen of them left alive, but they each grabbed a missile launcher and fired it at the approaching aircraft.

"Incoming," one of the pilots yelled.

By the time Roger's men had fired, the helicopters were within eight hundred meters and the helicopters had no time to evade the missiles.

"Shit, I just lost eight ships," Captain Shaaban said.

"Unfortunate, but make damn sure you finish them off before we get there," Colonel al-Jabiri said.

When the convoy roared past their position, Roger and his men lay dead amongst the burning wreckage of their pickup trucks and the downed choppers.

"Damn, I can't believe those inbred country bumpkins managed to take down eight of my helicopters," Colonel al-Jabiri said when he caught sight of their ragtag collection of vehicles. When the column was two miles from the Canadian border Colonel al-Jabiri radioed the Night Hunters. "Captain Shaaban, execute Dragon's Breath."

All but two of the Night Hunters reversed course and headed back south as the convoy raced across the border. The Night Hunters were flying nap-of-the-earth, four abreast, but as they approached the air base they redeployed into a side-by-side formation that extended for hundreds of yards on either side of Captain Shaaban's aircraft.

"Attention all units, on my mark," Captain Shaaban said. "Execute."

The long line of choppers immediately began ascending at their maximum rate of climb, and when they reached seven hundred meters they launched every onboard missile they had. They were only two kilometers from the air base when they launched, and as hundreds of the Ataka-B air-to-ground missiles streaked toward the aircraft lined up in neat rows, the Night Hunters reversed course and headed north.

"What the hell?" said Master Sergeant Warren, one of six airmen on duty in the control tower when the first missile hit one of the B-52s. He was about to sound the alarm when two of the missiles struck the control tower, sending the burning bodies of the airmen flying through the air as the shattered control tower crashed to the ground. By the time the onslaught of missiles stopped, the runways were rivers of fires from the jet fuel on board the shattered hulks of the aircraft.

As Night Hunters crossed the Canadian border, Colonel Fakhoury's phone rang.

"You can pull back now," Ehsan Hashmi said.

"Excellent," Colonel Fakhoury said. "Load the dead and wounded on the trailers. We're leaving."

A few minutes later General Stenson's aide said, "General Glasgow says that he has to speak with you immediately."

"What now?" General Stenson asked.

"The base has just been hit by a massive air assault," General Glasgow reported.

"How bad?"

"We've lost all but one of our alert aircraft, and all of our runways are out of commission."

"That's catastrophic. Your command represents a large portion of our strategic response capability."

"Trust me, I know that."

"Damn it, I should have forced us to go to a heightened DEFCON condition."

"Wouldn't have mattered," General Glasgow said. "We'd already implemented FPCON delta, so we'd locked down the base and doubled the perimeter security, but even DEFCON three doesn't call for air cover."

"I'll need a full assessment of your battle readiness ASAP," General Stenson said.

"You'll have my formal report by morning, but we're no longer operational."

CHAPTER 19

General St. James had been pacing behind the controllers in the command center for several minutes before he said, "I need a status update."

"We've haven't had any contact with the aircraft in over ten minutes. I've vectored an AWAC into the area, but it's going to be another fifteen minutes before we know anything," the head controller said.

"Let me know if you hear from them, but they're probably all dead. I'd better escalate this," the general said as he started toward his office.

"Sir, I've got General St. James on the line," Colonel Ridgeway said.

"Who the hell is General St. James?" President Wilkes asked.

"He's coordinating the air strikes that General Stenson ordered," General Lehman said.

"Put him on the speaker so everyone can hear," President Wilkes said. "Let's hear what you've got."

"We've lost four squadrons of F-16s, seventy-two aircraft in all, and we still haven't got them stopped."

"How the hell can a bunch of low-life terrorists pull off something like that?"

"I'm not trying to make excuses, but these aren't your

garden variety terrorists, they're using Soviet R-74M2 missiles."

"Soviet? Surely you're not trying to convince me that the Soviets are behind this," President Wilkes said.

"No, sir, but the Soviets have been selling some pretty sophisticated stuff to the highest bidder. They were able to engage our aircraft from more than a hundred miles away, and we think they may be using Soviet S-400 missile batteries."

"Pure conjecture at this point," President Wilkes said.

"Conjecture? What the hell does it take to convince you?" General Lehman asked.

"More than you've shown me so far," President Wilkes said as he struggled to not lash out at the general.

"General St. James, we appreciate the update, and General Stenson will be getting back to you on our next steps," President Wilkes said.

"Next steps?! We need to go after them with everything we've got," General St. James said.

"I hear you, but we'll handle it from here," President Wilkes replied. "General Lehman, I want you to make sure that General Stenson doesn't take any further action unless he clears it with me first."

"Yes, sir. If you don't mind, I'll go next door and give him a call."

"Please do," President Wilkes said. "Colonel Ridgeway, I need to speak with Governor Ludwig."

"Yes, sir, but General Stenson needs to speak with you."

"General Lehman, you might as well hang here with me," the president said. "General Stenson, I appreciate you having General St. James brief us."

"Thanks, but that's not why I called. A second group has looted Minot and Bismarck."

"Is this the same bunch that just shot the shit out of General St. James's men?"

"No. The tactics and the equipment are similar, so they're probably related, but that's not the worst of it. Before they bugged out they launched a massive airstrike against the Minot Air Force Base."

"How bad?" General Lehman asked.

"According to General Glasgow, the Fifth Bomb Wing is no longer operational."

"Son of a bitch," General Lehman said. "Now will you do something?"

"You need to calm down," President Wilkes said. "Continue, General Stenson."

"We're at Force Protection Condition delta, but we need to move to DEFCON four," General Stenson said.

"These were horrific events, but I doubt any of these attacks could lead to a nuclear engagement," President Wilkes said.

"Sir, I've got the governor on the line," Colonel Ridgeway said.

"Mr. President, I appreciate the call, but I believe the incident is over," Governor Ludwig said.

"Great, but what have you learned about the other attacks?" President Wilkes asked.

"What the hell are you talking about?" Governor Ludwig asked.

"The attacks on Minot, Bismarck, and the Minot Air Force Base."

"Communications are down all over the state, so I wasn't aware of any of that."

"When we're done, General Stenson can get you up to speed."

"If you wouldn't mind, I'd like to do that right away."

"No problem, Colonel Ridgeway will transfer you."

"This is getting worse by the minute," General Lehman said.

"Colonel Ridgeway, I need Director Burnside and Secretary Baker ASAP," President Wilkes said. "General Lehman, I'll need a complete report on this debacle ASAP, and the air base attack is to be need-to-know only."

A few minutes later General Stenson's phone rang.

"The man's an imbecile and a coward," General Lehman said.

"What's the president done now?" General Stenson asked.

"Not one damn thing. He even chewed my ass out over you authorizing the air strikes."

"That's bullshit. Had I known they were going to attack the air base, I'd have done a hell of a lot more."

"Don't blame yourself, it caught everyone by surprise."

"If it were up to me I'd beef up their security with the Third Armored Cavalry Regiment out of Fort Hood, Texas."

"Then do it, but don't tell anybody," General Lehman said.

"Understood. Who knows, maybe we'll get lucky, and he won't get reelected."

"Fat chance, the last poll I saw had him ahead by twenty points, but I'm going to call Walter and let him know how I feel."

"Go for it, but if we ever go down that road, there's no going back," General Stenson said.

"I've been expecting your call," Walter Jefferson said.

"I've had it with Wilkes," General Lehman replied.

"I know you're upset, but it might not be much longer."

"Are you just saying that to shut me up?"

"No, sir, I'm not. I'm not prepared to discuss it, but are you and General Stenson still on board?"

"Damn straight."

"Good, and I hope we'll have some prior warning, but it all depends on whether my source can get me the intel in time."

"Sounds pretty ominous to me."

"I'm afraid it could be, but she hasn't been able to find out any specifics yet."

"She?"

"Sorry, I shouldn't have said that. Let's drop it for now, but hang in there." After a long pause Walter Jefferson asked, "General, are you still there?"

"Sorry, I shouldn't be telling you this, but the president has asked Attorney General Timbal to launch an investigation into your involvement with the militias."

"Shouldn't you have led off with that?"

"Probably, but I have to admit that I don't want the president to figure out it was me that tipped you off."

"Actually I can understand that, but don't worry, I'll keep you out of it."

By the next afternoon, riots had broken out across much of the nation, and Harvey Gabriel was back in the Oval Office trying to convince President Wilkes to take some action.

"Mr. President, the people need to hear what you're doing to ensure that these terrorist attacks won't escalate," Harvey Gabriel said.

"You're probably right, but I'm not changing course this close to Election Day. Let's set up a press conference for this afternoon, and I need you to write up some nonspecific bullshit that will get me by for now."

"You're the boss. I don't suppose you'll be taking any questions afterward?"

"Hell no, and don't schedule it for more than fifteen minutes."

Instead of quieting the criticism, President Wilkes's statements ignited a firestorm of indignation as angry demonstrators took to the streets to demand action.

Six days later, the president called Harvey Gabriel into the Oval Office. "We need to get to work on my next press conference," he said.

"Sure, but you'd better take a look at this first. It was the lead story in today's *Wall Street Journal*."

President Wilkes's face lost most of its color as he read the article. "Where the hell did they get these photographs, and do we know what part two is going to cover?"

"The photos were taken by an unnamed civilian contractor who was working at the base when the attack occurred. The second part runs tomorrow, and it's all about Roger Newsome's exploits."

"I've got a fund-raiser in Philadelphia tomorrow, so we'll work on it when I return."

Three days later, the president called Harvey Gabriel back to the Oval Office. "Good lord, did you listen to that nitwit on NPR this morning? You'd have thought I was encouraging the attacks," President Wilkes said. "And it sure didn't help any that Roger Newsome's pack of militia rednecks managed to shoot down eight of their aircraft."

"He was pretty brutal," Harvey Gabriel said. "But they're not going to let up until you come forward with a believable strategy to stop them."

"So you've gone over to the warmongering side of the house, have you?"

"Hardly, but these bastards have slaughtered Americans on our own soil, and it seems to be escalating. That last raid was the closest thing to an invasion that this country has seen since the war of 1812."

"Now you're being dramatic."

"Maybe a little, but people are scared, and there

have even been several instances of the police joining the demonstrations."

"I know, but I'm still hoping it will blow over."

"Doesn't sound like much of a plan, but are you still wanting to hold another press conference?"

"Not right now."

Very early the next morning, Daoud Mansouri walked into the fish market where they'd set up shop for the day and asked, "Are you ready for me yet?"

"Yes, but you'll have to overlook the smell," Dizhwar Akram said.

"It's not that bad, and it beats getting blown to hell. I read the overnight reports on the way over. Is there anything hot this morning?"

"Have you seen this week's cash flow numbers yet?"

"No, but since you're asking, they can't be good."

"Catastrophic is the word that comes to mind. Ehsan Hashmi drew seventy million, and he's saying he needs another thirty immediately."

"Do we know what he spent it on?"

"Of course, he keeps meticulous records. He made a six-million-dollar payment to Hani Aboud, he sent another five million to fund the Mexican operation, and he spent the rest on the package from our Pakistani friend."

"Good, that means he's getting close to pulling the trigger on the main event, but I still wish we didn't have to use a third party for something this important," Daoud Mansouri said.

"Ehsan swears that Annas Elmaleh is the only one who could pull this off," Dizhwar Akram replied.

"Do we have a date yet?"

"All he'd say was very soon. On the positive side, they did take eighty-three more girls hostage during the last raid."

"Excellent, and what happened to the money from his last raid?"

"He didn't want to get caught with all that cash, so it's on the way here in air cargo containers."

"Is he still planning an East Coast operation?"

"He wouldn't say."

The next morning Walter Jefferson was sitting in the conference room in his house, rereading the article about Roger Newsome's exploits. When he finished, he decided it was time to implement another piece of his long-term strategy. He went to the conference room and sent out a meeting invitation for 2 P.M. that afternoon, along with the file containing what he wanted to cover with the militia leaders.

"Gentlemen, I appreciate you taking this meeting on such short notice," Walter Jefferson said.

"We were very sorry to hear about Roger Newsome and his men, but at least they went down fighting," Jeb Butts said.

"His death was a great loss, but that's why I wanted to talk with all of you. I'm starting a youth movement to ensure we have a steady flow of new recruits, and I wanted to see if you would help me roll it out."

"Send me what you've got, and I'll see what we can get going," Jeb Butts said.

"Excellent. I'll cover all of your expenses," Walter said.

"Most generous." Clyde Thomas nodded. "But I'm afraid the press is going to accuse us of trying to brainwash the recruits."

"Or that we're trying to form some sort of cult," Willy Wood said.

"Take a look at the curriculum, and if you don't want to participate, you don't have to," Walter Jefferson said.

"Like I said, you can count me in," Jeb Butts said.

"Me too," Terry Gould said.

"Some of them didn't seem too keen on your youth movement," John Jay said after the call.

"They'll come around, and if not, we can always replace them," Walter Jefferson said.

"Just give the word. We still on for your other project?"

"Definitely, and I need you to start putting together another rapid response team, but don't tell anyone."

"Purpose?"

"Problem resolution, and they need to be willing to do whatever it takes."

"If you're okay with mercenaries there's no shortage of that kind of talent."

"Not an issue, at least you know where they're coming from."

"Consider it done. Anything else?"

"I need you to take over Roger Newsome's group."

"You want me to command his militia?" John Jay asked.

"Yes, but not in the way you're thinking. I'd like to use them as my personal protection detail, but their level of discipline is atrocious."

"Doable, but I'm going to need some help."

"Whatever you need," Walter Jefferson said.

"If you want it quick, I'll have to bring somebody in from the outside."

"No problem, as long as they don't mind getting a little bloody."

"If he does he's not the right guy."

Two weeks later, another wave of Daoud Mansouri's recruits were about to strike.

"It's too damn early for me," Misty Groom said.

"I know, but we've got to be out of here before my dad comes in to open up at six," Marsha Winkle said as she unlocked the overhead door to her father's garage in Queens, New York.

"I can't believe we're actually going through with this," Misty said.

"Me either, and my dad is going to be furious."

"Your dad is the type of person that we're trying to reach. I can't believe he didn't catch us while we were putting this together."

"I told him the boys were helping us rebuild the van and your car, and I guess he was just glad that I was taking an interest in something other than partying."

"He sure does get wound up when he's had a drink our two."

"It was his unrelenting tirades about the Arab and Muslim worlds that finally pushed me into converting. I'm so glad you found the ISIS website, it has made everything crystal clear to me."

"I'm not sure that I would have found the courage if Daoud Mansouri hadn't taken the time to respond to me."

As they started their vehicles and drove away, there were over thirty more around the country doing the same thing.

"Move on, this is an unloading zone," said the crossing guard in front of the Washington Market School in New York City.

There were over sixty children gathered in front of the redbrick building's entrance when Misty Groom detonated her bomb. The powerful explosion splattered the crossing guard's body in every direction, and shattered Misty's car into thousands of pieces of hot metal and glass. The deadly wave of shrapnel ripped a bloody path through the crowd of waiting children, and the concussion blew the glass out of the windows on both sides of the street and turned the window-mounted air conditioners into deadly projectiles.

Sergeant Maples was working a traffic accident just down the block when the explosion erupted. "Dispatch, there's been a huge explosion in front of Washington Market School. You need to roll the fire, medics, and some backup," he said.

"Any casualties?"

"I'm about a half a block away, but there were a bunch of kids in the street, so it's going to be bad."

"There are multiple units on the way."

"I'm on my way down there to see what I can do."

Marsha Winkle's target was the PS 234 Independence School, but she got held up in traffic and was almost twenty minutes late.

The children had already gone inside when she arrived, and she didn't know what to do. Large metal pipes buried in concrete protected the entrance to the school, but as she circled the block she spotted an unprotected service entrance. They'd used plastic explosives in Misty's car, but they'd stripped all of the seats out of her van so they could pack it full of barrels of fertilizer and diesel fuel, patterned after the bomb that Timothy McVeigh had used in the Oklahoma City bombing.

Marsha drove to the end of the block to turn around. She took a deep breath and hit the gas. By the time the van smashed through the double doors of the service entrance, it was going over seventy miles per hour. Marsha had triggered the device just before the van hit the building, but it had a three second delay, so the van was over thirty feet inside the building when it exploded.

"Nine-one-one, what's your emergency?"

"This is the SkyFox HD news helicopter. PS 234 just exploded."

"That's at two-ninety-two Greenwich isn't it?" the 911 operator asked.

"It's definitely on Greenwich, but I couldn't tell you the building number. You won't be able to miss it, because the whole damn thing is in flames."

For the first time in months, President Wilkes was eating a late breakfast with his wife, Rachel, when Mary Counts rushed in with a note from Director Gillespie. As he was reading the note, Rachel watched all the color drain out of his face. She asked, "What's wrong?"

"There have been at least thirty car bomb explosions in the last thirty minutes."

"Where?"

"They were all at schools in fifteen different states."

"Oh dear God, no," Rachel said.

"I'm sorry, but I need to get on this," President Wilkes said as he got up to leave.

"Of course, and I'll say a prayer for all of them."

"Net it out for me, Colonel," President Wilkes said when he entered the Situation Room.

"Not many details yet, but it's bad," Colonel Ridgeway said.

"That seems to be a recurring theme of late. Where did they detonate the bombs?"

"All but one of them occurred in the drop-off areas of the schools."

"Bastards. What the hell do they hope to gain from killing innocent children?"

"Innocent lives mean nothing to them because they use terror as a tool to gain control over the people."

Almost twenty minutes passed before the director of national intelligence called to update President Wilkes.

"How bad is it?" President Wilkes asked.

"Horrendous," Frank Gillespie said. "We've had thirty-six separate attacks, and the first casualty count is one thousand and thirty-six killed, and another three hundred seriously wounded, and that number doesn't include at least ninety-one crossing guards and parents. However, the attack on PS 234 in New York City is going to run the number of deaths up substantially."

"Why?"

"The blast collapsed the entire building, and they don't believe anyone made it out alive."

The president bowed his head to say a prayer before he asked, "Has anyone taken credit for the attacks?"

"No, but in two instances the suicide bombers were teenage girls."

"I really didn't need any more of this kind of shit," President Wilkes said.

Self-centered bastard, the director thought.

"I need to address the nation, so I'll need a complete report by this afternoon," President Wilkes said.

Due to the number of attendees, President Wilkes held the press conference in the East Room of the White House. He spent the first twenty-five minutes sharing the details of the attacks before he opened it up for questions.

"Mr. President, have we been able to identify the perpetrators?" asked Gerald Johnson, a reporter for *The New York Times.*

"We've identified two of them, but we haven't been able to tie them to a specific group, and so far no one has taken credit for the attacks."

"Were these terrorist attacks or not?"

"We don't know. The only common thread that we've found in the two we've identified is that they were both recovering drug addicts."

"Drug addicts don't bomb schools," Gerald Johnson said.

"Is there any chance that these attacks could happen again?" asked Sara Gibson, a reporter for *The Washington Post.*

"Unlikely."

"How can you say that?" asked Thad Purvis, a reporter for *The Wall Street Journal*. "You don't have a clue why these attacks occurred."

"At this time we don't believe they are likely to be repeated. Thank you for coming, and that's all the questions I have time for tonight."

"What did you think of my press conference?" President Wilkes asked his wife as he was getting ready for bed that night.

"I think you need to get your head out of your ass," Rachel said.

"What?"

"You know damn well that ISIS is behind these attacks. Why aren't you doing something about it?"

"You too?"

"Me too, for sure. What the hell has happened to you? It seems like you're afraid to do your job."

"The election is in four days, and I'll take care of it after I'm reelected."

This isn't the man I fell in love with, she thought to herself. "There are more important things than an election," she said.

"Not to me."

President Wilkes was in the Oval Office by five the next morning, and when he finished reading the overnight updates, he called Larry Ragsdale at home. "Every news and talk show host in the country is unmercifully raking me over the coals," he said. "You need to help me come up with some positive news."

"We're doing everything we can, but I wouldn't worry about it. According to the latest poll, your numbers are holding up just fine."

"I'm considering turning General Stenson loose on these scumbags," President Wilkes said.

"This isn't the time to do anything rash," Larry Ragsdale said. "Stay the course, and it will all work out."

"I pray you're right. Hell, even my wife was giving me shit about it."

"I know it's been hard on you, but trust me, everything is going to be fine."

JOHN JAY HAD been gone for a couple of days on an assignment for Walter Jefferson, and he hadn't checked in like he was supposed to.

"Where are you?" Walter asked.

"I'm on my way back, but it turned out to be far more difficult than I'd anticipated."

"Well, am I going to have to read your mind?"

"I'd rather not discuss it on an open line," John Jay said.

"Fine. When do you get back?"

"It's going to be several hours yet."

"Come see me as soon as you land."

"It's going to be pretty late for you."

"Doesn't matter because I'm not going to sleep until I hear how you've done."

John didn't get back to the ranch until almost 2 A.M. Walter was sitting on the couch in front of the fireplace in the great room, sipping a glass of brandy.

"I don't think I've ever seen you take a drink before," John Jay said.

"I rarely drink, but I needed something to calm my mind down."

"What's the big deal? We've dealt with far worse than this."

"I know, and I wish I could explain it, but ever since I found out that the president was having me investigated, I haven't been able to think about anything else."

"Well you can stop worrying about Timbal's investigation. I've convinced him to give you a clean bill of health on everything."

"He took the money?"

"No, I had to take another path, and that's why I was out of touch for a while."

"Are any of his family members missing?"

"No humans, but he did suffer a horrible accident at his horse farm. Someone broke in and slit the throats of his three grand champion stallions."

"Sorry I missed that," Walter said. "Have you made any progress on upgrading Roger's group?"

"In a big way. I've persuaded Oliver Porter to come to work for us."

"Never heard of him."

"Nor should you have. He's a disgraced CIA agent who spent most of his career training security forces for our Third World allies."

"Sounds good, but why isn't he still with the CIA?"

"He went off the reservation during an extraordinary rendition operation he was in charge of in Morocco and slaughtered six U.S. citizens."

"Is he stable enough to be trusted?" Walter asked.

"He'll be fine as long as we don't let him interrogate anyone."

CHAPTER 20

On the weekend following the presidential election, Banna Abadi was sitting in her one-room flat in New York City when she received an unexpected phone call.

"It's so good to hear your voice again," she said when she realized who it was. "When are you coming home?"

"I just called to tell you that I love you, and to thank you for always being there for me," Isben Abadi said.

"I love you too, but I'm your mother, and you never have to thank me for anything."

Just before the phone went dead, Banna Abadi heard a man's voice scream, "What the hell are you doing?"

When Isben tried to get up off the floor, Annas Elmaleh kicked him in the ribs. Isben was an athletic two hundred and twenty pounds, but Annas's kick had driven him three feet across the dusty cement floor.

Annas was only five foot eleven and a hundred and eighty pounds, but he was a highly trained martial artist, and at one time had been one of the most feared assassins in the world.

"Stay down there, you worthless dog. You were warned not to contact anyone."

"I just wanted to say good-bye to my mother."

"Disobey me again and you're dead. Now get up, the truck will be here shortly."

When the rented semitrailer pulled into the decrepit old garage in the industrial district of Vancouver, British Columbia, Annas Elmaleh hurried to close the overhead door behind it. When they opened the trailer door, Isben Abadi caught his first glimpse of the large brushed-metal box. It was securely strapped down in the middle of the otherwise empty trailer, but its nondescript appearance belied the horror it contained. The other members of the team rushed over to offload the container, and Isben could see that they were in their early twenties like him.

"The shipment was late in arriving, so we're short on time," Annas Elmaleh said. "While they're making the final preparations to the payload, I've got a video that Daoud Mansouri wanted you to watch before you take off."

Annas Elmaleh started the video on his phone and handed it to Isben Abadi.

"I wanted to take this opportunity to assure you that our people will be telling the story of this day forever," Daoud Mansouri said. "This moment will go down in the Islamic State's history as the first step to eradicating the infidels that have inflicted their evil ways on our people, *Allahu Akbar,* and now I'll let you hear from a few of the true believers that have gone before you."

When the video was finished, Isben Elmaleh said, "You've got ten minutes before takeoff, so why don't you use the time to make your peace with Allah. If you'd like, you can use my phone to record a final message to your family, and I'll make sure that they get it."

As Isben knelt on his prayer rug, he was at peace with his decision. As he thought back to how he'd arrived at this moment in time, he could see the irony in it all. His mother had immigrated to the U.S. as a child, and she'd never spoken of the horrors her family had endured in Iraq before they'd sought political asylum. Isben had never known his grandfather, but he'd found his diaries while he was helping his mother clean out the attic. His grandfather's decision to help the Americans had enabled him to get his family out of the country, but he'd spent the rest of his life regretting his decision as he watched his family slowly move away from the Islamic values that had anchored his life. By Isben's second year in college he'd begun to study everything he could find on the Islamic State, and he'd quickly come to realize that he shared many of the same beliefs. When Isben had first contacted them via their website, he'd expected to be sent to Syria for indoctrination and training, but instead Daoud Mansouri had persuaded him to stay in school, and to begin taking flying lessons. He'd known that he'd get the call someday, and two years later, Daoud Mansouri had contacted him.

When Isben Abadi finished his prayers, he recorded a final message to his mother, and walked out to where the helicopter was being readied. He returned the phone to Annas Elmaleh, and climbed into the pilot's seat of the S-61V Sikorsky helicopter. Annas Elmaleh's men had stolen it from a local construction company a few days before, because it could lift up to eleven thousand pounds.

"You've got plenty of fuel, but make sure you stay below a hundred feet so they don't pick you up on radar," Annas Elmaleh said.

"I understand, and praise be to Allah for allowing me this honor," Isben Abadi said.

After he got the Sikorsky started, he revved the engine for liftoff, and came to a hover over the container. The ground crew secured the cable to the load, and ran back out of the way as the chopper lifted it free of the ground.

When Isben Abadi turned the Sikorsky out over the

waters of the Salish Sea, the container was only a few meters above the waves. Annas Elmaleh had been adamant that he had to trigger the device at precisely 1330 Pacific, so Isben was paying close attention to his airspeed.

As Isben Abadi made his way toward Puget Sound, his mind was racing with the implications of what he was about to do. However the wind picked up as he entered Puget Sound, and he had his hands full keeping the load under control. He glanced nervously at his watch as he entered Elliott Bay and realized that he was ahead of schedule, so he quickly recomputed his airspeed and adjusted the throttle. When he caught sight of CenturyLink Field he began his ascent.

Bill Turner had been saving for months so he could take Jaden, his eleven-year-old son, to the Seahawks game. They were seated in section 325 behind the south end zone, and their view of Seattle's downtown skyline was spectacular.

"How's your hot dog?" Bill asked.

"It's great," Jaden said. "Dad, what's that helicopter carrying?"

When Isben was directly over the field, he muttered, "Forgive me, Mother," and flipped the switch to detonate the device. The electronic trigger was programmed to send a text message to Annas Elmaleh, confirming the detonation before it set off the device.

"I don't know, but it might be a part of the halftime show, I'll—"

Bill never finished his sentence, as the fireball from the nuke vaporized the stadium.

"It's done," Annas Elmaleh said when Ehsan Hashmi answered his cell phone.

"*Allahu Akbar,*" Ehsan Hashmi said. "Hang on, and I'll get you paid. Okay, if you'll check your account, the money should be there."

After Annas Elmaleh had verified the twenty-five-million-dollar deposit, he said, "Good working with you, but don't ever contact me again. I don't need the Americans crawling up my ass.

"Let's get the hell out of here," he told the pilot of his rented Citation X.

A couple of minutes later the Citation X accelerated down the runway of Vancouver International Airport, and when it lifted clear of the runway the pilot retracted the landing gear, triggering the plastic explosive charges hidden in the wheel well.

Ehsan Hashmi was sitting in the airport parking lot when the Citation exploded. *He won't be needing the money anymore,* Ehsan Hashmi thought as he opened his laptop to rescind the bank transfer. When he finished, he opened a chat session and typed, "There is fire in the sky, and the stage has been cleared."

"*Allahu Akbar,*" Dizhwar Akram exclaimed when he received the message. "I've just received the confirmation from Ehsan Hashmi. The operation has gone off as planned, and our mercenary problem has been taken care of."

"I told you to have faith, and it would all work out," Daoud Mansouri said.

"Are you watching the Seattle game?" John Jay asked when he came rushing into Walter's office.

"I was going to, but I just got off the phone with Governor Ludwig," Walter Jefferson said. "Why, has something happened?"

"There's been some sort of explosion, but the network isn't giving any details yet."

"Explosion?"

"The MetLife blimp was doing an overhead shot of the game when a heavy-lift Sikorsky helicopter passed directly underneath it, and then wham, the brightest light I've ever seen."

"What's the name of that new guy we just recruited?"

"There have been so many lately, you'll have to give me a hint."

"You know, the egghead from Michigan State?"

"Oh the NEST guy, that would be Tony Ferguson."

"See what he knows, and while you're doing that, I'll try to reach General Lehman or General Stenson."

Marjorie Paterson had been watching the game, and she called her boss seconds after the explosion. "I'm sorry to disturb you on the weekend, but I think there's been a major incident on the West Coast," she said.

"What sort of incident?" asked Simon Dobbs, the director of the Department of Energy.

"There's been a horrendous explosion at the Seahawks game."

"I'm sorry, Marjorie, but how is that an issue for the DOE?"

"I think it was a terrorist attack. The MetLife blimp was broadcasting the game live, and it showed a helicopter passing directly underneath it just before it exploded."

"Are you sure it was an explosion?"

"It was definitely an explosion."

"I'll get them to check it out."

The director was about to hang up when Terry Jacobs finally answered.

"Sorry, boss, I was in the bathroom," explained Terry Jacobs, the weekend supervisor.

"Marjorie swears there's been an explosion at the Seahawks game," Director Dobbs said.

"Damn, she's right. The satellite is showing a nuclear explosion near Seattle."

"Oh, lord, give me strength. Get the Aerial Measurement System birds in the air, then we need to get the ARAC team started plotting where the radiation is going to hit."

A couple of minutes later, Terry Jacobs came back on the line. "The AMS aircraft should be on location in about ninety minutes, and I've alerted ARAC. Anything else?"

"Patch me through to Tony Ferguson."

"Tony Ferguson speaking, how may I help you?" asked the commander of the Nuclear Emergency Support Teams. After graduating from Michigan State with a doctorate in nuclear physics, Tony had worked for the DOE for a few years before joining the NEST team. He had brown hair and eyes, and was five foot eleven and a hundred and ninety pounds. He'd played lacrosse in college, and still ran at least four miles every morning.

"Have you heard the news yet?" Director Dobbs asked.

"Sorry, boss, I didn't check the caller ID. Heard what news?"

"There's been a nuclear explosion on the West Coast, and I need your team on site as soon as possible."

"No problem, but could you be more specific?"

"Sorry, I'll have them send you the exact coordinates en route, but it was near the Seahawks stadium."

"We're on it, but what are we looking at?"

"No idea, but I'll forward the AMS data to you as soon as it comes in."

When the director hung up, Tony Ferguson called the Davis-Monthan Air Force Base in Arizona.

"NEST command, Captain Lawrence speaking."

"Captain, this Tony Ferguson, and I've got an incident on the West Coast."

"We just heard the news. What are you going to need?"

"I'll need one of your C-5As, and I want it loaded with the following: two portable labs, three of the hardened positive air MRAPs, a hundred of the RST's Demron W class-two suits, and one of the remote-controlled excavation backhoes. We'll be at your location in ninety minutes, and I'll need that aircraft loaded and ready to go."

Tony's personal cell phone rang. "I'm rather busy at the moment, what do you need?" he answered.

"Sorry, but Walter Jefferson would like your take on what just went down in Seattle," John Jay said.

"There's been a confirmed nuclear explosion at or near CenturyLink Field. I'm putting my team together right now, and we're on our way out there to do the initial damage estimates. Look, I need to go, but I'll get you an update when I can."

When Tony and his team landed in Arizona, the C-5A was fully loaded and ready to go. Their aircraft taxied up beside the C-5A, and Tony and his team literally ran onto the waiting aircraft. As aircrew started buttoning it up, Tony Ferguson headed to the flight deck to talk to the pilot.

"I'm Tony Ferguson," he said as he stuck his head through the cockpit door.

"I'm Colonel Whittle. Take a seat, and we'll visit once we're airborne."

"Flynet One, you're cleared for takeoff, and God-speed," the control tower radioed.

"Roger that, tower, Flynet One is rolling," Colonel Whittle replied.

Once the massive aircraft was at cruising altitude, Colonel Whittle told his copilot, "Major, you've got the aircraft." He turned to Tony Ferguson. "We've been cleared direct to Sea-Tac, and if the weather holds, we should be on the ground at the Seattle/Tacoma International Airport in a little over an hour. But if you wouldn't mind, I'd like to know what we're getting into."

"I'll tell you what I know, but it's not much," Tony Ferguson replied.

CHAPTER 21

Earlier that day, President Wilkes and Vice President Regal had been meeting in the Oval Office with a few of their supporters to discuss his objectives for his second term.

"Congratulations on your reelection," offered the Speaker of the House, Terrance Finnegan, as he sat down in front of the president's desk.

"Thanks, Terry, but I couldn't have done it without all of you," President Wilkes said.

"Nonsense, you've done a stellar job," said Michael Carmichael, the president of the Senate pro tempore.

"You've got that right," Vice President Timothy Regal said. "I can still remember all of the doubters when you first took office, but you've done every damn thing you said you would."

"And more," Terrance Finnegan said. "Although for a while there, I was afraid they might lynch all of us when you pushed through your plan to nationalize heath care by forcing everyone onto Medicare or Medicaid."

"That and the budget cuts you've made to their sacred cows. I listened to an NPR broadcast on the way over, and you should have heard them whining about the cuts to the farm subsidies and that last round of military budget cuts."

"You've got to admit that it takes talent to piss off both conservatives and liberals," President Wilkes said.

"I've never understood how they can be called conservatives when all they do is spew hate and intolerance," Vice President Regal said.

"Me either, but they're right about one thing, we desperately need something to make the public feel safe again," President Wilkes said. "This latest rash of incidents has everyone on edge."

"We have a few thoughts . . ." Larry Ragsdale started to say, when Special Agent Edgar Robertson interrupted the meeting.

"I told you that I didn't want to be disturbed," President Wilkes said.

"Frank Gillespie is on line one, and he said that he needs to talk with you right now," Special Agent Robertson said.

"Put him on the speaker," President Wilkes replied. "What's got your panties in a wad, Frank?"

"We've had a confirmed nuclear explosion on the West Coast," the director of national intelligence said.

"Oh, God. You said the West Coast, but you didn't say where exactly."

"Sorry, the Seattle area, CenturyLink Field."

"Shit, that's where the NFL game of the week is being played," Vice President Regal said.

"Director, I want you and the rest of the NSC on site ASAP," President Wilkes ordered.

"I'm on my way," Director Gillespie replied.

"I'll have a security team at your location in twenty minutes," said Special Agent Robertson.

"I can drive myself."

"Do as he asks, Frank," President Wilkes said.

"Fine, but I think it's silly. I've just texted Colonel Ridgeway, and he'll have our initial synopsis of the situation ready for you in a few minutes. I'll be there as soon as I can."

"Sorry to cut this short, but I need to get on top of this," President Wilkes told the group when he hung up.

"We understand," Michael Carmichael said. "And let us know if there's anything you need from us."

"If this is half as bad as it sounds, I'll be calling on all of you."

When President Wilkes and Vice President Regal got off the elevator in the basement of the West Wing, an armed security team met them.

"What's this?" President Wilkes asked.

"This is our new level-one protocol," Special Agent Robertson said.

They'd just completed a major upgrade to the huge White House Situation Room, and neither one of them had seen it yet.

"Damned impressive," Vice President Regal said.

"Yes, sir, it is," Air Force Colonel Ridgeway said as he handed the president a briefing folder.

"Anything new in here?" President Wilkes asked.

"Not much, but we're downloading a video of the explosion."

"Where did that come from?"

"NSA extracted it from the live feed from the Seahawks game."

"What have I missed?" Director Gillespie asked when he walked in twenty minutes later.

"Nothing, we just got here ourselves," President Wilkes said. "Once we have everybody, we'll start with a video clip from NSA, and then you can take over."

"Do we have an ETA on General Lehman?" Director Gillespie asked.

"He lands in ten minutes, and the rest of the council just arrived," Colonel Ridgeway replied.

"That should give me enough time to gather casualty estimates and an updated overview of the situation," Director Gillespie said.

As the council members filed in, President Wilkes was taking a roll call on his iPad and making notes on possible tasks for each one of them. When General Lehman arrived, the president entered his name, and mentally verified his entries.

Starting to his right was Vice President Regal; General Curtiss Lehman, the chairman of the Joint Chiefs; Frank Gillespie, the director of national intelligence; Andrew Milliken, the secretary of state; Aryeh Behrmann, the secretary of defense; Benjamin Sparks, the secretary of the Treasury; and Jerry Jones, the new assistant to the president for national security affairs.

"Okay, we're all here, let's see the video," President Wilkes said.

When it popped up on the two-hundred-inch, ultra-high-def monitor, it was like being there in person. The camera operator in the gondola had been focused on the game, but when he noticed the helicopter he'd instinctively panned the camera toward it.

"I'm going to slow the playback so I can point out a couple of details," Colonel Ridgeway said. "The blimp never changes course, so we don't believe the pilot ever saw the chopper. The chopper is an S-61V Sikorsky, and if you'll focus your attention on this portion of the screen you can see the large metal container at the end of the cable."

When the chopper was directly over the playing field, the screen erupted in a massive burst of light as the weapon detonated. No one said a word as they struggled with the enormity of what they'd just witnessed.

"Any better estimates on the strength of the explosion?" President Wilkes asked.

"We still believe it was between seven hundred and fifty and a thousand kilotons," Director Gillespie said.

"My God, the Hiroshima and Nagasaki bombs were less than twenty-two kilotons," Vice President Regal said.

"That's true, and we all know how many deaths resulted from those," Director Gillespie said. "Now I'd like to walk you through our casualty estimates. The weapon went off at thirteen-thirty Pacific," he explained as he used the laser pointer to highlight the location of the explosion on the satellite photograph of the area.

"The stadium seats sixty-seven thousand, and it was filled to capacity. It was ground zero so we can assume an almost one hundred percent causality rate at the stadium."

"Horrific," Jerry Jones said.

"It gets worse. Downtown Seattle is less than a mile from ground zero, and if the explosion was in the one megaton range, it would have leveled everything for a two-mile radius."

"No survivors?"

"There might be a few, if they were in basements, or a substantial structure."

"So net that out for us," President Wilkes said.

"It's almost a certainty that the casualties will exceed three hundred thousand."

"Lord save us," Vice President Regal said.

"I hope He hasn't forgotten us, but I think we're on our own with this," President Wilkes said.

"There can be no doubt that this was a terrorist attack, and that they were trying to maximize the casualties," General Lehman said.

"True, but no one has taken credit for the attack," Director Gillespie said.

"We spend a fortune on border security, how the hell could this happen?" asked Benjamin Sparks, the Treasury secretary.

"I can answer that," Jerry Jones said as he took control of the screen with his laptop and clicked on an icon for the info center of the U.S. Customs and Border Protection website.

"The United States has over five thousand miles of border with Canada and almost two thousand with Mexico. Our maritime border includes ninety-five thousand miles of shoreline. Each year, more than five hundred million people cross the borders into the United States, some three hundred and thirty million of whom are noncitizens. There are almost a hundred and twenty million vehicles that enter the U.S. annually, and over twenty-two million cargo containers. So no matter how much money we spend, a determined foe will find a way in."

"I apologize for my comment," Secretary Sparks said. "It's easy to forget what an almost insurmountable task it is."

"To hell with the geography lesson, what about all those people?" Secretary Behrmann asked.

"FEMA needs to get all over this," Vice President Regal said.

"I'm not letting anybody in there until the NEST teams have finished their assessments," President Wilkes said. "Director Bainbridge said that they'll have their teams in the air within the hour, and their first assessments before morning."

"That's a long time to wait," Secretary Sparks said.

"It can't be helped, the local authorities don't have the equipment to enter the blast site," President Wilkes said.

"Rod Clawson, the director of the NSA/CSS would like to speak with you," Colonel Ridgeway said.

"I hope you have some good news for us," said President Wilkes.

"Afraid not, but I do have a video of the event," Director Clawson said.

"We've already seen the video," replied the president.

"This is from a high-resolution satellite, and it will give you a much better perspective of the event."

"Proceed," President Wilkes said.

"In the interest of time I'm only going to play the last two minutes."

They watched as the helicopter crossed the coastline and moved over the stadium, but this time they witnessed the full effects of the blast as the searing heat from the thermal wave incinerated and then the shockwave flattened the surrounding countryside before the mushroom cloud blocked their view.

"I can't even imagine the horror those poor people experienced," Secretary Sparks said.

"Don't take this the wrong way, but they didn't suffer for very long," said Director Clawson.

"I suppose that's a blessing, but I'd like to take a moment of silence for everyone that just lost their lives," President Wilkes said.

"Continue, Director," President Wilkes said when they'd finished.

"It was a nuclear explosion, with a yield of approximately a thousand kilotons. A nuclear explosion has three distinct forms of damage: thermal, blast or shockwave, and finally radiation. The thermal fireball would have been approximately ten million degrees, with a diameter of approximately eleven hundred and twenty meters. Which would have gouged out a crater that is at least sixty meters deep and three hundred meters in diameter."

"What does that mean for the stadium?" Vice President Regal asked.

"The thermal blast was traveling at the speed of light and would have incinerated everything in its path, so CenturyLink and Safeco Fields are gone."

"What about the city?" President Wilkes asked.

"Downtown Seattle is less than thirteen hundred meters away, and the wave of thermal energy would have swept through it in less than a second, leaving nothing but massive fires and devastation behind. Which brings us to the second factor: the shockwave. At that distance, the overpressure and the winds would have been devastating. But since the explosion occurred at a height of a thousand feet, when the shockwave struck the ground it was reflected and formed a second wave that was traveling directly behind the first one. The reflected wave would have been traveling much faster than the incident wave, and when they merged into a single wave, called a Mach stem, it would have doubled the overpressure of the first wave, which further magnified the horrific damage as it expanded outward from ground zero. Given the proximity, there won't be much left of downtown, and you should expect massive casualties."

"What about the radiation?" General Lehman asked.

"The initial burst would have killed anyone within a couple of miles, and the distance the fallout will spread is going to be highly dependent on the winds."

"That was very informative, Director Clawson," President Wilkes said. "You can stay on if you'd like."

"We need to move immediately to DEFCON one," General Lehman said.

"Without a doubt," Secretary Behrmann said.

"I hear you, but I'm going to go with DEFCON two for now," President Wilkes said.

"How in God's name can you justify that?" General Lehman asked. "We've just been nuked."

"True, but we don't have any idea who we would

nuke in return, so we'll go to a two until we do. Is that all you have?"

"For the moment, I'm afraid it is."

"I'm sure everyone could use a break, so let's take ten minutes before we get FEMA and homeland on the line," President Wilkes said.

"Are they on yet?" President Wilkes asked when they returned.

"They'll be on screen in a moment."

"Mildred, why don't you go first," President Wilkes said.

"We've been trying to coordinate with the Washington State government, but the governor, Jim Ride, was at the game, and his office is assuming he's dead," said Mildred Burnside, the director of FEMA.

"The lieutenant governor, Jeremy Watland, was vacationing in Yellowstone, but we finally reached him about twenty minutes ago. He's invoked the Washington State disaster plan and activated their National Guard units."

"Do we need to provide transportation?" President Wilkes asked.

"I've already had the air force send in a helicopter to airlift him out of the park, and they've got a KC-130 standing by to take him the rest of the way. As soon as he lands, the National Guard has a helicopter standing by to ferry him back to the capitol in Olympia."

"Does he need anything from us?"

"He wanted you to declare the state a federal disaster area."

"Done, and I think it would be prudent to include California, Oregon, and Arizona," President Wilkes said.

"I concur."

"Have any of those states taken any action?"

"Margaret Trubridge, the governor of Oregon, has declared the state a disaster area, and is responding with all available resources. When I talked to Jim Tuttle, the governor of California, he was going into a meeting with his emergency management team, so I would expect some sort of action out of them before morning."

"Anything out of Arizona?"

"Nothing, but I'll reach out to Governor Chavez when we're done here, and see what he's planning."

"We don't need a bunch of gawkers getting sick from the radiation," President Wilkes said. "General Lehman, I want you to cordon off the blast site as soon as you can."

"We've issued a recall for all off-duty personnel and canceled all leaves, but it's going to take us some time to gather enough manpower to secure a perimeter of that size."

"I understand, but you need to make it your highest priority," President Wilkes said. "Director Burnside, how large does the perimeter need to be?"

"Not a clue," Director Burnside said. "General, can you help me out?"

"It depends on the winds, but to be safe, I'd estimate we'd need to cordon off a perimeter of at least thirty miles."

"We'll go with that for now," President Wilkes said, "Homeland, you're up."

"We've instituted an Imminent Threat Alert, and the FAA has grounded all nonmilitary flights in the U.S.," Secretary Baker said.

"What about border security?" Vice President Regal asked.

"We've closed all the ports of entry until we have enough manpower to search every vehicle in or out of the country. We've also frozen all the incoming shipments at the seaports until we can inspect them."

"Disruptive, but necessary steps," President Wilkes said. "Anything else?"

"That's all I have for now."

"Until we can gain control of this situation we're going to meet every day," President Wilkes said.

"Do you have the schedules worked out?" General Lehman asked.

"No, but Colonel Ridgeway will send you the specifics once we do. I don't care if you attend in person, but if you are off-site, make damned sure you're using an NSA certified circuit."

CHAPTER 22

As Tony Ferguson's aircraft approached its destination, Colonel Whittle said, "We've been cleared to begin our descent, and we should be landing at Sea-Tac in about twenty minutes."

"Could you make a pass over the city before we land?" Tony Ferguson asked.

"I'll check," Jeff Whittle said.

"The local air traffic control is down, but we've been cleared to orbit the city for as long as you need."

There was a thick haze in the air, but once they'd descended to five thousand feet, the scene became readily apparent.

"Oh my God," Colonel Whittle said.

"What's wrong?" Tony Ferguson asked as he unbuckled his seat belt and moved up behind the pilot's seat. "Damn, this weapon had to have been at least a megaton to have caused all of this," he said as they orbited the smoking devastation.

As they passed over the area where the stadium had been, Tony Ferguson asked, "Isn't this where the stadium should be?"

"Yes, it used to be where that big smoking crater is," Colonel Whittle said.

"You can land, there's nothing else to see here," Tony Ferguson said.

"About that, the airport's instrument landing systems are down, and I haven't been able to contact the control tower. So I'm going to have to wing it, if you want me to try to land."

"I need you to land if at all possible."

"Then I'll give it a try. You'd better go on back and warn your team that it could get rough."

"Buckle up, because this could get hairy," Tony said as he sat down beside Jeff Bloomberg, the excavation crew team leader.

"How long do you think we can stay on location?" Tony asked when he saw that Jeff was studying the AMS data they'd just received.

"If these readings are correct, I'd estimate about two hours a shift," Jeff Bloomberg said. "Where are we going to start?"

"I was going to start with the stadium, but there's a huge crater where it used to be."

"That must have been one hell of an explosion."

"The first estimates pegged it at less than a megaton, but it had to be at least that. The city doesn't look much better, but we might find some survivors in the basements."

"If it's that bad, I doubt we'll find any."

"It could be a fool's errand, but I want to take a look," Tony Ferguson said.

"No problem, just don't get your hopes up."

"We're making our final approach into Sea-Tac, so make sure you're in your seats and buckled up tight," Colonel Whittle announced.

Between the smoke and the low-hanging clouds, they had zero visibility until they broke through at an altitude of less than a hundred feet.

"What is all that shit?" the copilot asked when

they saw the shattered aircraft burning furiously on the end of the tarmac. "You'd better go around," he said.

Colonel Whittle checked his altitude and airspeed, and said, "Too damn late now."

The 737 on the end of the runway was almost unrecognizable as they skimmed over the top of the emergency vehicles fighting the raging inferno. As soon as they'd cleared the wreckage, Colonel Whittle cut the engines and slammed the gigantic aircraft down onto the tarmac. The C5A Galaxy bounced a couple of times before he hit the thrust reversers and jammed down hard on the brakes.

The aircraft violently decelerated for several seconds before he made a hard left turn off the main runway. As they were taxiing, Tony Ferguson returned to the cockpit.

"The main terminal is a mess, so I'm going to park at the Clay Lacy FBO," Colonel Whittle announced.

"I don't care where you park, but be quick about it, because the radiation levels are pretty damned high," Tony Ferguson said.

There were twenty high-end private jets parked at the FBO, but none of them looked to be airworthy.

"This is as close as I can get," Colonel Whittle said as he stopped on the taxiway in front of the FBO.

"Good enough," said Tony Ferguson. "Keep your men on board. I'm going to send you down to San Jose as soon as we get oriented."

Once the colonel got the nose of the aircraft open, they double-timed it toward the entrance to the FBO. The front of the building had been all glass, but the blast had imploded it, and there were shards of glass scattered across the lobby.

"Who's in charge here?" Tony Ferguson asked as they picked their way through the debris.

"I'm Becky Turner, and I guess I am, since everybody else is gone," said the clerk sitting at the front desk.

"Where did they all go?" Tony Ferguson asked.

"What the hell happened? We all saw a huge flash of light, and heard the explosion, but I had to go pee, and when I came back out everyone had left. I tried to call my husband to come and get me, but the landlines are out, and I can't get a signal on my cell phone."

"There was a nuclear explosion near Seattle."

"My family is in Seattle. Are they going to be all right?"

Tony closed his eyes for a second or two before he said, "Becky, there's no good way to tell you this. If they were in the city, they're probably dead."

Tony managed to catch her when she passed out from the shock.

"What happened, boss?" Jeff Bloomberg asked.

"I just told this young lady that her family was probably dead."

"Shit. Is there anything I can do?"

"See if you can find anybody that's still in charge around here."

Ten minutes later Jeff came back and said, "Boss, other than the firefighters, everyone else has bugged out."

"The radiation levels are much higher than we expected, so I want you to go back out there and tell those firemen to let that shit burn, and that we're going to transport them to the San Jose relief center.

"Becky, I know this is hard, but I'm going to send you down to the relief center as well."

"What about my husband and daughter? I can't just abandon them."

"If you'll give me your address we'll check on them when we go into the city."

"I thought you said that everyone was dead?"

"It's a long shot, but if they happened to be in a basement or a really sturdy concrete-and-steel structure, they might have survived."

"Today is laundry day, and our machines are in the basement."

"I promise you that we'll check it out," he said. "Chris, would you mind taking Becky out to the plane?"

When Jeff returned, Tony told the team, "I saw that there are showers in the pilots' lounge, so we're all going to scrub up before we suit up and head out."

"Is that really necessary?" Chris Matthews asked.

"The radiation levels are much higher than I'd expected, so just do as I ask."

When they were suited up, they walked outside to the hardened MRAP they were going to use as a rolling command post. It was outfitted with anti-radiation sheathing and a positive air filtration system so that they could enter the area around ground zero. Normally the trip into downtown Seattle was less than a thirty-minute drive up State Highway 509, but it was slow going because the roadway was littered with vehicles.

Chris Matthews was driving the MRAP, and shortly after he'd made the turn onto Fourth Avenue, he caught sight of the rim of the smoking crater.

"May God have mercy on their souls," he said.

"What's wrong?" Tony Ferguson asked.

"That how I've always imagined Hell might look."

"Let's keep moving."

"I'm going to have to backtrack, and see if I-5 is passable."

I-5 was in bad shape as well, but after almost three hours they reached the downtown area.

They'd gone less than a mile when Chris Matthews said, "This is as far as we go."

Tony went up front to get a look for himself. "This

is even worse than it looked from the air," he said when he saw the massive debris piles from the collapsed buildings. "Jeff, get the drone fired up so we can look for a way around this mess."

They launched the drone, and as they surveyed the area, Jeff Bloomberg asked, "What is all that shit?"

"Cars, trucks, vans, you name it, but it looks like there's a way around this mess if we backtrack a couple of blocks."

"It's going to be dark by the time we get there," Chris Matthews said.

"We've got lights. Let's keep moving," Tony Ferguson said.

Almost an hour later he said, "Stop here, this is the address she gave me."

"My God, what a mess," Jeff Bloomberg said. "There's no way anyone could have survived in there."

"We're here, so let's fire up the robotic sled and take a look around," Tony Ferguson said. "Becky said there was a laundry room in the basement, and maybe we'll get lucky."

They had to stop several times to use the sled's remote-controlled backhoe to clear away the debris, but they finally reached the staircase to the basement.

"There's a metal door down there, and it looks intact," Jeff Bloomberg said.

"I'm going down there to take a look around," Tony announced.

"Let me go, I'm a lot better at this sort of stuff than you are," Mike Dubois offered.

"I made the promise, not you."

"Don't be pulling that bullshit on me, this is what we all signed on for."

"You're sure?"

"Damn straight, let me be the hero for a change."

"Okay, but the radiation levels are off the scale, so

your suit isn't going to hold up for more than about twenty minutes."

"Then I guess I'd better hurry."

Mike was six eleven, and weighed well over three hundred pounds, but he was as strong as a bull and agile for a big man. As he moved quickly through the still-smoking piles of debris, he was carrying an adult's and a child's anti-radiation suit with him. The steel door was locked from the inside, but one kick from his size-fifteen boots and it swung open. He jammed the door shut behind him and turned on the LED lights on his helmet.

Mike had searched the laundry room and was about to give up when he heard a soft cough from behind the line of dryers.

"Wake up, we need to get out of here," he said when he located Becky Turner's husband and daughter.

"I've found them, and they're both alive, but they're both out cold."

"Do you need help?" Tony Ferguson asked.

"I'll holler at you if I can't manage."

Ten minutes later, Tony Ferguson said, "Mike, you're taking too long. You need to get your ass back out here."

"I'm on my way, boss," Mike said as he threw them over his shoulders and started up the stairs.

"My god, man, we'd have come out and helped you carry them," Chris Matthews said.

"That wasn't what took so long, it was almost impossible to get them into those damned suits."

"Are they going to live?" Mike asked as their doctor, Charlie Montgomery, worked on them.

"I've given them both an injection of potassium iodine, and a new drug the Israelis provided a few months ago for that mess in Dubai. They're both stable, and I think they've got a chance, but we need to get them airlifted out of here ASAP."

"This is Flynet command, and I need an immediate air evacuation for two survivors we've recovered."

"Roger that, we'll have a medevac chopper there within the hour."

"We've already taken more exposure than I'd intended," Tony Ferguson said. "So we're going to hitch a ride back on the chopper."

Tony gave Director Dobbs a verbal report on the way, and as they were landing in San Jose, he said, "I'll get all of this written up so that the retrieval teams will know where we've already looked."

President Wilkes hadn't slept very well, but he was up and in the Oval Office by five the next morning.

"Any updates?" President Wilkes asked.

"Not yet, but Tony Ferguson and the NEST team have been on site, and they should be checking in shortly," Mary Counts said. "Harvey Gabriel left you a message late last night, and he'd like some of your time this morning if possible."

"Good, because I need to put out an announcement on this as soon as possible, and I also need to talk to Nancy Baker."

He'd just finished reading his messages when Mary buzzed him, and said, "I've got Director Baker for you."

"Good morning, Director Baker. Have you got an update for me?" President Wilkes asked.

"I do, and Secretary Behrmann has moved mountains since last night. The army and the marines will have reinforcements in place at the major ports of entry by tomorrow morning. The air force will have drones monitoring the border checkpoints, and we'll be using satellites to monitor the rest of the borders."

"How's that going to work?"

"General Stenson will be pre-positioning ten-man rapid response teams so that they can reach any portion of the country in an hour or less."

"Great, I'll work all of that into my press release for later today. Anything else I can use to help calm the country's fears?"

"Nothing firm yet."

The president was jotting down notes for Harvey when Mary came back in. "You need to watch this," she said as she turned on the TV.

"This is George Sandoval with *Good Morning America,* and we're preempting our normal programming to bring you scenes from several of the demonstrations taking place around the country. After that we'll be showing you a satellite video we acquired from a source out of China that shows the actual moment of detonation in Seattle yesterday. We're going to start with the demonstrations in Chicago, where there have already been hundreds of arrests and at least four deaths. The smoke you're seeing is coming from downtown Chicago. The CPD commander on site is reporting at least two city blocks in flames, and that the CFD commander has just issued a fourth alarm.

"Now on to Detroit, where police are reporting twenty-five deaths, and as many as two hundred wounded. The chief of police has just put another six hundred riot police on the street to quell the looting, and the mayor has instituted a dusk-to-dawn curfew for the entire city. He's also warned that they will be taking a zero tolerance policy toward looters, and that he's authorized the use of deadly force."

They'd been watching the program for almost half an hour when the president said, "I've seen enough, turn that shit off. Is Harvey here yet?"

They hadn't noticed him, but Harvey had been standing in the doorway for several minutes, watching the telecast. "Are you ready for me?"

"Hell yes, I need to get something out there before they break in here and lynch me."

"It's not that bad yet," Harvey said as he sat down.

After he'd scanned the president's notes he said, "Excellent. This will make a good start, but we need to get some more details about what you're going to do for Seattle."

"I'm sorry but my blood pressure is acting up, and I've got to lie down for a little while," President Wilkes said. "Mary, I need you to hook Harvey up with FEMA and homeland so he can get the latest updates. When General Lehman arrives, tell him to go ahead with the NSC meeting without me. Harvey, once you're satisfied with the press release, just go ahead and send it out."

After he'd checked him out, the White House doctor was afraid the president was about to have a stroke, so he gave him a shot and a sedative and sent him straight to bed.

"Who do we have on?" President Wilkes asked when he sat down in the White House Situation Room the next morning.

"General Lehman, FEMA, homeland, NSA, DOE, and the vice president are on," Colonel Ridgeway said.

"I'd like to start by thanking all of you for the progress you've made on your assignments. I've added Director Clawson to our group for the duration of this emergency, and he's going to kick it off."

"You all should have received the National Nuclear Security Administration's initial assessment," Director Clawson said. "It contains a complete overview of the radiation's airborne measurements, and the on-site visits carried out by the various teams. The appendix contains the detailed reports from the NEST team that physically surveyed ground zero. We've rescued a few survivors, but most of them probably won't survive long term."

"Have we identified the bastards that did this?" Vice President Regal asked.

"The NEST team has processed the samples from the

blast site, and we've identified the manufacturer of the weapon."

"I'll bet it was Iran," Vice President Regal said.

"No, the weapon was Pakistani."

"I can't believe Pakistan would attack us after all the help we've given them to eradicate the Pakistani TTP," President Wilkes said.

"After discussing it with all of the other agencies, we don't believe they were involved in the attack or even had prior knowledge of it," Director Clawson said.

"What did they have to say when you told them it was one of theirs?" President Wilkes asked.

"At first they tried to deny it, but once we showed them the proof, they admitted that they had five weapons stolen from their storage facility outside Islamabad a few months ago. However, it gets worse. They think that elements of ISIS may already have the other weapons in their possession."

"That's what you've been trying to sell all along, but as I told you before, show me the proof," President Wilkes said.

"Whether you believe it was the Islamic State or some other rogue organization, there are definitely four more devices in the wind. As to the proof, we're working on that. We've identified the ship the terrorists used to smuggle the weapon into Canada, and we're currently interrogating the contract drivers they used to transport the weapon."

"Good, maybe we can finally get some actionable intelligence," President Wilkes said. "Are you ready to discuss the casualties?"

"I'll let the DOE take over from here."

"We now believe the initial estimates were too low," Director Bainbridge said. "The bomb was a surface detonation, and it caused a lot more radioactive fallout than we had originally modeled."

"What are we doing about it?" President Wilkes asked.

"The local authorities have issued the evacuation orders, but they're having a hard time getting the word out, because the electromagnetic pulse from the blast destroyed virtually all of their communications infrastructure. The Washington State National Guard is going door-to-door in the affected areas, but they're at extreme risk as well, because they don't have the proper equipment."

"Then get them the equipment," President Wilkes said.

"We're working on it, and we'll be delivering an additional shipment of potassium iodide pills this morning," said Mildred Burnside, the FEMA director.

"That's just not going to cut it. What about that new drug the Israelis sent us a while back?"

"We've already used up the original shipment, but there's a planeload due in this afternoon, and they've given us the formula so we can manufacture it ourselves."

They continued working on their logistical efforts for the rest of the morning, and just before lunch, Colonel Ridgeway handed Director Clawson a note.

"Something wrong?" President Wilkes asked.

"No, for a change it's some positive news."

"Out with it."

"During the interrogation one of the truckers admitted that he'd taken a photograph of the man that hired them," Director Clawson said.

"So we finally caught a break," Vice President Regal said.

"Yes, and it turned out to be a Pakistani mercenary by the name of Annas Elmaleh."

"A mercenary? Then we still don't know who's behind this?" the president asked.

"No, but the—"

"This is total bullshit. We know that Elmaleh has worked for ISIS in the past," General Lehman interrupted. "And we just need to get off our dead asses and wipe these sorry sons of bitches off the face of the earth."

"Slow down, we don't want to get ahead of ourselves," President Wilkes said.

"Ahead of ourselves?! You cowardly bastard, they've murdered hundreds of thousands of our countrymen."

"By God, sir, you're not going to disrespect me. If you don't think you can work with me, I can damn sure get someone else."

"Sorry, but it's killing me to see our people being slaughtered, and not do something about it."

"I can appreciate that, but that's the last time I'll tolerate that sort of bullshit from you. Director Clawson, get us back on topic," President Wilkes said.

"As I was about to say, the Canadian Security Intelligence Service believes Annas Elmaleh was on board a private jet that exploded during takeoff that same afternoon."

"Think, or know?" President Wilkes asked.

"He was last seen boarding the aircraft, but they haven't gotten the results of the DNA tests back yet."

"Offer them any assistance they need, but I want an answer," President Wilkes said. "Director Clawson, do you have anything else?"

"No, I don't."

"We're not going to accomplish much else today, so we'll meet back here at oh-six-hundred tomorrow."

When the president got back upstairs to the Oval Office, his press secretary, Harvey Gabriel was waiting.

"How'd we do?" President Wilkes asked.

"All of the major networks are going to carry your press conference, and you're scheduled to go on at eight P.M. Eastern," Harvey Gabriel said.

"How are you coming on my talking points?" President Wilkes asked.

"Take a look," Harvey said as he slid the script across the desk.

"I'm good with everything except the last part," the president said. "I'm not ready to place the blame on anyone yet. If I say it was the Islamic State, the public is going to expect an immediate response."

"So it wasn't ISIS behind all of the attacks?"

"I didn't say that, but even if it was them, they're spread across the Middle East, Africa, and probably Canada, and it's going to take a hell of an effort to eradicate them."

"What's your point?"

"They're not going anywhere, and for the time being I want to focus on getting the Seattle mess cleaned up."

Later that night, Walter Jefferson was sitting in front of the fireplace in his great room when his encrypted satellite phone rang.

"Once again the gutless bastard isn't letting us go after them," General Lehman said before Walter Jefferson could even say hello.

"Slow down, General. Just be patient for a little while longer."

"This shit has got to come to an end or I'm going to kill him with my bare hands."

My kind of guy, Walter thought. "Now, now, General, just hold it together for a little while longer. Can you do that for me?"

"I'll do my best, but if this shit continues, I'm not going to promise anything."

When he'd finished with the general, Walter called John Jay into the great room. "I've got a few small tasks for you and your boys," he said.

"Good, we're getting bored just sitting around waiting. What have you got in mind?"

"I need you to go to these cities and stir up some trouble."

"No problem, anything in particular you'd like us to do?"

"No, just use your imagination, but make sure that whatever you do inflames the situation."

"Excellent, it will give me a chance to observe some of the new recruits I've just brought on board."

Three days later, the president arrived in the Oval Office at 4 A.M., and Mary Counts was already there with his daily briefing folder.

"You're up awfully early," President Wilkes said.

"I stayed up half the night watching the news, and I knew you'd expect a report on everything that happened overnight."

"Usually they just call me if it's that bad."

"It was bad, but there wasn't anything you could have done about it."

"I needed the rest, but what's going on?"

"There were six demonstrations that escalated into full-blown riots."

"That's not that shocking."

"True, but this time there were close to a hundred police killed during the confrontations."

"Damn, you'd better let me see what you've got."

When he finished the reports, he said, "Someone has to be orchestrating this. Common rioters don't use machine guns or IEDs. I'd better get Nancy Baker working on this."

CHAPTER 23

General Lehman was still agitated when the NSC met the next day, but he managed to control himself until they were about to adjourn for the day.

"You can sugarcoat a turd, but it's still a turd," General Lehman said. "The Islamic State is a plague to humanity, and we need to exterminate them."

"Calm down, General. Until I see some proof, we're not exterminating anyone."

"Gutless bastard," the general muttered.

"You insubordinate son of a bitch," President Wilkes said. "I'm going to think about it overnight, but I'm probably going to replace you."

"You do whatever you think's right," General Lehman said.

"I'll ha—He hung up," President Wilkes said. "I've had it with that man."

"I don't blame you, but he's quite good at his job," Vice President Regal said.

"I know. We'll discuss it in the morning. And on that note, I think I we're done for today," President Wilkes said. "Our next meeting will be at ten A.M. tomorrow, and I want all of you on site. Colonel Ridgeway, would you make sure General Lehman gets the word?"

General Lehman had immediately called Walter Jefferson to vent.

"General, can I get a word in please?" Walter Jefferson finally interrupted.

"Sorry, but I'm done playing nice with that asshole."

"You've made that quite clear, and your timing is impeccable, because I was just about to call you."

"Why?"

"An unforeseen turn of events has forced me to move up our timetable. Hang on, I'll be right back." The line went quiet for almost three minutes before Walter Jefferson said, "I've just sent you the updated plan. Make sure General Stenson gets a copy."

"Not a problem, he was my next call."

"If either of you have an issue with it, or can't do it, I need to know right away."

General Lehman opened the file and studied it for a few minutes. "How did you come by this?" he asked.

"My sources will remain anonymous, but trust me, it's going down. Can you handle your end?"

"There's a couple of new wrinkles to it, but I'll get with General Stenson and put it in motion."

"I've got General Lehman on line one for you," General Stenson's aide said.

"I've just forwarded a file I got from Walter Jefferson," General Lehman said.

"How could he know all of this, and our intelligence agencies not have a clue?" General Stenson asked.

"I think he has someone on the inside, but it doesn't matter, this simply can't be allowed to happen."

"Agreed. I'm going to drop off now so I can get the team moving on this."

"General Stenson, what's up?" asked Lieutenant General Walter Lacy, the commanding officer of Fort Bragg's Special Operations Group.

"Liberty Tree is a go," General Stenson said. "However, several things have changed, and I've just sent you the updated plan."

"Got it, and I'll contact the team after I've read it."

General Lacy called Colonel Downey. "Colonel, I need to see you ASAP," he said.

"Sorry for the drama, but they've pulled the trigger on Liberty Tree," Lacy said when Colonel Downey arrived.

"It's about damn time. We're prepped and ready to go," Colonel Clayton Downey said.

"I agree, but the circumstances have changed, and you'll have to make some fairly major adjustments."

"It's a little late for that."

"Can't be helped. The Islamic State is going to try to assassinate the president in the morning, and your team is going to stop them."

"How is that so different from our plan?"

"You're right, they would both result in a change of leadership, but we're not going to let those scumbag terrorists assassinate the president of the United States. Take a look at it, and let me know what you think."

"This doesn't leave any margin of error."

"Can't be helped."

"If time allowed, I'd add another fifty men to the op."

"You'll just have to make do, but the rest of the troops will be standing by on the outskirts of the city to take over once you've completed your portion of the operation. I just wish I still had a part in it."

"You're not running the show?"

"General Stenson has assumed full operational control. He wants to avoid the regular com channels, so he'll contact you on this encrypted sat phone when the time comes."

"Is our equipment in place?"

"It is, and it's a good thing that General Stenson let

us use some of his black ops funds to lease those hangars."

On his way out, Colonel Downey called his XO, Lieutenant Sam Stallings.

"Lieutenant Stallings, contact the team and have them meet us at home base."

Colonel Downey had been in the army for almost twenty years, and they'd offered the deputy commander promotion to him before Colonel Tompkins, but he couldn't see himself stuck behind a desk for the rest of his career. The colonel was an extraordinary soldier, and even at forty-three, he was one of the most athletic soldiers in the division. He'd spent most of his career in special ops and was a highly proficient marksman and quite adept at all forms of hand-to-hand combat. His hair had turned gray years ago, but his blue eyes were still twenty-twenty. His most valuable trait was his uncanny ability to adapt to rapidly changing conditions during a firefight.

As Colonel Downey left the base his mind was racing through the implications of what they were about to do. As he was on his way to meet up with his team, Ehsan Hashmi was planning another raid. This time he was going to target New York State, so he'd consolidated all of their forces to the farm they'd leased south of Winnipeg.

"I don't think it's a good idea to put all of our assets in one place," Colonel al-Jabiri said.

"The farm covers three sections, so if you're that worried about it, park the choppers on the far side, set up the S-400s in the middle, and if you put the tents on this side, you should have plenty of separation," Ehsan Hashmi said.

"Sir, this just came for you in this week's courier pouch," the lieutenant said as he handed him the envelope.

"What's it say?" Colonel al-Jabiri asked.

"It's a note from Daoud Mansouri. He sends his congratulations for a job well done, and he's summoned me for a face-to-face meeting," Ehsan Hashmi said.

"What about the operation?" Colonel al-Jabiri asked.

"I shouldn't be gone very long, but if I'm not back you know what to do."

"With the way they're scrutinizing international travel, I doubt you'll be able to get there."

"I'm going to see if Mr. Trope can finagle something for me."

"The smuggler?"

"He's proven quite resourceful in the past."

Trope had a warehouse on the outskirts of Winnipeg, so Ehsan went to see if he could help.

"So do you have a solution for me?" Ehsan Hashmi asked.

"I do, but I hope you're not claustrophobic," Mr. Trope said.

"I'm not."

"Then follow me, and I'll show you what I've put together."

He unlocked the doors to an air cargo container and said, "This is a sealed container, and it's got enough food, water, and oxygen for a week, but it's going to be cramped."

"Let's do it."

"Fine. You'll leave on tonight's flight out," Mr. Trope said.

"The men are all present," Lieutenant Stalling announced when Colonel Downey entered the hangar.

"Good, but before I address the men, I need you to walk me through what we've got on board the choppers."

"The eight ground support choppers are configured

with M230 thirty mm chain guns, M-134 miniguns, and nineteen-round seventy mm FFAR rocket pods. The rocket pods are loaded with the laser-guided hydra-70 missiles, and the remaining four helicopters are configured to carry our twelve-man assault teams."

"Did they get the navigation systems updated?"

"About an hour ago."

"Good. I'm ready to address the men.

"They've green-lighted Liberty Tree, and we'll be wheels up at oh-five-hundred," Colonel Downey said.

The men immediately started high-fiving each other, but Colonel Downey said, "Quiet down. I know we've spent the last six months training for this day. However, we've received some new intelligence that has necessitated some rather significant changes to the operation. So gather around, because we've got a lot of work to do before morning."

They spent the better part of five hours rehearsing the updated mission plan, and when they finished Colonel Downey threw random questions at them until he was convinced they had it down pat.

"I think we're ready. We're on lockdown, so grab a cot and try to get some rest, because this is the most important mission of our lives."

At 7 P.M. that night, Secretary Behrmann called his brother at his home in Tel Aviv.

"Good evening, brother," Lieb Behrmann said.

"Sorry if I woke you."

"Not an issue. I don't sleep much these days."

"I understand completely, but I wanted to let you know that we have identified the weapon used by the terrorists."

"Iranian?"

"No, it was Pakistani. It was stolen by the TTP, and resold to a Pakistani by the name of Annas Elmaleh."

"Damn, our source was correct. I just wish we could have taken him out before this all went down, but don't worry, we'll find the bastard."

"No need, he was killed in an aircraft accident shortly after the attack."

"Accident my ass, somebody was cleaning up loose ends."

"You're probably right, and we still don't know who he was working for."

"We've heard rumors he's been working for Daoud Mansouri."

"The caliph of the Islamic State?"

"That's him."

"Thanks. We'll look into it, but that's not why I called. I caught wind of something that I need your people's help with," Secretary Behrmann said.

"Sure, but you have far more assets than Mossad."

"True, but I'm not sure who I can trust. Will you help me?"

"Of course. Send me what you've got, and I'll get my people moving."

President Wilkes had already gone to bed when Pete Kincaid, one of his largest contributors called.

"Thanks for taking my call," Pete said.

"It's always good to hear from an old friend, but why so late?"

"I've got something I need to pass by you and Timothy, and I need to do it first thing in the morning," Pete said.

The president checked his appointment calendar. "I've got a horrible schedule for tomorrow."

"I really need for this to happen."

The president took another look at his schedule and said, "I can give you twenty minutes at six fifteen in the morning, and Timothy will be with me, so just call my direct number."

"I really appreciate it."

"There, I've done as you've asked," Pete Kincaid said. "Now I'd like to see my family."

"No problem," John Jay said as he shot him in the back of the head.

Once Colonel Downey's teams were airborne the next morning, there wasn't much conversation. When the choppers neared the city, the pilots activated their terrain-following navigation and descended until they dropped off the radar grid.

Damn, I was hoping I'd hear something by now, Colonel Downey thought when they were within twenty-five miles of the White House.

"All aircraft, we're going to land in the park up ahead," Colonel Downey ordered.

"Are we on schedule?" John Jay asked.

"I am, but I just talked to Charles Whitaker, the pilot of the other bird, and the remote controls shorted out and he's going to have to pilot the aircraft," said Paul Whipple, the militiaman remotely piloting the captured Soviet Mi-28NE Night Hunter helicopter.

"Are they going to be able to carry out the mission or not?"

"They've stripped out the remote controls, and he's in the air, but he's at least forty minutes behind schedule."

"Damn it to hell," John Jay said. "We can't wait, so they'll just have to do the best they can."

They had an onboard camera pointed at the Islamic terrorists they had strapped into the front seats, and John Jay said, "It's too bad those two assholes are going to miss all of the fun."

"No surprise there, you gave them enough clonazepam to knock out a horse," Paul Whipple said.

"Make sure you keep low enough to stay off the radar," John Jay said.

"I can't get any lower without hitting something."

"Here's your coffee, Mr. President," Mary Counts said as she set a carafe of coffee on the Resolute desk.

"Sorry I'm late, but what was so urgent?" Vice President Regal said as he sat down at six thirteen that morning.

"A couple of things. Pete Kincaid called last night, and he wanted to visit with both of us this morning. I've decided to can General Lehman, and I wanted to get your opinion on his replacement," President Wilkes said.

"That's an easy call, you should promote Admiral Kennedy, but what does Pete want with us?"

"No idea, but he was adamant that he speak with us this morning."

"We've got incoming," one of the White House perimeter guards radioed when he spotted the helicopter.

"Target your missiles right there," John Jay said as he pointed at the screen.

Paul Whipple centered the target and unleashed all sixteen of the helicopter's Ataka-B air-to-ground missiles.

"We've got multiple missiles inbound," the sentry warned.

"I think he—" Vice President Regal never finished his sentence, as the missiles struck the Oval Office.

"Good shooting, now ram that bastard down their throats," John Jay said.

There was a wall of fire and smoke obscuring the building, so all Paul Whipple could do was hold his course and hope for the best. When the chopper smashed through the jagged opening left by the missiles, the Semtex exploded, igniting the fuel, and sent a gigantic fireball racing through what remained of the Oval Office.

Colonel Downey's squadron was still sitting in the park when General Stenson finally called.

"They were off on the time, it's going down right now," he said.

"Son of a bitch, we're on our way," Colonel Downey replied. "All units, move out. Stay below the radar for as long as you can," he told his pilot.

As the alarms were sounding throughout the White House compound, the automated systems had already contacted the D.C. emergency management center.

General Stenson knew their emergency response protocols so he knew where to call next.

"This is General Albert Stenson, and I need to speak to Director Timmons immediately."

"This is Director Harvey Timmons, and this had better be dammed urgent, because I'm up to my ears in shit," said the secretary of homeland security and the Emergency Management Agency.

"I know, but I have a special operations team that's responding to an attack on the White House, and I need you to stand down all of the emergency responders until I give you the all clear."

"Just who the hell do you think you are? My people are en route, and this is our responsibility, so you're the one that needs to stay out of it."

"You hardheaded son of a bitch. The White House is under attack, and I don't have time to try to sort out friend from foe, so stand down."

"Multiple vehicles inbound, take them out," Colonel Downey said.

As the convoys of police, fire, and emergency services vehicles raced toward the White House, two of the choppers banked to target them. The pilots couldn't help feeling a sharp pang of remorse as they centered them in their heads-up displays and triggered their M230 chain guns. The 30 mm cannon rounds shredded the onrushing line of vehicles, turning the street into a killing field.

"Heads up, there's another group at ten o'clock."

A second pair of helicopters launched a barrage of antitank missiles at a small convoy of armored SWAT units speeding toward them. As the destruction unfolded in front of him, the SWAT commander managed to turn away before they destroyed his SUV.

"Command, this is Captain Louis with SWAT team four, and we've just come under heavy fire from what looks like army helicopters."

"The bastard did it," the director muttered as he keyed the mike to the radio. "This is Director Timmons, and I'm ordering all units to stand down and return to base. Again I repeat, all units stand down and return to your home bases, and await further instructions."

"You bastard, you've killed a lot of good people," Director Timmons said.

"I warned you," General Stenson said. "I'll let you know when my men have the situation stabilized."

As his teams were about to enter the White House's defense perimeter, Colonel Downey radioed, "Citadel command, this is SOCOM flight Halo One, requesting permission to land."

"Halo One, permission denied, and do not attempt to land or we will fire on you."

"I repeat, this is SOCOM flight Halo One, we are inbound and requesting permission to land."

"Permission denied, exit the area immediately. This is your last warning."

"Roger that, Citadel, but we are going to land, and if you fire on us, we will respond."

"We've got a number of army Black Hawks that are preparing to land," Special Agent Guthrie said.

"Tell them to get the hell out of here, we've got enough problems."

"I did, but they're going to land anyway."

"Attention all available security personnel, we have

an Angels Red, I repeat: Angels Red, and lethal force is authorized."

"Execute Safe Sky," Colonel Downey said.

Colonel Tompkins's men knew where every antiaircraft battery, missile launcher, and sniper position was located so they targeted them when they opened fire.

"Nine o'clock," Colonel Downey's pilot said when he saw the rapid response team come charging outside.

The door gunner swiveled his General Electric M134 minigun toward them and unleashed a six-thousand-round-a-minute stream of 7.62 metal-jacketed slugs.

When one of the other agents saw the team being slaughtered, he radioed, "Team one is down, I repeat team one is down."

The backup team grabbed their weapons and headed outside to try to repel the air attack. As the savage firefight raged outside, the internal response teams had finally managed to extinguish the fires and clear enough of the debris to reach what was left of the Oval Office.

"Wanderlust and Joker are down," Special Agent in Charge Tommy Henderson announced.

"The medical team is on the way," Special Agent Jeffcoat said.

"Not necessary, they're both deceased."

"Are you absolutely certain?"

"I'm sure," Special Agent Henderson said as he tried unsuccessfully to keep from puking at the sight and smell of their horribly burnt and mangled bodies.

When he managed to stop puking, Special Agent Henderson ordered the Speaker of the House and the president of the Senate pro tempore protected, using their code names. "Control, have the Capitol Police secure Raven and Cowboy until we can get our teams over there to transport them to the secure locations."

A few minutes later Special Agent Jeffcoat reported,

"The Capitol Police said that they've already been picked up."

"By which agency?"

"They said a team of army rangers just left with them."

"Army? What the hell is going on?"

Special Agent Henderson mentally ran down the presidential succession list and said, "Send a team for . . . Hell, we never assigned them code names. Reroute the pickup teams and have them transport the secretary of state and the secretary of the Treasury to separate secure locations."

"They're on their way," Special Agent Jeffcoat said. "Is there anything you need?"

"A couple of body bags, and some more people to help gather up the body parts."

"Don't kill anyone you don't have to, but you've got your assignments," Colonel Downey ordered as the choppers sat down on the White House lawn. "Now move out and report in as soon as you've secured your objectives."

As the teams went about their tasks, Colonel Downey and six of his men made their way toward the Oval Office. When the Secret Service agents saw them coming, they went for their weapons.

"Stand down," Colonel Downey ordered. "There's no need for this, it's over."

One of the agents panicked and raised his weapon, but before he could get off a shot, the colonel put three 9 mm rounds in him from his MP5 submachine.

"Now lower your weapons. No one else needs to die," Colonel Downey said.

"Stand down, men," Special Agent Henderson said. "Are you assholes responsible for all of this?" he asked.

"No, we had a report that there was going to be an attack, but we got here too late," Colonel Downey said.

"We've been ordered to secure this facility, and that's what I'm going to do. I need you to surrender your weapons, and my men will escort you outside. Before you go, I need to know where you are holding Colonel Williams, so I can secure the football."

"We moved him to the basement, but it won't do you any good, because we've already had them deactivate the president's and the vice president's authorization codes."

"Not my problem. My orders are to deliver the colonel and the football to General Lehman."

"I was just watching the news reports out of D.C., and it looks like your plan is working," John Jay said as he sat down on the couch in Walter Jefferson's office.

"So far so good, but what are you doing back?"

"I decided it could wait. With everything that's happening right now, I think it's time to put Lou Burke in charge of your security."

"Is he ready, and more importantly, is his team ready?"

"They are, but I wanted you to meet him in person before he takes over."

"Then let's do it."

"I can't tell you what an honor this is to finally meet you," Lou Burke said.

Walter had already studied his background, but he asked, "Tell me a little about yourself."

"I grew up in New Orleans, and I entered the army when I graduated from Tulane University. After I graduated from OCS at Benning, I did a couple of tours in Afghanistan and Iraq, and after that I went through airborne training, and then RASP II training at the Ranger School at Fort Benning. A couple of years later, I joined the Seventy-fifth Rangers, and carried out dozens of missions all over the world."

"Why'd you get out?" Walter Jefferson asked.

"I had a slight misunderstanding with an Iraqi colonel during a joint operation near Kirkuk."

"Explain."

"We had a disagreement on tactics, and I might have overreacted a bit."

"Quit beating around the bush," Walter Jefferson said. "You shot him in the head, and took control of the situation."

"True, but if I hadn't, we'd have all been killed."

"What's the big deal? You shot a raghead," Walter Jefferson said.

"Exactly, but they court-martialed me, and I got two years hard labor in Leavenworth and a BCD."

"John speaks highly of your skills, and that's good enough for me," Walter Jefferson said as he shook Lou's hand. "When can you start?" he asked.

"He just did," John Jay said. "He's got his core team in place, and he's working on ramping up the rest of the support structure."

"How many men are you going to have when you're finished?" Walter Jefferson asked.

"Approximately three hundred, but I've already got fifty top-notch agents for your personal security team, along with ten pilots and the administrative support staff," Lou Burke said.

"If you need more, get them. Sorry to cut this short, but I've got a call in ten minutes."

"One thing before you go," John Jay said. "We're ready to activate the new structure for Roger Newsome's old group."

"I thought you said it could take two or three months."

"I did, but Oliver Porter already has eight thousand tier-one special ops troops ready to deploy."

"Excellent. If you're around this afternoon, let's discuss how we can best utilize them."

CHAPTER 24

As the events at the White House were playing out, a convoy of black Cadillac Escalades was leaving Washington, D.C. at a high rate of speed. One of them was carrying the Speaker of the House and the president of the Senate pro tempore, and the rest were carrying the members of President Wilkes's cabinet. There was a bulletproof, soundproof panel separating the passengers from the driver, and the glass was so dark that they couldn't see anyone in the front of the vehicle.

"Do you have any idea what's going on?" asked Michael Carmichael, the president of the Senate pro tempore, as they left the city.

He was third in line on the presidential succession list, and had been a senator from Indiana for forty years and was the current chairman of the Senate's Armed Forces Committee.

"Hell no, and when I tried to ask one of them, he told me to shut up and not to cause any trouble," said Terrance Finnegan, the Speaker of the House.

Terrance Finnegan was the representative from West Virginia. He was sixty years old, with dark brown hair and blue eyes. He was an ex-marine, and in his younger days quite a hell-raiser before he'd settled down and gotten married.

"What did you say?"

"Not a damn thing. I'm not going to argue with a bunch of wild-eyed soldiers carrying machine guns."

"I guess we'll know when we get there, but at this rate of speed, it shouldn't take that long. I saw a long line of buses pulling up as they were whisking us away, and I'll bet they were there for the rest of Congress."

"You're probably right. God only knows what's going down, but it can't be good."

A few miles down the road their SUV exited the interstate as the rest of the small convoy continued on. They drove for another twenty minutes before they turned down a side street into an industrial area.

"What the hell is going on now?" Terrance Finnegan asked.

Before Michael Carmichael could answer, the glass panel slid open, and the front-seat passenger shot them both dead with his silenced .40 caliber Beretta.

"Damn, that sure made a mess," the shooter said.

"Doesn't much matter. They're going to run it through the crusher and then melt it down anyway," the driver said as he pulled into the salvage yard.

Director Timmons was sitting at his desk when his phone rang at twelve-thirty that afternoon. "It's about time you called me back. I demand to know what's going on," he said.

"I know you have questions, but it will all become clear in a little while," General Stenson said.

"What the hell are you talking about?"

"If you'll look out your window, you should see my men cordoning off the building. Martial law has been declared nationwide, and the military is going to be providing all security functions until further notice."

"You're taking over D.C.?"

"Not just D.C. We've got units in every major city in the United States."

"You can't just come in here and take over. Who declared martial law?"

"The chairman of the Joint Chiefs, General Curtiss Lehman, issued the order twenty minutes ago," General Stenson said.

"He's not in the line of succession for the presidency," Director Timmons said.

"None of the people on the list are available, so the general is going to fill in for now."

"This is treason, and you'll never get away with it."

"We'll see. They'll be coming for you in a couple of minutes, and I suggest that you go along quietly."

"I'll do no such thing."

"Your choice, but I would strongly advise you to rethink your decision."

When the buses started pulling up in front of the capitol, Captain Willy Larson, the head of security asked, "What the hell are all these army trucks doing here?"

"No idea, but I can go out and ask them," Larry Flint said.

"No need, I'll take care of it. Major, what the hell is going on?" Captain Larson asked.

"My orders are to secure this facility and transport all of the members of Congress to a secure location," Major Trimble said.

"First I've heard of it. You'd better wait here until I can verify your orders with my boss."

"Take him," Major Trimble said.

Captain Larson tried to resist, but one of the soldiers clubbed him in the face with his rifle butt.

"Take it easy," Major Trimble said. "We don't want to kill anyone we don't have to."

When the soldiers burst into the Senate chamber and the House floor, several of the members of Congress tried to make a break for it, but they didn't get very far before the soldiers captured them. As the soldiers unceremoniously herded them outside and onto the waiting buses, several of the passersby were posting live videos of it to the web.

"Are they going to kill us?" asked Marvin Bridges, a senator from West Virginia.

"Nah, they wouldn't have gone to all this trouble if they were going to kill us," replied Sherrie Bromberg, a senator from Kansas.

The buses carrying the members of Congress had already left by the time the Night Hunter helicopter being piloted by Charles Whitaker arrived at the Capitol Building. The congressional staff was still milling about on the stairs in front of the Capitol, so Charles didn't realize that the members of Congress had already left.

"Heads up. We've got incoming," Major Trimble said when he saw the Night Hunter unleash a barrage of missiles into the Capitol Building. As the building erupted into a massive cloud of fiery debris, Major Trimble screamed, "Take that asshole out."

Two of his men took a knee and fired their FM-92 Stinger missiles at the low-flying helicopter. The missiles struck home, sending the mortally wounded chopper pinwheeling into the dome of the Capitol.

"Lieutenant, get some men over there and pull those people off the stairs before they're incinerated," Major Trimble said as the inferno consuming the building sent flames hundreds of feet into the air.

The buses carrying the members of Congress drove straight through, and five hours later they arrived at their destination.

"This is the Greenbrier hotel. We used to come here during the summer when I was growing up," said Gerald Rupert, the representative from West Virginia, as they drove past the sprawling white hotel.

The bus passed by the massive white columns framing the front lobby, and it didn't stop until it reached a drab green wooden fence that framed a cement ramp that sloped down to an underground entrance.

"We're at our destination," the guard said. "When the door opens, I want you to follow me, and please don't try to escape, because you won't like what happens next."

The guard led them down the cement ramp to the west entrance of the bunker, which was a relic of the Cold War. They entered the facility through a silver metal door with a sign on it that said HIGH VOLTAGE. The hundred-thousand-square-foot facility had been completed in 1961, and was built to withstand a nuclear attack. It was dug deep into the hillside underneath the Greenbrier's West Virginia wing, and the walls and ceilings were three to five feet thick steel-reinforced concrete, covered by twenty to sixty feet of dirt. It had eighteen dormitories that could accommodate over eleven hundred people. It was designed to be self-sufficient, with its own generator, water supply, hospitals, etc., and it even had meeting rooms for the full House and Senate, along with the governor's hall and the mountaineer room. There were four entrances, three from the main hotel, and the west basement entry that was guarded by a twenty-five-ton blast door that could be opened with only fifty pounds of pressure.

The guard led them down the ramp and herded them into the House of Representatives meeting room where Colonel Whipple was waiting to address the group.

Colonel Whipple was the executive officer of the West Virginia militia, and he was in charge of the bunker. He had long, dark brown hair and beard, and spoke with a slow Southern drawl. At first blush he didn't come off as all that bright, but he'd graduated from Marshall University in Huntington, West Virginia with a double major in mathematics and computer science.

"I apologize for all of the drama, but this is going to be your home for a while. Let me begin by assuring you that you're in no danger. However, any attempts to escape or to cause trouble will be dealt with harshly."

"Why are we here?" asked Ted Nelson, a senator from Texas.

"I'm not privy to that information, but I'm sure you'll be briefed at the appropriate time. The 'bunker,' as this facility was known during the Cold War, was built at the direction of President Eisenhower, and was constructed to house a thousand or more people in the event of a nuclear attack. We've made extensive renovations to modernize the facility, and each of you will be issued a laptop to use while you're with us. There's no Internet access, but the Wi-Fi network will let you access the facility's digital library, which has a comprehensive selection of books, music, and videos to keep you entertained. There are two fitness centers, as well as racquetball courts and saunas. Meals are at oh-seven-hundred, twelve-hundred, and eighteen-hundred hours, and we've got a good crew of chefs to fix your meals. Now, if you'll follow the guide that brought you in, they'll show you to the section where you'll be staying."

Walter Jefferson was on his way to the hangar on his ranch when General Lehman called. "General, I wasn't expecting to hear from you today. I thought you were holding a press conference."

"I go on in twenty minutes, but I just found out that President Wilkes's cabinet and the members of Congress aren't where they're supposed to be, and I'm not pleased that you've deviated from the plan."

"Nothing to worry about. We decided to move them to more secure locations."

"Fine, but I still need to know where they are," General Lehman said.

"In due time. Right now you've got more important matters to attend to."

General Lehman paused before he replied. "I've got to go, but we need to talk about this."

The telecast was being held in the Pentagon's largest briefing center, but when General Lehman walked in, it was standing room only. "Where the hell did all of these people come from?" General Lehman asked. "This was supposed to be by invitation only."

"They've all got valid invitations, we just never expected all of them to show up," Major Grooms said.

As the general stepped up to the podium, he cut a dashing figure in his full dress uniform, covered in medals. There were two army rangers in full battle gear flanking the podium, and as Lehman removed his hat to start the broadcast, his silver-gray hair glistened in the bright lights.

"My fellow Americans, I come before you tonight with a heavy heart. This morning, at a little after six A.M. Eastern Time, we lost two great Americans when President Richard Wilkes and Vice President Timothy Regal were assassinated by elements of the Islamic State. As horrific as that is, I also realize that a number of you have lost loved ones in this and other attacks that have transpired around the country. These radical extremists have proven that they will use any means, no matter how heinous, to destroy our way of life, and the time has come for all of us to step forward and be counted.

"I'm not sure who first quoted this ancient proverb, but it think it's an apt representation of the situation we find ourselves in: 'In adverse circumstances, actions that might have been rejected under normal circumstances may become the best choice.' The myriad of threats that we're facing today demand an approach that some of you may find distasteful, but to quote a variation of the phrase coined by the ancient Greek physician Hippocrates: 'Desperate times call for desperate measures,' which is why at noon today I declared martial law. The United States military has officially assumed command and control of the United States government."

The room immediately erupted into cacophony of screams of outrage and disbelief as almost everyone in the room stood up to protest.

"Quiet," the general bellowed over the din. "Shut the hell up, I'm not finished."

When the pandemonium didn't subside, he grabbed a machine gun from one of the rangers and triggered off a burst into the ceiling, sending all the civilians in the room diving for cover.

"That's better," he said as he laid the machine gun on the podium. "Please get up so I can continue.

"These measures are intended to be temporary, and once we've eliminated the threats, we'll reinstate civilian control of the government. Until that time, we've sequestered the members of Congress, the Supreme Court justices, and all of the federal judges in secure locations until the danger is past."

Once again the room erupted into yelling and cursing, but when he grabbed the machine-gun again, the noise quickly subsided.

"The military will be responsible for maintaining order until we can stabilize the situation, at which time we'll rescind the martial law decree. To achieve this we'll utilize manpower from selected federal, state, and local law enforcement agencies, but in all cases, the military will be the final authority. If anyone is contemplating the use of civil disobedience, I'll warn you now that we won't hesitate to use lethal force to maintain order. That's all I have, and now I'll take a few questions."

"Have you been able to properly secure our nuclear arsenal?" asked Walter Grub, a *New York Times* reporter.

"Great question, and yes, that was one of our first priorities. The ability to launch nuclear weapons now lies within the military command structure."

"Would you mind telling us who that is?"

"Not at all. The primary launch authority lies with me, and Air Force General Tony Gibbs is responsible for the secondary authorization. Admiral Kennedy is my alternate, and General Otis Biggalow is General Gibbs's alternate."

"I can appreciate what you're trying to do, but you don't have enough manpower to provide security nationwide," said Jamie Preston, the Fox News anchor.

"You're correct, Ms. Preston," General Lehman said. "Walter Jefferson, who is a senior member of our leadership team, and his organization, the Combined Militias of the United States, will be providing the additional manpower as needed."

"Are you out of your mind?" Jamie Preston asked. "They're nothing but a bunch of rednecks with guns."

"Mr. Jefferson is a highly respected member of the business community, and has been a presidential candidate. Many of the militia's members are ex-military, or have law enforcement backgrounds. I also have Mr. Jefferson's personal guarantee that his organization will follow the directives and standard operating procedures that we've instituted."

The general took questions for another five minutes, but they were all along the same lines, so he said, "Please don't misunderstand that what I've laid out is up for debate, and I can see that further discussion isn't going to add any clarity, so I'm going to end here. Good night, and God bless America."

Walter Jefferson, John Jay, and Lou Burke had watched the broadcast in Walter's great room, and when it was over, John Jay said, "Jamie Preston was way out of line with that comment about you."

"Sticks and stones, but put her on the list," Walter Jefferson said.

"What's this list you're referring to?" Lou Burke asked.

"It's a list of people that may need John's special attention."

"Attention?"

"The form of attention will depend on the circumstances, but all options are on the table. Any issues with that?"

"Nah, I was just wondering."

Later that night, General Lehman and the other members of the Joint Chiefs were gathered in a Pentagon conference room for a videoconference with the nine Unified Combat Commands. He would have liked to hold the meeting face-to-face, but the room they were using was loaded with the best gear they had.

It was only twenty by twenty, but it had twenty-foot ceilings, and the high-definition screen for the ultra-high-def projector was four hundred inches by four hundred inches, so they wouldn't have any problem seeing the commanders.

As General Lehman reviewed his notes, he fully understood the quandary that he faced. By law, the commanders held the command and control authority for all branches of the United States' military forces stationed in their areas of responsibility. By law the Joint Chiefs had no operational control over them, and the chain of command went from the president to the secretary of defense to the combat commanders, but that had all changed when they'd usurped the civilian government.

"I apologize for the short notice, but I felt it was imperative that we were all together when I brief the UCC leaders," General Lehman told the other members of the JCS.

"My God, I still can't believe this is really happening," said Admiral Pete Donnelly, the chief of naval operations.

"We've been discussing the possibility for months, and you've been saying that you were behind us all the way."

"True, but I never really believed it could happen."

"We were forced to act when they assassinated the president and vice president, and the task of wiping these Islamic bastards off the face of the earth has fallen to us."

"Easier said than done," said General Terry Willowby, the commandant of the marines.

"I'll say. Some days it seems like we're fighting the Lernaean Hydra from Greek mythology," Admiral Kennedy said. "Every time we cut one head off, they grow two more."

"True, but that cowardly bastard of a president would never really let us go after them. He always wanted to take the safe way out, and use drones or an occasional air strike," said General Otis Biggalow, chief of staff of the army.

"I hate to speak ill of the dead, but I'd agree with that," said General Tony Gibbs, chief of staff of the air force.

"Why so quiet, General Goldstein?" General Lehman asked.

"I'm all for killing the bastards, but I'm more concerned with how we get the domestic unrest under control," replied the chief of the National Guard Bureau.

"I'm with Frank on this one," said Admiral Southby, commandant of the Coast Guard.

"I'll be happy to address your concerns after this call," General Lehman said. "But right now I need you all to focus, because it's imperative that we get the UCC on board.

"Lieutenant, we're ready for them now," he told his aide.

"Thank all of you for joining us tonight," General Lehman continued. "As I'm sure you're all aware, our nation has suffered another horrific tragedy today, with the deaths of President Wilkes and Vice President Regal."

"That's a bit of an understatement," quipped Admiral Clyde Hooks, commander of the U.S. Strategic Command.

"Why isn't Secretary Behrmann briefing us?" asked General Lawrence Drummond, commander of the United States European Command.

"Secretary Behrmann is currently indisposed, and for now, you'll be taking your orders from the JCS," General Lehman said.

"That's bullshit," cried Admiral Samuel Crawford, the commander of the United States Pacific Command.

"It is for a fact," added General Patrick Volkey, commander of the United States Special Operations Command said. "We all saw your press conference, and we know that you've seized control of the government."

"Unfortunately we've been forced to take drastic measures to deal with the current situation. This country needs the military's leadership if it's going to survive, and by God we're going to provide it.

"We've all sworn an oath to protect this country, and

as the operational commanders of our military forces, I expect each of you to step up and help us eradicate ISIS so we can get back to our normal democratic process."

"Fine words, but all you've done is set yourselves up as a military dictatorship, and I'll have no part of it," Admiral Crawford said.

"Let's not be hasty," General Albert Stenson said. "The Islamic State is a terrible threat to our way of life, and I can fully support what General Lehman is trying to achieve, as long as he gives us his word that it's only temporary."

"I'd like to hear you say it, but I'd really like it in writing if possible," said Air Force General Norman Mathis, commander of the United States Central Command.

"You have my word as an officer and a gentleman that this is only temporary, and I'm more than willing to put it in writing, but first things first. As our first order of business, we have to develop a strategic approach to deal with the terrorists.

"Admiral Hooks, I'd like you to take the lead on that."

"Aye, aye," Admiral Clyde Hooks said. "Are there any constraints on the tactics or resources I can use?"

"None. Recommend whatever it takes to get the job done, and I don't give a damn if the UN or anyone else likes it."

"When do you need it?"

"ASAP, and while you're working on that, I want General Stenson to formulate a plan to wipe out those assholes that nuked Seattle."

"Do you know their location?" Admiral Hooks asked.

"They're somewhere in Canada, but President Wilkes wouldn't let us go in after them. So gentlemen, can I count on your support?"

One after another, they all grudgingly agreed to go along.

"Thank you. I'll let you get some sleep now," General Lehman said as he motioned the lieutenant to break the connections.

"That didn't go as badly as I'd feared," General Lehman said.

"True, but I sensed that several of them had reservations," Admiral Donnelly said.

"Hell, I still have some myself," General Willowby said.

"You wouldn't be human if you didn't, but we've got to see this through, or our country is doomed," General Lehman said. "Once again thank you for your support, and I'll brief each of you as soon as we have a plan of attack for Canada."

"You look like hell," General Lehman said when General Stenson sat down in his office in the Pentagon the next morning.

"I couldn't sleep, so I stayed up all night working on the plan."

"Good, I just wish we knew where they were."

"That part was surprisingly easy. It only took NSA a couple of hours to pinpoint their current location."

"I imagine that they've moved back away from the border."

"No, virtually all of their forces are bivouacked about ten miles south of Winnipeg, and it looks like they could be contemplating another raid. I've got a plan to take care of them once and for all, but you may not have the stomach for it."

"Let me be the judge of that."

They spent the next two hours going over the general's handiwork. "Damn fine plan, but I see what you meant by having the stomach for it. How long will it take to get ready?"

"Twenty-four hours."

"Let's do it."

"Are we going to give the Canadian government a heads-up?" General Stenson asked.

"Hell no."

After Ehsan Hashmi was on his way, Colonel al-Jabiri and Colonel Fakhoury spent the next day redeploying their forces as they'd discussed. There was a dilapidated old house on the farm, but it was in such bad shape that they were all staying in tents.

It was almost midnight when Colonel al-Jabiri asked, "Did you get the radar going again?"

"Yes, it was just a blown fuse," Lieutenant El-Shennawi said.

"I'm going to have a cup of coffee and call it a night, but make damn sure your men stay alert."

As Colonel al-Jabiri was turning in for the night, there were two squadrons of B2 bombers approaching from the south.

"Attention alpha squadron, execute Colonel Haick," the squadron commander said.

Colonel Haick's squadron dropped their payload of AGM-158 JASSM-ER terrain following missiles and reversed course, while bravo squadron continued on to the target. Once his squadron was out of radar range they started climbing, and Colonel Haick asked his weapons officer, "How long until impact?"

"First impact in sixty seconds, but one of the missiles went off course and self-destructed."

When the first wave of missiles struck, the blasts from the missile's thousand-pound warheads reverberated across the countryside, sending flames and debris rocketing into the previously tranquil night sky.

"We're under attack," Lieutenant El-Shennawi said as Colonel al-Jabiri came running out of his tent in his underwear.

"No shit. What have you got on radar?"

"Radar is down," Lieutenant El-Shennawi said. "But it doesn't matter, because none of the missile launchers survived the first strike."

"We need to get to the choppers," Colonel al-Jabiri said. "Colonel Fakhoury, I want your men armed with Stingers and standing by."

Colonel Fakhoury was just getting his men organized when the next wave of missiles struck the camp, killing Lieutenant El-Shennawi and hurling Colonel al-Jabiri's unconscious body into the thick brush behind the tents. When Colonel Fakhoury saw them go down, he decided to make a run for the choppers. The visibility was almost nonexistent as he and his men ran across the field to where they'd parked the Night Hunters.

"Shit," the colonel said when he reached the collection of shattered, burning hulks. "Forget the choppers, we'll take the trucks," he screamed.

The colonel and a few of the others made it to the pickups, but the second squadron of B2Bs arrived and began carpet bombing the farm with sticks of seven-hundred-and-fifty-pound bombs.

By the time the last bomb fell, there were less than twenty ISIS troops still alive, and they were wandering around in shock and confusion.

"We've got to get out of here," one of the survivors said.

When they couldn't find a serviceable vehicle, he said, "Forget the trucks, let's make a run for it."

"I've got movement on the south side of the field," one of the B2B pilots said.

"Air Three, we've got targets at these coordinates," the B2 squadron commander said.

"We're inbound," replied Major Dawkins, the commander of the F-16 squadron escorting the B-52s.

"Drop on my command," Major Dawkins said when he spotted heat signatures near the far tree line.

"Three, two, drop."

The small band of survivors were frantically running for the safety of the forest when the stick of GBU-31 JDAMS, tipped with thousand-pound warheads, stitched a fiery path through their ragged group, hurling the bloody shards of their shattered bodies across the countryside.

"That should do it. You can call off the rest of the aircraft," Major Dawkins said. "Ranger One, you're up."

"Roger that," Colonel Downey said. "We're inbound, but we're going to make a low-level recon before we land."

When his squadron of fifty UH-60L DAP helicopters made their low-level passes over the enemy encampment, it was evident there wouldn't be many survivors.

"Echo team, land on the north side of the clearing, and begin your sweep for survivors. Air Three will maintain air cover, but I don't think we'll need more boots on the ground." The airstrikes had completely decimated the ISIS encampment, and after they'd spent thirty minutes searching for survivors, Colonel Downey said, "The operation is complete."

"Then get the hell out of there before the Canadians do something stupid," General Volkey said.

"Sir, Prime Minister Colbert is on the phone, and he's demanding to talk with you," Captain Marks said.

"Prime Minister Colbert, what can I do for you tonight?" General Lehman asked.

"You know damn well why I'm calling. I demand an explanation for your attack on my country."

"Demand? Your country has been harboring those murderous bastards for months."

The phone went dead for several seconds. "How long have you known?"

"We discovered that President Wilkes had known almost from the beginning, but he never had the balls to call you on it."

"I can sympathize with that. I discovered the truth not long after my predecessor committed suicide, but I couldn't figure out how to unwind it. I know that's no excuse, but there it is."

"Both of us find ourselves in rather difficult situations, so let's forget about it and move on."

Early the next morning General Lehman had just gotten to the Pentagon when he got a call from Walter Jefferson.

"I just heard the news," Walter said

"News?"

"Don't play dumb. You've wiped out the Islamic State's Canadian contingent."

"I was going to call you as soon as I got out of the JCS meeting this morning."

"I thought that we'd agreed that you'd give me a heads-up anytime you were going to go big on an operation."

"In principle I'm fine with that, but I'm not going to ask permission from you or anyone else to do my job."

"That wasn't our agreement," Walter Jefferson said.

"Like I said, I'll keep you in the loop when it doesn't jeopardize an operation."

"Fine, but on a more positive note, it sounded like the operation was a success."

"We killed them all, but they had a shocking amount of really high-end Soviet gear."

"Not surprising, they'll sell to anybody that's got the cash," Walter Jefferson said. "I'm going to let you go for now, but do try to keep me in the loop."

"You look pissed, boss," John Jay said when Walter hung up.

"I am, but we'll deal with it another time. Changing subjects, have you heard anything about a militia meeting in Vegas?"

"No, but I can ask around."

"Do, but keep it on the down low. Why haven't we announced Oliver Porter's new position?"

"My bad. They might have invited him to the meeting if they'd known he was running Roger's old group."

"I doubt that. I'm pretty sure they distrust anyone that's associated with me."

CHAPTER 25

Two days and four countries later, Ehsan Hashmi finally reached Mosul.

"Welcome to Iraq," Dizhwar Akram said. "I know you've had a difficult journey, so we've got a hotel room all ready for you. You're scheduled to meet with Daoud Mansouri in the morning, and I'll have a car pick you up at six."

"Congratulations on a great victory," Daoud Mansouri said when Ehsan Hashmi arrived at the fish market where Daoud's office was that day. They'd set up the furniture between two of the massive cement columns that held up the roof of the massive marketplace. The lights were shimmering across the film of water that covered the cement floor where the vendors were laying out the fresh-caught fish of the day.

"All praises to Allah, it was a remarkable success," Ehsan Hashmi said. "After President Wilkes tightened their border security, I was afraid we might not pull it off."

"Smoke and mirrors, he was just pandering to the voters," Dizhwar Akram said.

"I was surprised that you'd summon me in the middle of our operations," Ehsan Hashmi said.

"It was fortuitous that I did," Daoud Mansouri said. "Your entire team has been killed."

"I don't understand, Colonel al-Jabiri wasn't supposed to launch the operation for another forty-eight hours."

"He didn't, the Americans hit them on the Canadian side of the border."

"They invaded Canada?"

"No, they used cruise missiles and followed that up with carpet bombing."

"I didn't think they had it in them," Ehsan Hashmi said.

"You assassinated President Wilkes and Vice President Regal. What did you think they would do?" Dizhwar Akram asked.

"I did no such thing," Ehsan Hashmi said.

"They're sure as hell blaming us for it," Daoud Mansouri said.

"Why would I do that? It would be sure to set them on a quest to destroy us, and besides that, they'll have them replaced within hours."

"I wish that were true. Their military has taken control of the government, and General Lehman, the chairman of the Joint Chiefs, has vowed to exterminate us."

"That's not good, but he can't act without congressional approval, and as dysfunctional as they are, it'll take them months to authorize it."

"Congress is no longer in play, and they've removed the Supreme Court justices and all of the federal court judges."

"I sure never saw a military coup coming," Ehsan Hashmi said.

"You forgot to mention that dip-shit militia leader, Walter Jefferson, who has thrown in with them," Dizhwar Akram said.

"I did some research on him before we launched the North Dakota raid, and I wouldn't sell him short," Ehsan Hashmi said. "He's a bit of an enigma, but he could be a formidable foe."

"Whatever, but I am worried about the American military launching large-scale operations against us," Daoud Mansouri said. "I need you and the team to come up with a strategy if they do decide to come after us."

"Okay, but there's no way in hell we can go head-to-head with them," Ehsan Hashmi said. "If it's going to come down to a fight to the death, we'll need to try to buy some more nukes."

"I've got no problem with that, but you've spent most of our available cash, so you'd better put something together to restock the coffers."

"Walter Jefferson is on line one," said Major Charlie Benson, General Lehman's aide.

"Give me five minutes, and you can put him through," General Lehman replied.

"Sorry for the wait, but I wasn't expecting your call," General Lehman said.

"No problem, but I'm terribly concerned with the number of Muslims running around loose in this country, and I want to do something about it," Walter Jefferson said.

"Slow down. Most Muslims aren't sympathizers with the Islamic State. Hell, I've got several good friends who are Muslim."

"I'm not just talking Muslims, it's all Arabs and anyone that has converted to Islam. God knows we've had enough of these lone wolf attacks from these self-radicalized fools, and there's no doubt in my mind that they're all trying to bring this country to its knees."

Oh shit, General Lehman thought.

"You might have a point, but why are you all worked up about this right now?" General Lehman asked.

"I know you've got your hands full, so I'd like to take the lead on shoring up our domestic security."

"I'd hate to see us start some sort of witch hunt like they did during World War II with the Japanese internment camps, but I'll give it some thought."

"Okay, but I'd like an answer by the end of the week."

"You don't look pleased," John Jay said.

"General Lehman is holding up my plan for the enemy sympathizers."

"Trouble with him again? You want me to take care of it?"

"Not yet. How long before our other projects get moving?"

"There will be a few this week, but next week is the real start of it."

"Excellent, that should help move things along."

A few days later, General Lehman had just stepped off the elevator in the Pentagon when Major Benson came rushing up.

"General, we've got big problems in New York City."

"Slow down. What sort of problems?"

"There've been a series of attacks in the New York City subway system."

"What sort of attacks?"

"There have been six knife attacks, two with a sword or an axe, and we don't have the specifics on the rest yet."

"Sounds more like a typical day in the city than terrorists," General Lehman said.

"I'd agree if they hadn't beheaded the victims."

"Oh shit. Did they get them stopped?"

"They think so. The Transit Authority cops killed most of them, but in a couple of instances the crowd took matters into their own hands."

"See what else you can find out, and I need to talk to General Stenson."

Every day that week there was some sort of incident, and by Saturday, General Lehman decided to call an emergency meeting of the Joint Chiefs.

The White House was still a mess so they were holding their meetings in the JCS conference room in the Pentagon, often referred to as "the tank." Unlike the White House Situation Room, "the tank" was low tech, with paintings on the walls instead of high-resolution monitors, and a massive solid oak conference table. The other members were already seated around the conference table when General Lehman sat down at the head of the table.

"I need a plan to put a stop to this shit," General Lehman said. "Admiral Kennedy, how do we identify the potential offenders before they can strike? Are they being guided by the Islamic State?"

"The NSA has already accumulated thousands of terabytes of usage data from the various ISPs around the country, but it turned out to be far more daunting than they'd anticipated."

"So they've given up?"

"No, they've made a breakthrough, but we had to give complete immunity to an elite group of hackers, and commandeer half the data processing power in the federal government to do it. The hackers have managed to develop a series of search algorithms to scan the databases and identify a pool of potential threats."

"That's great news, but why am I just now hearing about it?"

"They've got the lists, but the numbers are so vast that it makes it unrealistic to try to contact even a percentage of them directly."

"Same old shit. For a second there you had my hopes up," General Lehman said.

"We need to increase the manpower in the targeted areas, but that will probably just send them elsewhere," General Biggalow said.

"Do it," General Lehman said. "At least we can say we're doing something."

"General Stenson and I were just discussing manpower needs, and he's going to need some of Walter Jefferson's men to even do that," Admiral Kennedy said.

"I'll let him know, but make damn sure we keep an eye on them, because I don't need them killing a bunch of innocent civilians."

"Why don't you trust him? He's delivered on everything he said he would."

"I can't put my finger on it, but there's just something not right about him."

"I'm sorry, but I don't agree," Admiral Kennedy said.

The next morning General Lehman hadn't left home yet when he got an unexpected phone call from Walter Jefferson.

"I'm glad you called, Mr. Jefferson, I needed to talk with you," General Lehman said.

"Good, we can kill two birds with one stone," Walter Jefferson replied. "Why don't you go first?"

"Admiral Kennedy needs some more of your men."

"It's about time. I'll have Peterson give him a call."

"That'll work. What did you have for me?" General Lehman asked.

"I need you to set up a meeting on the twentieth of next month, with all of the combat commands," Walter Jefferson said.

"I can do that, but they're going to want an agenda."

"Understandable, but I don't want to taint their thinking, so I'll wait to hand it out at the meeting."

"Your call. I haven't seen some of them in ages, so it'll be good to catch up."

"Why don't you host a dinner for them the night before? That will give you some time to catch up before the meeting."

"That's a great idea, I'll see what I can get set up."

"Don't sweat that, I'll have Amy Walsh make the arrangements for you. That way we can get right down to business the next day."

"Thanks, and we'll come ready to work."

"Congratulations, today marks the three-month anniversary of your new republic," John Jay said when he saw Walter hang up.

"Hardly what I had in mind, but it's a start," Walter Jefferson said. "Is everything in place for tomorrow?"

"It is, but you do realize that if we're ever found out, we'll go down in history as monsters."

"Of course I do, but the reward is well worth the risk. It's my hope that what we are about to achieve will be the first step toward my ultimate objective to spread democracy worldwide."

"I'm not sure the rest of the world is going to share your vision."

"You're probably right, but the world has lost its way, and I feel that it's my destiny to lead it out of the darkness."

The next morning, General Lehman was about to call General Biggalow when Major Benson burst into his office.

"Sorry to disturb you, but all hell's broken out in Dallas."

"What now?"

"There's an active shooter incident at the Skyline High School in Dallas."

"Damn, not another one. I need General Lacy."

"You calling about Dallas?" General Lacy asked.

"I am. Do we have anything in the area?"

"The closest would be a special ops team in Laredo."

"Who's in command?"

"Colonel Stimple. They have seventy-five men, ten MH-60M, and eight UH-60L DAP Black Hawk helicopters."

"Get them in the air, and contact the local authorities and let them know we have a team on the way."

"The army has a special ops detachment on the way," Police Lieutenant Randy Turk said.

"Too late for that," Police Captain Jewel said. "The murderous bastards are trying to break into the library and the auditorium, where most of the students are sheltered.

"Lieutenant Bridges, you're a go for breach," Captain Jewel said.

"Go for breach," replied Lieutenant George Bridges, the SWAT commander.

"SWAT One, you've got the cafeteria. SWAT Two, you've got the auditorium, and don't stop for anything," Lieutenant Bridges said.

"SWAT Three, I want you to sweep the halls, and guide the medical teams to any survivors you find. All units, the EOD team is standing by if you encounter any explosive devices. All units, execute."

The attackers had chained the front entrances shut, but the SWAT teams blew the doors open with explosive charges and rushed inside.

"Lord, please let them save those kids," Captain Jewel prayed as the blasts shook the building.

It broke their hearts as the members of SWAT 1 and 2 had to bypass the dead and wounded children in the halls.

"There they are," said the SWAT 1 team leader when he spotted the four black-clad figures. The SWAT teams were all carrying the newly issued Heckler & Koch HK UMP machine guns, and they opened fire on the masked intruders as soon as they had a clear field of fire. They only fired for a few seconds, but the hail of .45 ACP rounds quickly neutralized the killers.

"This is Swat One, the perpetrators are down, and you can tell them it's all right to open the doors to the cafeteria."

"This is Swat Two, the intruders have been neutralized, but we have two men down and require immediate medical attention."

A few minutes later, SWAT 3 radioed, "The hallways are clear, but we have many casualties, and we need all available medical personal ASAP."

"Major Benson, have we received an update on the Dallas situation?" General Lehman asked ninety minutes later.

"No, sir, not yet."

"Then I want to talk with whoever's running the show down there."

"This is Captain Jewel."

"Captain, this is General Lehman, and I need to know what the hell is going on down there."

"Sorry, I thought we'd sent you a status update. The incident was resolved about forty-five minutes ago."

"How bad?"

"I don't have the final tally yet, but it's bad. So far we've confirmed sixty dead, and a hundred and one wounded, with thirty of those in critical condition."

"What about the terrorists?"

"There were eight of them, and they're all deceased."

"Good riddance, but I wish you could have taken one alive, so we could interrogate him."

"They weren't all male. Three of them were teenage girls."

"Excuse me? I thought they were terrorists."

"I guess you could call them that, but they were either past or present students at the school."

"That's horrible, but at least it wasn't the Islamic

State this time. Captain, I appreciate you taking the time to update me, and I'll recall the special ops team.

"Major Benson, I need Director Berkley," General Lehman said.

Once he had Director Berkley on the phone, General Lehman said, "Director, I need your best forensic team in Dallas."

"No problem, but if it's for the attack on the high school, the local team is top notch," replied Charles Berkley, the director of the FBI.

"Your call, but I need answers, and I need them fast."

Twenty-four hours later, the FBI director called with the report.

"So what did you figure out?" General Lehman asked.

"I'll send you our written report, but the bottom line is that all of the attackers were either students or ex-students, and recent converts to Islam."

"Damn, it was ISIS, I just didn't want to believe it. I know you said that you're sending the report, but run it down for me."

"The assailants were between the ages of sixteen and nineteen, and judging by what we've found on their computers, they'd been studying Islamic State terror tactics, and were acting together."

"Why would kids do something like that?"

"The messages they'd posted on their social media pages and scrawled on the walls in the school stated that the attacks were in retribution for the drone attacks we've been carrying out against the ISIS leaders."

"Please tell me that they weren't Americans."

"Six of them were born here, and the other two were naturalized citizens."

"How in God's name could Americans stoop that low?"

"Actually that's not the way they would have seen it. They saw it as their duty to defend their faith."

"That's pure propaganda, truly religious people don't murder innocents."

"I hear you, but from their point of view, that's what we do every day when we indiscriminately kill innocent civilians with our drones."

"That's different, we're trying to eradicate dangerous criminals."

"They would have disagreed."

"It almost sounds like you're on their side."

"Hardly, but although I abhor their methods, I do understand what motivated them."

"Keep that shit to yourself."

"Understood, but you should be expecting more attacks like this. When we had our Internet bots crawl the Internet for leads, we discovered many thousands of similar posts."

"Can you track them down?"

"That's the same thing Walter Jefferson asked me."

"How the hell did he get involved?"

"He started pumping me for information not long after the attack, and he intimated you were both working on it. Sorry if I shared something that I shouldn't have."

"Don't worry about it."

The general had just hung up when Rod Clawson, the director of the NSA/CSS called.

"Tell me you've got some good news for me," General Lehman said.

"Maybe. We've discovered where they're holding the president's cabinet and the members of Congress."

"Where?"

"If you don't mind I'll send you the details via courier."

"Getting paranoid in your old age?"

"Damn straight."

Late that night, General Lehman was studying the data from Director Clawson when he realized what he had to do. He threw on a uniform, and sped through the deserted city streets toward his office in the Pentagon.

"Good morning, General Lehman, although it's quite late in Virginia," said General Lawrence Drummond, the UCC of the European Command.

"Early morning, but time is short."

"That sounds a little ominous."

"Ominous doesn't do it justice. I've just sent you an overview of a mission I need you to take on."

"Never a problem," General Drummond said.

"You'd better take a look before you say that."

It was a one-page document, so it only took him a minute to read it. "It's mind-boggling that he'd think we'd let him get away with this," Drummond said.

"It is, but it just goes to show what he's willing to do to achieve his goals. So, are you still in?"

"Hell yes, but it's going to take me a few days to put it together."

"No problem, in fact I'd like the timing of the operation to coincide with the dinner we're hosting for the combat commanders, and feel free to improvise in any manner you need to."

"Okay, but if you'll allow it, I'd like to lead the mission. I hate putting my commanders in this kind of a jam."

"Not a good idea. Why don't you send your XO to the meeting in your stead? Just don't tell anyone ahead of time. That way you'll be able to deal with any wrinkles that might come up."

"That's a good idea, and thanks for entrusting this to me."

"I hope you can say that when it's all said and done. One other thing: I'm going to have Admiral Crawford stay behind as well. That way we'll have someone we can trust on the other side of the globe."

The next day, Lieb Behrmann received an unexpected call.

"Sir, there's a General Lawrence Drummond on the line, and he'd like to speak with you," Lieb Behrman's executive assistant said.

"Put him through.

"General, we've never spoken, but my brother had always spoken highly of you," Lieb Behrmann said.

"He's a good man."

"Is? I was under the assumption he was dead."

"He's alive and kicking, but I need your country's help to rescue him."

"Go on."

General Drummond spent the next half hour laying out his plan, and when he finished, Lieb Behrmann said, "We're in. Colonel Neri commands unit two-twelve of our special forces, and I'm going to have him flesh out the details for both operations. He'll lead the Lake Placid mission."

"Good, and I'll provide the transportation for the hostages and your teams."

Walter Jefferson was checking his e-mail at the desk in his bedroom when he received an unexpected late-night call.

"Excuse the hour, but I have something that I need to tell you," Charles Berkley said.

"Never a problem, but couldn't it have waited until morning?" Walter Jefferson asked.

"I should have called you days ago, but I slipped up and let General Lehman know that we'd been discussing how to identify the Americans that might be considering joining the Islamic State's cause."

"What were you thinking?"

"I didn't do it on purpose."

"How did he react?"

"I could tell that he wasn't pleased, but he really didn't say that much."

"It'll be fine, but you need to get your shit together, because I'm counting on you and your team's help."

"Whatever you need," Charles Berkley said.

"What are you doing up so late?" John Jay asked when he saw Walter's light on as he walked by on his way to his room.

"I just got off the phone with the director of the FBI. He screwed up and let General Lehman know that we'd been talking."

"Do I need to have a word with him?"

"No, I still need his help to carry out my plan. How are you coming with our other project?"

"You'll start seeing the results on Friday, but I hope you know that this is going to be difficult to control once it gets started."

"I'm counting on it. I forgot to ask you this morning. How many of Oliver Porter's teams have we gotten deployed?"

"He's got just over fifty percent of them in the field, and he hopes to deploy the rest by the end of the month."

"Excellent, but before he sends them all out, make sure he checks to see if Lou Burke needs any of them."

CHAPTER 26

When Major Benson entered his office on Friday morning, General Lehman knew there was something wrong by the look on his face. "Now what?"

"We're getting reports of vigilante attacks against Muslims in the Dallas–Fort Worth metroplex," Major Benson said.

"What makes them think it's vigilantes?"

"There are several videos of the attacks on YouTube, but this is by far the worst of them," he said as he queued up the video. It looked like a peaceful middle-class neighborhood until they saw the angry mob rush the house. They watched as they kicked in the front door and dragged a man outside. When his terrified family came rushing outside to try to save him, they grabbed them and started pummeling them as well. The mob was screaming curses at the family as they forced them to watch as they threw a rope over a tree limb and strung him up. As he slowly choked to death at the end of the rope, several of them spray painted RAGHEADS GO HOME and REMEMBER SKYLINE on their house in three-foot-tall red letters. The video ended with the mob drenching the man's still-twitching body in gasoline and lighting it on fire.

"That was truly disgusting. Get Director Berkley for me," General Lehman said.

"I just watched a horrific video of the violence occurring in Dallas, and I want those animals tracked down and prosecuted," he said.

"Fine, but does that mean you're going to release the judges so we have a court to try them in?"

"Just catch the bastards, and then we'll talk about what comes next."

The mob hadn't bothered to try to hide their identities, so it only took the local FBI agents a couple of weeks to round up most of the perpetrators.

"I've got good news," Director Berkley said.

"That's a commodity that's been in short supply around here," General Lehman said.

"We've arrested the bulk of the mob that murdered Mr. Nasiri."

"I'm ashamed to admit it, but I never even knew his name. Good work."

"Thanks, but what do you want us to do with them now? You still haven't released any of the federal judges, and it won't end well if they go to trial in the local courts."

"I'm not sure. Can you give me a couple of days to try to work something out?"

"Sure, but I wouldn't wait too long, the press has started running articles about the arrests, and it could turn ugly quickly."

Walter Jefferson was eating lunch in his office when the general called. "What's up, General?" Walter Jefferson asked.

"I need your help," General Lehman said.

"Shoot."

After the general had explained the situation, Walter said, "You're in luck. I've been working on a plan to deal with the lack of a functioning federal court system, so if you don't mind, we'll handle it from here."

"Are you sure? There are over a hundred prisoners."

"We've got it. You've got bigger issues to deal with.

"Amy, see if you can find John Jay for me," Walter Jefferson said.

"What's up, boss?" John Jay asked when he walked in.

"Have Jeb Butts send some of his men to Dallas to pick up the rioters that the FBI arrested," Walter Jefferson said.

"No problem, but what's he supposed to do with them?" John Jay asked.

"Have him put them up on his dude ranch down by Laredo, and don't let them talk to anyone, because I don't need any flack out of the general. Are you ready for next week?"

"The team is already in place."

"Maybe I wasn't clear on my expectations," Walter Jefferson said. "This is the most important mission I've ever tasked you with, and I want you to see to it personally."

"I've got every confidence in the team that I sent, but I can sure do that."

"Good, and make damn sure you contact me as soon as it's done."

"Okay, but what's the big deal?"

"I've got this on a very tight timeline, and if you don't verify that it's taken care of, I'll have to cancel my broadcast."

"Boss, it's none of my business, but how are you going to explain that you know those kinds of details so soon after the attack?"

"The restaurant we're using has a closed-circuit video system that streams to their off-site security company."

"That seems a little odd."

"It's owned by a rather unscrupulous character, and he likes to know who's there before he comes in for the night."

The first thing on Monday morning, General Stenson was on the phone to General Lehman. "Did you know Walter Jefferson is holding a prime-time TV broadcast tonight at nine Eastern?"

"I sure as hell didn't. What he's going to be covering?" General Lehman asked.

"Nobody seems to know, but he's convinced all the major networks to carry it, and he's scheduled it for a full thirty minutes."

"I haven't seen anything on the schedule. I wonder when they're going to put the word out."

"They're not, they're just going to preempt regular programming."

"This sounds pretty shaky. I'd better see what the hell he's up to, and I'll call you back as soon as I find out."

"Please do, and are we still on for tonight?"

"Yes, they've all landed, and we're supposed to meet them at the restaurant at six thirty. Dinner's at seven."

"Walter Jefferson's office," said Amy Walsh, Walter's executive assistant.

Amy was fresh out of college, and really didn't have any experience, but she was a drop-dead gorgeous redhead with a killer body. She realized that was probably why she'd gotten the position, but the money was unbelievable, and so far the job wasn't that difficult.

"Amy, this is General Lehman, and I need to speak with Walter if he's available."

"Sorry, General, he's in an all-day meeting and won't be out until just before the press conference tonight. I can take a message, and see if he's got time to call you back during one of the breaks."

"That would be fine. Tell him that I'd like to discuss

the purpose of tonight's press conference, and if possible, before he goes on the air."

"I'll see that he gets the message. Is there anything else I can do for you?"

"There is one other thing, and you might know the answer. What did he do with the prisoners they picked up from the Dallas County Jail last week?"

"He didn't say, but I'll put your question on the note as well.

"General Lehman just called for you," Amy said as she handed Walter the note.

"What did he want?" Walter Jefferson asked.

"He wanted to discuss your press conference, and he wanted to know what you did with the Dallas prisoners."

"What did you tell him?"

"Nothing, I figured if you wanted him to know, you'd have already told him."

"Smart girl."

"You going to call him back?"

"Nope, but I do need to talk with John when he lands," Walter said as he pitched the note into the trash.

"His flight doesn't land for another thirty minutes, but I'll leave him a voice mail to give you a call."

"Good, and when you're done with that, would you mind getting General Stenson for me?

"What the hell did you tell General Lehman?" Walter Jefferson asked.

"Nothing, I just gave him a heads-up that I'd seen the notifications that you sent to the networks concerning tonight's press conference."

"Why would you do that?"

"He knows that my teams monitor everything, and I was afraid he'd become suspicious if I didn't give him a heads-up. I knew you wouldn't take his call, so I didn't think it was a big deal."

"It's not, I was just making sure you hadn't gotten cold feet."

"Hell no, it's time we put an end to all of this turmoil."

"So the meeting is still on then?" Walter Jefferson asked.

"Of course, and I've got my talk all prepared. I just hope that I can persuade most of them to go along with it."

"I don't think it's going to be an issue."

"I wish I shared your confidence. This is a huge shift in strategy, and I'm almost sure a couple of them are going to take exception to it."

"You let me worry about that. I just need you to deliver the message."

"I'll handle it, but I'm more than a little concerned myself."

"I understand, and that's definitely one of the subjects we're going to discuss when we get together tomorrow," Walter Jefferson said.

Forty-five minutes later John Jay called.

"What's up, boss?" John Jay asked.

"I've added another name to your list," Walter Jefferson said.

John opened the encrypted e-mail and said, "I'm somewhat surprised, but consider it done."

As General Lehman's car pulled up in front of the restaurant where they were meeting, his cell phone rang.

"I'm stuck in traffic, and I'm going to be about twenty minutes late," General Stenson said.

"No problem, I'll buy the boys a couple of drinks while we wait," General Lehman replied.

One of Walter Jefferson's operatives inside the NSA was monitoring all of General Lehman's and General Stenson's communications, so a couple of minutes later

John Jay received a text message on their change of plans. Amy Walsh had reserved a private room at the Italian restaurant for their get-together, and they all stood when the general entered.

As General Lehman moved around the table shaking hands with the UCC leaders, he said, "Gentlemen, you might as well make yourselves comfortable. General Stenson is delayed in traffic, but he should be here in time for dinner."

As they sat back down, General Lehman said, "Waiter, we'd like to order some drinks."

As the waiter was taking their drink orders, they heard screaming and the sound of automatic weapons fire.

"What the hell?" General Volkey said as four machine gun–toting, black-clad men burst into the room and opened fire without saying a word. The commanders were all on their feet by then, but none of them had any weapons, so they died without being able to put up a fight.

"Do you want us to behead them, boss?" one of the fighters asked.

"No time. Push the table out of the way and pile the bodies up so that we can burn them."

When his men finished piling the bodies up like cordwood, the team leader said, "Cover the bodies with the thermite blankets and set the timer for one minute."

They'd slaughtered the other patrons and restaurant staff on the way in, and as they worked their way around the overturned tables and the dead bodies, the team leader said, "I've changed my mind. Behead a few of these fools and bring the heads outside, but be quick about it, the police will be here shortly.

"Arrange the heads around the pole while I take care of this," the team leader ordered when they came running outside carrying the bloody heads. He climbed the pole to attach an ISIS battle flag to it, but as he slid back down, the plate glass windows stretching across the front of the restaurant exploded from the heat of the raging inferno inside.

"Shit, that's hot," one of the men said as the molten shards of glass hit them.

As a thick black cloud of smoke billowed out of the building, the team leader said, "That's sure to draw a crowd. Load up and get out of here."

As the team was getting into the van, he removed the black hood covering his face and then the black jumpsuit.

"Aren't you coming with us?" the driver asked.

"No, I've got a loose end that I need to take care of," John Jay said as he started casually walking away from the restaurant.

When General Stenson's car finally reached the block the restaurant was on, the police had it cordoned off, and there were fire trucks, ambulances, and cop cars everywhere.

It was a one-way street, so the car-service driver couldn't turn around.

The driver got out and walked down the block to talk with one of the policeman standing guard. When he returned, he said, "Sorry, sir, they've got a hell of a mess going on down there, and we're going to be stuck here for a while."

"Damn. How much farther is it to the restaurant?"

"It's at the end of this block, but the cop said that's where the fire is."

"Oh hell," General Stenson muttered. He tried calling General Lehman several times before he finally gave up.

They'd been sitting there for several minutes when

General Stenson's cell phone rang, and he assumed it was General Lehman returning his call. "General Lehman, is everyone alright?" General Stenson asked.

"Where are you?"

"About a half a block from the restaurant, and it looks like—"

"Shit the bed," the driver said when the .45 caliber round shattered the side window, splattering General Stenson's brains all over the other side of the limo. Panicked, the driver threw off his seat belt and tried to open his door, but the next bullet struck him in the side of the head, killing him instantly.

John Jay put a couple more bullets into each of them before he pitched the silenced pistol through the shattered window. As he turned and walked away, he was speed dialing Walter's number.

Walter Jefferson was preparing to go on the air as Colonel Neri's teams were about to make their assault on the rustic Whiteface Lodge in Lake Placid, New York. Walter Jefferson hadn't wanted any unwanted attention, so they'd confiscated the lodge to hold the members of President Wilkes's cabinet.

The vibrant multicolored fall foliage on the tree-covered slopes of the Adirondack Mountains provided plenty of cover for Colonel Neri's team to make their approach to the lodge. When the snipers were in position, Colonel Neri said, "All units execute."

The ten snipers centered the sentries in the crosshairs of their Barrett XM500 .50 caliber sniper rifles, and within seconds the guards had been neutralized.

"Clear," reported Sergeant Brickner, the sniper team leader.

"All units move out," Colonel Neri said.

As Colonel Neri's Sayeret Maglan Special Forces troops rushed through the entrances to the lodge, they had their 9 mm MTAR21 X95S assault rifles at the ready.

"Heads up," Colonel Neri said when he spotted two machine gun–toting guards coming down the stairs.

The colonel and the four special forces troops shadowing him each put a burst of 9 mm rounds into the hapless guards. Dead from the hail of bullets, the guards came tumbling down the wooden staircase.

"Keep moving," Colonel Neri said as he bounded up the stairs to search the rooms on the second floor.

"While they were doing that, Lieutenant Bergen's squad searched the first-floor rooms, and Sergeant Bruckner's squad took the top floor.

"None of the hostages are in their rooms," Lieutenant Bergen said.

"Ditto here," Sergeant Brickner reported.

"The second floor is empty as well," Colonel Neri said. "Spread out and find them."

"We've found them," Lieutenant Bergen said. "They're all in the Kanu dining room."

"Secure the staff, and we'll be right down," Colonel Neri said.

While his men used the plastic zip ties to secure the staff, Colonel Neri walked over to the hostages and said, "I'm Colonel Neri of the Israeli Special Forces, and we're taking you out of here."

"Did my brother send you?" Secretary of Defense Behrmann asked.

"We can discuss that later. Right now I need you to get up and come with me."

"Thank the lord, we'd about given up hope," Frank Gillespie said as he threw his napkin on the floor and stood up.

"Wait, we're missing someone. Where is Secretary Milliken?" Colonel Neri asked.

"His heart couldn't stand the strain, and he died shortly after we arrived," Secretary Behrmann said.

"We're ready for pickup," Colonel Neri called over his headset as they made their way toward the front entrance.

By the time they reached the front porch of the rustic lodge, the helicopters were starting to land on the lawn. Colonel Neri gathered the cabinet members around him and said, "All of you will be coming with me. Sergeant Brickner, your team will lead us out to the choppers," he said.

The sergeant and his team of snipers immediately surrounded the cabinet members and started hustling them toward the waiting choppers.

"Shit, where'd that come from?" Sergeant Brickner asked when a rifle shot from the third-floor balcony blew out the side of Benjamin Sparks's head.

"Damn," Colonel Neri said as one his snipers put a .50 caliber round through the guard's head before he could fire again.

Once they were airborne, Aryeh Behrmann spoke. "I really appreciate you saving our ass, but how in the world did you find us?"

"I'm afraid that's out of my pay grade."

"Who the hell cares?" said Nancy Baker, the secretary of homeland security.

"I'll just be glad to get back to Washington so we can take care of this mess," Frank Gillespie added.

"I'm afraid that's not where we're headed," Colonel Neri said.

"Where then?" Secretary Behrmann asked.

"My orders are to drop you off at EUCOMM command in Stuttgart, Germany."

After a short flight, they landed at Adirondack Regional Airport, where General Drummond had a Boeing 777 300-ER waiting for them.

The starboard engine was already running when they pulled up alongside the aircraft, and as they were boarding the pilot started spinning up the port-side engine.

"In a hurry?" Aryeh Behrmann asked.

"Damn right we are," Colonel Neri said. "I want to be long gone before they discover we've got you."

As their plane crossed the shoreline and headed out over the Atlantic, Colonel Neri sent General Drummond a one-word text message. When the general's phone beeped, and he saw the message: FREEDOM, he knew they'd pulled off the first phase of their objectives.

At precisely the same time as Colonel Neri's team was heading over the Atlantic, four more squads of the elite Israeli commandos were moving quickly toward the four entrances to the bunker, where Walter Jefferson's men were holding the members of Congress.

Disguised as tourists, the teams had checked into the Greenbrier hotel in Sulphur Springs, West Virginia two days before, and had blended in with the rest of the guests until they were ready to strike. As commandos approached the entrances to the underground facility, they slipped their earbuds in, opened their duffel bags, and assembled their weapons. Each team had a well-endowed bikini-clad young lady with them, and as they neared the entrances to the bunker, they sent them on ahead to distract the militia members guarding the entrances.

"I've lost my way, could you tell me where the sauna is?" the scantily clad young woman asked the militia members guarding the entrance.

"Where are you from, sweet thing?" one of the guards asked as he stared down at her ample bosom.

She never got to answer, as the silenced rounds from the special ops snipers blew out the backs of their heads.

"Oh shit," she screamed as she got splattered with one of the guards' blood and brains.

"Here's your five hundred bucks, now get lost," said Colonel Minkel, the leader of the raid.

"One is clear," Colonel Minkel called to the other teams.

As soon as the other teams had reported in, Colonel Minkel said, "We're a go for entry, and we don't have time for prisoners."

As the teams entered the bunker, they went directly to their assigned locations.

They'd studied the captives' schedules, so they knew the prisoners would all be eating dinner. As they made their way toward the two cafeterias, they killed every militia member they encountered.

"Major Whipple, we need help in section two."

"We all do, but I don't have any to send you," Major Whipple said.

"Listen up, people, we're taking you out of here," Colonel Minkel announced at the top of his voice when they entered the main cafeteria.

"It's about damn time," said Michael Carmichael, the president of the Senate pro tempore. "Where are you taking us?"

"I'll explain later. Now please get up and follow us."

"Did you get through to the command center?" Major Whipple asked.

"The phone lines are out, and they're jamming our radio frequencies."

"Keep trying, if we don't get some help we're going to lose the whole facility."

"Should we use the emergency dispatch system that John Jay briefed us on?"

"He said to only use it in the case of an extreme emergency, but I guess this qualifies," Major Whipple said as he removed the protective cover and flipped the switch.

The members of Congress were hustling toward the exits when a series of very large explosive charges detonated, burying everyone inside under thousands of tons of earth and rock. As the bunker imploded a large section of the West Virginia wing of the Greenbrier hotel collapsed in on it.

WALTER HAD FLOWN to the CBS Studio Center in Studio City, California to do his broadcast, and he was getting nervous because he hadn't heard from John Jay yet.

"Have you got everything you need?" Amy Walsh asked as they made their final preparations for Walter's press conference.

"No, but I've still got a few minutes yet," Walter Jefferson said. "How do I look?"

"Very distinguished. I don't mean to rush you, but the producer just called, and he's got a question for you."

"Amy said you had a question," Walter Jefferson said.

"Do you really think it's a good idea to have armed militia standing in full view of the audience?" the producer asked.

"Is that a problem?"

"Given what just happened at the White House, I thought that you might want to use regular military service members."

"I see your point, but I'd rather stick with the plan. How long until I go on the air?"

"You've got twelve minutes."

"I'm not feeling well, so if I'm not back by then, just tell them that I have taken ill and that we'll reschedule."

"Okay, but the networks are really going to be pissed if you cancel now."

Walter Jefferson was standing in the bathroom anxiously awaiting the call, so he answered it on the first ring. "I was getting worried. How'd it go?" Walter Jefferson asked.

After John had explained the wrinkle with General Stenson, Walter asked, "And everything else went as planned?"

"It did."

"Good work, and make sure the security company forwards a copy of the video to us," Walter Jefferson said.

As he straightened his tie in the bathroom mirror, he realized his pulse was racing, and he loved it.

"I was getting worried. Everything is ready, and you go live in thirty seconds," the producer said as he motioned for the production crew to turn up the lights.

"Good evening, ladies and gentlemen, and for those of you who don't already know me, I'm Walter Jefferson. I deeply regret that my first official act as the chancellor of the United States is to deliver some tragic news. This evening, at approximately six forty-five P.M. Eastern Standard Time, a group of Islamic State terrorists assassinated—no, slaughtered—the chairman of the Joint Chiefs, General Curtiss Lehman. General Lehman was killed at an off-site meeting with the all of the Unified Combat Command leaders. Present at the meeting, and also murdered, were Admiral Clyde Hooks of the U.S. Strategic Command, General Lawrence Drummond of the European Command, Admiral Samuel Crawford of the Pacific Command, Air Force General Norman Mathis of the Central Command, Marine General Paul Cassidy of the Southern Command, and General Patrick Volkey of the Special Operations Command.

"In a separate, but we believe related incident, General Albert Stenson of the Northern Command and his driver were gunned down en route to the same meeting.

"And last, but certainly no less tragic, the cowards slaughtered forty-eight patrons and staff from the restaurant. Our prayers go out to all of the family members affected by these heinous crimes, and I give each of you my solemn vow that we will avenge their deaths many times over.

"Before I continue, I'd like for all of us to observe a moment of silence, so that each of us can say a prayer for them and their families, and for all of the others that have been murdered by these animals.

"Thank you. Now I'm going to clarify my earlier statement about assuming the role of chancellor of the United States. General Lehman had the foresight to prepare a succession plan, and I'm next in line. Since I'm a civilian, and not in the presidential line of succession, I'm going to use the title of chancellor while I'm in charge of the country's affairs.

"Our nation has suffered many unanswered atrocities from these so-called jihadists, but that inaction ends today. As a first step toward regaining control of our domestic situation, I've signed an order authorizing the creation of six holding camps that are strategically located across the United States. Elements from law enforcement, the various branches of the military, along with members of the Combined Militias of the United States, have already begun rounding up the IS/Muslim sympathizers from around the country. The detainees will be transported to the closest holding facility, where they will go before a military tribunal. If they're found to be a threat, they will be held there until we can determine a proper course of action. We're also investigating several other groups that could be a threat to the stability of the country, and they will be dealt with accordingly. We're making every effort to identify the potential traitors, but I'm asking all of you to help us identify potential enemies. To facilitate the process, we've put up a website where you can make an anonymous report about a group or individual that you think might be a threat.

"As a first step to secure our borders, we're denying entry to any non-U.S. citizen, and prohibiting all foreign travel by U.S. citizens until we can get the online clearinghouse up and running. Until we can get the new national ID program in place, I'm mandating a dusk-to-dawn curfew for every city with a population of over a hundred thousand.

"I often use quotes from one of my more famous ancestors, Thomas Jefferson, but in this case, as Mr. Spock so famously said in the movie, *The Wrath of Khan*, 'The needs of the many outweigh the needs of the few.'

"In closing, I'm asking that each of you help me pull our nation back from the edge of the abyss. Good night, and God bless America."

How the hell could he already know all of that? the producer thought. *We just received the news of the attack, and the police are saying that it may be weeks before they can identify the victims.*

Walter Jefferson's speech had been carried on every major network, and before the strobe lights had time to cool, a copy of his speech was circulating on the web.

The next morning, Dizhwar Akram had set up their temporary office in a downtown espresso bar, but he was pissed because there hadn't been enough room for Daoud Mansouri's desk.

"I'm very sorry, but we couldn't get your desk in here," Dizhwar Akram said.

"No worries, I'll sit at the bar. Could someone fix me a cup of coffee?" Daoud Mansouri asked.

"Here's your coffee and some dates. We just pulled this down, and you need to watch it," Dizhwar Akram said as he hooked up his laptop to the TV behind the counter.

When they finished watching Walter's speech, Daoud Mansouri asked, "What the hell was Ehsan Hashmi thinking?"

"It couldn't have been him. He had an emergency appendectomy two days ago, and he hasn't been released from the hospital yet."

They hadn't gotten back to the ranch until after midnight, but Walter Jefferson was already sitting on his veranda when Amy Walsh came out and said, "I'm sorry to disturb your breakfast, but this is important."

"Son of a bitch. Is John back yet?" Walter Jefferson asked after he'd read the note.

"Weather delay out of Dulles, but he should be here by noon."

"I need to see him as soon as he lands."

"Damn, who shit in your Post Toasties?" John asked when he walked into Walter's office.

Walter handed John the note and asked, "How the hell could this happen?"

"No clue, because Porter had his best men at both locations. However, the bunker debacle was probably caused by the emergency system I had them install when we did the renovations."

"Why would our people kill themselves like that?"

"They didn't know what it was going to do. I told them it would lock down the facility and dispatch an emergency response team."

"Devious as hell, I like it." Walter chuckled. "I guess that solves our congressional problem, but we've got to find those cabinet members."

"Understood, but they'll be long gone by now. How much shit are you getting from your broadcast last night?"

"Actually it hasn't been as bad as I'd feared, but I've

got a call with the combat commanders' executive officers in a few minutes. Once I've promoted them I'll have a better sense of how much pushback I'm going to get from the military."

As the executive officers of the various combat commands were coming online, Walter was noting their names, and which command they had. When the Pacific Command joined the call, Walter was shocked to see Admiral Crawford.

"You're supposed to be dead," Walter Jefferson blurted out.

"To quote Mark Twain, 'The reports of my death have been greatly exaggerated.' "

"Let me second that thought," General Drummond said as he joined in.

Walter didn't miss a beat as he said, "How did you survive?"

"I wasn't at the meeting," Admiral Crawford said. "General Lehman ordered me to send my XO."

"Ditto for me," General Drummond said. "He must have suspected something was amiss."

"Obviously he was right," Walter Jefferson said. "Since you're both still in place, I'll move on to the other commands."

Walter was seething, but he managed to hold it together for the duration of the call. When he'd finished promoting the new leaders of the Unified Combat Commands, he went to wake up John.

It took John several seconds to answer his door, and when he opened it, he could tell Walter was past pissed. "Walter, what's wrong?"

"You swore that you'd killed them all, yet I was just on a videoconference with the combat commands, and who did I see? General Drummond and Admiral Crawford, that's who."

"Impossible, my team killed everyone in the room,

and they told me that there was only one empty seat when they burst in."

"Didn't you ID them?"

"The room was a slaughterhouse when I got back there, so I didn't bother verifying their identities. I guess I've really screwed the pooch this time."

"I'm not really mad at you. General Lehman is what happened. I just wish I knew how much he really knew, and who he'd shared it with. We'll need to get rid of anyone that he might have told."

"That's going to be a big list," John Jay said.

"I don't care, just take care of it."

"I'm supposed to be in San Francisco next week, do I need to reschedule?"

"Just put some of Porter's men on it."

"I'll brief him before I take off. What's next for you?"

"Now that General Lehman is out of the way, I'm going to relocate to the White House."

"Then I'll change my return flight to Dulles," John Jay said.

"Don't bother, it's going to take me several days to get moved."

John's flight to SFO got diverted to San Jose because of the weather, so he was scrambling to make his meeting.

"All we have left is an SUV," the girl at the Hertz counter said.

"I'll take it."

John walked outside and boarded the bus to the car lot.

"Stop your sniveling, and shut the hell up," the hulking middle-aged man growled.

"I'm sorry I spilled my drink on you, but please don't hurt me again," his terrified young wife sobbed.

"I'm going to show you what sorry means when we get to the car," he said as he grabbed her arm and squeezed as hard as he could. She grimaced in pain, but managed not to cry out.

None, of my business, leave it alone, John thought as the bus stopped to let them off at their vehicles. John took a moment to check his messages as the couple got off the bus, but as he was walking to his vehicle, he saw them loading their luggage into an SUV parked next to his. John had been emotionless since he'd been wounded, but something about the man touched something buried deep inside his psyche. They were the last vehicles left on the lot, so there was no one else there to hear the man slap his wife and pin her up against the vehicle.

"Please, Harry, don't hit me again."

"You're going to learn some manners if I have to beat you half to death doing it," he said as he drew his massive fist back to punch her in the face.

"Ugh," was the only sound he made as John cupped his hand over his mouth and rammed his Ka-Bar Becker BK9 Combat Bowie through his back and deep inside his heart.

John pulled Harry backward and let his still-twitching body fall to the ground in front of his startled wife. John could see the abject terror in her eyes as he said, "Don't scream, I'm not going to hurt you."

John wiped the blade of his knife clean on the man's white shirt and got into his vehicle and left.

As he was driving away, he thought, *I've got no idea why I did that, but it sure felt good.*

John called Walter from the car and told him what had happened.

"Sounds like a real asshole, but don't worry about it, I'll handle the authorities," Walter said.

It took Walter almost ten days to set up the move, but when his armored limo pulled up at the White House, Colonel Ridgeway met him.

"Chancellor Jefferson, I'm Colonel Ridgeway. I'm in charge of the White House Situation Room, and I'll be helping you get settled in. Mrs. Wilkes has already moved back to Virginia, so I had the movers put your belongings in the residence."

"Thanks, but I'd like to get my office up and running as soon as possible," Chancellor Jefferson said.

"I figured, however the Oval Office reconstruction won't be finished for several months."

"What do you suggest?" Chancellor Jefferson asked.

"There are several office suites on the basement level of the West Wing, and that would give you easy access to the Situation Room."

"Then that's what I'll do."

CHAPTER 27

A week after the rescue mission, Aryeh Behrmann was sitting in General Drummond's office in the Special Operations Headquarters in Stuttgart, Germany.

"I've got a call with Admiral Crawford in ten minutes. Would it be all right if I fill him in on the Lake Placid operation?" General Drummond asked.

"Not yet," Aryeh Behrmann said.

"He's going to be upset when he does find out."

"Just blame me. I'd like to listen in, if you don't mind?"

"Thanks for calling me back," General Drummond said.

"Sorry for the delay, but I wanted to get my commands moved to FPCON delta before we talked," Admiral Crawford said.

"I did that as soon as I learned of General Lehman's death, and I instructed them to only accept orders that come directly from my command."

"Damn it, I should have done that," Admiral Crawford said. "I'll take care of it as soon as we're finished, but I wish we could lock down the nukes."

"We're working on that."

"I'm pretty sure Walter Jefferson wasn't expecting to see us on the call."

"No, he wasn't, but he never batted an eye," General Drummond said. "So, what do you think of our self-appointed chancellor?"

"I think he's a devious power mad little bastard who will leave no stone unturned to achieve his goals, but do you have any idea what happens now?"

"From what little our new chancellor has shared, it looks like we're going after the Islamic State and their new allies."

"I've got no problem with that, but how about domestically?"

"Hard to tell, but he'll have to do something pretty drastic to get it back under control."

"I think we should talk on a regular basis, and let's keep that between us for now."

"I don't know him, but it sounded like the admiral would be on our side when the time comes," Aryeh Behrmann said.

"He's a good man, but this is going to be difficult for all of us," General Drummond said. "When are you going to make the announcement?"

"I'll have a better sense of the timing after tonight's meeting with a few of the key members of NATO. Were you able to persuade the Russian president to attend?"

"It wasn't a problem, he'd already let me know that he'd be willing to help out."

They were meeting in an upstairs conference room in the European command center, but other than the guards, everyone else had gone for the day.

The room was set up to hold fifty people, so they were gathered at one end of the room. Secretary Behrmann had met most of them before, but he had no idea what to expect this time. He took his place at the head of the table and said, "Thank you for agreeing to meet with me."

"Not a problem, that's what allies are for," British Prime Minister Marjorie Williams said.

Marjorie was a thirty-eight-year-old, brown-eyed, petite brunette, and the only woman in the room. She'd only been in office for six weeks, and none of the other leaders knew much about her.

"Prime Minister Williams is right, but we're all hoping that you have a plan to regain control of your government," said German Chancellor Helmut Duisenberg.

Chancellor Duisenberg was almost eighty, but his mind was still sharp, and at six foot four and two hundred and forty pounds, he was an imposing figure. His hair, handlebar mustache, and bushy eyebrows were snow white, and his complexion always made him look a little flushed.

"I'd be lying if I said I had a ready-made answer," Aryeh Behrmann said.

"Refreshingly candid, but Chancellor Jefferson is in control of your nuclear arsenal, and that could be catastrophic for all of us if you can't regain control," said the president of Russia, Valery Gorelov.

President Gorelov had been the head of the KGB before he'd assumed the presidency eleven years before, and since then he'd ruled the country with an iron fist. He was fifty-five years old, with sandy blond hair and electric blue eyes, and he could be quite charming when the situation called for it.

"That will all change when I assume the presidency," Aryeh Behrmann said.

"I don't mean to be rude, but you're number six on the succession list," said the French president, Nicolas Lebrun.

President Lebrun was fifty-five years old, with silver hair, brown eyes, and was a small man at five foot three and a hundred and twenty pounds. However, his diminutive size belied a fiery temper and a completely fearless approach to life.

"Correct, but unfortunately the others are all deceased."

"I'm terribly sorry, I wasn't aware of that."

"Chancellor Jefferson isn't likely to publicize it," Aryeh Behrmann said. "Once I make the announcement, I'm counting on a significant portion of the military recognizing my legal authority over them."

"I'm sure that given a choice many of them would, but Chancellor Jefferson has done a good job of consolidating his power base," Belgian Prime Minister Guy Goossens said.

Prime Minister Goossens's family was extremely wealthy, but he'd dedicated his life to public service. He was seventy-one years old and had been in office for thirty-one years, but he'd shown no signs of slowing down. He was completely bald, and the thick lenses of his glasses made it difficult to see his brilliant green eyes.

"I'm not saying it won't be difficult, but what choice do I have?"

"None, and my country stands ready to support you in any way we can," Prime Minister Williams said.

"We're not a member of NATO, but we'll back you all the way," President Gorelov said.

"Thank you, and I've spoken with my brother Lieb, and the Israeli government has pledged its unqualified support as well."

They spent the rest of the evening working on strategies, and by 3 A.M. they had a tentative set of plans.

"I can't thank all of you enough for the support you've shown tonight, and with your help we'll succeed," Aryeh Behrmann said.

The next morning, FBI Director Berkley received an unexpected call.

"Chancellor Jefferson, what can I do for you today?" Director Berkley asked.

"I want you to begin forwarding me the names you've been mining from the Internet," Walter Jefferson said.

"Okay, but I can't guarantee the validity of the assumptions we're making."

"I understand, but could you cross-reference them to their ethnicity and/or country of origin?"

"Sure, but you're going to be accused of racial profiling."

"Will you do it or not?"

"Of course I will, but what are you going to do with the data?"

"Let me worry about that."

"It will take us a little while to make the tweaks, but you should have the first batch by the end of the month."

"When you're finished with that, I need you to find out what the hell happened at Lake Placid and in West Virginia."

"We're working on that, but everything at the West Virginia site is buried under a mountain of rock."

"Then concentrate on Lake Placid," Walter instructed.

"Amy, I need you to schedule a video call with the militia leaders at three P.M. tomorrow," he said.

"Good afternoon, gentlemen," Walter Jefferson said when the militia leaders had all joined the call. "When we finish construction on the holding facilities in Arizona, Nevada, Utah, and New York, I'm going to start sending you a weekly list of the suspected enemy sympathizers in your areas."

"For what purpose?" Willy Wood asked.

"I want you to pick them up and transport them to the nearest holding facility."

"It's about time," Jeb Butts said. "I'm tired of these assholes disrupting our lives."

"Damn straight," Terry Gould said. "Although I'd rather just line them up and shoot them."

"That's harsh," Willy Wood said.

"We're not going there, at least not yet," Walter Jefferson said. "Do any of you have any qualms about this?" He paused. "No? Then I'll expect you to be ready when the time comes."

Thirty days later, Walter Jefferson received an early morning call from homeland security.

"Your militias are getting way out of line," Director Baker said.

"Good morning to you too, Ms. Baker," Walter Jefferson said.

"Sorry, but yesterday afternoon four of Clarence Booth's men murdered three sheriff's deputies."

"I'm sure there's a good explanation."

"That's bullshit. They were looting a store owned by the family they'd just picked up, and when the deputies tried to stop them, they shot them down."

"I've authorized them to confiscate any and all property from the terrorists they apprehend, and from what you've told me so far, it sounds like the sheriff's deputies should have stayed out of it."

"There's no way those people were terrorists. Their family has lived in that town for four generations, and their grandfather was the town's mayor for over twenty years."

"What's done is done, but I'll ask them to tone it down a bit. Are you making any headway on securing the borders?"

"Some, I guess," she said hesitantly. "You know what? That's total bullshit. There's really no way to secure them. There are simply too many miles of open territory."

"Finally, an honest person, and it just so happens that I agree with you. That's why I'm going to pursue another solution to the problem."

I wonder what he's going to pull now? she thought to herself.

When Walter hung up he called Amy Walsh into his new office. "I want you to set up a meeting with what's left of the Joint Chiefs."

"When and where?"

"Next Tuesday at six A.M., and we'll hold it here in the Situation Room."

The Joint Chiefs were used to meeting in the Situation Room, but they were shocked when they realized that the entire White House staff had been replaced by members of Oliver Porter's black-clad special operations group.

The only remaining member of the staff was Colonel Ridgeway, because unbeknownst to them, he'd been one of Walter's true believers all along.

"This is downright disturbing," General Willowby said when he saw the three lightning bolts on the patches of their coal black berets.

"I appreciate you making the time to meet with me," Walter Jefferson said.

"No problem, and we stand ready to assist you in any way we can," said Admiral Kennedy.

"Thank you, Admiral, and as our first order of business, I'm naming you the new chairman," Walter Jefferson said.

"Thank you, sir. I'll do my best to fill General Lehman's shoes."

"I have no doubt, but let's move on to the real purpose of the meeting. The iPads that Colonel Ridgeway is passing out contain the presentation we're going to be discussing. The late Admiral Hooks developed the basic framework of the plan; however, we've made some extensive modifications to it. I'll give you a few minutes to read through it before we continue."

When Walter saw they were starting to have side conversations, he said, "It looks like most of you are finished, so we'll get started. Up to now our attempts to bolster border security have been an abject failure, which is why we'll be launching a pair of operations, code named North Wind and South Wind."

"If I understood the material correctly, you intend to invade Canada and Mexico," General Willowby said.

"That's right, and I'd like to hear your thoughts on the overall initiative, but before you weigh in, I need you to understand that the goals of the operation aren't up for debate."

"I'd be shocked if the UN Security Council didn't immediately authorize sanctions, and possibly direct action against us," General Biggalow said.

"There's a very strong possibility of all that, and rather than agonizing about it, I've had elements from Oliver Porter's commands seize the UN building this morning. They're currently transporting the diplomats and their staffs to JFK, where they will be put on planes and sent home. In a simultaneous operation, Oliver Porter is coordinating a similar series of operations with the appropriate state militias, and by tomorrow morning they will have closed every embassy and diplomatic mission in the country."

"Are you out of your mind?" Admiral Donnelly asked. "It would take me a week to count all of the international laws you've already broken."

"The United States is done bowing down to that herd of losers."

"They'll slap us with embargoes and sanctions to isolate us from the world's economies, and we don't have the resources to go it alone," General Gibbs said.

"Not your problem," Walter Jefferson said.

"NATO won't stand idly by while we invade a member nation," General Biggalow said.

"Canada made a deal with the devil, and they're going to have to pay the price, and the Mexicans haven't done anything to help us control the southern borders."

Walter let them vent for a few more seconds before he slammed an iPad down on the conference table, sending pieces flying. "Enough!" he yelled. "What I need to know now is that each of you will faithfully carry out my orders without hesitation. But before you answer, there will be ramifications if you refuse. We'll go around the table, and all you have to say is yay or nay," Walter said.

Everyone answered affirmatively until they reached General Terry Willowby, the commandant of the marines.

"I'm sorry, but this is insanity, and I'll not be a party to it," General Willowby said.

"Your call. Colonel Ridgeway will escort you out."

The door had just closed when they heard the unmistakable sound of a gunshot from the hallway.

"What the hell just happened?" General Goldstein asked.

"That was the ramification I alluded to earlier," Walter Jefferson said.

"You had him killed?" General Gibbs asked.

"No, that was his decision."

They worked for another thirty minutes before Chancellor Jefferson dismissed them.

Half an hour after they'd left the White House grounds, General Drummond received an encrypted e-mail detailing everything that had just transpired.

"Sorry for the wait, but I wasn't expecting to hear from you today," Admiral Crawford said when he joined the video call with General Drummond.

"I'd considered holding off until our regular call," Drummond said. "But I knew you were good friends with General Willowby."

"Has something happened to Terry?"

"Chancellor Jefferson had him killed."

The admiral closed his eyes and bowed his head for several seconds. "Sorry, I was saying a prayer for my friend," he said.

"No need to apologize."

"This sure as hell removes any doubts that I had about how this is going to play out for us."

"Damned straight, and you should beef up your personal security," General Drummond said.

"It wasn't why I did it, but I've just moved my flag to the *Gerald R. Ford*."

"That should work for now. I've relocated to the Supreme Headquarters Allied Powers Europe in Casteau, Belgium, which is just north of Mons."

"How come?"

"I wanted to be in a secure location when our dumbass chancellor launches his invasion."

"Excuse me?"

"The same source that tipped me off to General Willowby's death says that Walter Jefferson intends to invade Canada and Mexico."

"That's insanity, the JCS would never go along with that."

"Unfortunately they all did, except for Willowby, and that's what got him killed."

"What the hell do we do now?"

"It's time to bring him on board," Aryeh Behrmann said.

"Who was that?" Admiral Crawford asked.

"That was Secretary of Defense Behrmann, who's about to become the new president of the United States," General Drummond said.

"How's that work? He's way down the list."

"Several weeks ago, all the members of Congress and Benjamin Sparks, the secretary of the Treasury, were killed during a joint rescue mission with the Israelis."

"How did Chancellor Jefferson keep something like that quiet?"

"All the public has ever known was that the military was holding them in seclusion, so it wasn't that difficult. However, an Israeli special ops team successfully extracted the surviving cabinet members. Secretary Behrmann is next in line for the presidency, and we've been working on a plan to restore democracy to our country."

"Why tell me now?"

"We've reached the point where we need to involve a wider range of potential allies, and we want you to handle Asia and the Pacific for us. Since Chancellor Jefferson has men virtually everywhere, we'd like you to contact them in person."

"Hot damn, you can count me in," Admiral Crawford said. "Japan is going to be pissed that we didn't contact them before the Chinese, but I'll smooth it over with Prime Minister Kaneshiro."

"Any questions?" General Drummond asked.

"Why is the chancellor so hell-bent to launch these invasions?"

"He's convinced it's the only way to secure the borders."

"I'm not sure he's wrong, but what do you intend to do about it?"

"Since I'm the Supreme Allied Commander of Europe and the ACO, President Behrmann has asked me to work with the NATO Military Committee to develop a contingency plan."

"Sounds good. Just let me know what you need me to do," Admiral Crawford said.

Late the next morning, Chancellor Jefferson was working in the Situation Room when Amy Walsh said, "Sorry it took so long, but I've located Mr. Porter."

"You're a hard man to get ahold of," Chancellor Jefferson said.

"Chancellor Jefferson, I wasn't expecting to hear from you until Friday," Oliver Porter replied.

"I've got something I need you to take care of."

"No problem. What have you got?"

"I want you to take control of the militias in Georgia, North Carolina, and West Virginia."

"Issues?"

"They're critical to my plans, and I don't have time to worry whether they're going to back my play."

"I'll contact them immediately."

"I guess I wasn't clear, I want you to permanently remove the leadership. Is that going to be an issue?"

"Hell no. Do you care if I fold them in with my guys?"

"Whatever works, but are they up to it?"

"Probably not all of them, but I'll transfer the ones that can't hack it to the border and transportation security divisions."

The setting sun was casting a fiery glow on the windows of the second-floor conference room at SHAPE headquarters in Casteau, Belgium, when the NATO commanders sat down around the table.

"Thank you for taking the meeting on such short notice, and I hope that none of you object, but I've asked General Kozlovsky to sit in," General Drummond said.

"We were all praying that your cryptic message was a joke," French General Thibault Beauregard said.

"How I wish it were," General Drummond replied. "I don't have the specific date of the attacks, but we have credible intelligence that the United States is going to invade Canada and Mexico."

"Is this some sort of sick joke?" British General Sir Richard McConnell asked.

"After the shit your government pulled outside of Winnipeg, I'll believe anything," Canadian Lieutenant General Terrance Couturier said.

"There's no way we can let that happen," General McConnell said.

"Let's face facts," German General Fredrick Fenstermacher said. "Even with the tremendous cutbacks the Americans have instituted, none of our countries has the wherewithal to go up against them."

"We could make it a joint NATO task force," General Janssens said. "There's no way they'd fire on coalition troops."

"I beg to differ, Chancellor Jefferson just had the commandant of the Marine Corps executed for not going along with his scheme," General Drummond said.

"We can't stand by and do nothing," General McConnell said. "We should at least send a few squadrons of fighter aircraft to shore up the Canadian defenses."

"That's a good first move," General Drummond said. "General McConnell, would you mind coordinating with the other members to get that done?"

"No problem, and we should ship them as many SAM batteries as we can scrounge up."

"And some attack helicopters as well," General Fenstermacher said.

"I can handle the SAM batteries and the helicopters," Russian General Kozlovsky said.

As they continued working on the problem, General Drummond made sure that each of them had a meaningful part in the planning and execution. A little before midnight General Drummond said, "We've made a good start, but this has to stay need-to-know. If Chancellor Jefferson discovers what we're up to, he'll move up the operations."

"We've accomplished quite a lot, but despite everything we intend to do, neither the Canadians nor the Mexicans are going to last very long," Russian General Kozlovsky said.

"Probably true," General Drummond replied. "But it sounds like you have something else to say."

"I think it would be prudent to include an exit strategy for the Canadian forces. That way they can preplan a fighting retreat, and allow us to save some of their assets."

"Go on."

"President Gorelov has agreed to provide asylum and guarantee their safety until you can determine next steps."

"How can you guarantee their safety?" General Armistead asked. "Your country isn't in any better shape than the rest of us."

"True, but unlike most of you, we still have a believable nuclear first strike capability."

"Ah, the old mutually assured destruction ploy," General Drummond said. "When the time is right, we'll take you up on your very generous offer."

When General Drummond finished briefing Aryeh Behrmann, he said, "I know you're busy, but I've got another project that I need done." He handed the general a USB drive and said, "This has the name and address of everyone I need you to retrieve."

"Damn, this is a lot of names," General Drummond said after he'd opened the file. "What the hell do you need with all these people? Wait, I recognize some of these, they're former members of Congress."

"I had to dig pretty deep, but there are enough people there to restore a semblance of our government. I couldn't find enough retirees from the judicial branch, so we're going after the most qualified people I could identify."

"Are you going to try to form a cabinet?"

"I am, and they're in there as well. In all, there are a thousand and fourteen names on the list, and I need every one of them."

"Assuming we're successful, where do you want them?"

"President Gorelov is going to let us use the building known as the Russian White House as our base of operations."

"Where's he going?"

"They've been quietly renovating the Kremlin, and he's already in the process of moving his residence and the government offices."

"What does he expect in return?"

"He said that he sees it as a necessary move to keep his country safe, but if the truth be told, I don't think he's willing to take a chance on Walter Jefferson's mental stability."

"That could be the truth, but keep your eye on him, because he rarely says what he means, and not only is he tricky, he's every bit as ruthless as our new chancellor."

EARLIER IN THE year Clyde Thomas's mother had died, and he'd sold off their liquor stores so he could focus all of his attention on the Nevada militia. His best friend, Tommy Mazola, was the head of security for Caesars Palace, and when the militias had taken over the security for Las Vegas, Tommy had let Clyde move into one of their high-roller penthouses. In return, Clyde made sure none of Tommy's properties had any issues from the police.

"Thanks for calling me back," Clyde said as he looked out at the nighttime grandeur of the Las Vegas strip.

"Your message sounded urgent," said Willy Wood, the leader of the New York militia.

"I'm terribly concerned with some of the things our fearless leader is up to."

"Join the club, but you need to be careful who you say that to, he's a dangerous man to cross."

"For sure, but I think it's time to man up and deal with it."

After a lengthy pause, Willy asked, "What did you have in mind?"

When Clyde finished laying out his thinking, Willy didn't say anything.

"You still there?" Clyde Thomas asked.

"Yes, but are you sure it will work?"

"No, but it's all I could come up with."

"What the hell, count me in."

It was almost midnight when Chancellor Jefferson woke up Colonel Ridgeway with an urgent call. "Colonel, I'm going to be out of touch for a few days, and I don't want anyone to know that I'm gone," Chancellor Jefferson said.

"That won't be a problem, I'll just say you're in a high-level strategy meeting and can't be disturbed. Do you need me to arrange transportation?"

"Not necessary."

"When are you leaving?"

"I'm on my way out, and make damn sure you keep this quiet."

When Chancellor Jefferson's Gulfstream landed at the Beijing Nanyuan Airport, the ground controllers guided his aircraft to a large hangar in a secluded portion of the airport. As soon as the aircraft had taxied inside, the Chinese soldiers closed the massive doors behind it. The Chinese leader, President Zhao, met Chancellor Jefferson at the bottom of the aircraft's stairs.

"It's good to finally meet face-to-face," President Zhao said as they shook hands.

"It is, and thank you for taking the meeting," Chancellor Jefferson said.

"Your proposition intrigued me, but if this goes south we could send the entire world up in flames."

"As the old saying goes, 'Go big or go home.' "

They met for two days, and as Chancellor Jefferson was about to board his aircraft to leave, they shook hands. President Zhao asked, "We're in agreement on this, but do you have any idea when we'll need to act?"

"No, and that's why it's critical we complete our preparations as soon as possible."

"Then I'll go ahead and get a firm commitment from our other partners."

CHAPTER 28

Thirty days later Director Clawson walked into Walter Jefferson's office in the basement of the West Wing and said, "Thanks for seeing me on such short notice, but we could be in trouble."

"That's nothing new, but could you be a little more specific?"

"In the last twenty-four hours, twenty-four squadrons of fighter aircraft have landed at the Montréal–Pierre Elliott Trudeau International Airport."

"Whose?"

"It's all over the board. Twelve were Dassault Rafale B fighters, six were Eurofighter Typhoons, and six were Saab JAS 39 Gripens."

"NATO! Somebody has been running their mouth. Amy, I need to speak with Admiral Kennedy ASAP.

"I need you to launch the operations immediately," Walter Jefferson said.

"Impossible, the divisions for the Mexican operation won't be in place for at least a week," Admiral Kennedy said.

"Screw Mexico, just go with North Wind."

"I really need another week."

"Don't make me replace you."

Eighteen hours later, Admiral Kennedy launched Operation North Wind.

"The Americans are making their move," Canadian General Tibbits said. "Our spotters are reporting large-scale movement of their ground forces."

"Damn, I was hoping the intel was wrong," Canadian Army Lieutenant General Armistead said. "What have we done?"

"I've authorized AIRCOM to scramble the NATO aircraft as soon as they have a radar fix, but I'm going to hold our aircraft in reserve until we can verify their points of attack."

"Alert General Boulanger's command, and tell them that we'll transmit the details once we've verified them."

General Boulanger was a Canadian three-star general, and the current commander of the Canadian Joint Operations Command. He was a hardened combat veteran with nerves of steel. He'd held many commands during his twenty-five-year career, but his most successful was when he'd commanded a multinational division made up of three thousand special ops troops. He'd led them all over the world on a three-year mission to track down and kill high-ranking members of al-Qaeda. He was fifty-two, but his wavy black hair only had a few streaks of gray in it, and at five foot eleven and a hundred and eighty pounds, he was still fit and trim.

"Lieutenant, I've got a large number of aircraft inbound from the southeast, air speed eight hundred and seventy kilometers, altitude thirteen thousand meters, at approximately eight hundred kilometers out," said Sergeant Manning, one of the Canadian radar operators.

Royal Canadian Air Force Lieutenant Jameson double-checked his operational orders before he said, "Issue a level one alert to all squadrons, and scramble the NATO aircraft."

"AIRCOM command to Napoleon One. There are

many bogies approaching from the southeast, and you're cleared for immediate departure."

"Napoleon One, roger that," Colonel Manseau said.

Since the French had contributed the lion's share of the aircraft, they'd put Colonel Manseau in command of all of the NATO squadrons.

"This is Napoleon One, and we'll take the lead. Napoleon Two and Three will follow in five-minute increments."

"Napoleon Two, roger that," said Colonel Broomfield of the British Royal Air Force.

"Napoleon Three affirmative," said Colonel Christoferson of the Swedish Air Force.

"General you're needed in the command center," Captain Todd said.

"What's up?" RCAF General Harold Tibbits asked when walked in.

"We've identified thirty-five heavy bombers on radar, but our ground spotters are reporting a large number of aircraft making nap-of-the-earth approaches."

"What have we done so far?" General Tibbits asked.

"We've scrambled the NATO aircraft, and they—"

"Excuse me, I need to take this," General Tibbits interrupted as he answered his phone.

"General Tibbits, I've got you on with General Thibault Beauregard, and he's going to brief us on the situation," General Armisted said.

"Four armored columns just crossed the border, and they're headed to Toronto, Montreal, Ottawa, and Quebec," General Beauregard said. "From the radio traffic we've intercepted, we know that they're from the III Corps Command Group, under the command of Lieutenant General Fred Avery. The four columns are all similar in makeup. They have a battalion of heavy armor, a squadron of attack helicopters for close air support, and six squadrons of F-16s providing air cover."

"Excellent, they're sticking with their plan," General Armisted said. "General Tibbits, execute CRAF order one-twenty-one."

"Roger that," General Tibbits said. "Captain Todd, launch the NATO aircraft."

"Bagotville, this is AIRCOM. Scramble all aircraft and contact AIRCOM control on three-eight-four-point-five when airborne," Captain Todd said.

The Canadian forces were sitting in their aircraft on the taxiway, waiting on the order to launch.

"Roger three-eight-four-point-five. Snake One, out," Colonel Siebel said as he made the turn onto the main runway and went to maximum thrust. When he reached takeoff speed he pulled the nose up and retracted his landing gear before sending his CF-18 almost straight up off the end of the runway.

"Cold Lake, this is AIRCOM, scramble all aircraft. Contact AIRCOM control on one-two-six-point-six when airborne, and be aware Bagotville is en route."

"Contact one-two-six-point-six on departure. Tiger One, out," Colonel Louis Cote said as he hit the afterburners on his CF-18.

Thirty minutes after they'd begun their ground attack, Admiral Kennedy called Chancellor Jefferson to give him an update.

"The four field commanders are reporting very light initial resistance," Admiral Kennedy said.

"I told you they wouldn't put up much of a fight," Chancellor Jefferson said. "How long until they reach their objectives?"

"If everything stays to schedule, we should be there within twenty-four hours."

As the NATO squadron closed on the American aircraft, Colonel Manseau's Dassaults had the lead. The combination of their Thales/SAGEM's OST Infrared Scan and Track optronics and MBDA's MICA IR medium-range missiles allowed the Rafales to supplement their radar-guided missiles with passively targeted, no-warning attacks on enemy aircraft from beyond visual range.

"Napoleon One, launch missiles and follow me," Colonel Manseau said.

Four minutes later, Colonel Sampson, the squadron commander providing air cover for the Ottawa column, said, "Bogies at angels thirty, and they're a hundred miles out."

Seconds later the missiles began blasting the American F-16s out of the sky.

"Command, this is Otter One, and I've just lost most of my aircraft to an enemy attack," Colonel Sampson said.

"Say again, Otter One."

"I said that we've suffered eighty percent causalities, and we have many bogies closing on us."

"Attention Otter Two, this is North Wind command. Go to burners, and provide assistance to Otter One."

"On our way," responded the Otter 2 commander, Colonel Smiley.

"Attention all aircraft. Drop tanks and follow me," Colonel Smiley said.

As the now closely bunched American squadrons closed in on the NATO forces at Mach 1.8, the NATO squadrons went into a steep dive and turned back to the north.

"The cowards are making a run for it," Colonel Smiley muttered.

He was already nearing his aircraft's top speed, so Colonel Smiley had to throttle back as he pushed over to follow them down.

As F-16s raced after them, the turbulence was bouncing them around pretty badly. "Keep the hammer down, we can't let them escape," Colonel Smiley said.

The NATO aircraft led the Americans over Major Bassonet's PAC-3 Patriot missile batteries, which were well camouflaged, so Colonel Smiley never knew they were there before the major ordered, "All batteries fire."

"Missiles, break right, and take evasive action," Colonel Smiley ordered when his missile warning sounded.

As the F-16s desperately tried to evade the missiles, the NATO squadron reversed course.

"This is Napoleon One, and you're free to engage at will," Colonel Manseau said.

With a large number of the Americans' aircraft destroyed by the SAMs and their formation in a shambles, the dogfight was horribly lopsided. Twenty minutes later the countryside was littered with the funeral pyres of the American aircraft, but by then the NATO squadron was low on fuel.

"AIRCOM, this is Napoleon One. We're low on fuel and requesting an immediate vector to the nearest airfield," Colonel Manseau said.

"Turn right, and descend to five thousand feet. You're cleared direct to Bagotville. Alberta Four, you're cleared to engage."

"Follow me," said RCAF Colonel Charles Sieben, the commander of the second wave of CF-18 Hornets.

When they were within range, Colonel Sieben said, "All aircraft, prepare to drop on my command."

"Drop and follow me," Major Gabriel said as he released his full load of thousand-pound, Mark 83 bombs.

"Where the hell is my air cover?" asked Colonel Waters, the commander of the Ottawa task force, when the JDAMs started hitting the column.

"Major, why aren't your men shooting those bastards down?" Colonel Waters asked.

"No excuses, they caught us with our pants down,

but we're on it now," replied Major Tuttle, the commander of the Americans' Patriot missile batteries.

A few seconds later, their truck-mounted missile launchers had acquired their targets and launched their PAC-3 Patriot missiles.

"Press on, men, we've got to take a chunk out of their asses, or our boys are going to get slaughtered," Colonel Sieben said.

As the CF-188s expended the rest of their ordnance, several of them risked blacking out as they threw their aircraft into violent twists and turns to evade the Americans' missiles, but they were taking heavy losses.

As Canadians were desperately pressing their attack, the NATO contingent had landed, and the ground crews were working feverishly to get them rearmed and refueled.

"How long?" Colonel Manseau asked.

"We're working as fast as we can," Sergeant Smythe said.

"Sorry, I know you are, but I need a time."

"Twenty minutes."

"AIRCOM, this is Napoleon One, we'll be available in thirty," Colonel Manseau said. "Will this be a ground support, or air action?"

"Air. They've scrambled virtually everything they have."

"Dear God, we'll never be able to handle that many."

After a short pause, AIRCOM said, "Have them rearm your aircraft with the Meteors."

"There are only enough for one sortie."

"We realize that, but we've got to slow them down. You're to fire your missiles at maximum range, and contact AIRCOM for instructions."

"Roger that. What frequency should I use?"

"They're monitoring all of our frequencies, so they're

bringing you a satellite phone–enabled laptop, and we'll transmit your next set of orders via that."

"You're good to go, Colonel, and they said to give you this," Sergeant Smythe said as he handed him the gear.

"Let's hit it," Colonel Manseau yelled at the pilots in the ready room.

They took off four abreast to get airborne as quickly as possible, and immediately went to afterburners.

"Mind your spacing, and prepare to launch," Colonel Manseau said as they clawed for altitude.

When they were 120 km from their targets, Colonel Manseau said, "Fire all missiles."

Once the weapons were away, Colonel Manseau said, "On me, break right," before he threw his fighter into a hard right turn.

"Form back up on me," he said as they completed their gut-wrenching turns.

"AIRCOM, Napoleon One standing by," Colonel Manseau said.

A few seconds later, an encrypted file appeared on his laptop with the vectors to rendezvous with the refueling tankers.

As the NATO aircraft raced north, their missiles were closing in on the Americans' formation.

The Meteor missile's onboard systems were configured to switch from passive to active target acquisition at the last possible moment, to reduce the chances of an enemy aircraft being able to evade the attack.

"I've got a missile warning," the copilot on the lead B-52 said.

"Activate countermeasures," the pilot said as he banked to evade the missiles. The Meteors had been designed to take down cruise missiles as well as the fifth generation Soviet aircraft, so the lumbering B-52s never stood a chance.

"It's not working," the copilot said a couple of seconds before one of the missiles blew off their left wing.

The rest of the squadron didn't have any better luck, as the barrage of missiles decimated their formation.

"Sir, we've just lost contact with Bomber One," Commander Travis said.

"Lost contact?" Admiral Kennedy asked.

"We're almost certain they've been shot down."

"Their countermeasures should have been able to handle a missile attack."

"Maybe, but we've already had multiple ground confirmations of aircraft down."

"Where the hell were their escorts?"

"Most of them were lost as well, but there was an OC-135 in the area, and it recorded a portion of the attack."

"Put it up."

As soon as the admiral saw the missile, he said, "No wonder, that's a Meteor, and it was designed to handle everything from next-gen aircraft to ballistic missiles, but I didn't think they were even in production yet. And what the hell happened to the reinforcements?"

"They'll be on station in about twenty minutes, but they'll have to be refueled before they can engage."

"Contact the ground commanders and have them hold up."

"Everyone but General Richardson's column has already halted."

"If they're holding their own let them keep at it."

General Richardson's command was approaching the border, and he'd sent the 160th Special Operations Aviation Regiment MH-60 Black Hawks on ahead to secure the bridges they needed to continue their advance.

"There they are," Major Burnside said as the two bridges came into sight.

As the line of Black Hawks separated and prepared to drop the rangers, nothing seemed out of the ordinary.

Their gunships had already taken out the sentries, so they were able to land without incident.

"We'll be standing by," Captain Hurd said as Major Burnside exited the chopper.

"Affirmative, but you're sitting ducks out here," Major Burnside said. "You can wait at that abandoned truck stop we just passed."

Once the helicopters were gone, Major Burnside said, "I want two machine gun teams on either side of the approaches to cover the Javelin teams. Lieutenant Turk, spread your Stinger teams out along both bridges."

After he'd gotten the teams lined out, Major Burnside decided to get Captain Hurd to do a quick recon of the area.

"Red One to Air One, come in please."

After he'd tried several times, he asked, "What the hell is wrong with the radio?"

The sergeant did an equipment check and said, "The equipment's fine."

The Canadian forces were hidden on the other side of the river, and when the helicopters had gone, Captain Froude, General Boulanger's aide, said, "We've got all of their communication channels blocked."

"Excellent, send the order to execute," General Boulanger said.

A minute later, two squadrons of the escort version of the Eurocopter Tiger attack helicopter swooped down on the bridges from both directions. "We've got incoming," Lieutenant Turk said.

The choppers were flying side by side about twenty meters above the river, and when they opened up with their 30 mm cannons, it sent the rangers scrambling for cover.

"Let them have it," Lieutenant Turk said as he retrieved an FIM-92F missile tube from one of his men lying dead on the bridge, but before he could launch it, a 30 mm round decapitated him.

"Focus your fire on their missile teams," the commander of the Eurocopter squadron said when he saw two of his choppers explode and cartwheel into the river.

General Boulanger watched the American rangers valiantly trying to fight off their assault for almost ten minutes before he ordered, "Captain Deschaine, send your teams in."

They'd concealed sixteen LAV-25s nearby, and their exhausts spewed black diesel smoke as they surged forward and opened fire with their 25 mm M242 Bushmaster chain guns and their twin M240 7.62 mm machine guns.

"If you don't get that damned radio working, we're screwed," Major Burnside said as he ducked behind a bridge rail.

"I'm doing the best I—" the radio operator was saying when a burst of 25 mm cannon shells ripped him almost in half.

Ten minutes later, Captain Deschaine said, "The bridges are clear, but I hated killing all those good men."

"They didn't leave us any choice, but check for survivors before you go."

General Richardson's column wasn't encountering any serious resistance as they raced up the Autoroute Robert-Cliche toward Quebec City, but as they neared the river crossing, he realized Captain Richardson hadn't checked in on time.

"Are we having communication issues?" General Richardson asked.

"Let me check," replied Captain Metz, General Richardson's aide.

A couple of minutes later he said, "Sorry for the delay, but they've been jamming our communication channels for almost thirty minutes."

"Shit, step on it," General Richardson told his driver.

"Thank God," General Richardson said when he saw that the Pierre Laporte and the Quebec Bridges over the Saint Lawrence River were still standing.

"Major Todd, secure the Pierre Laporte Bridge," General Richardson said. "Major Rickles, secure the Quebec Bridge, and find out what's up with Major Burnside."

"It looks like Major Burnside did his job," Captain Metz said.

"I'm glad, because we really need those bridges."

The reinforcements were almost halfway across the bridges when Captain Deschaine said, "Blow the bridges and fall back."

When their sappers triggered the explosives, the thunderous explosions reverberated up and down the river. The series of carefully placed charges took out the bases of both bridges, and General Richardson watched in horror as the bridges collapsed into the river.

Simultaneously, the Canadian soldiers dug in on the other side of the river, and opened fire with mortars and heavy machine guns.

"Sir, you should take cover," Captain Metz said, after a mortar round landed less than fifty yards from the command vehicle.

General Richardson didn't respond until he'd finished scanning the other side of the river with his field glasses.

"Okay, we can go now," General Richardson said to his driver. "Let's go back to that truck stop we passed a ways back, and I'll set up my command post there."

"Major Gar, concentrate your fire along the riverbank," General Richardson said as they left.

"Yes, sir," replied Major Gar, the commander of the column's armored battalion.

As the American tanks began shelling the Canadian forces with their M256A1 120 mm smoothbore guns, the Canadian tank commander, Colonel Gagnon said, "Target their trucks and mobile artillery batteries."

When the Canadians' Leopard 2A7+ main battle tanks open up with their Rheinmetall 120 mm L/55 smoothbore cannons, their shells tore huge gaps in the Americans' miles-long line of vehicles.

As effective as they were being, Colonel Gagnon realized they didn't have the manpower to stem the Americans' advance for long.

"Keep moving, they've started to bug out," Major Gar said when he saw the Canadian forces begin their retreat.

General Boulanger waited until the Americans' armor had entered their predetermined field of fire before he said, "All batteries open fire, and fire for effect." He had prepositioned their heavily camouflaged M777 Howitzers twenty kilometers away, and when the barrage of 155 mm Excalibur GPS-guided munitions was added to the Leopard's fire, the effects were devastating. However, the general had realized they'd be wiped out if they tried to slug it out. So they had the artillery pieces mounted on flatbed trailers, and when they'd fired sixty rounds each, the fleet of Volvo tractor-trailers hauled ass. The Leopards pulled out at the same time, but their top speed was only 45 mph so they hadn't gotten very far when the next wave of F-16s arrived.

"There they are," said Major Grubbs, the squadron commander. "Alpha squadron will take the lead, and the rest of you follow in order."

Fifteen kilometers farther down the road, the Canadians had prepositioned five SAMP/T Aster 30 SAM missile batteries to cover the tanks' retreat.

"Fire all missiles," Colonel Tremblay said when they had radar lock.

Each of the Aster units had two trucks carrying eight ready-to-fire missiles, and ten seconds later they'd fired all eighty of their Aster 30 block 1 missiles.

"Reload and prepare to move out on my command," Colonel Tremblay said.

As Major Grubbs's squadron descended through twenty thousand feet, his missile warning sounded.

"Missiles, take evasive action, but continue pressing the attack."

The countryside was soon littered with the burnt and twisted airframes of the destroyed aircraft, but sixteen of the aircraft had managed to evade the missiles.

The surviving F-16s were down to five thousand feet when the Canadian rangers unleashed the Mistral missiles mounted to their Renault ACMAT trucks.

"Shit, more SAMs," the lead pilot said just before one of the missiles blew the tail of his aircraft off.

"All tank commanders report," Colonel Gagnon said.

"Eight Leopards destroyed, and three damaged," Captain Troupe said.

"We're moving out, but I'm leaving you two trucks," Colonel Gagnon said. "If you can't get the damaged units moving in the next twenty minutes, destroy them and follow us," Colonel Gagnon said.

When they didn't receive an update from Major Grubbs, General Richardson said, "Colonel Peters, take a couple of your birds forward and find out what the hell is going on."

"I'm on it," replied Lieutenant Colonel Peters, the squadron commander of the AH-64D Longbow helicopters.

An hour later, Colonel Peters returned for a face-to-face briefing with General Richardson.

"Well?" General Richardson asked.

"They've taken a burnt earth approach as they're retreating northward."

"I expected that. They're still jamming most of our frequencies; was that why we haven't been able to contact the rest of our air cover?"

"That might be some of it, but from what we just saw, most of them have been shot down."

"They're all dead?"

"Not all, we picked up six fighter jockeys that managed to eject, and there're probably more."

"Major Greely, have Major Spring get his recon forces out there and see what they can find," General Richardson said. "How's your unit doing?" he asked.

"We need to refuel and rearm, but we're in pretty good shape. Do you want us to try to provide air cover?" Colonel Peters asked.

"No, your helicopters wouldn't stand a chance against their aircraft."

"Probably true, but we're willing to try."

"A brave offer, but I'm not moving another inch until we can regain air superiority."

"That makes sense, but it may be easier said than done. One of the pilots we rescued said that he'd never seen that many SAMs."

"I've had several reports like that, but I can't understand how they were that effective against our countermeasures."

"I might have the answer for you. The same pilot was adamant that they were Meteor missiles, but he had to be mistaken, because they never went into production."

"No, he could be right. It was a joint NATO program, and when we dropped out, NATO continued on their own."

"Damn politicians," Colonel Peters said.

"Amen, brother, but to paraphrase Alfred, Lord Tennyson, 'Ours is not to reason why, but to do or die,'" General Richardson said. "But let's get back to work. I need you to find me a bridge that's still intact."

"I've got Admiral Kennedy for you," said Major Greely, General Richardson's aide.

"I know you're in the middle of a shit storm, but I need a status update," Admiral Kennedy said.

"We're just outside of Quebec City, but they've blown both bridges, and if we don't find another one, we'll have to wait for the corps of engineers to put up a temporary bridge."

"Casualties?"

"They've hit us pretty hard, but we've neutralized the immediate threats, and what's left of their forces are retreating northward."

"That's what I'm hearing from the other commands as well, but we sure weren't expecting this much resistance. Whoever put the threat assessment together sure blew it out their ass."

"Big time. Hell, we've lost over fifty percent of our fighter aircraft, and forty percent of our bombers. If I didn't know better, I'd say they had a copy of our battle plans."

"Maybe they did. I doubt that everyone on our team is comfortable with what our fearless leader is doing," Admiral Kennedy said.

"Very true."

"Hang in there, and I'll get you some help when I can."

Chancellor Jefferson was monitoring the operations for the Situation Room in the basement of the White House, but he hadn't had an update in a couple of hours and he was getting impatient.

"Clyde Thomas is upstairs, and he says that it's imperative that he speak with you," Colonel Ridgeway said.

"I'm about to get on a call, but I can give him a few minutes," Chancellor Jefferson said.

"What the hell are you doing in D.C.? You're supposed to be finishing up the construction projects," Chancellor Jefferson said when Clyde walked in.

"That's why I'm here. Several of us really don't like what you're doing."

"Several?! Who else is in this little pity group of yours?"

"Can I sit down?"

"Sure, but who else has concerns?"

Clyde put his briefcase on the table and entered the code to unlock it.

"Quit screwing with that, and answer my question," Chancellor Jefferson said.

Clyde's hands were shaking as he opened the lid and retrieved the silenced 9 mm Beretta. Gun in hand, he stood up to get a clear shot at the chancellor, but before he could get a shot off, Walter pulled his .45 caliber Sig from the holster concealed in the small of his back and put two shots in Clyde's chest and one between his eyes.

Amy Walsh was in the next room and when she heard the gunshots she came running in.

"Oh my God," she said when she saw Clyde bleeding out on the floor.

"Calm down and get Colonel Ridgeway in here, and then I need to see John Jay," Chancellor Jefferson said.

Thirty minutes later, John Jay ambled through the door.

"Two in the chest, one in the head. Classic," John Jay said. "What went down?"

"The bastard tried to kill me," Walter Jefferson said.

"Obviously, but luckily he wasn't very good at his craft," John Jay said.

"Luck had nothing to do with it."

"You want me to take care of the body?"

"Nah, Colonel Ridgeway will dispose of that asshole."

"So what did you need?"

"I want you to take care of the rest of the sorry bastards that were in on this."

"Any thoughts on where to start?"

"I'd start with Willy Wood. Sorry, we'll have to finish this later, because I have to take this call," Chancellor Jefferson said when the videoconference popped up.

"You're late," Walter Jefferson said.

"I had a hard time reaching General Richardson," Admiral Kennedy replied.

"Going that badly?"

"No, in fact, he's done better than the others, but like the other three operations, they've suffered significant causalities."

"Regrettable, but a necessary sacrifice. When do they expect to reach their objectives?"

"The Canadian forces hit us really hard at first, but most of them have started retreating northward toward the Nunavut province and the Northwest Territories."

"That's great, but you still haven't answered my question."

"They should all reach our original objectives in the next forty-eight hours."

"See, that wasn't so hard."

"Do you want us to pursue them?"

The chancellor paused before he said, "Maybe later. First we need to consolidate what we've taken and get the buffer zones properly established."

"Sounds reasonable. Any further thoughts on next steps?"

"Once we've sealed off our northern borders, I want you to move forward with the Mexican campaign."

"Okay, but we've used up a large portion of our air power, so it could get dicey if the Mexicans decide to put up a fight."

"I'll admit that the Canadians' effort surprised me, but South Wind is a better plan, and it's highly unlikely the Mexicans will put up much resistance."

"General Richardson made an odd comment on our call today. He said it almost seemed like they had our battle plans."

"I'm sure it was just his imagination, or maybe he was trying to make excuses for how they struggled against a vastly inferior force."

"That's harsh. He's a good man, and a fine commander."

"Whatever, but all of you need to do a better job with the Mexican operation."

"I know you don't want to hear it, but I tried to warn you that we weren't ready."

"Just get it done, or I'll find someone who can. Where are we at on finding the cabinet members?"

"Nowhere."

"Keep on it, some of those assholes are quite capable of causing trouble."

While Chancellor Jefferson was busy mapping out their next moves, the coalition forces were doing the same.

General Drummond and Aryeh Behrmann were sitting in a second-floor conference room at SHAPE headquarters in Casteau, Belgium, when they called General Boulanger to get an update.

"From the reports we've gotten so far it sounds like you've held your own," General Drummond said.

"We have, but we won't survive another effort like that," General Boulanger replied.

"You should be all right, they're moving on to Mexico," General Drummond said.

"How could you possibly know that?"

"You forget I'm still on the team."

"Even with inside knowledge, I don't see how we can stop them."

"Our only hope is to work together. I know you've lost a lot of aircraft, but we're sending you replacements, and I hope to have a supply chain opened up through Russia within the month."

"The Russians are going to help out?"

"President Gorelov is convinced that Chancellor Jefferson's ambitions extend far beyond our current borders."

"America has never been about subjugating others."

"Times change, and I honestly believe he's closer to Adolf Hitler or Joseph Stalin than he is to Thomas Jefferson."

"I pray that you've misjudged him, but since the Russians are willing to help out, we could use some manpower."

"They've got no shortage of that. I'm also meeting with the UN Security Council on Tuesday, and I'll see what they're willing to do."

"I thought the UN was dead and buried."

"They're going to resume operations next week in the Reichstag building in Germany."

"There's got to be a bit of irony in that," General Boulanger said. "If that's all you need, I need to get on another call."

"How is our Russian facility progressing?" Aryeh Behrmann asked when the general disconnected.

"They finished sweeping the facility for bugs this morning," General Drummond said.

"Was that really necessary?"

"They found over eleven thousand."

"Damn, I guess old habits die hard. So when can we move in?"

"The important stuff is in place, so I've scheduled your aircraft for oh-six-hundred tomorrow morning, and the remainder of the items on your shopping list should arrive in about two weeks."

"Great. I'm going to make my announcement as soon as we have everything in place, but do you have a feel for how it's going to be received by your troops?"

"It's going to be a crapshoot," General Drummond said. "It all hinges on how convincing you are that your new government has validity. I didn't mention this before, because we weren't sure we could pull it off, but we've established end-to-end control of the segment of the NCCCS infrastructure that controls the nukes in Admiral Crawford's commands as well as mine."

"Does that mean you could stop the chancellor from using the weapons?" Aryeh Behrmann asked.

"Affirmative. All of the assets are under our exclusive control, and Admiral Crawford and I have established a new set of protocols for their use."

"That's great news, but there are still a great number of devices under that maniac's control."

"Very true, but it gives us a little bit of leverage."

"I suppose, but I doubt he'd ever believe we'd actually use them."

The next evening, Willy Wood's car and driver were waiting outside when he and his wife left the historic Italian restaurant Barbetta in Times Square. There was a light mist falling when they left the restaurant, and Willy was surprised when his driver didn't get out to open the door for them.

"Just a second, and I'll walk you out," the doorman said as he opened a large umbrella.

"Thanks, Tony," Willy Wood said as he handed him twenty bucks. "See you next week."

"What's the matter, Pete, you afraid of a little rain?" Willy Wood chided his driver as he slid in and closed the back door to the stretch limo. The darkened glass panel separating them from the driver slid open, and John Jay shot Willy's wife in the head with his silenced pistol.

"You murderous bastard," Willy Wood said as he went for his own pistol.

"Don't," John Jay said. "I need you to answer a few questions for me."

"Go to hell," Willy said as he jerked his pistol out.

"Dumb-ass," John Jay said as he pumped two rounds into Willy's head.

"Where have you been?" Chancellor Jefferson asked when John Jay returned to the White House the next morning.

"I was in New York city trying to clean up after General Lehman."

"How's that going?"

"Not that well. I had to kill Willy Wood before he could tell me anything."

"Oh well, here's a complete list of the militia leaders and where they're located."

"Any that you couldn't live without?"

Walter mulled over his answer for a second or two before he said, "Nah."

CHAPTER 29

The next day Admiral Kennedy was at the White House for an afternoon meeting with Chancellor Jefferson. When Admiral Kennedy sat down in the Situation Room across from the chancellor, he said, "I need to tell you something before we get started."

"It had better be good news," Chancellor Jefferson said.

"Not so much. We've lost control of all of our offshore nuclear assets."

"What the hell does that even mean?"

"We can't launch them, and we couldn't prevent them from being used against us."

"I didn't think that could happen."

"They had to have inside help to do it, but the bottom line is that it's been done."

"It's those damned combat commanders again. Oh well, I'll deal with them later. How's South Wind coming along?"

"We'll be ready in twelve days."

"Why are you still dragging your feet on this?"

"I'm not, I just don't want to go off half-cocked like last time."

"Whatever, but it had better not get delayed again."

Later that week, General Drummond was holding a

planning session with the NATO commanders in the ad hoc command center they'd set up in one of the larger conference rooms at SHAPE headquarters.

"Chancellor Jefferson's forces are scheduled to move on Mexico in eight days," General Drummond said.

"I'd hoped for more time," said General Thibault Beauregard.

"How are we coming with the supplies and reinforcements?"

"The SAM batteries were delivered last week, and the artillery should be in place today."

"Manpower?"

"We have four divisions of Brazilian troops, and two from Argentina," Lieutenant General Terrance Couturier said.

"How about air support?"

"We couldn't scrape up everything you requested, but we've managed to deliver four squadrons of Dassault Rafale B fighters, and two squadrons of the Eurofighter Typhoons."

"Were you able to work out anything with President Perez's team?" General Fredrick Fenstermacher asked.

"Yes, General Aguilar and I put together a strategy much like the one we used in Canada," General Sir Richard McConnell said. "The hope is that the American forces will react as they did in Canada."

"I'm not comfortable hoping for the same outcome," General Drummond said.

"Do you have any other options that you'd care to share?" General Thibault Beauregard asked.

"Point taken," General Drummond said. "Weren't the Israelis sending some hardware?"

"They did, but the bulk of it isn't going to make it in time," General Fredrick Fenstermacher said. "However, a couple of lasers made it, so we'll try them out during the San Diego attack."

"Time will tell, but I believe they made a grave tactical error when they expanded the operation to five divisions," General Drummond said. "It doesn't leave them with any reserves, and they don't have nearly enough aircraft to maintain air superiority."

Eight days later, Admiral Kennedy was sitting in the Pentagon's operations center when he said, "All units report."

"South Wind One is in position and awaiting orders," said General Leroy Tuttle, the commanding officer of the Tijuana division.

"South Wind Two is in position and ready to go," reported General Raymond Ramirez, the commander of the Nogales division.

"South Wind Three is good to go," said General Teddy Peterson, the commander of the Ciudad Juarez division.

"South Wind Four awaiting orders," announced General William Strong, the commanding officer of the Del Rio division.

"South Wind Five, standing by," said General Perry Miller, the leader of the Nuevo Laredo division.

"All commands, execute," ordered Admiral Kennedy.

They'd been assembling their forces for weeks, so the American commanders knew the Mexican army was expecting their attacks. As the South Wind operation kicked off, the aircraft squadrons assigned to each division launched their first sorties to clear the path for their armored forces.

An hour into the Tijuana operation General Tuttle asked, "How are the sorties progressing?"

"We've lost a couple of aircraft to ground fire, but we haven't encountered any enemy aircraft yet," U.S. Air Force Colonel Smily said.

"How about their ground forces?" General Tuttle asked.

"We've destroyed a small armored column, as well

as their artillery batteries, and it looks like the rest of them are bugging out."

"You're good to go, Colonel Faust," General Tuttle said.

"Roger that, we're rolling," replied Colonel Faust, the tank commander.

The sixty-five M1 Abrams main battle tanks belched black smoke as they fired up their powerful gas turbines and lurched forward toward the Mexican border.

"The Americans have just crossed the border and they're headed straight for you," Lieutenant Alfonso of the Mexican army reported.

"Are they following the route we're expecting?" Colonel Soto asked.

"Affirmative."

"Pull back to checkpoint three."

The Abramses were eight miles into Mexico when Colonel Soto ordered, "Let them have it."

Their antitank weapons had an effective range of several thousand yards, but Lieutenant Perez waited until the column of tanks was only fifteen hundred yards from his men before he radioed, "All units, open fire."

His men were working in the fields, disguised as farmhands, and when they got Lieutenant Perez's order they quickly removed the camouflage from their tripod-mounted antitank missiles and opened fire.

Colonel Faust was in the lead tank, and when he saw the swarm of missiles coming at them, he cried, "My God, where's that coming from?"

"Phase one complete. We're pulling back to the next checkpoint," Lieutenant Perez said after they'd fired all their missiles.

"All units commence phase two," Colonel Soto ordered.

The next layer of their defense was being commanded by Lieutenant Bustos and they were using the

MBDA MILAN 3/ADT/ER missiles that NATO had shipped them. As the remaining Abramses moved into range, Lieutenant Bustos's men began picking them off.

"Colonel Faust's column is reporting heavy casualties," Major Hoyer said.

"From what? They don't have any air cover and they don't have any armor," General Tuttle said.

"I don't know, he got cut off before he could elaborate."

"Get someone out there to find out what the hell is going on."

Twenty-five minutes later, Major Hoyer returned. "I've got Colonel Faust's XO, Major Leslie for you."

"What the hell is going on out there?" General Tuttle asked.

"When we first crossed the border we were ambushed by a large body of infantry using some sort of tripod-mounted antitank weapons. We fought through the first group, but we're still coming under heavy fire, and we've lost over half of our units."

"Totally unacceptable, and why isn't Colonel Faust making this report?"

"He was killed in the first volley."

"Congratulations, you're now a colonel, and you're in charge," General Tuttle said.

"Yes, sir," Colonel Leslie said. "What are your orders?'

"If they're taking out Abramses, I need to know what they're using."

"I'll get you a report ASAP."

"See that you do, and we can't afford to lose any more tanks, so hold where you are until I can get some gunships in there to provide air cover. Major Hoyer, contact Colonel Robinson, and have him get some of his gunships out there."

A half an hour later, Major Hoyer said, "Colonel Leslie needs to talk with you."

"What did you find out?" General Tuttle asked.

"They're using MILAN 3/ADT/ER missile systems."

"That's some pretty sophisticated stuff. I didn't think they were even in production."

"I don't know about that, but that's what my guy says they are."

"I'll take your word for it, and your air cover should be there shortly."

"Sir, I've got one more thing I'd like to share with you."

"Go."

"Most of them weren't regular army."

"Great, now you're going to tell me that a bunch of peasants kicked the shit out of you."

"My liaison officer from the Mexican army says that they're members of the Padaras cartel."

"Cartel? Is he sure?"

"The bodies all bore the distinctive cartel tattoos, and he swears that no nonmember would dare wear that ink."

"Shit, the cartels are a lot better funded and armed than the Mexican army, and we sure as hell weren't expecting them to work together.

"Major, I need Admiral Kennedy," General Tuttle said.

"How's the operation going?" Admiral Kennedy asked.

"Not well. We've already lost over half of our Abramses."

"I thought you were going to use airstrikes to clear out their armor."

"We did. This was infantry, armed with antitank missiles."

"That's hard to believe."

"I know, but it looks like NATO has been feeding them arms, because they're using the next-gen MILAN 3/ADT/ER missiles."

"That would do it," Admiral Kennedy said. "I'll give the other groups a heads-up. Anything else?"

"The Padaras cartel has joined the fight."

"Crap. We'll just have to show them the error of their ways. Any more good news?"

"No, but we should be back on schedule before nightfall."

All the columns had armor except for General Miller's Nuevo Laredo division, but Admiral Kennedy had planned a major air campaign to assist them.

"This is Red One. We are inbound and will be on target in five," said Colonel Laramie, the commander of the B-52 squadron.

"We have twenty heavies, two hundred kilometers out," said Major Cardenas, the commander of the Soviet S-400 Triumf launch vehicles.

"Fire on lock," Colonel Burgos said.

Eleven seconds later there were thirty-two missiles on their way toward the incoming bombers. The B-52s were opening their bomb bay doors to begin carpet bombing the Mexican forces when their missile warnings began sounding their strident alerts.

"All aircraft launch countermeasures and begin evasive maneuvers," Colonel Laramie ordered.

The squadron deployed their flares and chaff as ordered, but by the time they had a visual on the incoming Soviet 40N6 missiles the lumbering bombers had no chance. The Russian missiles decimated the B-52 squadron, but the commander of the Mexican forces didn't realize that the remainder of the American aircraft was coming in nap-of-the-earth over the gulf. The squadron of B1B bombers, or "the Bone," as it had been nicknamed, released their weapons at their maximum effective range.

"Damn, I think that's the first time I've ever seen a whole squadron go Winchester on someone," Major

Easley said as they turned and accelerated toward their next objectives.

"Stay off the radio," Colonel Loomis said.

The squadron commander monitored the weapons until they impacted the unsuspecting enemy positions.

"We've neutralized their SAM batteries, said Colonel Loomis, the commander of the stealth bombers. " We're moving on to our next objectives."

"Roger that, but we lost contact with Colonel Laramie's command. Have you seen any sign of them?" asked General Miller, the commander of the Nuevo Laredo operation.

"Possibly. We were seeing a lot of smoke coming from what looked like crash sites."

"How about your team?"

"I've had to send two aircraft back to base due to equipment malfunctions, but we're still combat effective."

"Attention all commands, execute phase two," General Miller said.

As their light assault vehicles and ground troops surged forward, they didn't meet any meaningful resistance for the first three hours. However, as they started the fourth hour of the operation, General Hermosa launched his counterattack.

"Heads up, you've got multiple vehicles approaching from the west," reported Sergeant Walton, the lead scout.

"How many?" Major Clark asked.

"At least a hundred, but it could be a lot more. I'll—"

"Sergeant, come back, you got cut off."

After multiple tries, Major Clark said. "All units halt, and prepare for an attack."

The leading edges of the American column were crossing a small stream when they received the order to halt.

"All units, return to this side of the stream," Major Clark said.

As the officers tried to get their men reorganized, the Mexican army's lead elements came flying over the small hill in front of them. They were in everything from Humvees to converted dune buggies, but they were all sporting either a heavy machine gun or a rocket launcher mounted to the tops of their vehicles.

"All units open fire," Major Clark said.

The din from the explosions and gunfire was deafening, but the skirmish was over within twenty minutes as the Mexican army retreated over the hilltop.

"Cease fire," Major Clark said. "All unit commanders report.

"Yes, sir, that's right, we've managed to beat off their counterattack, and we've only suffered thirty causalities," Major Clark said.

"We're behind schedule, so you need to get moving," General Miller said.

"I really could use some air support."

"There's two squadrons of F-16s inbound, and I've got two AC-130W Stingers headed your way."

"We've slowed them down," said Captain Hernandez, the commander of the Mexican counterattack.

"Fall back to your next checkpoint, and await further orders," Colonel Jimenez said.

"Is everyone in position?" Colonel Jimenez asked his aide.

"Awaiting orders," Lieutenant Garza said.

"You're free to engage when you have a target," Colonel Jimenez said.

"I've got thirty-six aircraft approaching from the east, and they're thirty kilometers out, at an altitude of forty kilometers," Lieutenant Padilla reported.

"Fire on lock," Captain Rojas said.

Within seconds, their S-400 SAM systems had launched all of their missiles.

Almost simultaneously, the American squadron commander ordered, "All aircraft fire on my command." A few minutes later Colonel Lewis said, "Fire."

"We've got multiple missiles inbound," Lieutenant Padilla said a few seconds later.

"Ready the lasers," Colonel Jimenez said.

"Standing by."

"Make sure the units are on auto-tracking, and initiate," Colonel Jimenez said.

They only had two of the Rafael Advanced Defense Systems' Iron Beam systems, and they had no idea what to expect. The Iron Beam systems started firing as soon as they had radar lock, and in less than sixty seconds all of the incoming missiles had been destroyed.

"Damned impressive," Colonel Jimenez said.

Colonel Lewis never knew their attack had failed, because the Russian 40N6 missiles had already decimated the two squadrons of F-16s.

General Antonio Fernandez had been keeping his aircraft in reserve, waiting for the appropriate time to commit them.

"Are our aircraft in position?" General Fernandez asked when he received the news that they'd successfully fended off the American airstrikes.

"On station, and awaiting orders."

"All units attack," General Antonio Fernandez ordered.

General Fernandez was only forty-five years old, and his meteoric rise through the ranks had been fueled by his savagery and single-minded determination to control the cartels.

In addition to the S-400 missile systems, President Gorelov had sent them fourteen of their fifth-generation fighters to supplement the NATO aircraft. Much like the F-22 Raptor, the Russian Sukhoi T-50 PAK-FA had been built as an air superiority fighter, and they had been a welcome addition to their capabilities.

"Target is in range," Russian Colonel Joseph Vereshchagin said. "Fire all missiles, and follow me," he ordered.

Each of the T-50s carried eight X-38 GLONASS satellite guided missiles, tipped with cluster bomb warheads. Like the aircraft, the missiles presented little to no radar signature, so General Miller's command post never realized they were in danger until the missiles reduced his command post and everything surrounding it into a blazing inferno.

An hour later, Major Hoyer returned and said, "I've got the sitrep you requested."

"What the hell took so long?" Admiral Kennedy asked.

"Sorry, but I wanted to gather a complete picture before I got back to you."

"Let's hear it, and start with General Miller's command."

"That's what held us up. We couldn't reach his command until a few minutes ago."

"I needed to know that."

"I understand, but the solar flares are playing havoc with our communication channels, so we assumed it was just a glitch."

"So what the hell is going on down there?"

"A few hours after they launched their operation, General Miller and his entire staff were killed in an airstrike."

"What happened? We've got complete air superiority, and I know that he'd set up a robust SAM site to protect his command post."

"I can't answer that."

"Let's hear the rest of it."

"General Tuttle's command has met unexpectedly

stiff resistance, but Generals Ramirez, Peterson, and Strong are reporting light to no resistance, and expect to reach their first day objectives ahead of schedule."

"That's a bit of good news. Any updates on Tuttle's situation?"

"They've upped their initial loss estimates to sixty-six percent of their tanks destroyed, with another ten percent damaged but repairable."

"Leave me what you've got and I'll go through it, but before you go, I need you to schedule a call with Chancellor Jefferson for twenty-one hundred," he said.

"I apologize for the hour, but I wanted to have my shit together before I briefed you," Admiral Kennedy said when he made contact with the White House Situation Room.

"Not an issue," Chancellor Jefferson said. "I've been following the operation's progress all day."

"Then you already know about General Miller's death?"

"A regrettable loss."

"It is, and we've lost the bulk of his staff as well."

"What's your plan?"

"I've already dispatched Lieutenant General Benjamin Lacy to assume his command."

"The commander of the special operations group?"

"That's right, and he's a damn good man."

"How soon can he take over?"

"He'll be there by morning. I've already briefed him on the situation, and he's bringing his staff with him, so they should hit the ground running. I ordered him to stay off the front lines, because we can't afford to lose any more senior officers."

"Good, but we need to get this wrapped up quickly."

After the general had spent another forty-five minutes covering where they were, they called it a night.

"That didn't sound too bad," John Jay said.

"I suppose it could have been worse," Chancellor Jefferson said. "How are we progressing with the next phase of the camps?"

"Fine, but the shit is going to hit the fan when their real purpose becomes known."

"Screw them. By then it will be too late to stop us."

General Lacy's helicopter touched down near what was left of General Miller's command post a little after sunrise.

"Welcome to hell, General," Major Bowers said as he saluted General Lacy.

"It sure sounded like you boys have been getting your asses kicked."

"A bit of an understatement," Major Bowers said.

"Well, we're going to put a stop to that. Major Bowers, you've done an admirable job, but this is my XO Colonel Downey, and he and his team are going to take over."

"Just let me know if there's anything I can do to ease the transition," Major Bowers said. "Most of our communications gear was destroyed in the attack, but I'll see what I can scrounge up."

"That won't be necessary. I've been ordered to set up my command post on our side of the border, so I'm only going to be here for a short time."

"Colonel Downey, what sort of equipment are you going to want?" Major Bowers asked.

"I like to stay mobile, so I won't be working out of a command center," Colonel Downey said.

"Colonel, have we received the satellite photos I requested?" General Lacy asked after the major had left.

"They should be in your in-box."

"Where the hell did they get gear like that?" Colonel Downey asked as they viewed the high-resolution images.

"The analyst report said most of it was from NATO,

but that Israel and Russia have both kicked in," General Lacy said.

"Damn, there's nothing like taking on the whole world."

"That's what happens when you turn your back on your friends," General Lacy said.

"Are we backing the wrong play?" Colonel Downey asked.

"We can have *that* discussion another time. Right now we need to get this situation stabilized. You need to get your best officers out there on the front lines to make sure nobody loses their nerve."

"Right away."

"I've got to get my ass back to Laredo, but I'll call you first thing in the morning," General Lacy said.

"General Lacy has assumed command of the American forces," Colonel Jimenez said.

"Then you'd better warn our commanders to stay alert, because he's an aggressive son of a bitch," General Fernandez said. "I remember what he did to clean up that mess in Venezuela, and he's not going to sit on his hands waiting for orders."

"Were you up all night?" Colonel Downey asked as they started their videoconference the next morning.

"I got a couple hours of sleep," General Lacy said. "I've sent you a file of what I've come up with. Look it over, and let me know what you think."

After several minutes, Colonel Downey asked, "You did all of this last night?"

"What do you think?"

"We're going to be badly outnumbered, so would you mind filling in the blanks?"

"Since we don't have any heavy armor, we'll use your M117 Guardians to make a frontal attack on their main body."

"Their infantry has had great success against our armor."

"I'm counting on them committing their reserves, and as soon as they do, you'll execute a double-envelopment maneuver. You'll have twenty-five Downeys, and seventy-five 6X6 Cougar MRAPs for the left and right flank, and the Downeys will provide covering fire while they unload the infantry."

"Which puts the Mexicans in a crossfire," Colonel Downey said.

"Exactly."

"I like it, but you're definitely not leaving me anything in reserve."

"I'm not, but if we do this right, we can finish them off."

"When do we go?"

"Yesterday would be good."

"Got it."

A couple of hours later, Colonel Jimenez interrupted General Fernandez's briefing. "The American forces are on the move."

"Where?" General Fernandez asked.

"The main body is on Highway 850, headed toward Monterrey."

"I didn't think they'd recover this quickly. Is everyone ready?"

"In position, but I don't like depending on Joaquin Moreno Lazcano's men."

"Why not? They've stood up to everything we've thrown at them," General Fernandez said.

"And now you're going to trust them with something this important?"

"Joaquin may be a lot of things, but he never reneges on a deal."

"Get ready, here they come," said Pablo Velasquez,

the leader of the Lazcano cartel's men. "Now," he yelled over his headset.

As the massive IEDs they'd positioned along the highway detonated, the first eight ASVs disintegrated into thousands of pieces of hot metal fragments.

"Go around that, and keep moving," Major Leadbetter said when he saw the cloud of fire and smoke from the explosions.

"They're not stopping," Ricardo Garza said.

"All units execute," Major Leadbetter ordered.

As they began their double flanking maneuver, the Guardian's auto loading 105 mm M68A2 cannons were firing six rounds a minute at the enemy's front line, and the Downeys unleashed a hail of bullets from their M2 .50 caliber machine guns.

When Major Leadbetter saw the MRAPs pause to start unloading the assault troops, he signaled the Downeys that were outfitted with MK19 40 mm grenade launchers to open fire.

As the American mortar shells began hitting his line, Pablo Velasquez said, "Mortars open fire."

The cartel's 60 mm mortars had been deployed to give them an almost hundred-meter field of fire on either side of the roadway, and as the mortar rounds began pounding the countryside they were exacting a heavy toll on the American forces.

By then the Guardians had finished reloading, so Major Leadbetter said, "All Guardian units, target those mortar positions, and fire for effect."

As the 105 mm rounds tore through the Mexicans' mortar teams, their rate of fire fell off quickly.

Pablo Velasquez had almost ten thousand men hiding in the brush, and when he saw the tide of the battle turning on him, he ordered, "All units attack."

The cartel members were armed with everything from RPG-32s, M16s, AR15s, and AK-47s to a mix of hunting rifles and pistols, and although they weren't soldiers, they were all combat veterans who'd been hardened by years of pitched battles against the Mexican army.

"Major Tribble, dismount the rest of your troops," Major Leadbetter said when he saw the wave of ad hoc infantry charging at them.

Each of the hundred and fifty MRAPs carried eight heavily armed special operations troops, but they were badly outnumbered.

"We're getting our ass kicked out here," Major Leadbetter said.

"Hang in there, help's on the way," Colonel Downey said.

The Americans were taking a horrific toll on the cartel's forces, but they were suffering heavy casualties as well, as they were being steadily driven back toward their vehicles.

"Have your men take cover," Colonel Downey said.

A few seconds later a stick of GBU 39 bombs from the two AC 130s ripped a fiery path through the cartel's ranks, and before the dust could settle, four A10 Warthogs opened fire with their 30 mm cannons. The Warthogs tore huge gaps in the cartel's infantry before the Mexicans used their Russian-made 9K32 Strela-2 rocket launchers to shoot them down.

"All units pull back," Pablo Velasquez said. "Garza, jammers on."

After several attempts to contact Colonel Tompkins, Major Leadbetter said, "This is Major Leadbetter. If you can hear us, we've got them on the run, and we're going after them to finish them off."

They had a drone over the area so Colonel Downey could follow the action, and when he saw them going after them, he said, "Major Leadbetter, hold your position. Do not follow them."

After several more attempts, Colonel Tompkins said, "Captain Spade, what's wrong with this damn radio?"

The captain ran out to get a technician, while the colonel continued observing the action on the screen.

"Damn," Colonel Downey said when the saw the shoulder-fired antiaircraft missile coming at the drone.

After a couple of minutes, Captain Spade returned and said, "The equipment's fine, they're jamming all of our frequencies."

"Lieutenant Travis, get out there and tell them to hold where they are. Captain Spade, check and see if we have another drone."

As Major Ledbetter's forces closed in on the retreating cartel troops, they entered the small valley. Pablo Velasquez waited until the hard-charging Americans were inside the kill zone before he said, "Execute operation Tabula Rasa."

When the ATVs burst out of the dense brush to cut off their retreat, Major Leadbetter said, "Look out, they're behind us.

"I've stepped in it this time," he muttered when he saw the ATVs fire their first salvo of antitank missiles.

"Command, we're surrounded, and under heavy fire, and I need immediate air support," Major Leadbetter said.

When the ATVs paused to reload, the infantry concealed on the hillsides began laying down a murderous crossfire with their Russian Kord heavy machine guns.

Pablo Velasquez watched the carnage unfold for several minutes before he said, "Cease fire. Move in, and make sure they're all dead.

"*Jefe,* your plan worked to perfection," Pablo Velasquez said.

"Good. Make sure you leave a rearguard, and then get your ass back here," Joaquin Moreno Lazcano replied.

"My men have stopped their advance," Lazcano said.

"I owe you one," General Fernandez replied.

"Way more than one, and rest assured I'll collect."

"Lieutenant Travis is back," Captain Spade said an hour later.

"Send him in," Colonel Downey said.

"We had to make a run for it, but from what we could see, Major Ledbetter's command has been wiped out."

"Wiped out?"

"They were totally surrounded, and they couldn't have survived the kind of fire they were taking."

"Captain Spade, have all units halt and dig in," Colonel Downey said. "And I need General Lacy ASAP.

"We've suffered heavy losses and I've been forced to halt the operation," Colonel Downey said when he finally reached General Lacy.

"We had a good plan, what the hell happened?" General Lacy said.

"The flanking maneuver worked, but they suckered Major Leadbetter into an ambush."

"Damn, the admiral is going to have some explaining to do."

CHAPTER 30

Two days later, General Drummond was meeting with the NATO commanders in one of the SHAPE briefing rooms when Colonel Lee came in and said, "I've got the White House on videoconference in the Situation Room, and Chancellor Jefferson is demanding to speak with you."

"Didn't you tell him I was in a staff meeting?" General Drummond asked.

"Of course, but he said it was imperative that he speak with you immediately."

"It's about time," Chancellor Jefferson said when General Drummond sat down in front of the camera.

"Sorry, I was tied up," General Drummond said.

"I don't give a shit about your petty little meetings. I've just found out that you and Admiral Crawford have illegally seized control of the nuclear assets within your commands."

"We decided it was a prudent course of action."

"You may be the head of the NATO forces, but this is way out of your pay grade, and I demand that you immediately return control of the weapons."

"Not going to happen."

"You, sir, are relieved of your command."

"Again, not going to happen."

"You impertinent bastard, you will stand down."

"That's not your call anymore," Aryeh Behrmann said.

"Who the hell is that talking?" Chancellor Jefferson asked.

"The duly appointed president of the United States," Aryeh Behrmann said as he stepped into the camera's view.

"Behrmann! I'd hoped you were dead, but who died and made you president?"

"That would be President Richard Wilkes, and I've been sworn in by the chief justice of the Supreme Court, Christopher Doubleday."

"There's not a chance in hell that I'll let you return. In fact, I'm going to track down every one of you bastards and kill you. Hell, I'm going to kill your families and everyone in your bloodlines while I'm at it."

"We may have to serve in absentia for the time being, but no matter the cost, we're all committed to returning democracy to our nation.

"He hung up on me," President Behrmann said. "You don't think he was serious about killing our families, do you?"

"You're joking, right?" General Drummond asked. "The slimy little bastard would murder his own mother to stay in power."

"Then we need to relocate all of our families before he can carry out his threats," President Behrmann said.

"About that. I had a bad feeling about how this would play out. So when we started picking up the people on your list, I had the teams pick up every family member we could locate."

"Mine too?"

"Absolutely."

"Why haven't I seen any of them around here?"

"We decided it would be best to take them directly

to Russia," General Drummond said. "Now that the chancellor knows, when are you going to announce your presidency to the rest of the world?"

"I've got a couple of things I need to take care of first."

"When you're ready I'll contact President De Smet and make the arrangements for the broadcast."

When President Behrmann hesitated, the general asked, "Is there something else I should be aware of?"

"I wasn't sure that I was going to accept President Gorelov's offer of asylum, but this puts a new light on it, so I'm going to go ahead and relocate, but I don't want anyone to know yet."

"COLONEL RIDGEWAY, FIND John Jay and have him come down to the Situation Room," Chancellor Jefferson said when he'd hung up on President Behrmann.

"What's up, boss?" John Jay asked.

"I just had a conversation with the new president of the United States."

"What?"

"I said that I just talked with the newly appointed president of the United States."

"Impossible, everyone on the presidential succession list is dead."

"So we thought, but it seems Secretary of State Behrmann has survived, and he's been rebuilding the government in absentia."

"A fat lot of good that's going to do him. We've got complete control of the government."

"We'd better, because he's got a valid claim to the office. Get with the NSA, and have them find out where he's hiding."

"Sure, boss, but what then?"

"That will depend on where he's hiding.

"Colonel Ridgeway, I need Admiral Kennedy," Chancellor Jefferson said.

"Did we have a call scheduled?" Admiral Kennedy asked when he answered the phone.

"No, but there's something you need to know," Chancellor Jefferson said. When he'd finished explaining the situation, he asked, "Admiral, are you still there?"

"Sorry, but that was a lot to take in. Are you going to abdicate?"

"Hell no. I'm not going to let anyone take away everything I've worked for."

"But he has a valid claim."

"That might have been true in the past, but I'm not going to allow anything or anyone to derail my plans, and Admiral, I'm counting on your continued support."

"I'll hold up my end of the deal, but there are going to be a lot of people who will want you to step aside."

"People in hell want ice water. Just make sure you keep your people in line."

"I'll do what I can."

"That sure didn't sound like a solid vote of confidence," John Jay said.

"No, it didn't, but it could have been worse. Keep an eye on him, and if he starts wavering, deal with it."

Six weeks later, John Jay caught Chancellor Jefferson as he got off the elevator in the basement level underneath the West Wing.

"You're up awfully early," Chancellor Jefferson said.

"I wanted to make sure you'd seen the announcement about Aryeh Behrmann's press conference tonight," John Jay said.

"I learned about it last night, but President De Smet refused to cancel it."

"Great, more allies for Behrmann. We knew NATO

was helping him, and if the rumors are true so is Russia."

"Along with the majority of the member nations of the UN Security Council."

"That's a hell of a lot of firepower to take on. What are you going to do about it?" John Jay asked.

"Not much I can do, other than stay the course. They all depend on trade with us, and this newfound enthusiasm for Behrmann will fade once it starts hurting their pocketbooks."

"I thought your press conference went well," President Gorelov said when President Behrmann walked out of the Russian broadcast center. "But why didn't you allow any reporters to attend in person?"

"I don't want Chancellor Jefferson to know that I'm in Russia."

"So that's why you had us reroute the transmission to look like it was originating in Brussels?"

"Exactly."

"A little paranoid?"

"It was really my brother's idea. He's convinced that I could be in danger."

"That explains it, he's the most paranoid person I've ever met."

"Not without reason. There have been sixteen attempts on his life during the two years he's been prime minister."

"I had no idea."

"He's taken great care to keep that quiet, and I shouldn't have mentioned it."

"His secret is safe with me. How did you feel the press conference went?"

"As well as could be expected," President Behrmann said. "I was hoping for a few more questions, but it could have been because they were having to call their questions in."

"Possibly, but I did get the sense that they were taken aback by your announcement."

"I didn't feel like I had a choice."

"You didn't, and I think the world is starting to understand the risks that madman represents."

"Trust me, it keeps me awake at night."

"How's the Mexican operation going?" President Gorelov asked.

"We've stopped them for now, but it wouldn't have happened if several of the cartels hadn't joined in."

"I thought the Mexican government was going to back you?"

"They have, but their troops are poorly trained, and I don't think that they have the stomach for an all-out war with the United States."

"Who does? For a supposedly peaceful country, your countrymen are quite adept at warfare."

"Peaceful my ass. We've been in some sort of shooting war, albeit undeclared, for decades. We just like to delude ourselves into thinking that we're always on the right side of every conflict that we've jumped into. However, my family history has given me a much different perspective on the world than most Americans."

"How true, and if your presidency holds up, you're going to be the first Jewish president."

"I'm not sure that's much of a claim to fame, since I was just the last man standing."

"Who did you pick for your VP?"

"My first choice was General Drummond, but I couldn't afford to take him out of his current position, so I'm going to use Jim Rutherford."

"President Wilkes's previous assistant for National Security Affairs?"

"That's him. His wife, Denise, was a United States district judge in New York, so they brought him along. Why, do you know him?"

"Not well, but I worked with him on the situation in the Ukraine a couple of years back. I hate to cut this short, but I've got a previous commitment."

Late that night, President De Smet called President Behrmann at his new residence in the Russian White House. "Sorry about the hour, but I wanted to let you know that Chancellor Jefferson tried to persuade me to cancel your press conference," he said.

"What did you say?" President Behrmann asked.

"I told him to go to hell, and I don't think he knows you've relocated."

"Thanks for not telling him."

"Your secret is safe with me, but I still don't understand why you even care."

"Actually I don't, but my brother is convinced that I'm in mortal danger."

"He's a little paranoid, however I've found that he's usually quite perceptive."

After Chancellor Jefferson had slept on it, he realized there wasn't anything he could do to stop Behrmann short term, so he decided to accelerate his plans for domestic security.

"Colonel Tompkins, contact the JCS, and let them know that I'm holding an emergency meeting here at the White House," Chancellor Jefferson said when he walked into the Situation Room the next morning.

"When do you want them here?" Colonel Tompkins asked.

"Tomorrow afternoon at fifteen hundred hours," he replied.

"Thank you for getting here on such short notice," Chancellor Jefferson said when they were all seated in the Situation Room.

"Was it really necessary for us to meet in person?" asked Admiral Kennedy.

"Yes," Chancellor Jefferson said. "I need to look

each of you in the eye when I ask for your unconditional support on this new initiative."

Oh shit! they all thought to themselves as they remembered General Willowby's fate.

"Colonel Ridgeway is passing out the material for today's discussion, and I'll give you a few minutes to look it over before we get started." He gave them a few minutes to scan the material before he said, "Let's get started. We'll begin with the section labeled 'Holding Facilities.' Does anyone have any comments?"

"I've tried to keep an open mind, but what you're proposing could be construed as the first step to ethnic cleansing," Admiral Kennedy said.

"Actually, you're not that far off base," Chancellor Jefferson said. "The Arab/Muslim community presents a unique and very real threat to this country's security, and I mean to put an end to it."

"Surely you don't really believe that," said Admiral Pete Donnelly, the chief of naval operations.

"I do, and I believe history will show that they've been at the root of this country's problems for decades. We just haven't had the balls to call them on it."

"You haven't laid out any protocols for how they'll be dealt with once they're in custody," said General Clarence Houston, the newly appointed commandant of the Marine Corps.

"Those will be forthcoming, but rest assured they'll be structured to provide a permanent resolution."

"So you're going to deport them?" asked General Otis Biggalow, the chief of staff of the army. "That's never worked."

"That's one of the possible resolutions we're considering."

"What's with the section on seditious religious organizations?" asked General Frank Goldstein, the commandant of the Coast Guard.

"Nothing to concern us for today. I just wanted a placeholder in case the issue ever came up."

They knew the chancellor was being disingenuous, but none of them were willing to call him on it.

"Next we'll cover the modifications to the current curfews," Chancellor Jefferson said.

"You're expanding the curfews?" General Biggalow asked.

"Yes."

"I thought the metropolitan curfews were working, but even if they're not, we're already stretched to the breaking point."

"Turn to the section labeled 'Manpower,' " Chancellor Jefferson said.

"You're reinstating the draft?" General Houston asked.

"I am. With all of the threats we're facing, we're going to need a lot more manpower."

"How do you intend to pay for it?" Admiral Kennedy asked.

"Flip to the next page."

"Good lord, man, there will be riots in the streets if you raise taxes that much," General Goldstein said.

"Hardly. I'm only raising the effective rate to forty-five percent, and only on people earning more than three hundred and fifty thousand dollars a year."

"Yes, but you're also taking away all of the deductions for the people in those tax brackets."

"Cry me a river, and unlike those limp-dick politicians you're used to, I don't have to kowtow to the fat cats to raise money for reelection."

"I sure as hell don't have any sympathy for politicians, but none of this is going to be very popular with the American people," Admiral Southby said.

"That will soon pass if we can return stability and a sense of security to their everyday lives. The rest of the document is self-explanatory, so if none of you have any further questions or concerns, I think we're done for today."

Late that night, Walter Jefferson was about to call it a day when John Jay stopped by his office.

"I wasn't expecting you back for another couple of days," Walter Jefferson said.

"It didn't turn out to be that big of a deal. The arrogant bastards thought those retards they were using for security had their backs."

"So they're all gone?"

"Everyone on your list, and the bodies will never be found because I dissolved them in acid."

"As soon as their militias report their disappearance, I'll name their replacements."

"How did your meeting with the Joint Chiefs go?"

"None of them had the balls to speak out after what happened to General Willowby."

"I don't blame them. Aren't you worried that the militias are going to figure out who's behind the disappearances?"

"No, it's not like they're a bunch rocket scientists, but let me change the subject for a moment. I haven't been able to come up with a workable strategy to handle Aryeh Behrmann."

"Obviously it would be easier if we could get at him, but with NATO backing his play, I doubt there's much we can do short term, unless you're willing to go nuclear on him."

"I'd briefly considered that, but I'm not that desperate yet. It's getting late; let's revisit this tomorrow."

The next morning, John Jay joined the chancellor in the White House's family dining room. "You're up awfully early, I figured you'd sleep in," Chancellor Jefferson said.

"I'm afraid I don't sleep much anymore," John Jay said.

"Still having a lot of nightmares?"

"I suppose that's what they are. Some of them seem so real that I'm not sure they're not something I've experienced in my previous life."

"You still have a lot of gaps in your memory, don't you?"

"I guess I do, but the most troubling part is not knowing what's real and what's some hellish dream."

"I can't imagine anything worse. I've got access to the best doctors that money can buy, so if you'd like to try that avenue again, just let me know."

"No, thanks, I'm done letting some quack mess with my head."

"What have you got going on today?" Chancellor Jefferson asked.

"I'm supposed to tour the camp in Arizona this afternoon, and on the way back tomorrow I'm going to swing by the Lockheed Martin plant in Marietta, Georgia, to watch the first F-22 roll off the production line."

"It's about damn time."

"Actually I'm shocked they were able to resurrect the production cycle that quickly, given the number of contractors involved."

"Splitting the production up wasn't the brightest thing Congress has ever done."

"That just proves the old saying that the most efficient form of government is a benevolent dictatorship."

"I'm not a dictator."

"Sorry, I didn't mean any disrespect."

"I was just screwing with you. I don't give a damn what they think, as long as I can achieve the goals that I've laid out for this country."

"If you don't mind me asking, what would be your ultimate measure of success?"

"Success would be that this country is once again

dominant on the world stage, and that we aren't at risk from the enemies in our midst."

"I get the world stage, but I'm not sure I follow you on the whole 'enemies in our midst' thing."

"The Muslims, that's what I'm talking about. They want to inflict their sharia laws on us."

Damn, he's even more paranoid than I am, John Jay thought. He glanced at his watch. "I'd better get going."

After John left, Chancellor Jefferson called Colonel Ridgeway over. "Colonel, I want you to track down the officer in charge of mothballing the aircraft a couple of years ago."

"No need, it was Colonel Popov, and they're all stored at the Davis-Monthan Air Force Base in Tucson, Arizona."

"Thanks, that will be all for now."

"What's up, boss?" John Jay asked when his cell phone rang.

"While you're in Tucson, I want you to swing by the Davis-Monthan AFB, and see what it would take to reactivate the F-35s and the F-22s they've got stored there."

"No problem."

"And keep this to yourself for now."

"Welcome to Tucson," said Pete Dawkins, the facility supervisor, when John stepped off the plane. Pete had been in the construction business most of his life, but when his two sons had been slaughtered in a terrorist attack at one of their job sites, he'd joined up with the Arizona militia in hopes of avenging their deaths. He was sixty-five and had no military experience, but the militia had welcomed him in and given him a purpose in life.

"Let's get to it, I've only got a couple of hours before I've got to take off again," John Jay said.

"That should be plenty of time. Hop in the golf cart, and I'll show you the sights."

As they traveled down the road that ran through the middle of the compound, Pete said, "If you'll look to your left, these are the men's barracks."

"What's your capacity going to be?"

"We'll have enough room to house around forty thousand without going to bunk beds, and we've got plenty more land if we need to expand."

"I just reviewed the projected headcount for your facility, and that should suffice for now. How about the women's area?"

"That would be the buildings on your right, and we've got room for about twenty thousand, but again we can build more."

"That should work, because you're not going to be holding them very long."

They drove for another two miles before stopping. "This is the first of our furnaces, and over there is the main road we've built to handle all of the truck traffic from the mines," Pete Dawkins said.

"Excellent, and it looks like your team has done everything that we've asked. How long before you're operational?"

"If the rest of our materials ever get here, we can have it finished in around nine weeks."

"Still waiting on the girders and the rest of the furnaces?"

"That, and we're still short a hundred thousand feet of electrical cable."

"I'll light a fire under their ass on my way to Georgia."

"Not that it matters, but why all the furnaces? I've never seen a design like this. I can't figure out how we're going to be able to smelt ore with these, they look more like the emergency destruction furnaces we installed for the NSA a few years back."

"It will all be explained at the proper time. You just need to make sure they're online by the scheduled date."

"Not a problem, as long as we get our stuff."

"Thanks for the tour, and I'll be back after you go live," John Jay said as he boarded the Gulfstream G650ER.

"What's up?" Chancellor Jefferson asked when he saw the caller ID.

"I just left the Tucson plant, and I'm headed over to the base."

"Problems?"

"No, but the supervisor was asking a lot of question about the furnaces."

"What did you tell him?"

"I told him not to worry about it, and that we'd brief him at the proper time."

"Did he accept that?"

"For now."

"Do we need to take action?"

"I don't think he suspects anything, but I told Colonel Newton to keep an eye on him."

"Anything else?"

"Who's going to be heading up the women's portion of the plan?"

"Mary Beth Wilson, why?"

"Seeing the facility made me realize that this should give us a better selection of bimbos, and I wanted to get my order in."

"I'll have her give you a call."

Six days after his announcement, President Behrmann received a call from his brother.

"Good morning, Mr. President," Lieb Behrmann said.

"Good morning to you, Mr. Prime Minister," Aryeh Behrmann replied.

"So, brother, now that the cat's out of the bag, what comes next? Lieb Behrmann asked.

"Now we get to work on freeing our nation from that evil son of a bitch."

"Great, but how's that going to work? He's in control of most of your nuclear assets, and even after the ass kicking they just got, the most lethal fighting force in the world."

"I didn't say it was going to be easy. Did you have a reason for calling, or did you just want to bust my chops?"

"Sorry, I couldn't resist. I spent half the night on calls with the various leaders of the member nations in the UNASUR, and they're prepared to let you relocate your government to their headquarters in Quito, Ecuador."

"How the hell did you pull that off?" President Behrmann asked.

"When Mexico backed your play, I'd hoped it would open their eyes to the danger Chancellor Jefferson poses to the entire South American continent. But when the Russians and the Chinese went to bat for your new government, they realized that this could quickly escalate into World War III."

"That's good news, but I think I'll stay put for the moment."

"I understand completely, but I'd like you to at least begin a dialogue with them."

"Absolutely."

"I'll set up an introductory call for next Wednesday. Will that work for you?"

"Give me a second," Aryeh said as he opened his calendar. "I can do three to five P.M."

"I'll send you an invitation once I've got it confirmed. How's Mom liking Russia?"

"Rub it in, you asshole. Maybe I can persuade her to spend a couple of months with you."

"I've got to run, but don't hesitate to call if you need anything," Lieb said.

"How's Russia?" General Drummond asked when the president joined their daily videoconference call later that day.

"Freezing my ass off," President Behrmann said. "But make sure you keep that to yourself. I've only got a few minutes before my next meeting, so if you don't mind, I'll lead off."

"You're the boss, you can go whenever you want."

"I know your team has more than enough to worry about, but if my next call goes as expected, I'll need you to send one of your senior officers to Quito, Ecuador to act as a liaison to the UNASUR."

"No problem, I've got several who'd be good at that, but wouldn't a diplomat be a more appropriate choice?" General Drummond asked.

"Normally yes, but just work with me for the time being."

"You've got it."

"That's all I had, so I'm going to drop off, but if you wouldn't mind, copy me on the meeting notes so I can stay up to speed."

The days had run together for him as President Behrmann had gotten completely overwhelmed by his workload. As he was about to get on the call with Secretary Gutierrez he felt badly that he hadn't done his homework.

"Your brother is already on, and if you're ready, Secretary Gutierrez is standing by to join the videoconference," said Army Major Genevieve Black, the president's personal assistant.

"Help me out, I know he's the head of the UNASUR, but didn't he used to be the president of Argentina?"

"He was, and he was just reelected to his second two-year term with the UNASUR."

"Secretary General Eduardo Gutierrez, let me introduce you to the president of the United States and my baby brother, Aryeh Behrmann," Lieb Behrmann said.

"It's my great honor to meet you," Secretary General Eduardo Gutierrez said. "Although the circumstances could be better."

The secretary had just turned sixty, but his black hair and full beard didn't have a trace of gray. He'd been a force in his country's government for many years, and was an elder statesman in South American politics.

"The honor is mine, Secretary Gutierrez. Lieb has told me a great deal about the projects you've helped him with, and I hope that we can form the same level of trust and cooperation between us."

"If you're anything like your brother that won't be an issue. But enough small talk, what are you going to do about that psychopath that's running your country?"

"Right to the point, I like that. There's no easy answer, but with Mexico and the NATO nations' assistance, we've managed to stop their advances in Canada and Mexico."

"I'll admit to being shocked when I heard the news," Secretary Gutierrez said.

"It was definitely touch and go for a while, and if President Nunez hadn't persuaded the cartels to lend a hand, it wouldn't have ended well."

"They can be powerful allies, but their assistance will come at a price."

"I understand, but we'd run out of options," President Behrmann said.

"You are like your brother. You do whatever needs done, regardless of the risks. But speaking of deals, what is it that you hope to gain from an alliance with the UNASUR?"

"It's going to take a large group of allied nations to overcome Chancellor Jefferson. I've already secured agreements with several nations, including the NATO nations. But now that Jefferson controls most of Canada and a large portion of Mexico, the distances involved preclude any sort of ground assaults without your organization's backing."

"When your brother first broached the subject I took the liberty of polling our members, and they were open to the idea, but as I'm sure you know, Mexico has never been open to working with us."

"President Nunez now realizes it's just a matter of time before Chancellor Jefferson finishes them off. If your organization is open to it, he's prepared to become a permanent member of the UNASUR."

"Of course we are, because once that animal takes out Mexico, he'll be coming after us. President Behrmann, how would you like to proceed?"

"I don't have a name yet, but I'll have a liaison in Quito by the end of the month," President Behrmann said.

"Excellent, and that will give me time to get an office set up for him or her."

"Thank you, and I look forward to a long and productive relationship. Is there anything else that we need to discuss?"

"We can flesh out the details later, but if you want to make a ground assault you'll need to form an alliance with the Central American nations as well."

"I don't mean to interrupt, but if you don't mind, I can help you out with that," Lieb Behrmann said.

"No problem here, I've got complete confidence in your judgment," Secretary General Gutierrez said. "Gentlemen, if we're done, I'm supposed to take my wife out to dinner for our thirty-fifth wedding anniversary."

"You should have said something, we could have done this another time," President Behrmann said.

"Not to worry, she's used to it."

When the secretary dropped off, Lieb said, "That went well."

"Far better than I'd even hoped," Aryeh said. "What are the chances of getting the rest of them to join up?"

"After what Walter Jefferson has already done, it shouldn't be a problem. I'll start with the Organization of Central American States, and once they're on board, the stragglers will fall in line quickly."

"What do you think Chancellor Jefferson will do when he discovers what we're up to?"

"Hard to say, but if we manage to pull this off, we'll have him hemmed in."

"It's always dangerous to corner a wild animal."

When Chancellor Jefferson sat down in the Situation Room the next morning, he noticed his daily sitrep folder was thicker than usual. As he read the reports of the previous day's events, he was growing more furious by the moment. By the time he finished, he was thoroughly disgusted with the situation, so he called Admiral Kennedy.

"Yes, sir, what can I do for you this morning?" Admiral Kennedy asked.

"You can put a stop to all of these lone wolf attacks."

"They do seem to be escalating, but I've got to be honest with you. The military is ill equipped to stop them. The FBI or homeland would be better suited to the task."

"That's probably true, and besides that, they couldn't be any more incompetent than your bunch," Chancellor Jefferson said.

"Sorry little bastard," the admiral muttered after he'd hung up.

"Good morning, Chancellor Jefferson," said Charles Berkley, the director of the FBI.

"That's your opinion. I need you to get off your dead

ass and get these terrorist attacks stopped. I just know it's the damned Islamic State thugs again."

"I don't disagree, but it takes time to ferret them out, and even longer to get them in front of a judge."

"Screw that. I'm authorizing you to work directly with Director Clawson to track these people down and kill them."

"You mean take them into custody?"

"No, I mean kill them. If there's even a hint that they could be working with ISIS, I expect you to eradicate each and every one of them."

"Without any sort of due process?"

"A bullet to the head will suffice for due process. They're traitors and deserve no consideration whatsoever. Am I clear?"

"Crystal. Will you brief Director Clawson, or should I explain your expectations?"

"Just tell him what I said, and if he has any doubts or questions, have him call me, and this needs to happen yesterday."

CHAPTER 31

Five months later, Chancellor Jefferson angrily asked Amy Walsh, "Where the hell is John?"

"You sent him to Atlanta."

"I need to speak with him ASAP."

"What's up, boss?" John Jay asked.

"Aryeh Behrmann is turning the entire world against us," Walter Jefferson said.

"What's he done now?"

"He's persuaded the signatories to the Rio Treaty to include his government and to recognize him as the legal leader of the United States."

"Big whoop, none of them has shit for a military."

"They may not be top tier, but it gives him a lot of manpower."

"True, but none of them have sufficient training or leadership to represent much of a threat to us."

"It won't take General Drummond long to fill that vacuum, but even worse, Brazil and Argentina have pledged manufacturing and logistics assistance."

"That's not good, but what are you going to do about it?"

"I'm working on it."

"You want me to head back?"

"No, finish up what you're doing. I just needed to

vent to someone. Wait, how are the camps progressing?"

"Those are my next stops. I'm going to swing by and check on each one of them."

"Problems?"

"The influx of new arrivals has been far heavier than we'd anticipated, and except for the one in California, they're all over capacity."

"Time to begin phase two?"

"I'm afraid so, unless you want to put the project on hold until we can do some more construction."

"I wasn't ready to start yet, but I'll issue the order," Chancellor Jefferson said.

A few days later, Pete Dawkins received the new orders for the Tucson facility. "This can't be right," he said when he finished reading the instructions.

"What's the problem?" asked Colonel Ralph Newton, the commanding officer of the camp's Arizona militia detachment.

"Take a look for yourself," Pete Dawkins said. "But don't think for a moment that I'm going carry out any of that bullshit. In fact, I'm going to call John Jay right now."

Pete Dawkins sat back down at his desk and picked up the phone, but before he could dial the number, Colonel Newton shot him in the back of the head, splattering blood, bits of bone, and brains all over the desktop.

"Weak little man. I knew he wasn't going to last," Colonel Newton said.

"Lieutenant Stricker, I need you to come in here, ASAP."

"What the hell happened to Pete?"

"He had a little accident. We'll deal with that in a moment. Right now here's what I need you and the boys to do."

When Colonel Newton finished laying out what he needed done, Lieutenant Stricker said, "Damn, Colonel, I hate the Islamic State as much as the next man, but this just isn't right." However, when he saw the colonel's reaction, and glanced over at Pete, he said, "Don't get me wrong, I'll do my job."

"Where are you taking us now?" Jim Black asked as Lieutenant Stricker's men herded the male prisoners out of the barracks and onto the waiting buses.

"Work detail," the guard said. "Enough with the questions. Just get on the damn bus."

The buses were outfitted with an airtight, bulletproof panel that separated the guard and the driver from the prisoners. As the first bus pulled away from the barracks, the guard sealed the door and switched on the hydrogen cyanide gas vents in the back of the bus. When they'd gone about fifteen miles down the road, the guard turned off the gas supply and said, "They're done for. You can head back."

As the buses started lining up at a furnace, one of the militiamen working the furnace asked, "What the hell is going on?"

"If I were you I'd shut up and help us unload these bodies," Lieutenant Stricker said.

The massive furnace was already preheated to a thousand degrees as they piled the bodies onto the thirty-foot-square fire-resistant platform.

"That's about all we're going to be able to get on there," the furnace operator said.

"Then get on with it, we've got over two hundred more buses to unload," Lieutenant Stricker said.

The operator flicked the switch and the door to the furnace opened. The platform rotated inside, and the other half swung out and replaced it. When the exterior door sealed they heard the roar of the flames as the internal door opened to allow the superheated furnace to do its work.

"How long?" Lieutenant Stricker asked.

"In about twenty minutes there'll be nothing but a pile of ash, so we'd better get busy and load some more bodies onto this section."

While Lieutenant Stricker's detachment was disposing of the males in the camp, across the road Lieutenant Baker's men were cleaning out the women's barracks.

"Load the cute ones onto the even-numbered buses, and the rest go on the odd-numbered buses," Lieutenant Baker said.

"What's the difference?"

"The cute ones get sold off, the rest go over there," he said as he pointed to one of the red-hot furnaces.

Two days later, Major Black walked slowly into President Behrmann's office carrying the red folder they used for critical dispatches.

"Genevieve, what's wrong? You look like you've been crying," President Behrmann said.

She didn't say a word as she handed him the folder and tried to keep from breaking down completely.

"May God forgive them, because I never will," President Behrmann said when he finished reading the report. "Are you going to be all right, Genevieve?" he asked.

"My sister and her whole family were in that camp," she said as she fell to her knees, sobbing uncontrollably.

Aryeh rushed over to try to console her, and as he helped her to her feet, he said, "I'm so sorry, I didn't know that they'd been taken. Why didn't you tell me before?"

"You've got way too much on your mind already, and besides, I didn't think they were in any danger. I know that I'll probably go to hell for this saying this, but I want you to kill everyone responsible for this."

"You have my word on that. Why don't you take the rest of the day off?"

"No, I need to keep working or I'll go mad."

"I understand. Would you mind getting General Drummond for me?"

After the president had explained what had happened, General Drummond said, "I'm not trying to pass the buck on this, but you might want to touch base with Admiral Crawford on this one."

"Why him? He's on the other side of the world," President Behrmann said.

"I just finished reading the weekly MI-6 briefing, and if my memory serves me, he knows the author, Richard Dawkins."

"I'll reach out to him right away. Genevieve, I need Admiral Crawford."

"Sorry if I woke you," the president said when he saw the admiral was in his quarters.

"Not an issue, I had just finished reading the alert when Major Black called. I guess your Hitler analogy was spot-on," Admiral Crawford said.

"Tragically true. We can't let the murderous bastard get away with this," President Behrmann said.

"You'll think I've lost my mind, but how about the militias?"

"Actually, I find that an interesting proposition, but I doubt that we'd find much support there. What makes you even think they could be an option?"

"I don't get the full reports out here, but the weekly intelligence summary indicated a growing unrest among the militias, particularly the ones that have lost their leaders."

"That was extracted from an MI-6 report that General Drummond was referring to. He said that you had some previous history with the author. I believe he said his name was Richard Dawkins."

"Hell yes, I know him quite well, although I haven't seen him in several years. He and I pulled several ops together, more years ago than I'd care to remember. Where the hell did you run across him?"

"He's currently our MI-6 liaison, and General Drummond thought that since you already knew him you should be the one to make contact."

"Happy to, just send me his contact information," Admiral Crawford said.

"Fine, but don't take too long, because it looks like Jefferson is going to eradicate as many of his so-called undesirables as quickly as he can."

The next day Daoud Mansouri's bodyguards escorted him inside the empty aircraft hangar they were using for his office of the day. As he entered the cavernous building, he was mulling over the horrific series of setbacks his group had suffered over the previous weeks.

"What's the bad news this morning" Daoud Mansouri asked as he sat down at his desk.

"The American FBI has pretty much killed everyone that we've ever been in contact with," Dizhwar Akram said.

"You said they were getting more aggressive, but it usually takes them a lot longer to work through their legal issues."

"They're not going through the courts. They are simply tracking them down and killing them."

"What is their local law enforcement saying about that?"

"Not a word, and none of the killings are making the press either. Someone has put the word out, and no one is questioning anything."

"I don't suppose we should be surprised. Compared

to the number of people that are disappearing into the holding camps, this is nothing."

"And they call us animals. Have you had any luck contacting our teams in Mexico or Panama?"

"None, and we've got to assume they're all dead or on the run."

"What happened to our group in Iraq? We haven't seen or heard anything out of them in weeks."

"They're all dead. Turkey wiped them out with airstrikes and a full-scale ground attack."

"I thought we'd worked out an agreement with them?"

"We did, but the Kurds threatened to cut off their oil supplies if they didn't help them regain control," Dizhwar Akram said.

"It always comes down to the money, doesn't it? We're going to have to start all over again, but we need to raise a boatload of cash. Get Hashmi over here so we can get to work."

On Monday of the next week, John Jay was sitting in the White House Situation Room when he called Mary Beth Wilson to check on a shipment he was expecting.

"I was calling to see when the next shipment of bimbos was going to get here," John Jay said.

"You've already gone through three of them?" Mary Beth Wilson asked.

"Just two, the chancellor took the other one."

"But I sent him four. Oh well, we've got plenty, although I really had to beat the bushes for the redheads."

"Just make damn sure they're really redheads this time."

"I know, and I'm sorry about that."

"I'm really not that picky, so if you're running short, give them all to the chancellor, because he's pretty damned finicky."

"Trust me, I've learned that the hard way. Here's what I'm going to do. I'll have them expedite his delivery, and I'll make sure you get yours as soon as I can. Do you mind if I ask what's happening to them?"

"You really don't want to know."

After several videoconferences, Admiral Crawford had worked out a plan of attack with Richard Dawkins, but it had taken them another week to arrange a meeting with one of the militia leaders.

"How did the meeting go?" Admiral Crawford asked.

"Good," Richard Dawkins said. "I met with Jeramy Snoops, the new leader of the New York militia, and once I showed him the evidence we had on Jefferson's involvement in Willy Woods's death, he said that they'd try to work with us."

"Do you think he was serious?"

"Oh, hell yes. Willy was a lifelong friend of his, and I don't believe I've ever seen a man that mad before. Besides that, he was already convinced that it was just a matter of time before Chancellor Jefferson starts rounding up blacks."

"He's probably right. So what did you work out with him?"

"Nothing firm, but he said he was going to discuss it with the rest of his leadership team and get back to me."

"At least he didn't say no."

"Trust me, he's going to help us out. I just don't know the specifics yet."

After his meeting with Richard Dawkins, it had taken Jeramy Snoops a couple of days to calm down enough to work through what he wanted to do. Once he had his plan, he called a meeting at their headquarters in Queens, New York.

"What's up, boss?" asked Colonel Richard Deming, Jeramy Snoops's field commander.

"I found out who offed Willy," Jeramy Snoops said.

"I'll be happy to kill them for you."

"Not likely, it was Chancellor Jefferson."

"I told Willy not to trust that bastard, but what the hell do we do now?"

"Nothing right now, but that's not why I sent for you. I know you're aware of what's going on upstate."

"I am, but I can't believe it's happening here."

"If you're up for it, we're going to put a stop to it, at least in our neck of the woods."

"Lay it on me."

One week later Colonel Deming was sitting at a roadside park, waiting on the sun to go down. Colonel Deming had been a navy lieutenant commander until he'd gotten caught up in the budget cutbacks. He'd been a part of the Naval Special Warfare and had been assigned to Naval Special Warfare group 2, stationed in Little Creek, Virginia. During his last two years in, he'd led SEAL team 4, which had geographic responsibility for South and Central America. He was six feet tall and a hundred and eighty pounds of chiseled muscle. He had dark brown eyes and was always clean-shaven, and still wore his dark black hair high and tight.

"Everything ready?" Colonel Deming asked.

"All units are standing by, and the snipers are all in position," Major Green said.

As soon as it was dark enough, Colonel Deming ordered, "Sniper teams fire."

They had thirty snipers with eyes on every guard patrolling the perimeter of the massive prison complex, and when they received the word, they used their SR-25s and night vision scopes to put a 7.62 mm bullet through the heads of the guards.

"All clear," announced Sergeant Winters, the sniper team leader.

"Begin phase two," Major Green said.

Their sapper teams quickly cut holes in the twenty-foot-high wire fence, and quietly crept around the grounds planting their explosive charges to take out the lights, phone lines, and the facility's backup generators.

"Execute lights out," Colonel Deming said, and the sappers triggered their charges. The complex went dark.

"Lieutenant Bowie, move your ass," Major Green said.

Lieutenant Marvin Bowie was in charge of their ATVs. They'd been waiting a couple of miles down the road. "Move out," he said.

As they approached the main gate, Lieutenant Bowie said, "Take them out."

His gunner triggered the M134D minigun, and as the 7.62 mm rounds spewed out of the minigun at three thousand rounds a minute, the guard shack was immediately shredded.

"You know your assignments, get to it," Lieutenant Bowie said as one of his men opened the gate. "We're open for business," he said.

"We're on our way," Major Green said.

The ATVs took up positions around the sprawling complex to deal with any emergency responders as their assault troops rushed into the buildings to deal with the rest of the guards.

Twenty minutes later, Major Green said, "We're ready for the trucks."

Chancellor Jefferson's alarm had just gone off when Colonel Tompkins called.

"What's up?" Walter Jefferson asked.

"There's been an attack on the camp in upstate New York."

"I'll be right down."

"Here's what we know so far," Colonel Tompkins said as he handed him the notes he'd prepared.

He read it twice before he said, "I need to talk with John Jay."

"You calling about New York?" John Jay asked.

"You've heard?" Chancellor Jefferson asked.

"It's all over the morning news down here."

"Where are you anyway?"

"Florida. I had a little problem that I needed to take care of, but I can get up there by noon."

"Do that, but don't we have someone in the area?"

"No, the closest team is in Memphis."

"Get them on the road, because I want to know who had the balls to cross us."

"It was probably one of the militias."

"What makes you say that?"

"I think they've figured out that you were behind the militia leaders' deaths."

"If that's true, we'll need to deal with them quickly."

"Agreed, but it's going to get messy because there's a hell of lot of them, and the crazy bastards are armed to the teeth."

"Forget New York, I need you back in D.C.," Chancellor Jefferson said.

"Colonel Tompkins, I need General Tribble ASAP.

"Have you seen the reports on the New York attack?" Chancellor Jefferson asked.

"I have," General Tribble said. "It was a well-organized attack, and they're currently fleeing up the East Coast toward Canada."

"I want you to go after them, and I want them captured or killed ASAP," Chancellor Jefferson said.

"Any chance of some air support?"

"The Mexican operation has us tapped out. Is that going to be a problem?"

"No, we should be able to handle the rabble that attacked the camp, but it never hurts to ask," General Tribble said.

"Then get to it, and General, don't fail me."

Several hours after the attack in New York, Major Black burst into President Behrmann's office in the Russian White House, clutching a dispatch.

"What's up? You look like the cat that ate the canary," President Behrmann said.

"Close. Someone just freed all of the prisoners in the New York internment camp."

He read the note and said, "I need Admiral Crawford."

When the admiral appeared on the screen, President Behrmann asked, "Is this some of Jeramy Snoops's handiwork?"

"Could be."

"The report said they freed all the prisoners, but how in the world do you move that many people?"

"The camp is just off of Interstate 87, so it's not that far to the Canadian border, and they're probably using tractor-trailers."

"That makes sense, but they'd still have to traverse the safety corridor to reach the Canadian lines."

"True, but most of the manpower up there is militia. I'll call around and see what I can find out."

Two hours later, Admiral Crawford called back. "I was right about them using trucks to move the prisoners, but they've run into a snag and need some help. They'd rented a small fleet of cargo ships to ferry the prisoners to safety, but the Coast Guard intercepted them and forced them to turn back out to sea."

"Do you have a recommendation?"

"I think we should ask President Gorelov for help."

"Stay on the line and I'll give him a call."

"Sorry for the delay, but I'm still at home," President Gorelov said.

"I desperately need your assistance, and time is of the essence."

"I'll help if I can."

"There are approximately thirty-five thousand people on the east coast of Canada, and I need to get them out of there ASAP."

"Is this the group that just escaped from the New York facility?"

"It is."

"Hang on while I check on a couple of things," President Gorelov said.

Several minutes later, President Gorelov came back on and said, "Sorry for the delay, but that's a lot of people to move, and I needed to verify a couple of details before I committed to a course of action. I'll have five large cargo ships on location in twenty-four hours."

"That's quick work."

"I had them dump their cargos at sea, but there's one catch. You'll have to find a way to transport them out to the ships, because I've instructed them to remain in international waters."

"I understand, but I doubt that would mean much to Chancellor Jefferson if he discovers their purpose."

At 5 A.M. on the day after their escape, General Tribble called the Situation Room to brief Chancellor Jefferson. "Good morning, Chancellor Jefferson," he said.

"Only if you've taken care of our little problem."

"I'm working on it."

"Working on it, my ass, I warned you that I expect results. Do I need to replace you with someone more competent?"

"I'll get it done, but we can't go more than a couple of miles without being hit by IEDs or some sort of ambush. We're within a hundred miles of the prisoners, but it's slow going. We've only made three miles in the last four hours, and we've lost ten vehicles and a hundred men."

"Do whatever it takes to capture or kill all of those people, and I want it done ASAP."

"We'll do our best."

"I don't give a shit about your best, I want results."

"That was very pleasant," said Colonel Robbins, General Tribble's XO when the chancellor hung up.

"He's a disgusting little man, but he's also a murderous, unforgiving asshole. We move out in one hour, and we're going to push through to the coast, no matter the cost."

"We're going to lose a lot of men if we don't clear those damned IEDs before we proceed."

"Can't be helped. Give the order."

"General Tribble's command is on the move again, and if they can keep up the pace, they'll reach our current position in less than eight hours," Major Green said.

"Take Marvin's group, and see if you can slow them down," Colonel Deming said.

"Will do, and if I don't see you again, it has been a privilege to be part of your team."

"Same here, but don't count us out yet. When we finish loading the next wave, I'll send Major Nelson's men to help out."

They'd posted their request for help transporting the refugees on every type of social media, and as the flotilla of mismatched crafts made their way to and from the waiting ships, it was quite a sight.

"How much longer until we make contact?" General Tribble asked.

"At this pace we should be there in three hours," Colonel Robbins said.

"They'll reach your position in five minutes," Major Green's scout said.

"All units, attack," Major Green said as the lead vehicle reached their position.

As Lieutenant Bowie's ATVs came roaring out of the woods, the deadly buzz of their miniguns spewing out thousands of shells filled the air.

"We've got hostiles on both sides of the column," Colonel Robbins said.

"Halt the column and deploy into defensive positions," General Tribble said.

The column was being led by two groups of M7 Bradleys, and following about a hundred meters behind them were twelve M1128 Downeys sporting MGS 105 mm cannons.

"Heads up, they've got armor with them," Major Green said.

As the thousands of 7.62 rounds from their miniguns quickly shredded the M7s, the smoke from burning vehicles obscured the Bradleys' commander's vision.

"All units disperse and open fire," the Bradleys' commander said.

As the M1128s left the highway, they opened fire with their cannons. The militia's ATVs quickly shifted their fire toward the Downeys, but their 7.62 rounds couldn't penetrate the MGS's armor.

The firefight raged for over three hours before the last of the ATVs had been destroyed.

"All units cease fire," Colonel Robbins said. "All unit commanders report."

It took the colonel another twenty minutes to ascertain the damage from the attack.

"We're down to eleven operational M7s," Colonel Robbins said.

"Downeys?" General Tribble asked.

"One was damaged when it hit a culvert and overturned, but the rest are undamaged."

"Then let's move out," General Tribble said.

"General Tribble's men are on the move again."

"Any word from Major Green?"

"Earlier one of his units had reported him KIA, but we haven't heard anything from them in over an hour."

"Has Major Nelson's group made contact?"

"They have the column in sight, and they're in position."

"I should have held Major Green's command back until they could make a combined attack."

"If you had, we'd all be dead."

"Get the Russian captain on the horn."

"This is Captain Bezrukov."

"Captain, this is Colonel Deming, and we aren't going to be able to get the last wave of refugees out to your ships."

"Why not?"

"The American column is closing on our position. I've dispatched the last of our reserves, but that will only buy us an hour or so at most, and that's simply not enough time."

"How many more do you have left to move?"

"Hang on and I'll get you an exact number."

Five minutes later, Colonel Deming said, "I'm back. We have twenty-two hundred left."

When Captain Bezrukov didn't respond, Colonel Deming asked, "Captain, are you still there?"

"Sorry, I was redirecting my men. We've got a shallow draft vessel with us, and it should be able to get within about five hundred meters of the shoreline."

"Aren't you supposed to stay in international waters?"

"President Gorelov has authorized the change. One other thing. You and your men need to come along in the last wave."

Major Green's men attacked with shoulder-fired antitank missiles as the column rolled by their positions, but after forty-five minutes of savage combat, they'd been wiped out.

"I hope that's the last of them," Colonel Robbins said.

"How much longer?" General Tribble asked.

"I'm estimating no more than thirty minutes."

"See if you can speed that up, this has dragged on for far too long."

"Sorry to interrupt, but Chancellor Jefferson is demanding to speak with you," said General Tribble's aide, Major Winters, as he handed him the satellite phone.

"I'm kind of busy," General Tribble said.

"You'd better pray that your timidity doesn't let them escape," Chancellor Jefferson said.

"Are you threatening me?"

"It's not a threat, it's a promise. If you let them slip away, I'll have you tried and executed for treason."

So that's how it's going to be, you sorry piece of shit, the general thought. After several seconds, General Tribble said, "Rest assured that I'm going to do the right thing."

"You'd better," Chancellor Jefferson growled. "And call me when you've completed your mission."

Whatever, you arrogant asshole, the general thought.

"Attention all units, halt your advance immediately, and all unit commanders report to the command vehicle for an officers' call," General Tribble said.

Once the unit commanders were gathered outside his rolling command center, General Tribble said, "Men, I never thought I'd be saying this, but it is my personal belief that our commander-in-chief is leading our country straight to hell. I intend to move north to seek asylum with the Canadian forces, and you can either accompany me or continue the mission. All I ask is that you give your men the same option. I need you back here in one hour to give me your decisions."

Thirty minutes later the unit commanders were all back.

"Sir, I believe they've all returned," Major Winters said.

"I guess it's time to face the music," General Tribble replied.

"Hand your sheets to Major Winters," General Tribble said.

A few minutes later the major handed the general a single sheet of paper. The general's heart swelled with pride as he read the two words the major had written. "All in."

"I don't have the words to express my gratitude for your support, and I pray that I'm not leading you down the wrong path. Return to your units, we move out in thirty minutes.

"Major, see if the Canadians will respond on the NATO command frequency," General Tribble said.

"I've got General Boulanger on the line," Major Winters said a couple of minutes later.

"General Boulanger, thank you for taking my call," General Tribble said.

"I was shocked that you'd call, but what can I do for you?"

"We're located approximately three hundred miles south of your position, and I'm requesting asylum for my entire command."

"Is this a joke?"

"I assure you it's not. We're done taking orders from that maniac."

"Then come ahead, but don't try any funny business."

"Glad you made it," Captain Bezrukov said when Colonel Deming boarded his ship.

"Thanks for rescuing us, but I still don't understand

how we made it, because the group chasing us had more than enough time to reach us."

"We've just received a relayed message from General Boulanger, the Canadian commander. The American column that was pursuing you has requested asylum and is in the process of surrendering."

"Hot damn, that's great news. It's just too damn bad that so many good men had to die before he came to his senses," Colonel Deming said.

Chancellor Jefferson was working in his office just down the hall from the Situation Room, and when he realized what time it was he called Colonel Tompkins. "What's taking so long?" he asked. "General Tribble should have checked in hours ago."

"We haven't been able to raise anyone from his command," Colonel Tompkins said.

"Shit, that can't be good," Chancellor Jefferson said. "Keep trying, and I'll be over there in a few minutes.

"Amy, I need John Jay, and don't run off, I'm going to need you after I finish with him."

The horny little bastard is going to do me again, she thought to herself.

CHAPTER 32

"You look like you've got good news for a change," President Behrmann said when Major Black came into his new office at the Russian White House. When they'd done the renovations they'd turned the top floor into the presidential suite of offices. President Behrmann's new office covered one end of the floor, and the panoramic view of the city was magnificent.

"I do," Major Black said. "The Russians have picked up all of the prisoners from New York."

"That's great news."

"There's more. They also pulled out Colonel Deming and what was left of his team."

"That actually sounds a little grim."

"I'm afraid it is. Counting the colonel, there were only twenty survivors from his command."

"Anything else?"

"There's an e-mail from General Boulanger for you."

"What did he want?"

"It was marked for your eyes only, so I haven't opened it."

"This is great news," President Behrmann said.

"What happened?"

"General Tribble has requested asylum, and he's surrendering his entire command to General Boulanger."

"That is good news."

"I need Admiral Crawford."

"What's up? Major Black sounded awfully excited when she left the message to call you," Admiral Crawford said.

"General Tribble is surrendering his command to General Boulanger," President Behrmann said.

"Does that mean the rescue operation went off as planned?"

"They rescued all of the people from the camp, but most of Colonel Deming's men were KIA."'

"Unfortunate, but they knew the risks going in. Did General Tribble bring their equipment with them?"

"General Boulanger's note didn't give any details, but feel free to reach out to him for the specifics."

"Will do. Anything else?"

"Are you still in contact with Richard Dawkins?"

"Absolutely."

"Have him make arrangements to pull Jeramy Snoops out of there before Chancellor Jefferson takes him out."

Less than an hour later, Admiral Crawford called President Behrmann back.

"I just spoke with Dawkins, and he said that Snoops has already gone to ground and wasn't willing to abandon his men."

"Sounds like a stand-up guy," President Behrmann said. "But he's going to get himself killed."

"Snoops told him that he was going to organize a guerrilla war against the chancellor."

"Have Richard tell him that we'll lend any assistance we can, and make sure we get them some secure communications gear so we can contact them."

Three days later, President Behrmann was just about to go downstairs for lunch when his brother called.

"Congratulations, you're now a member of the

Organization of Central American States," Prime Minister Lieb Behrmann said.

"You're the one that did most of the work," President Aryeh Behrmann replied.

"Happy to help. What's your next move?"

"I'm considering relocating to Quito, Ecuador."

"I'm not sure that's a prudent move. That would put you within easy striking distance of Jefferson's airpower."

"I know, but it feels like someone is looking over my shoulder twenty-four/seven."

"That's because they are." Lieb chuckled. "Just live with it for a while longer. Hang on a second, my assistant just came in and handed me an urgent dispatch.

"Oh, dear God," Lieb exclaimed.

"Has something happened?"

"SHAPE headquarters has just been hit."

"Terrorist attack?"

"Undetermined, but there are several news helicopters broadcasting live video from the scene, and they're reporting that the entire complex is nothing but a pile of flaming rubble. I'm going to hang up and see if I can reach General Drummond.

"Genevieve, I need General Drummond," President Behrmann said.

"I'm sorry, but I couldn't help overhearing, do you think they're all right?"

"Too soon to say."

Several minutes later Major Black returned and said, "I haven't been able to reach anyone."

"See if you can contact President De Smet."

"All the phone circuits were busy, but Colonel Perry got through on a satellite video link to their emergency management center," Major Black said.

"Great, transfer it in here."

"Sorry, they haven't finished the wiring yet, so you'll have to take it downstairs."

"President De Smet, I'm sorry to bother you at a time like this, but I need to know what's going on at the NATO complex."

"I've got my people en route to the disaster, but Casteau is forty-five miles southwest of Mons, so they're just now arriving on the scene."

"But my brother said it's being broadcast live on TV."

"It is, but the city is in chaos, and I've gotten conflicting stories on what's happening."

"Anything is better than nothing."

"Fine, here's what I've heard. At approximately fifteen hundred hours local time, the SHAPE complex was destroyed by a series of massive explosions, and from the footage I've seen, I wouldn't expect many survivors."

"The facility has state-of-the-art security, what the hell happened?"

"Unclear at this time, but we've had several reports of aircraft flying low over the area, shortly before the explosions."

"Walter Jefferson's handiwork," President Behrmann muttered under his breath.

"Sorry, I missed that," President De Smet said.

"Sorry, just thinking out loud," President Behrmann said. "I'll let you go, but please keep me in the loop.

"I need Admiral Crawford," President Behrmann said.

"What do we know so far?" Admiral Crawford asked as soon as the video connection was made.

"I take it you've heard the news?" President Behrmann asked.

"The Internet is a wonderful thing. My XO just downloaded a cell phone video that's on YouTube, and it showed four B2 aircraft dropping sticks of what looked to be five-hundred-pound GBU-38 JDAMs."

"No wonder the complex is gone, a B2 can carry what, thirty bombs?"

"Actually, it's eighty, but with four aircraft, thirty each would have been more than sufficient. This has to be Chancellor Jefferson's handiwork. How do you want to respond?"

"I haven't even thought about that yet. Do you have any recommendations?"

"I'm afraid our options are rather limited," Admiral Crawford said.

"Yes, I suppose they are. Admiral, under the circumstances I've got to assume that General Drummond has been killed in the attack. So I'm promoting you to fleet admiral, and placing you in command of all of our forces. I also need you here with me, so make the arrangements as soon as possible."

"Aye, aye, sir, but I hope the promotion is temporary."

"I'd second that thought, but I think the chances of that are very slim."

Early the next morning, the secure video channel that had replaced the old Russian hotline started flashing.

"Sir, you've got an incoming call on the Russian hotline," Amy Walsh said.

I wonder what President Gorelov wants, Chancellor Jefferson thought. "I really don't have time to mess with him right now, but I suppose you'd better go ahead and put him through.

"President Gorelov, what can I do for you today?" Chancellor Jefferson asked before he bothered to look up at the screen.

"You cowardly bastard," President Behrmann said. "You've murdered thousands of innocents."

"Behrmann? I thought you were in Belgium."

"Obviously. I suppose I can understand why you'd try to kill me, but why kill all those other people?"

"I've got no sympathy for them because I consider them all enemy combatants. When you decided to challenge me, you should have expected the gloves to come off."

"So that's how it's going to be?"

"It is, and you can tell that scumbag brother of yours that I'm coming after him as well."

"I've got no concept of your kind of hate. I was going to say that you'd come to regret your actions one day, but I doubt that you're actually capable of remorse."

You have no idea, Walter thought. "I don't have any more time to waste on you," Chancellor Jefferson said, "but you'd better make peace with your so-called God."

Walter hadn't bothered to close his office door, so Amy Walsh had heard both sides of the conversation.

"You didn't mean that, did you?" Amy Walsh asked.

"Damn right I did, and you'd better not speak of it to anyone."

"I promise I won't," Amy said with a slight tremble in her voice.

"Have we heard from Mary Beth Wilson today?"

"No. Do you want me to track her down for you?"

"Maybe later. Take your clothes off and get over here."

"Please, you said that you wouldn't make me do that anymore."

"I lied, and now get over here, you sexy little bitch."

She started to protest, but when she saw the look on his face, she started stripping.

When Walter was finished with her, he said, "Put your clothes on and get back to work, and get John Jay for me."

Three days later Admiral Crawford finally made it to Moscow.

"It's good to finally meet you in person," President

Behrmann said when he got up to shake the admiral's hand.

"Thank you, Mr. President," Admiral Crawford said. "Have they found General Drummond yet?"

"Possibly, but we're still waiting on the DNA tests. How was the flight?"

"My plane had mechanical problems, and I was afraid that I was going to be stuck in Shanghai for another day, but the Russians let me hitch a ride."

"I'm just glad you made it," President Behrmann said.

"How's the plan for a counterattack coming?" Admiral Crawford asked.

"I've read at least twenty proposals, but saw nothing that I would be willing to do."

"I don't think there's much you can do, given our rather limited resources."

"Our current dilemma is similar to the one Charles de Gaulle found himself in during World War II."

"I beg to differ. We have over four hundred thousand troops, almost a third of our nuclear arsenal, and the bulk of the most powerful navy in the world, so we're not completely helpless."

"All true, but I can't imagine a scenario where I would be willing to use nuclear weapons against our own people."

"And therein lies the problem," Admiral Crawford said. "We're fighting a civil war, and just like the first Civil War, we're pitting our people against their friends, neighbors, and even brothers, but like Lincoln, we can't let our determination waver."

"What really disturbs me is that we're starting to see the same type of mentality that occurred during Adolf Hitler's rise to power," President Behrmann said. "I can still remember my great-grandmother talking about what happened to many of her friends and family during that time, and there are some horrifying similarities to what's occurring."

"I pray to God that you're wrong, but that's all the more reason for us to press onward," Admiral Crawford said. "What do you want me to focus on first?"

"Now that we've gotten all of the South American countries on board, I want you to help me prioritize our equipment needs and get to work on short-and long-term strategies," President Behrmann said.

"Happy to, but did you already have something in mind?"

"I'm no strategist, but I'd like to see us quickly reclaim control of the North American continent, and with as few casualties as possible."

"Got it, but quickly regaining control with the fewest casualties may be at odds with each other."

"I understand, but do the best you can. Major Black will get you set up in an office, and make sure that you receive all the documentation we have."

Earlier that day, Chancellor Jefferson had been hard at work in the Situation Room when John Jay came in.

"Well?" Chancellor Jefferson asked.

"They missed him," John Jay said.

"Shit. I thought you had it all arranged."

"We did. They disabled his aircraft when it landed to refuel in Shanghai, but before the team could take him out, the Russians picked him up."

"We may have shot ourselves in the foot on this one. Admiral Crawford is a much better strategic thinker than General Drummond ever was."

"Sorry."

"Don't worry about it, we'll work through it."

"If you don't have anything else, I'm headed out to Phoenix to check on the new militia leader out there," John Jay said.

"I'm good for now, but check in every once in a while, just in case.

"Amy, I need you," Chancellor Jefferson said.

Shit, not again, she thought to herself as she got up from her desk.

She'd started unbuttoning her blouse as she entered his office, but he said, "No not that, at least not right now. I need General Gibbs."

Thank God for small favors, she thought to herself. "I believe he's in California this week, but I'll track him down."

"Sorry, sir, I was doing my annual inspection tour at Vandenberg," General Gibbs said.

"No problem, but are you alone?" Chancellor Jefferson asked.

"No, my aide is in the room."

"Please ask him to step outside."

"Okay, he's gone, but for future reference, he's cleared at the highest levels."

"Not for this he isn't. I need you to take care of a problem for me, and I want you to involve the smallest number of people you can."

"What do you need?" General Gibbs asked.

When Chancellor Jefferson finished explaining his expectations, General Gibbs said, "You can't be serious."

"I'm deadly serious, and if you can't or won't do this, I'll have to replace you," Chancellor Jefferson said.

"No, I'll do it, but this could start World War III."

"I'm not worried. When it comes down to the nut cutting, none of them will respond."

"Christ, I hope you're right. When do you want this done?"

"ASAP, but use someone you can trust."

"No worries there, my men will do as they are told."

A week later Colonel Lukanhesko contacted President

Gorelov with an urgent alert. "Mr. President, our acoustic listening posts in the Ural's have picked up an American B2 bomber, and it's headed straight at Moscow."

"Why haven't you shot it down?" President Gorelov asked.

"I've scrambled our fighters to intercept, but we're having a difficult time pinpointing its location, so you need to take the appropriate precautions."

"I'll do that, and good hunting," President Gorelov said. "And call me when you've taken care of the threat."

As President Gorelov stepped into the elevator to descend into the building's underground bunker, he called President Behrmann.

"President Behrmann, you need to go immediately to the bunker in the basement of your facility," President Gorelov said.

"What's—" President Behrmann tried to ask before President Gorelov interrupted.

"No time, get to the bunker now, and call me back when you're locked in."

"Okay, we've reached the bunker and sealed the door," President Behrmann said as the ten-ton blast door swung shut.

"Good," President Gorelov said. "Our acoustic listening posts are tracking one of your bombers, and it's headed toward Moscow. Given what just occurred in Belgium, I would hazard a guess that they're after you again."

"Chancellor Jefferson again? The little bastard sure doesn't quit coming."

"He's a dangerous adversary, and seems to care little for international law. We're trying to intercept the aircraft, but the technology of your stealth bombers makes that a difficult proposition. I'll let you know as soon as the threat is past."

The Russians had scrambled fifty of their T-50 fifth-generation fighters, but they were having a hard time pinpointing the bomber's position.

The squadron commander knew he was running out of time when he said, "All aircraft disperse along these coordinates, and try to obtain a visual fix on the enemy aircraft."

The B2 was a little over three hundred kilometers from Moscow when Lieutenant Chudakov spotted the bomber. "I've got a visual on the intruder, what are your orders?" he asked.

"You're weapons free," the squadron commander said.

"Understood," Lieutenant Chudakov said as he dove to attack the intruder. "I can't get a missile lock."

"Do whatever you have to, but that aircraft has got to be stopped."

"Affirmative," Lieutenant Chudakov said as he went to full throttle and hit the afterburners.

The bomber crew never knew the Russian aircraft was even there before it rammed them amidships. Lieutenant Chudakov was doing over Mach 3 when he hit the bomber, and both aircraft disintegrated from the immense impact of the midair collision.

When the Russian squadron commander reached the crash site, he said, "Command, the enemy aircraft has been destroyed."

"Excellent work. What's the name of the pilot that shot it down?"

"It was Lieutenant Chudakov, but he had to ram the aircraft to get it stopped."

"President Behrmann, the threat has been taken care of," President Gorelov said.

"Thank God. Did the bomber turn back, or did your men shoot it down?" President Behrmann asked.

"Lieutenant Chudakov rammed the bomber," President Gorelov said.

"More lives sacrificed to that madman. If the lieutenant had a family, I'd like to make sure that they're taken care of."

"Not to worry, we take care of our own. Speaking of taking care of someone, I'm going to call your chancellor, and I'd like you to sit in with me."

When President Behrmann got to President Gorelov's newly renovated office in the Kremlin, President Gorelov said, "Why don't you sit over there so he won't see you right away. I want to see his reaction when he realizes you're still alive."

"President Gorelov is on the hotline for you," Amy Walsh said.

"I hope that he's going to report the unfortunate demise of President Behrmann." Chancellor Jefferson gloated.

"President Gorelov, what an unexpected pleasure."

"Lying bastard," President Gorelov said. "If you ever pull a stunt like that again, I'll nuke your sorry little ass off the face of the planet."

"I'm not sure why you're so mad, but I'll not be threatened by a Third World dictator like you. Your pitiful excuse of a country hasn't been a superpower in decades."

"Perhaps not, but I've still got enough ICBMs to take care of you."

"I'm not going to sit here and listen to this bullshit," Chancellor Jefferson said. "I had a problem, and I took care of it, so stop your sniveling and let's agree to move on."

"That's not going to happen as long as you're still in power," President Behrmann said as he moved into the picture.

"Son of a bitch, you're a hard man to kill," Chancellor Jefferson said.

"So it seems, but we're soon going to see if the same goes for you," President Behrmann replied.

"Do your worst. I may have missed you this time, but if it's the last thing I ever do, I'm going to kill you and that asshole brother of yours."

"Let me stop you right there, little man," President Gorelov said. "If you ever launch a missile or send an aircraft into my country again, it will be the last thing you ever do, and to be clear, that also goes for any nation that we have a defense treaty with."

"You can't threaten me."

"It's a promise, and just so you know, my country is committed to lending every assistance we can to President Behrmann's quest to retake his country."

"I'll—

"He hung up on me," Chancellor Jefferson said.

"He sounded serious," Amy Walsh said.

"I suppose he was." *This isn't working out at all,* Chancellor Jefferson thought.

Do you want me to get ahold of anyone for you?" Amy Walsh asked.

"Yes, but first I'm going to get ahold of you. Take your clothes off and get over here."

When he was finished with her, Chancellor Jefferson said, "Now I need John Jay, and when I'm finished with him, I'll need to speak with General Gibbs."

"How'd it go, boss?" John Jay asked.

"Missed again. I beginning to think this asshole has nine lives."

"I'd offer to take the job on, but there's no way I could get within a million miles of him."

"Very true, but that's not why I wanted to talk. That crap that went down in New York was pulled off by the New York militia, and we need to make an example out of them."

"What do you need from me?"

"I need you to track down that piece of trash that took over for Willy Wood and make sure he suffers the same fate."

"Do you have a location on him?" John Jay asked.

"I don't."

"No big deal, he shouldn't be that hard to find. Does it have to look like an accident?"

"Hell no, I want it to be very public. I want the rest of those redneck assholes to see what happens if you cross me.

"Amy, I'm ready for the general now.

"Once again you've failed me," Chancellor Jefferson said.

"I know," General Gibbs said. "It was unfortunate that the Russian pilot found them when he did. Another sixty seconds, and they would have launched their cruise missiles."

"Water under the bridge, but I'm going to need a couple of your bombers."

"What's the mission?"

After a lengthy pause, Chancellor Jefferson asked, "What's the narrowest point in Central America?"

"Give me a minute. That would be Darién, Panama. At that point the isthmus is only about thirty miles wide."

"Perfect. Here's what I want you to do."

When the chancellor finished, General Gibbs said, "I hope you know what you're doing."

"Behrmann has made agreements with most of the South American nations, and at some point they are going to try and mount a land offensive, and the only way they can do that is if they come through Central America."

"I suppose you're right, but this will be seen as a blatant war crime if they ever do defeat us."

"Just do your job."

"SIR, THERE'S BEEN another incident," Major Black said. "And Admiral Crawford is waiting outside to brief you."

"What now?" President Behrmann asked.

"At sixteen hundred hours today, there were at least six high-yield nuclear explosions near Darién, Panama."

"Why in God's name would that maniac bomb Panama?"

"We believe it was a preemptive strike to ensure that we couldn't move an invasion force through there."

"More lives lost to this monster. Find out if there's anything that can be done for them and get back to me.

"Genevieve, I need to speak with President Gorelov."

"President Behrmann, I've been expecting your call," President Gorelov said.

"I wanted to make sure that you're not considering doing something rash," President Behrmann said.

"Like nuking the sorry little bastard?"

"Exactly."

"I'd be lying if I told you the thought hadn't crossed my mind. However, I have already dispatched three bomber squadrons, and they're on their way to take out Elmendorf Air Force Base in Alaska."

"You're going to nuke Alaska?"

"No, they're using conventional weapons, and don't try to talk me out of it, because I'm not going to let this latest incident pass without a meaningful response."

"Wasn't going to, but I wish you had given us a chance to lend a hand."

"My people have it well in hand, but I would like you to come over in the morning, so we can give your little friend another call."

"Gorelov and Behrmann, why am I not surprised you two assholes are together?" Chancellor Jefferson said when they appeared on the screen in the White House Situation Room.

"Back at you, little man," President Gorelov said.

"You made a big mistake yesterday," Chancellor Jefferson said.

"I agree I should have nuked your ass instead," President Gorelov said.

"If you had, none of us would be talking, because I wouldn't have let that slide," Chancellor Jefferson said. "But what's done is done, and it's time to move on."

"And I'm just supposed to give you a free pass on nuking Panama?" President Behrmann asked. "Do you have any idea how many people you've needlessly slaughtered?"

"Couldn't care less. It was a necessary step to secure our borders, and I won't apologize for that."

"I'm not going to waste any more of my time trying to talk sense to a narcissistic sociopath like yourself," President Behrmann said.

"Narcissistic? Maybe, but our ancestors were right on with their belief in a manifest destiny. However, my vision of that is a little more global."

"You truly are insane, and don't think for a moment the rest of the world isn't going to hold you accountable for what you've done."

"I'd send the entire world up in flames before I'd let you stop me."

"I pray it won't come to that, but even that would be better than allowing you to continue with your crimes against humanity," President Behrmann said.

"Then bring it on," Chancellor Jefferson said as he broke the connection.

CHAPTER 33

"Boss, don't take this wrong, but have you lost your mind?" John Jay asked when the screen went dark.

"Don't start. I'm not the least bit worried about what Behrmann might do," Chancellor Jefferson said.

"It's not just him. He's got most of the world backing his play."

"Not all of it," Chancellor Jefferson said. "I'll have Amy set up a meeting with Admiral Kennedy and General Gibbs for tomorrow afternoon, and we'll get to work on our next moves. I'll want you and Porter there."

While Chancellor Jefferson was plotting his next moves, President Behrmann was doing the same.

"That's one arrogant son of a bitch," President Gorelov said when the chancellor hung up on them.

"I've got to be honest with you, I'm not sure I'm the man for this job," President Behrmann said.

"I realize that you find yourself in an unfortunate state of affairs, but like your President Lincoln, you've got to stay the course if your country is to survive. Have you thought through your next moves?"

"Most of the NATO military command was killed along with General Drummond, but once they've named their replacements, we're going to hold strategy meetings to determine our path forward."

"Give me a call when you're ready."

After several weeks of work, President Behrmann hosted a joint meeting with the UN Security Council and the new NATO commanders to present their plans.

They were meeting in the Diplomatic Reception Room on the ground floor of the Russian White House. The brilliant white columns spaced along the walls were outlined in gold, and the massive oak tables were arranged in a horseshoe with a polished titanium podium on a small raised platform in the center of the tables.

After Secretary General Pierre Clouatre introduced him, President Behrmann got up and walked to the podium.

"Not since World War II has the world faced a murderous madman like Chancellor Jefferson. He has no regard for international law or human rights, and he's willing to exterminate anyone who stands in his way. As the lawful leader of the United States government, I intend to regain control of the country. However, it's not going to happen overnight and the effort will cost a lot of lives on both sides. I also realize many of you will view this as a civil war, and may be unwilling to be drawn into the conflict. However, Chancellor Jefferson has already proven that it is only a matter of time before he tries to impose his vision of world order on all of you. Now I'm going to spend a few minutes laying out our plans to regain control. Before we resort to force, we're going to attempt to force Chancellor Jefferson to abdicate by isolating the United States from the rest of the world. Two weeks from now, with the help of our NATO partners and President Gorelov, we'll be instituting a complete air and sea blockade of the North American continent. We're going to block their access to the World Wide Web, and jam their satellite communications channels. One week before the quarantine goes into effect, we'll issue all the appropriate travel advisories, and e-mail everyone the details of what I've just covered. Now, if you have any questions, I'll try to answer them."

"Large portions of my country's exports are to the United States. Are there going to be any exceptions to the embargos?" the Chinese ambassador asked.

"I'm afraid not," President Behrmann said.

"At what point will you resort to force?" asked the Japanese ambassador.

"It would be premature to even hazard a guess."

President Behrmann spent most of the next hour answering various versions of the same questions before he said, "I think we'll end here. If we stay the course we can restore democracy to my country."

"I've just left an emergency meeting of the Security Council, and Behrmann has convinced NATO and the Russians to help him quarantine all of North America," the Chinese UN ambassador said.

"He's brighter than I gave him credit for," President Zhao replied.

"Do you want me to make this an issue with the Security Council?"

"No, I want you to catch the next flight to Beijing."

When the satellite phone in his jacket pocket rang, Chancellor Jefferson closed his office door before he answered it.

"President Zhao, what can I do for you today?" Chancellor Jefferson asked.

"Our ambassador attended a joint meeting of NATO and the UN last night where President Behrmann briefed the group on his plan to isolate North America."

"He doesn't have enough resources to pull that off," Chancellor Jefferson said.

"Alone no, but his list of allies continues to grow. We are not going to sit back and let that happen. Are you still on board with our agreement?"

"Yes. I'd hoped to regain control of the fleet before we had to act, but oh well. I'll issue the order for thirteen hundred GMT on Friday."

"Excellent. That should give me enough time to make our final preparations."

Three days later, Colonel Taan had just come on duty in the Taiwanese command center when one of the radar operators said, "Colonel, we have a large number of unidentified bogies inbound."

"Sound the alarm and alert the coastal command."

They'd just added two new destroyers to the command, bringing their number to eight. All of them were outfitted with the Aegis Combat System, but the new ones were the first they'd received that were also outfitted with the Aegis Ballistic Missile Defense System.

"All units, we have a level one alert, and you are free to fire on lock," said Captain Oong, the commander of the coastal defense group.

There were a hundred Deng Feng-15 missiles in the first wave, but the destroyers with Aegis systems enabled their RIM-67 missiles to neutralize the incoming missiles before they reached their targets. However there were three more flights of missiles right behind the first wave.

"We've managed to knock down almost all of the missiles, but we've expended all of our ordnance," Captain Oong said after they'd destroyed the last missile.

"Sir, we've got two more waves headed this way," the combat command center said.

"Stand by to deploy the Phalanx," Captain Oong said.

Unlike the previous missiles, these were the Chinese DF-21 antiship missiles, and even though the Phalanx's radar-guided 20 mm Vulcan Gatling guns were highly effective, the number of missiles overwhelmed their defenses.

Just before the burning hulk of his ship capsized and sank, Captain Oong radioed, "All our units have been destroyed and we're abandoning ship."

By the time the Chinese commander ceased fire, they'd fired almost eight hundred missiles. They'd spent years mapping out their targets, and as the Chinese troop ships approached the coast of Taiwan, there was only token resistance.

"General Haan's army has landed, and should attain all their objectives before nightfall," President Zhao's assistant said.

"Excellent, let's hope the admiral does as well," President Zhao said.

President Zhao had tasked Admiral Chung, the head of their submarine force, with the attack on the nearest elements of the Americans' Pacific Fleet.

There were four carriers in Admiral Tunney's combined task force, and they were on their way to implement the North Pacific portion of President Behrmann's blockade. The Chinese had been tracking them since they'd left Japan, and they had twelve of their submarines positioned along their route. When the carrier task force's escorts were within twenty kilometers, they surfaced and fired their supersonic YJ-18 antiship cruise missiles, tipped with 20-kiloton nuclear warheads. The American air cover launched a savage counterattack on the subs, but at that range they didn't have enough time to keep the tactical nukes from decimating the fleet.

"Have we heard from Admiral Chung yet?" President Zhao asked sometime later.

"No, sir."

"Then see if you can get him for me."

"Sorry it took so long, but I had to reposition a satellite so I could get a clearer picture of the situation," Admiral Chung said when he got on the line. "How'd we do?"

"From what we could tell we've sunk all four carriers, and close to a hundred percent of their escorts."

"Losses?"

"We haven't been able to reach any of our units, so I'm assuming they've all been sunk."

"Regrettable, but you've done well," President Zhao said. "I just hope Chancellor Jefferson holds up his end."

Admiral Crawford had started the day with thirteen operational carriers, counting the USS *Enterprise* CVN-80, which was docked in Haifa, Israel. The Israelis were integrating a radical new version of their Rafael Advanced Defense System's lasers into the ship's Aegis Ballistic Missile Defense system. The *Enterprise* was the third ship in the *Gerald R. Ford*–class of carriers, and in addition to the twin reactors that powered the ship, they'd added four more A1B gen-2 nuclear reactors to power the energy weapons systems. The upgraded reactors had a twelve-hundred-megawatt output, or roughly twelve times the capacity of the reactors used in the original *Nimitz*-class of supercarriers. The massive amount of excess power allowed them to gird the ship with the first generation of the electrically charged dynamic armor, and power the two Israeli graduated response lasers integrated into the ship's Aegis air defense system. The variable output lasers could operate from 5 watts to 2.5-megawatt range, enabling them to deal with a wide variety of threats. Its sister ships, CVN-78 and 79 were docked in Guam, awaiting orders to implement the Southern Pacific portion of the blockade. Since *Nimitz*-class carriers lacked the firepower of the *Gerald R. Ford*–class of the new supercarriers, Admiral

Crawford had combined the USS *George Washington* CVN-73 and the USS *John C. Stennis* CVN-74 carrier support groups. After a show of force in the Persian Gulf and stops in Bahrain and Qatar, they were transiting the Strait of Hormuz on their way to their assignment in the South Atlantic. As the waterway narrowed to just twenty-one miles, the Iranians opened fire with their homegrown Ghadir antiship missiles.

"Bridge, we've got a large number of incoming missiles on our port side," reported Commander Davis, the duty officer in the USS *John Stennis*'s combat information center.

The *Stennis* was Admiral St. James's flagship, and he was on the bridge when the attack began. "Flank speed, and all units, deploy countermeasures," he said. "CIC, notify command we're under attack."

The destroyers and frigates accompanying the CSG immediately opened fire with their antimissile defenses, but the Iranians kept firing wave after wave of missiles, until several of them were dead in the water and sinking. When the admiral ordered the carriers to flank speed the escorts couldn't keep pace. As they started to pull away from their surface escorts, the nuclear attack subs protecting them from underwater attacks were circling beneath them as they raced toward the relative safety of the Arabian Sea.

"Sir, we've just monitored a flash communication from the USS *John Stennis* and they're reporting that they're under attack from the Iranians," Colonel Akhavan said.

"See if you can confirm that," Israeli Prime Minister Lieb Behrmann said.

"The report is accurate," Colonel Akhavan said a couple of minutes later.

"Damn," Prime Minister Behrmann replied as he hit the speed dial on his phone.

"Prime Minister, what can I do for you today?" asked General Perlberg, the chief of staff.

"The Iranians have attacked an American carrier group in the Strait of Hormuz, and I'm ordering you to execute Plan One immediately."

"Yes, sir, and May God have mercy on their souls. Although I doubt they have any."

The carriers were only ten nautical miles from the open ocean when the Iranians opened fire with their Russian-made Raduga P-270 Moskit antiship cruise missiles. As they rocketed toward the fleeing carriers at Mach 3, the ship's Aegis Ballistic Missile Defense systems began tracking the incoming missiles with their SPY-1 radar systems. Once their computers locked onto the incoming missiles, the MK 41 Vertical Launch systems began firing their SM-3 missiles. The BMD systems took out 70 percent of the missiles, and as the remainder neared the carriers, their Block-1 Phalanx close-in weapons systems locked their 20 mm Gatling guns onto the missiles and began firing. Each of the Gatling guns was spewing out forty-five hundred rounds a minute, and several of the sophisticated Russian missiles struck home with their 320 kg warheads, but the massive carriers never slowed. As they entered the Gulf of Oman their air cover took out the last of the Iranian missiles.

"Cease fire, and slow to twenty knots so the escorts can catch up," Admiral St. James said. "All commands, report."

"We've taken multiple missile strikes, and two of our elevators are inoperable. We can still make flank speed, and we can land aircraft, but all of our catapults are out of action," reported Admiral Tucker, the commander of the *George Washington* CVN-73.

Due to the chaos the attack had caused, it took almost ten minutes for the rest of the survivors to report in, and after Admiral St. James had a grasp of their situation he contacted Admiral Crawford.

"The Iranians have hit us with a massive attack. Both carriers are badly damaged, and thirty percent of our escorts have been sunk, but we've entered the Gulf of Oman and are out of their range," Admiral St. James said.

"Are you still operational?" Admiral Crawford asked.

"Marginally, and if you'll authorize it, I'd like to launch a counterattack."

"Not necessary, I've just received a report that the Israelis have launched a massive missile-and airstrike on them."

"I hope they kill all of the bastards," Admiral St. James said. "Do we have any idea what set them off?"

"It wasn't just them. China has invaded Taiwan, and we think they've pretty much wiped out Admiral Tunney's group."

"Bastards."

"It gets worse. Chancellor Jefferson has launched multiple air strikes on the task forces in the Northern Pacific and the North Atlantic."

"How bad?"

"They sunk two carriers and several escorts, but he paid a heavy price because we shot down everything he sent."

"Good, but that's just more American lives sacrificed to the sorry little bastard's ambitions."

"True, and I'm afraid it's far from over. As soon as you can get underway, I want you to make for Hawaii, but I've got to go so I can brief President Behrmann."

"Sir, I've got Admiral Burton on the command channel, and he'd like to speak with you," Admiral Crawford's aide said as soon as he hung up.

"Admiral, I sure wasn't expecting to hear from you," Admiral Crawford said.

"I'm sick to my stomach that I didn't do this earlier, but I've just finished speaking with the commanding officers of every submarine under my command, and I've released them and recommended that they take their boats and join the fight against Chancellor Jefferson," Admiral Burton said.

"That's great news, but what are you going to do when Chancellor Jefferson finds out?"

"That's my problem, you just make sure you take care of my men."

"You have my word on that," Admiral Crawford said.

"I've got to go, but thank you for that," Admiral Burton said.

After he hung up, Admiral Burton took one last look at the picture of his dead wife on his desk before he put his gun in his mouth and pulled the trigger.

After Admiral Crawford finished briefing President Behrmann, the president called his brother, Lieb.

"That was a ballsy move you made," Aryeh said.

"I told you I'd watch your back," Lieb said. "I'd have finished them off, but they must have cut some sort of deal with the Chinese, because President Zhao called madder than hell and threatened to nuke us if I didn't back off."

"I think I have the answer to that. Do you have time to join a videoconference call this afternoon?" Aryeh asked.

"What time?" Lieb asked.

"Thirteen hundred GMT."

Lieb was the last to join the call. "Sorry I'm late, but a Hamas suicide bomber just killed forty people at the port in Haifa," he said.

"No worries," Aryeh said. "Since I called the meeting, I'll start. Before I get to the purpose of the call, I'd like to share a bit of good news. The remainder of the

United States submarine force is going to join us in our fight against Chancellor Jefferson."

"That's huge," Russian President Valery Gorelov said.

"More than you could know," President Aryeh Behrmann replied. "Following the latest attacks, we've discovered that Chancellor Jefferson and Chinese President Zhao met several months ago to form an alliance and have convinced Iran, Iraq, Afghanistan, Pakistan, and Syria to join them."

"That's why Zhao was mad," Prime Minister Lieb Behrmann said.

"I'm sure it is," replied President Aryeh Behrmann. "It's apparent that our plans to blockade the United States are no longer feasible, which makes it even more imperative that we implement phase two of our operation, which is to open up fronts on the northern and southern borders of the United States. President Gorelov will explain the portion of the operation that Russia is heading up."

"For the northern operation to succeed we must first secure Alaska," President Gorelov said. "The Canadian forces under General Armistead's command will launch an air and ground assault from the south, while Russian forces will mount an all-out air assault, followed by a flotilla of ships carrying supplies and reinforcements. Once we have control we'll expand the major ports to support our logistical needs. They haven't completed rebuilding the Elmendorf Air Force Base, so we don't expect the operation to take more than a few days. Once we have the situation stabilized we'll reinforce the Canadian Air Force with NATO aircraft, a hundred thousand additional ground troops, and two heavy tank battalions."

"Thank you, President Gorelov. Now Admiral Crawford is going to lay out our plans for the southern border."

"Currently we've got factories working day and night to build as many of the Soviet S400 missile batteries, the American Aegis Combat systems, and the Israeli Iron Dome Missile Defense systems as possible. We're adding the Israeli graduated response lasers, coupled with portable nuclear power generators to all of the systems, and once we're satisfied we can defend our positions we'll launch both operations. Unlike the northern operation, the southern operation doesn't require any military action since our allies still control all of South America. We're going to expand several of the existing deepwater ports to make sure we have sufficient logistical capacity, and we'll be building a large multinational air base in southern Brazil. However, before we can move the bulk of our ground forces into southern Mexico, we have to deal with the massive radiation contamination in Darién, Panama. We considered trying to decontaminate the area, but that would require far too much time and effort, so we've decided to build several hundred massive barges to ferry the men and equipment around the area. Once we have the men and equipment in place, we'll join up with the Mexican army and strike at Chancellor Jefferson's southern flank."

"Thank you, Admiral," President Aryeh Behrmann said. "I know this is a fifty-thousand-foot view, but what do you think of the plan?"

"What makes you think that Chancellor Jefferson is going to stand by while this all takes place?" Prime Minister Behrmann asked.

"We don't, but he's lost a significant portion of his air force, so with our combined air power we should be able to maintain air superiority."

"He's already shown he's not afraid to use nukes when he bombed Panama, so what's to stop him from using them against us?" asked Juan Trigueros, Spain's representative and the president of the UN General Assembly.

"It's a gamble, but given the number of nuclear weapons the Russians, the NATO nations, and we possess, it would be suicide for Chancellor Jefferson or his Chinese buddies to use theirs," President Aryeh Behrmann said.

"Mutually assured destruction worked against us for decades," President Gorelov said.

"Yes, but your people were sane," Prime Minister Lieb Behrmann said.

"Jefferson is many things, but I don't believe he wants to die," Juan Trigueros said.

"It makes me awfully nervous to chance the world's fate on the whim of a madman," Prime Minister Lieb Behrmann said.

"Do you have a solution for us?" President Aryeh Behrmann asked.

"As a matter of fact I do. We've developed and lab tested the technology for a space-based antiballistic missile system, but we never had the wherewithal to deploy it."

"An interesting proposition, but that would take years to deploy, and I'm afraid we don't have that much time," President Gorelov said.

"I agree, and we can have that discussion another time," President Aryeh Behrmann said. "Unless one of you has an objection, we're going to move forward with the operations I've laid out."

As winter fell on the North American continent, Chancellor Jefferson watched while President Behrmann, with the help of the Russians' air cover, managed to open up a supply chain to the Canadian forces.

When Chancellor Jefferson summoned him to the White House, Admiral Kennedy knew he was in for an ass chewing. They were meeting in the White House

Situation Room, and as soon as he sat down, Chancellor Jefferson started berating him.

"Admiral Kennedy, I think I've been very patient with you, but if you don't do something about what's going on in Canada I'll have to replace you," Chancellor Jefferson said.

"There no way in hell we can get anything up there at this time of year," Admiral Kennedy said.

"Then bomb the hell out them."

"With what? The plants haven't started delivering the replacement aircraft."

"Fine, but I'll expect some action when the weather clears," Chancellor Jefferson said.

"That was a waste of time," he said after the admiral left.

"True, but he's right," John Jay said. "Nothing can move up there at this time of year."

"Whatever. Speaking of failures, have you tracked down Snoops yet?"

"No luck so far. I even tortured several members of his militia to death, but nobody's talking."

"Stupid but loyal. Don't stop looking for that asshole. He's going to be trouble if we don't find him."

CHAPTER 34

Four months later, President Behrmann, Admiral Crawford, and President Gorelov were gathered in the situation center in the Russian White House.

"Admiral Crawford, is everything in place?" President Behrmann asked.

"Yes, sir, all units are standing by," Admiral Crawford said.

"Then issue the order to commence the operation," President Behrmann said.

Chancellor Jefferson was in his quarters just down the hall from the White House Situation Room when the alert came in. Admiral Kennedy was already there when the chancellor arrived.

"Colonel Ridgeway will lay out what we know so far," Admiral Kennedy said.

"At oh-five-hundred this morning, the Canadian army crossed into Alaska with two armored divisions and twelve thousand infantry," Colonel Ridgeway said. "Simultaneously, six squadrons of Russian fighters have shot down what little air cover we had left up there. In addition to the airstrikes, the Russians have troops and cargo ships headed toward the port in Anchorage."

"How have we responded?" Chancellor Jefferson asked.

"The air force has scrambled eight squadrons of F-16s and all the available B-52s," Admiral Kennedy said.

"Why aren't you using the B1s?"

"We're using them to keep the Mexicans under control."

"I thought you said we had the southern front under control?"

"To a point we do, but we've discovered that NATO has been using cargo vessels to smuggle fighter aircraft and SAM batteries into Veracruz. Our source said that they have received at least three squadrons of the Dassault Rafale B fighters, and that's just the ones he knew about."

The Port at Veracruz, also known as Heroica Veracruz, was one of the oldest ports in Mexico. Spanish explorers had founded it in the sixteenth century, however Admiral Ridgeway was using it because was only 8.7 kilometers from the local airport. Mexican General Fernandez was using the Veracruz International Airport as the staging area for all of his air operations.

"You were supposed to have taken out the airport and the port in Veracruz," Chancellor Jefferson said.

"We've tried, but between the fighters, the Israelis, and the Russian SAM batteries, it's suicide to even attempt it. About the only way you could take it out now would be with an ICBM."

As Chancellor Jefferson remembered his last confrontation with President Gorelov and President Behrmann, he thought, *Probably not a good idea. Aryeh Behrmann might not have the balls to retaliate, but that bastard Gorelov sure as hell would.*

They'd been discussing their options for a couple of hours when Colonel Ridgeway said, "The airstrikes didn't stop them, and we've just received a dispatch from Colonel Tobias, the commander of the Elmendorf Air Force Base, and he's surrendered the base and ordered all the other military units in Alaska to stand down and surrender. Since then the Canadian forces under General Boulanger's command have entered the city and now control the port in Anchorage."

"Cowardly bastard," Chancellor Jefferson said. "They should have fought to the last man."

"To what end?" John Jay asked.

Chancellor Jefferson brushed aside John's question and said, "Admiral, I want you to have Colonel Ridgeway send this executive directive to all commands. Any commander surrendering or ordering a retreat will be deemed a traitor and executed."

John felt his pulse race and his face flush at the comment, but he had no idea why.

"Isn't that a bit harsh?" Admiral Kennedy asked.

"Hell no," Chancellor Jefferson said. "Those damned Russians are meddling in my affairs again, but they've overplayed their hand this time."

"The order has gone out," Colonel Ridgeway said when he returned.

"Admiral, issue the order to execute Red One," Chancellor Jefferson said.

"What's Red One?" John Jay asked.

"Admiral Kennedy warned me months ago that this could happen, so we've been working on a little surprise for them," Chancellor Jefferson said.

Two hours later Admiral Crawford turned to President Behrmann and said, "Sir, Chancellor Jefferson's men have just shot down our air cover and sunk several of President Gorelov's ships that were unloading in Anchorage."

"There's got to be some sort of mistake, we had more than enough aircraft to control the situation."

"No mistake. They got hit by twenty or more squadrons of F-22s."

"Impossible, there never were that many F-22s."

"That may be, but that's what they're reporting, and General Boulanger is now reporting that all four American divisions are moving north at a rapid pace," Admiral Crawford said.

"President Gorelov, are your ships still in port?" President Behrmann asked.

"I believe so," President Gorelov said. "Why do you ask?"

"I'm considering having General Boulanger evacuate his men before they're overrun," President Behrmann said.

"They're not going to be able to take their equipment with them," President Gorelov said.

"Understood, but we can replace the equipment."

"Considering the circumstances, that's probably a prudent move," President Gorelov replied.

"Issue the order," President Behrmann said.

"Chancellor Jefferson is moving on the southern front as well," Admiral Crawford said.

"What would you recommend?" President Behrmann asked.

"I'm afraid there's not much we can do, but we can't afford to lose Veracruz, so I think we should advise General Fernandez to pull his men back to consolidate his defensive perimeter."

"Then do it."

The battles raged back and forth on both fronts for several days before the fighting finally died down. Chancellor Jefferson sat down in the White House Situation Room to call President Zhao.

"Congratulations, your plan worked," President Zhao said when he joined the teleconference.

"For the most part. We lost more aircraft than I expected in the Mexican operation, but we now control all of the country down to a few miles north of Mexico

City. However, I was pleasantly surprised with the ease that we finished off the Canadians. My only regret is that the Russians managed to evacuate most of their personnel."

"What's your next move?" President Zhao asked.

"I've ramped up our aircraft production, and I'm going to start deploying a new generation of submersible drones developed by the Defense Advanced Research Projects Agency."

"Is that the Antisubmarine Warfare Continuous Trail Vessel you've been testing?"

It was a top-secret project so Chancellor Jefferson was surprised President Zhao knew about it, but he never let on.

"That was an early prototype. These are basically unmanned nuclear-powered attack subs that can operate with little supervisory control but can also act as remotely controlled or piloted vessels depending on the circumstances of the specific missions."

"Your submarine technology is quite advanced. Why the shift to unmanned vessels?" President Zhao asked.

"Unfortunately the traitorous bastard that headed up my submarine force gave his commanders the choice to join President Behrmann, and most of them have."

"I'd burn the bastard alive if it were me."

"Couldn't, the coward killed himself."

"Is there anything we can do to help out?"

"We still need the shipments of steel and rare earth materials, and we could use as much of your manufacturing capacity as you can spare to rebuild our heavy equipment losses."

"Does that mean you'll give us access to your more advanced technology?"

"Of course, what about you?" Chancellor Jefferson asked.

"We need a dependable source of oil, and the drones have piqued my interest."

"No problem, but I'm afraid that we're going to have a hard time keeping the shipping lanes open," Chancellor Jefferson said.

"No worries. We've been secretly building a large fleet of advanced frigates, and we should be able to keep the sea lanes open," President Zhao said. "Once we've rebuilt, where do we want to begin knocking these bastards off?"

"If you don't have any objections, I'd like to start with the Israelis," Chancellor Jefferson said.

"After what they just did to Iran, that will resonate with our Middle Eastern allies."

Later that same day, President Behrmann and President Gorelov met in the new situation center in the Russian White House. The room was filled with state-of-the-art electronics, but the amphitheater-style seating, 8K resolution dual projectors, and high-end sound system that would put most movie theaters to shame were by far the room's most impressive features. They were hosting a teleconference with the NATO military commanders including Secretary Gutierrez of the UNASUR, Israeli Prime Minister Lieb Behrmann, Mexican General Fernandez, and Canadian General Boulanger to discuss their current circumstances.

"Gentlemen, let me begin by thanking all of you for your support," President Behrmann said. "However, as you all know, our operations haven't gone off as planned. Chancellor Jefferson's forces now control all of North America, except for the southern end of Mexico."

"What went wrong?" Secretary Gutierrez asked.

"In hindsight, it's obvious they were just waiting on us to make a move. We knew Chancellor Jefferson's ground forces drastically outnumbered ours, but we were counting on air superiority. However, he'd been secretly building a large fleet of F-22s, and once they were able to regain air superiority his forces were able to push the Canadian forces off the continent. Simultaneously his southern divisions launched an all-out attack to gain control of the rest of Mexico."

"In other words, we got our asses handed to us," President Gorelov said.

"I agree with President Gorelov's assessment, but my forces did manage to maintain a foothold in North America, and Veracruz has a deepwater port and a serviceable airfield," General Fernandez said.

"Good point. Why don't you give the group an overview of your situation?" President Behrmann said.

"Although they managed to drive us back, we've managed to hold them along a line ten miles north of Mexico City, and most of my forces, along with several of the cartel contingents, are still fully operational. We lost some of our equipment during the retreat, but we've reassembled the latest shipment of NATO aircraft and we have the new SAM batteries in place, so I believe we can hold at least for now."

"I don't mean to interrupt, but the UNSUAR and the Organization of Central American States stand ready to assist you in any way we can," Secretary Gutierrez said. "When Chancellor Jefferson nuked Panama, it removed any doubt in our minds about what he has in mind for the rest of us. We're willing to commit manpower, money, and whatever else is needed to take this madman down."

They continued talking for almost four hours before President Aryeh Behrmann said, "I think we'll call it a day. I'll send out the notes tonight, but I'll try to summarize what we've agreed to. The UNSUAR and the Organization of Central American States will deploy eleven divisions of infantry and four armored battalions to supplement General Fernandez's army, and as soon as feasible we'll establish a no-fly zone over the area. Simultaneously, NATO will implement a five-hundred-mile no-fly zone around Israel. Later this month Israel will begin receiving a hundred and fifty Soviet S-400 missile batteries, which will be coupled with their Iron Dome systems to turn the entire country into an A2/D2 zone. To beef up the rest of their defenses, we'll be sending them four armored divisions and thirty squadrons of fighters."

"What about Canada?" General Boulanger asked.

"President Gorelov is going to relocate you and your men to Severomorsk so that we can get you reequipped and ready to go," President Behrmann said. "However, I'm afraid it's going to be quite a while before we can get you back home. We'll meet as needed, and thanks again for your support. This won't happen overnight, but we will eventually prevail."

When everyone had dropped off, President Gorelov said, "That was well done. I sensed that you've decided to stay the course and do whatever it takes to prevail."

"I have, and I pray that I'm up to the task."